Unicorn Famous

Another Phoebe and Her Unicorn Adventure

Dana Simpson

Andrews McMeel
PUBLISHING®

Hey, kids!

Check out the glossary starting on page 173
if you come across words you don't know.

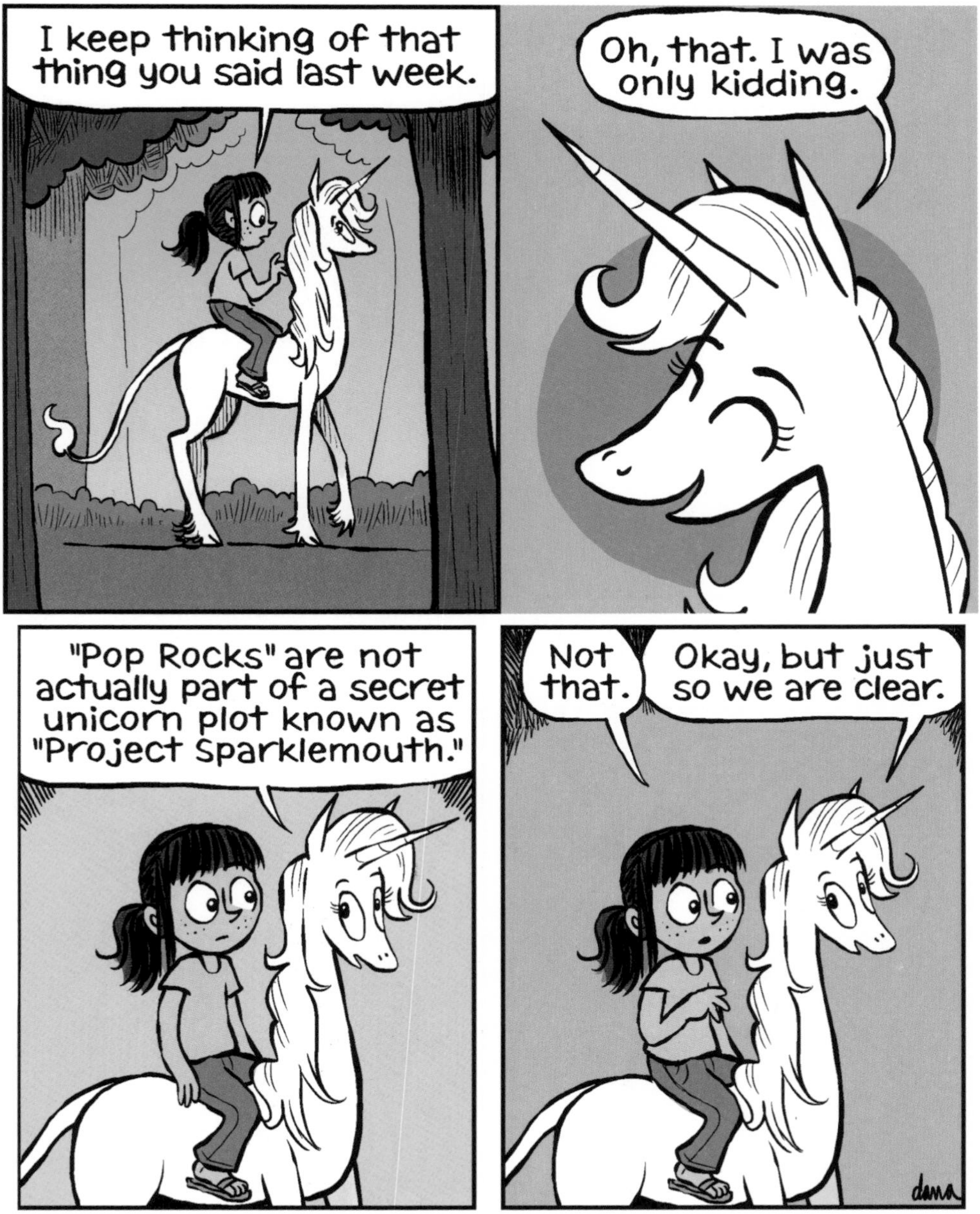

I keep thinking of that thing you said last week.
Oh, that. I was only kidding.
"Pop Rocks" are not actually part of a secret unicorn plot known as "Project Sparklemouth."
Okay, but just so we are clear.
Not that.
dana

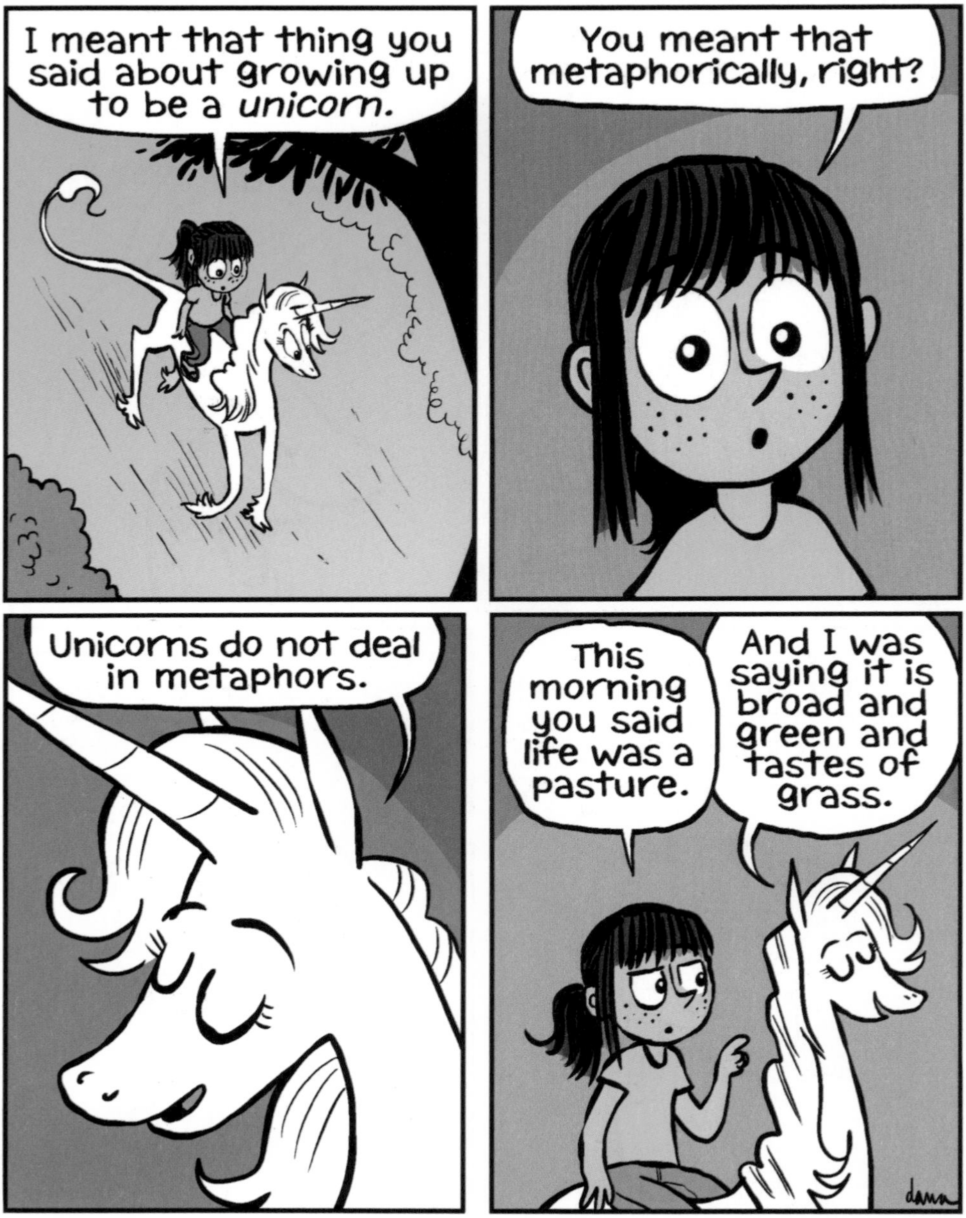
I meant that thing you said about growing up to be a *unicorn.*
You meant that metaphorically, right?
Unicorns do not deal in metaphors.
This morning you said life was a pasture.
And I was saying it is broad and green and tastes of grass.
dana

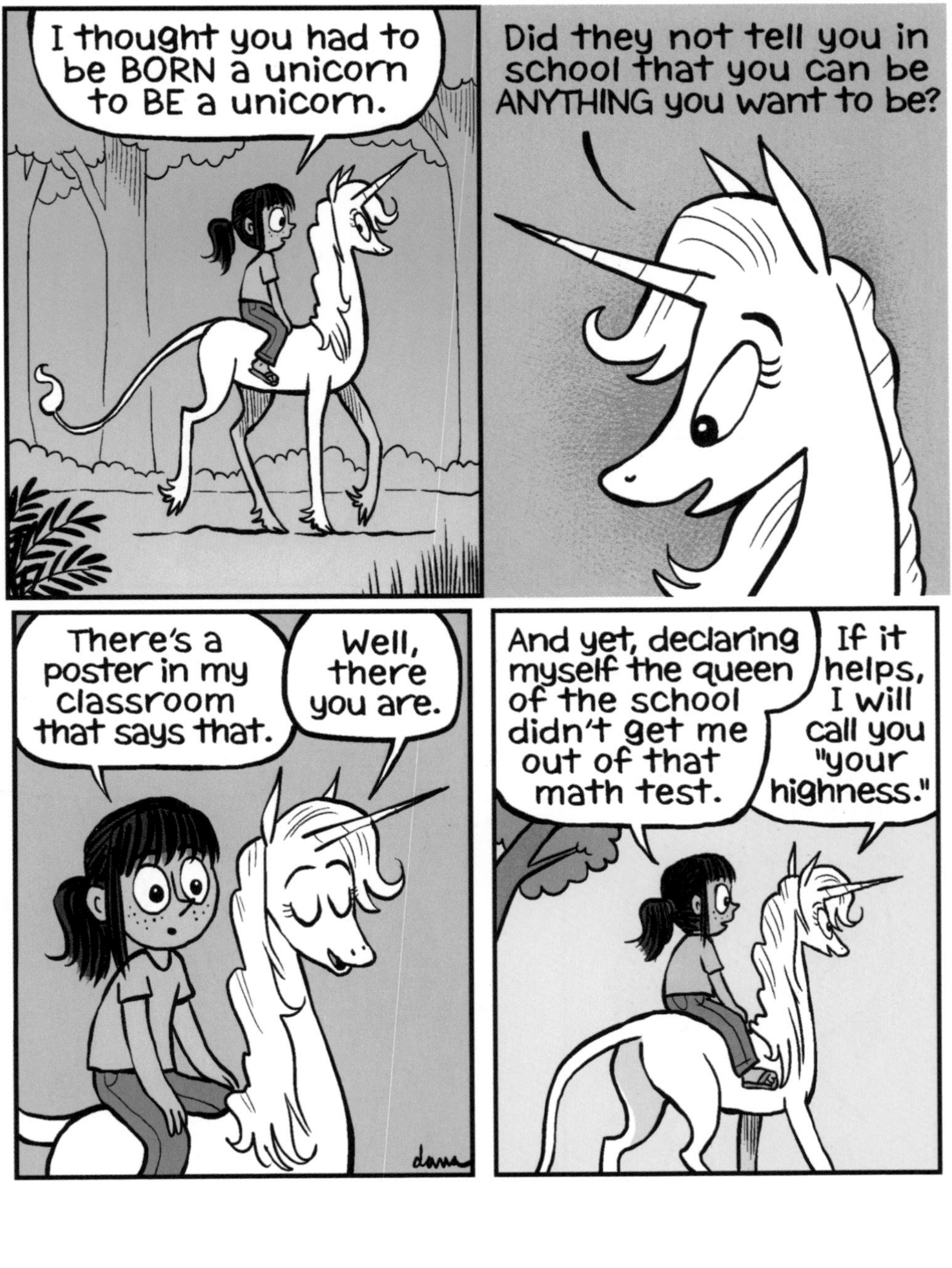
I thought you had to be BORN a unicorn to BE a unicorn.
Did they not tell you in school that you can be ANYTHING you want to be?
There's a poster in my classroom that says that.
Well, there you are.
And yet, declaring myself the queen of the school didn't get me out of that math test.
If it helps, I will call you "your highness."
dana

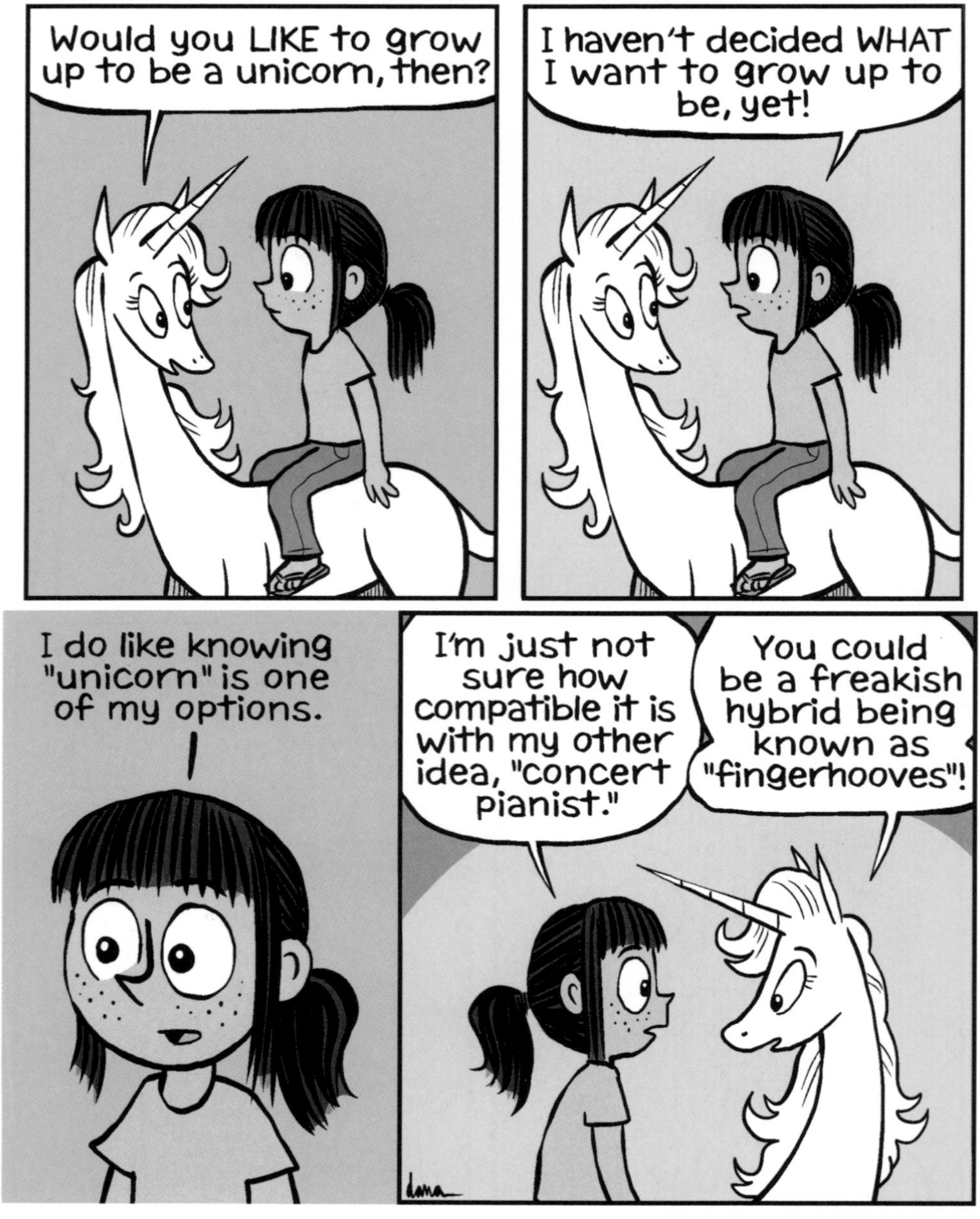

Would you LIKE to grow up to be a unicorn, then?
I haven't decided WHAT I want to grow up to be, yet!
I do like knowing "unicorn" is one of my options.
I'm just not sure how compatible it is with my other idea, "concert pianist."
You could be a freakish hybrid being known as "fingerhooves"!

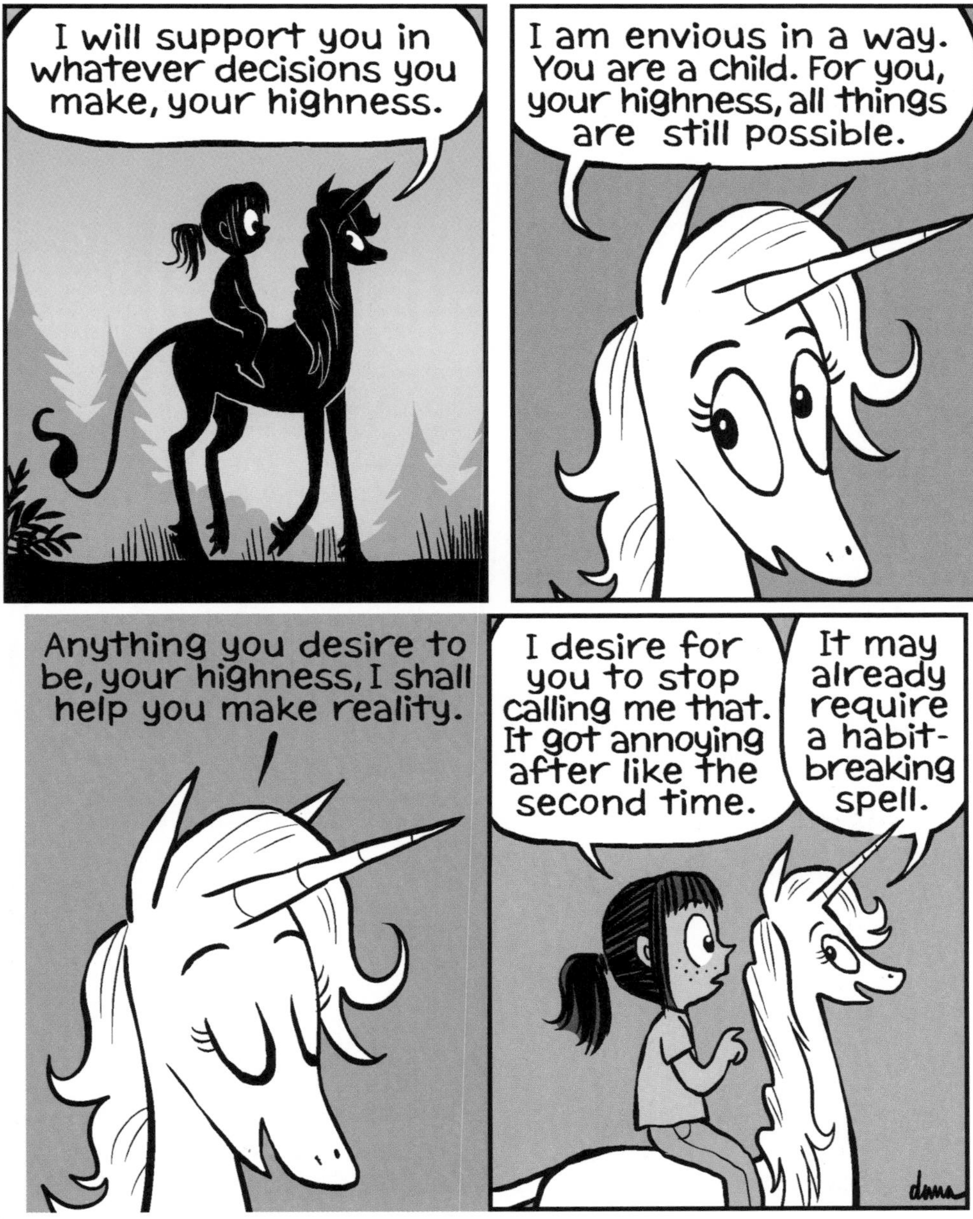
I will support you in whatever decisions you make, your highness.
I am envious in a way. You are a child. For you, your highness, all things are still possible.
Anything you desire to be, your highness, I shall help you make reality.
I desire for you to stop calling me that. It got annoying after like the second time.
It may already require a habit-breaking spell.
dana

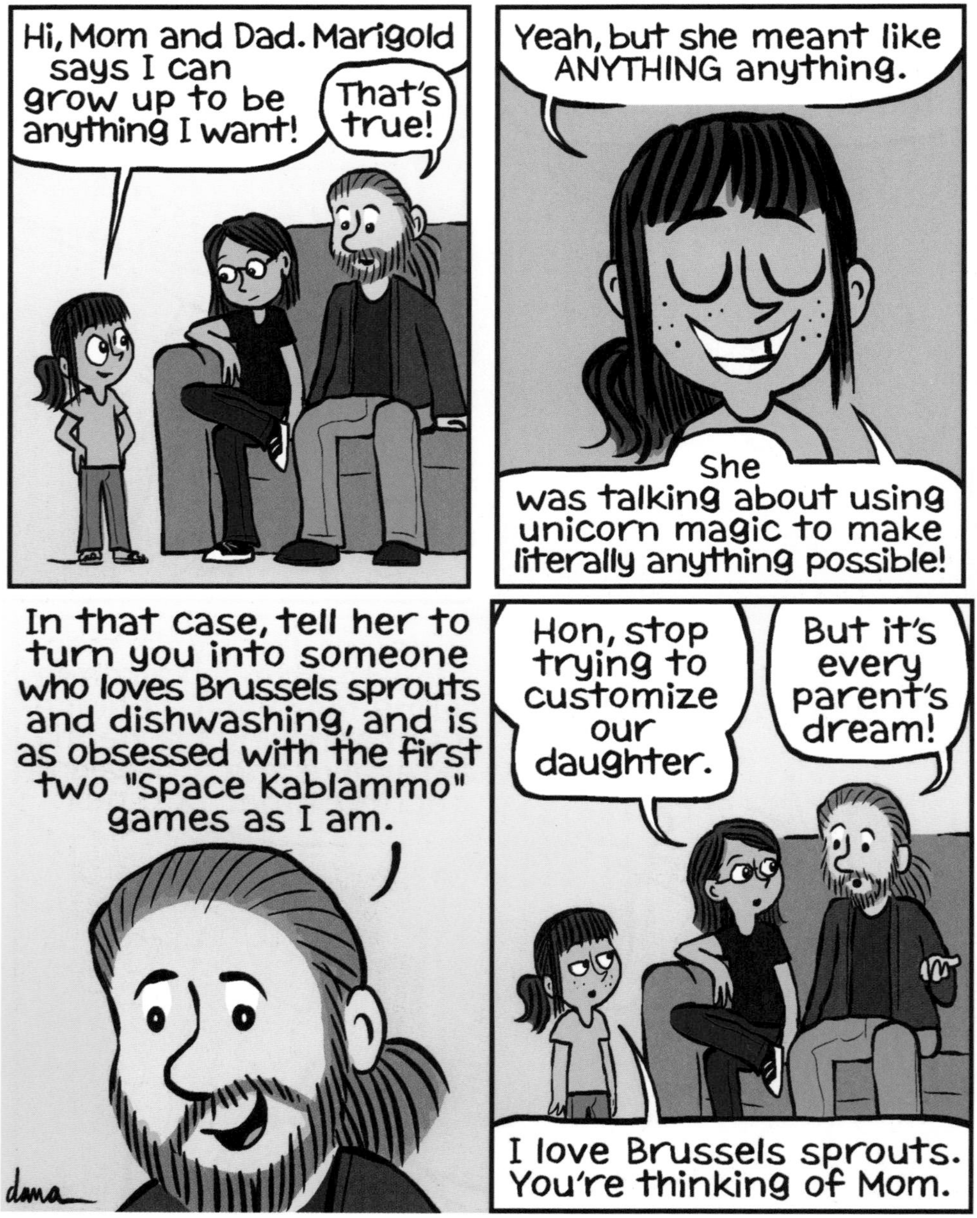
Hi, Mom and Dad. Marigold says I can grow up to be anything I want!
That's true!
Yeah, but she meant like ANYTHING anything.
She was talking about using unicorn magic to make literally anything possible!
In that case, tell her to turn you into someone who loves Brussels sprouts and dishwashing, and is as obsessed with the first two "Space Kablammo" games as I am.
dana
Hon, stop trying to customize our daughter.
But it's every parent's dream!
I love Brussels sprouts. You're thinking of Mom.

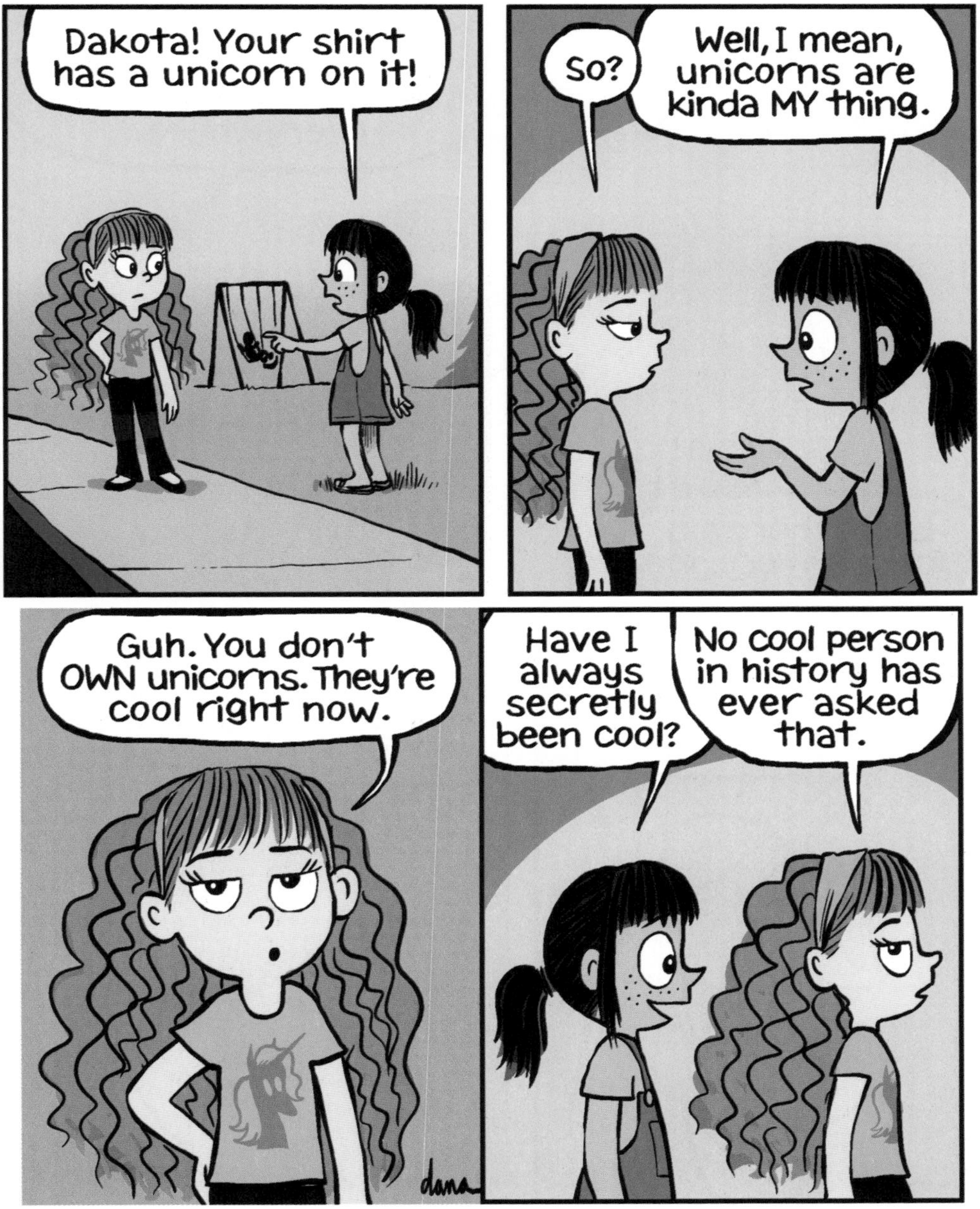
Dakota! Your shirt has a unicorn on it!
So?
Well, I mean, unicorns are kinda MY thing.
Guh. You don't OWN unicorns. They're cool right now.
Have I always secretly been cool?
No cool person in history has ever asked that.
dana

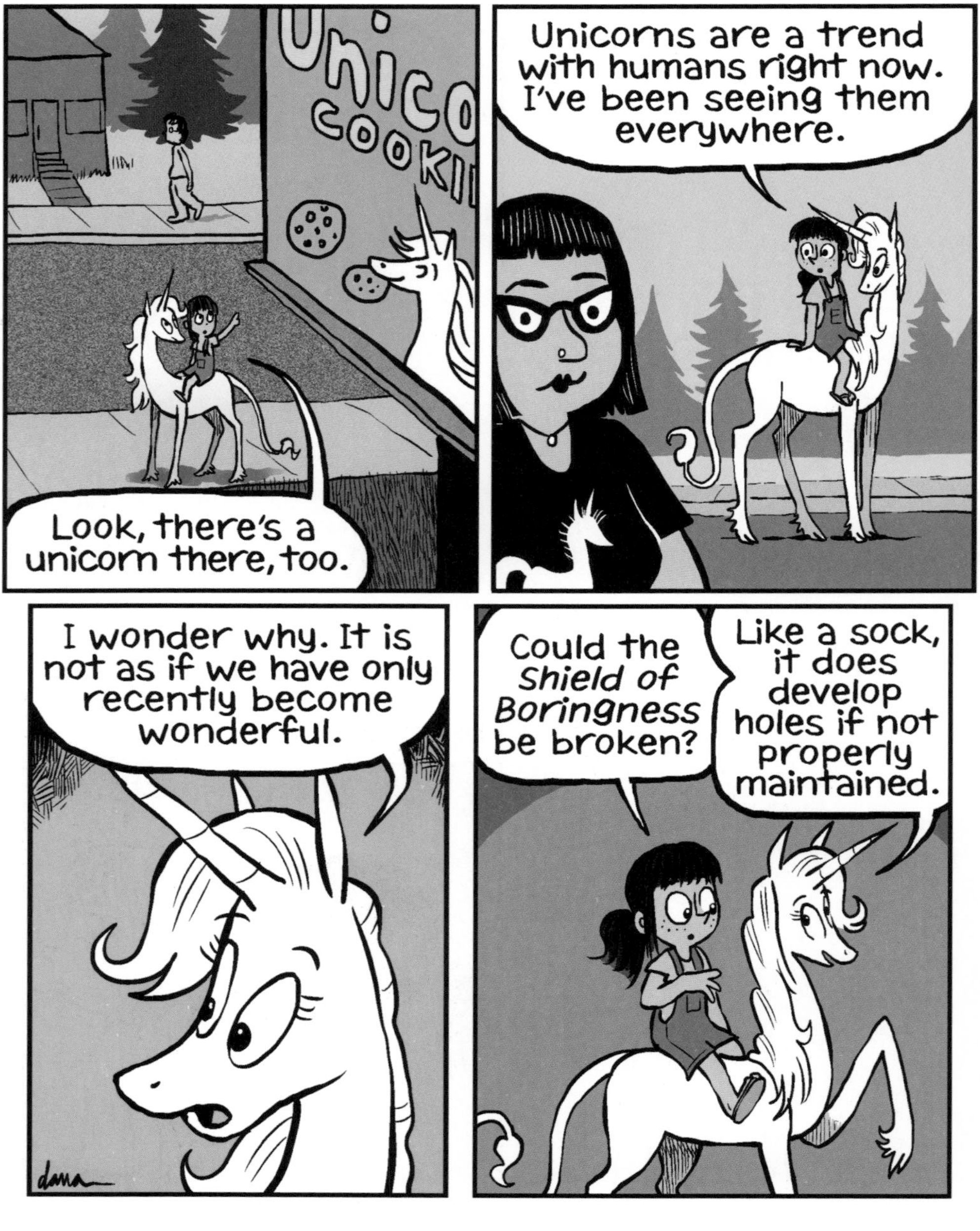
UNICO
COOKI
Look, there's a unicorn there, too.
Unicorns are a trend with humans right now. I've been seeing them everywhere.
I wonder why. It is not as if we have only recently become wonderful.
Could the *Shield of Boringness* be broken?
Like a sock, it does develop holes if not properly maintained.
dana

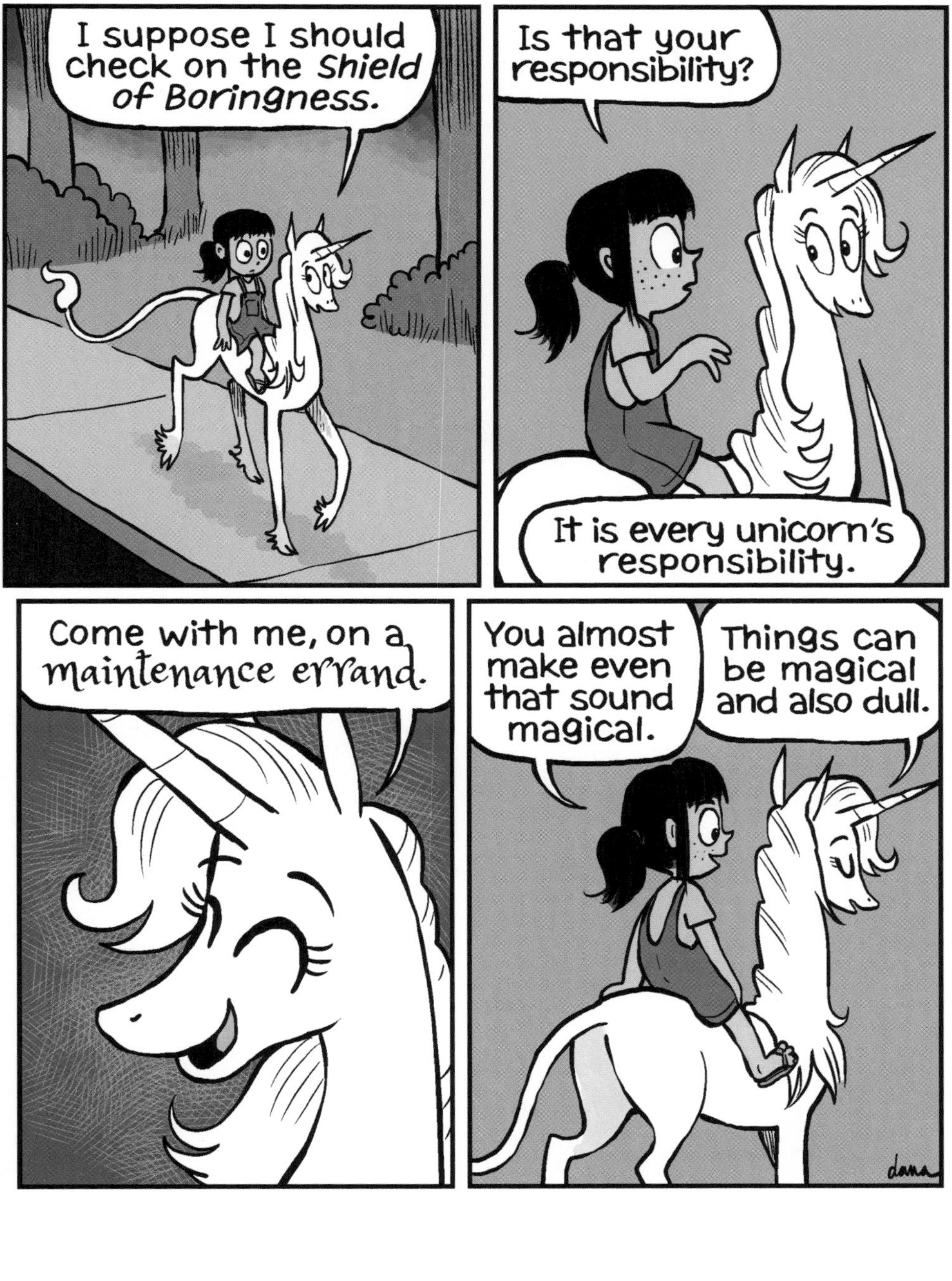
I suppose I should check on the *Shield of Boringness.*
Is that your responsibility?
It is every unicorn's responsibility.
Come with me, on a maintenance errand.
You almost make even that sound magical.
Things can be magical and also dull.
dana

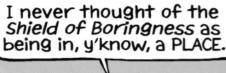
I never thought of the *Shield of Boringness* as being in, y'know, a PLACE.

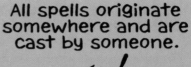
All spells originate somewhere and are cast by someone.

We must journey to the place where the local Shield of Boringness spell was cast, and consult the manual.

Spells have MANUALS?

In English, Goblin, and Colloquial Unicorn.

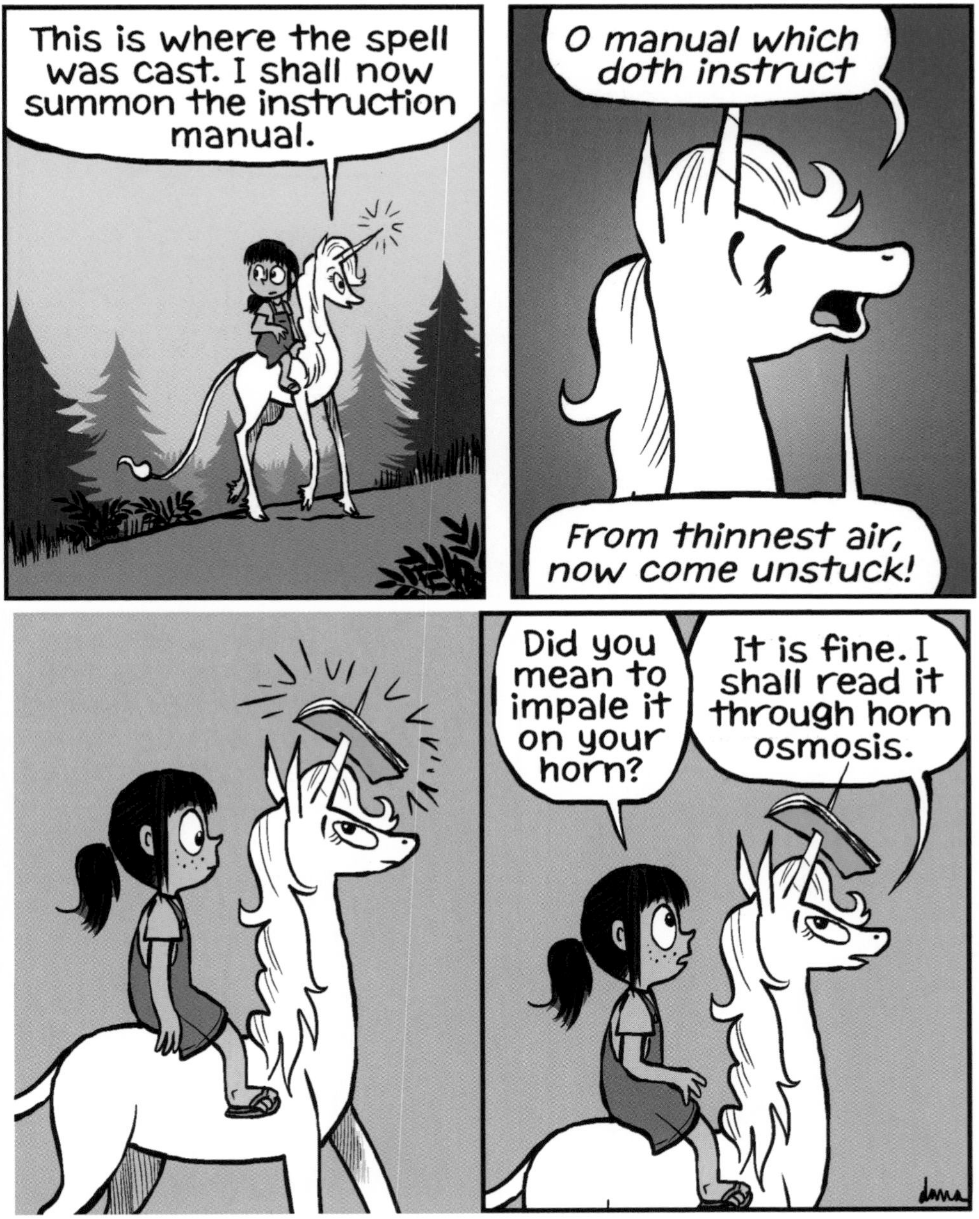
This is where the spell was cast. I shall now summon the instruction manual.
O manual which doth instruct
From thinnest air, now come unstuck!
Did you mean to impale it on your horn?
It is fine. I shall read it through horn osmosis.
dana

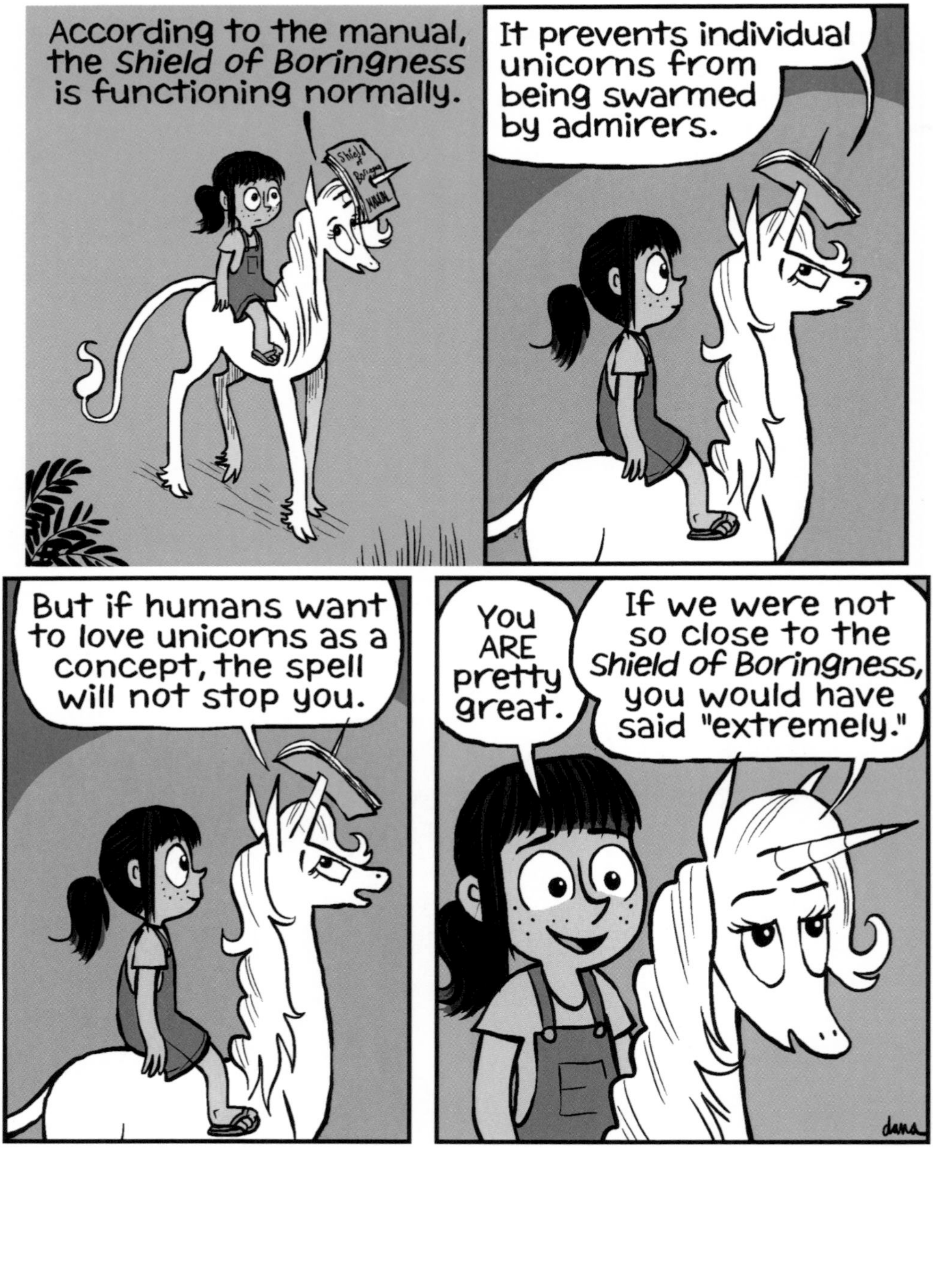
According to the manual, the *Shield of Boringness* is functioning normally.
It prevents individual unicorns from being swarmed by admirers.
But if humans want to love unicorns as a concept, the spell will not stop you.
You ARE pretty great.
If we were not so close to the *Shield of Boringness*, you would have said "extremely."
dana

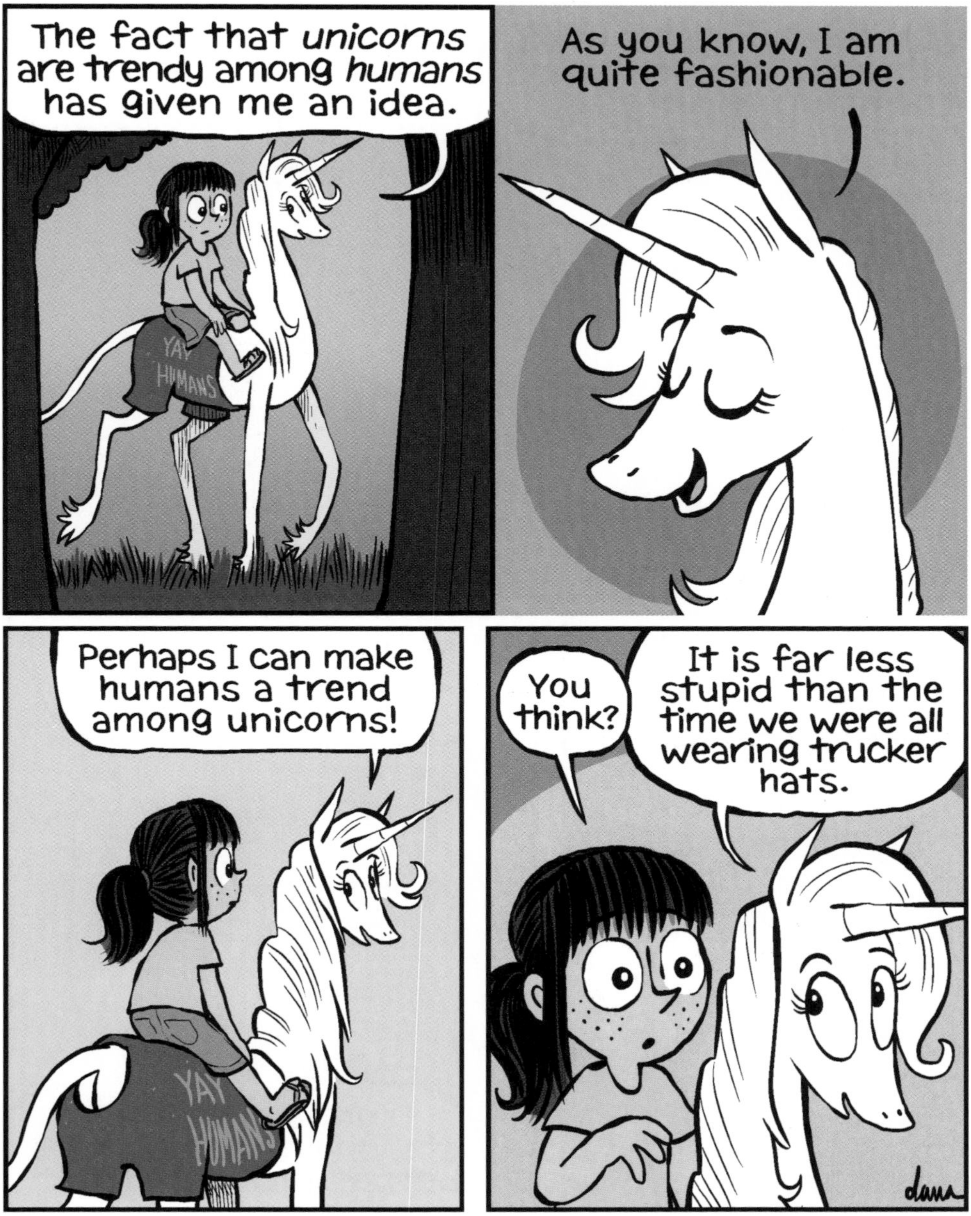
The fact that *unicorns* are trendy among *humans* has given me an idea.
YAY HUMANS
As you know, I am quite fashionable.
Perhaps I can make humans a trend among unicorns!
YAY HUMANS
You think?
It is far less stupid than the time we were all wearing trucker hats.
dana

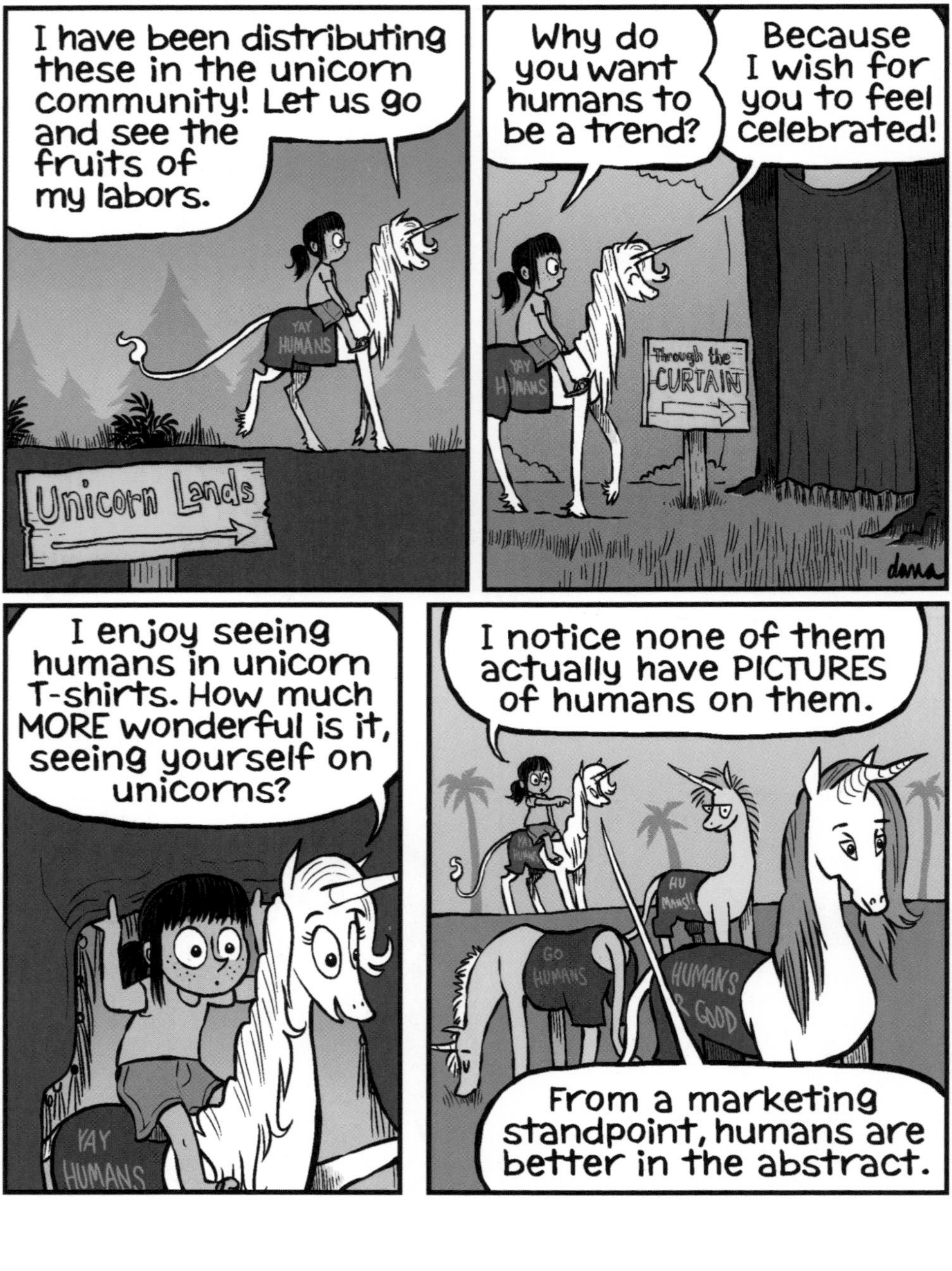
I have been distributing these in the unicorn community! Let us go and see the fruits of my labors.
YAY HUMANS
Unicorn Lands
Why do you want humans to be a trend?
Because I wish for you to feel celebrated!
Through the CURTAIN
YAY HUMANS
dana
I enjoy seeing humans in unicorn T-shirts. How much MORE wonderful is it, seeing yourself on unicorns?
YAY HUMANS
I notice none of them actually have PICTURES of humans on them.
YAY HUMANS
HU MANS!!
GO HUMANS
HUMAN'S R GOOD
From a marketing standpoint, humans are better in the abstract.

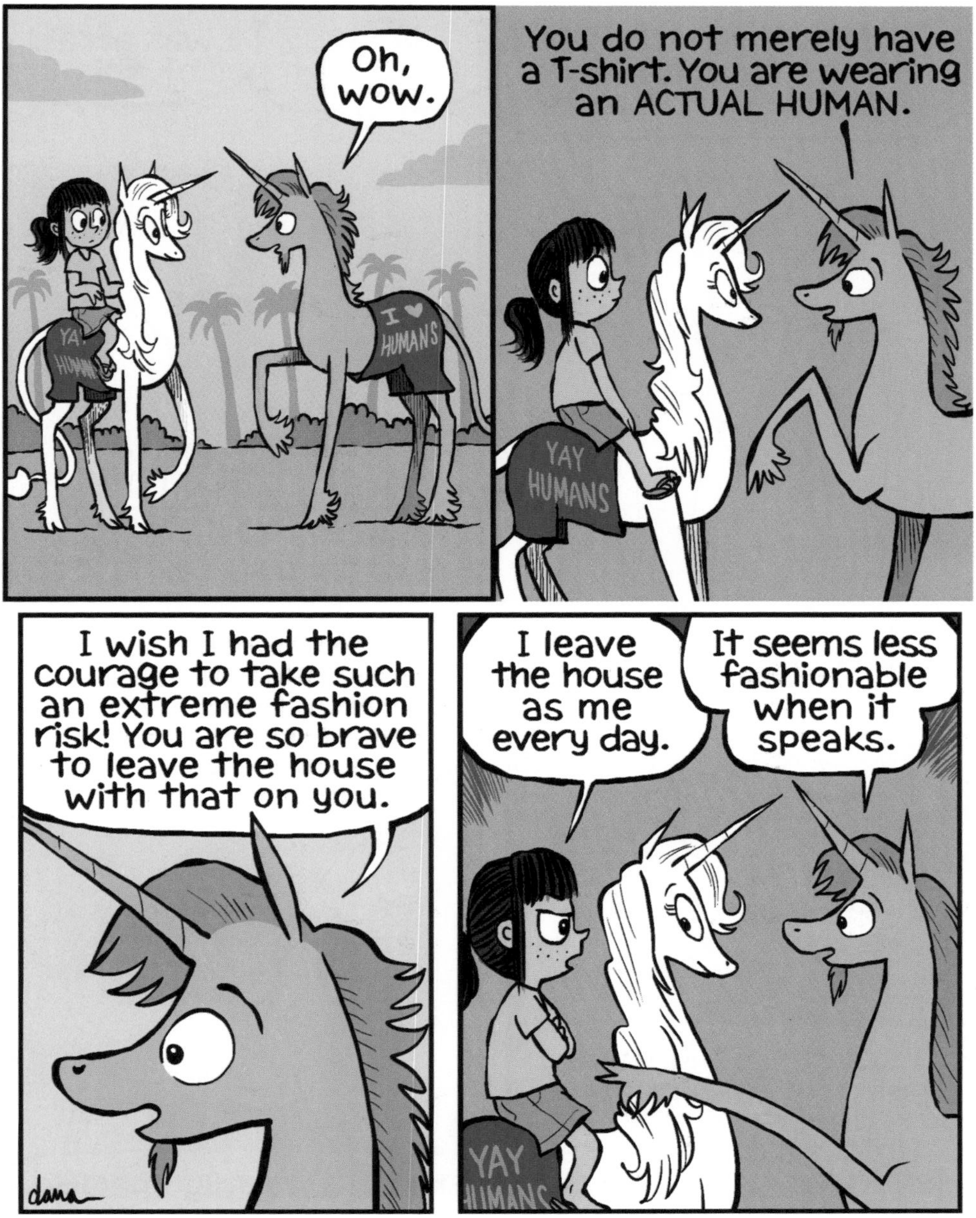
Oh, wow.
YAY HUMANS
I ♥ HUMANS
You do not merely have a T-shirt. You are wearing an ACTUAL HUMAN.
YAY HUMANS
I wish I had the courage to take such an extreme fashion risk! You are so brave to leave the house with that on you.
dana
I leave the house as me every day.
It seems less fashionable when it speaks.
YAY

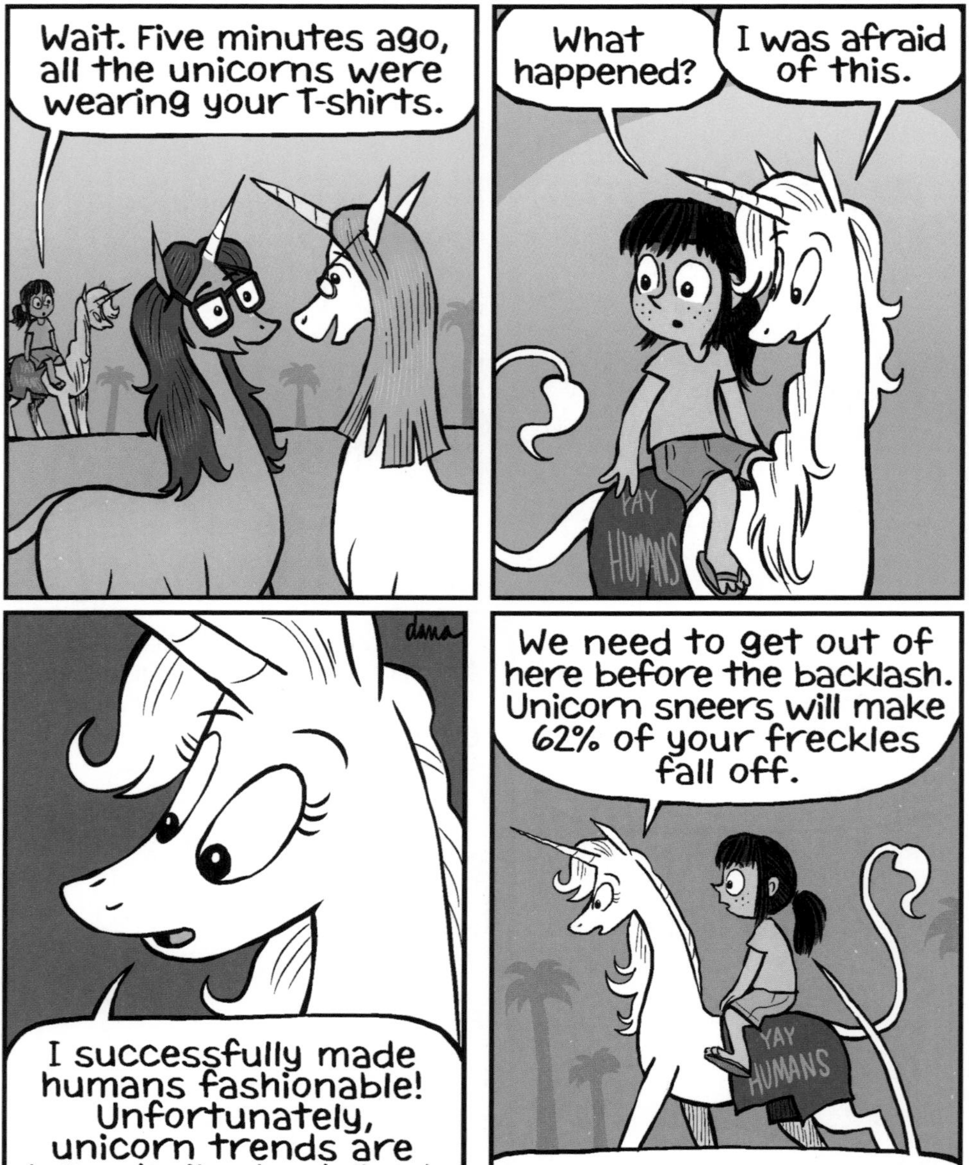
Wait. Five minutes ago, all the unicorns were wearing your T-shirts.
What happened?
I was afraid of this.
YAY HUMANS
I successfully made humans fashionable! Unfortunately, unicorn trends are legendarily short-lived.
We need to get out of here before the backlash. Unicorn sneers will make 62% of your freckles fall off.
YAY HUMANS
That's...weirdly specific.

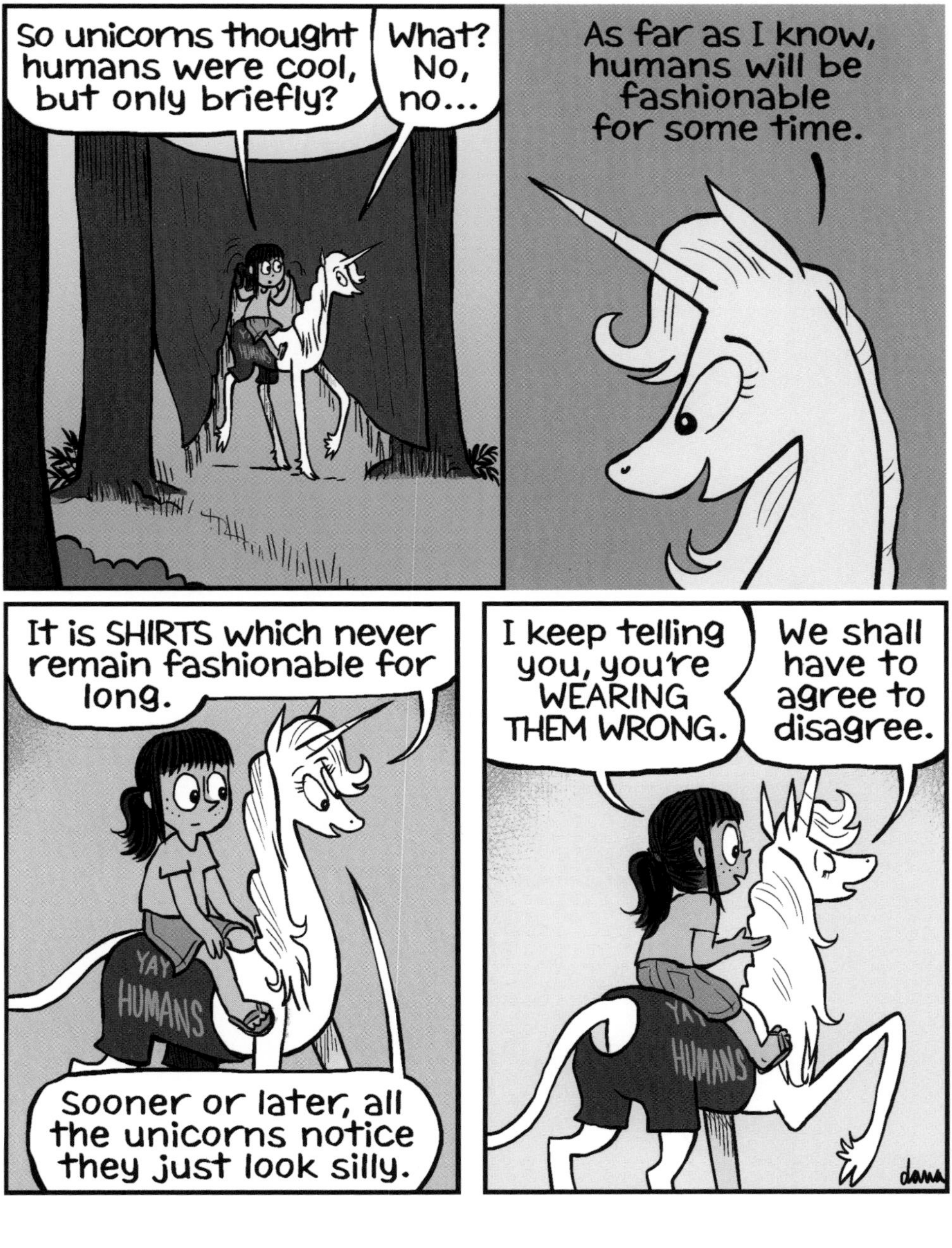
So unicorns thought humans were cool, but only briefly?
What? No, no...
YAY HUMANS
As far as I know, humans will be fashionable for some time.
It is SHIRTS which never remain fashionable for long.
YAY HUMANS
Sooner or later, all the unicorns notice they just look silly.
I keep telling you, you're WEARING THEM WRONG.
We shall have to agree to disagree.
YAY HUMANS
dana

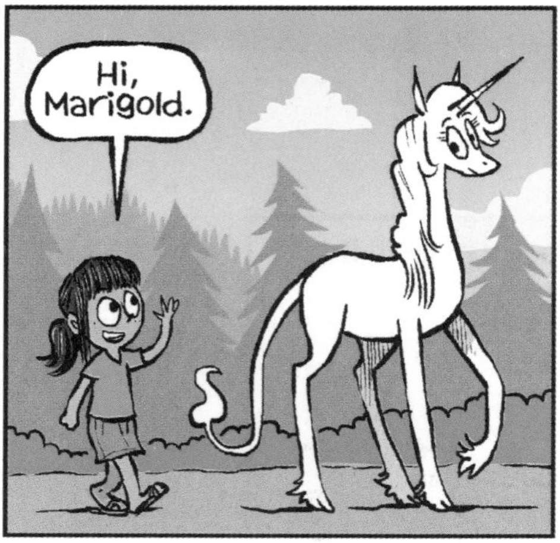
Hi, Marigold.

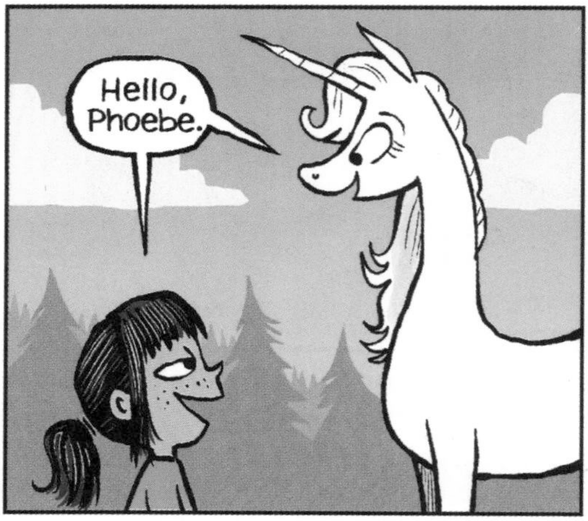
Hello, Phoebe.

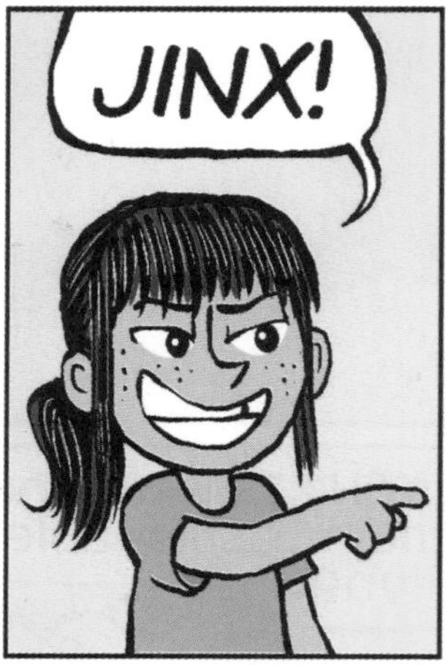
JINX!

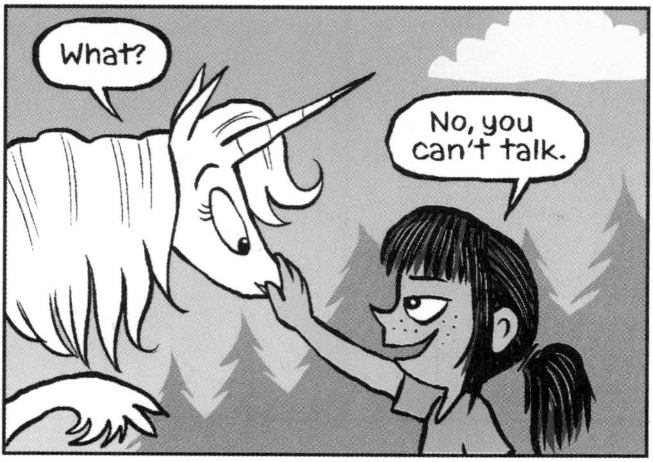
What?
No, you can't talk.

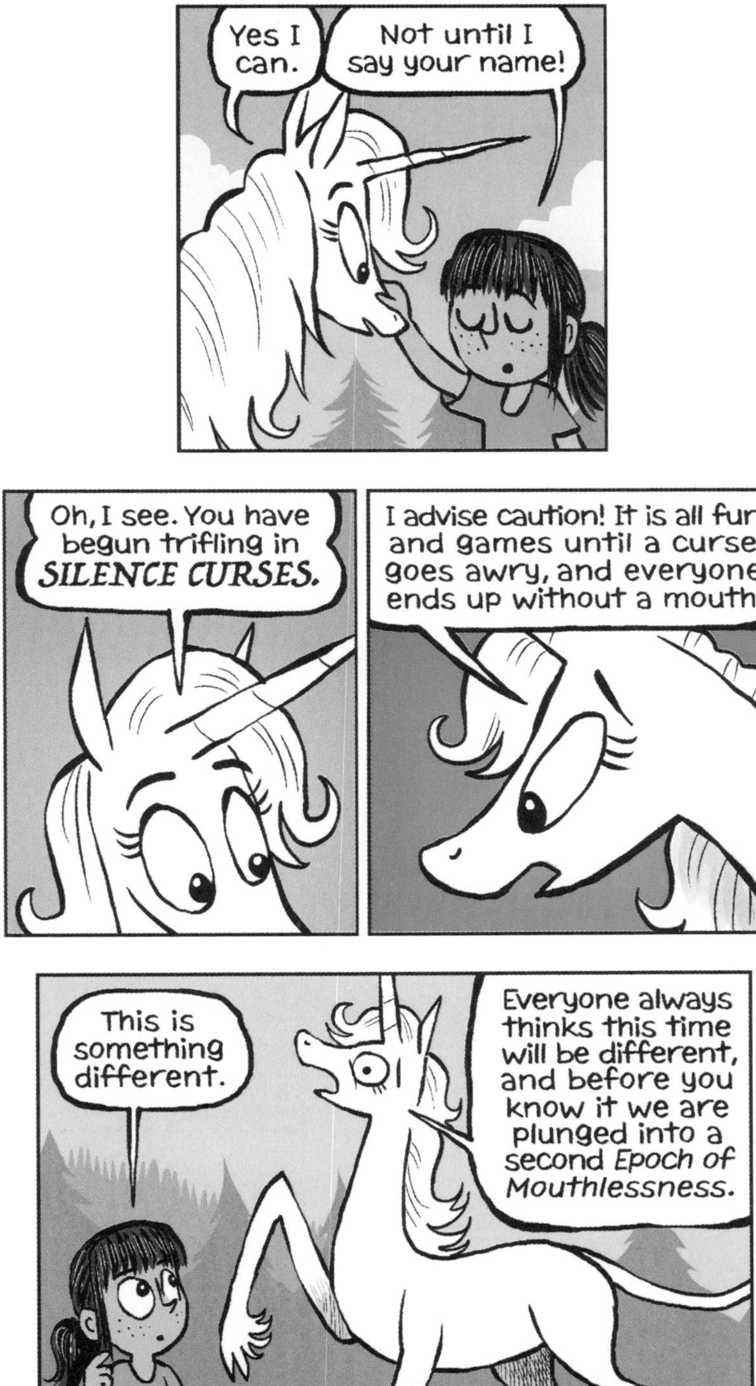
Yes I can.
Not until I say your name!
Oh, I see. You have begun trifling in *SILENCE CURSES.*
I advise caution! It is all fun and games until a curse goes awry, and everyone ends up without a mouth.
This is something different.
Everyone always thinks this time will be different, and before you know it we are plunged into a second *Epoch of Mouthlessness*.
dana

My best friend is a unicorn
She's long and tall and pale

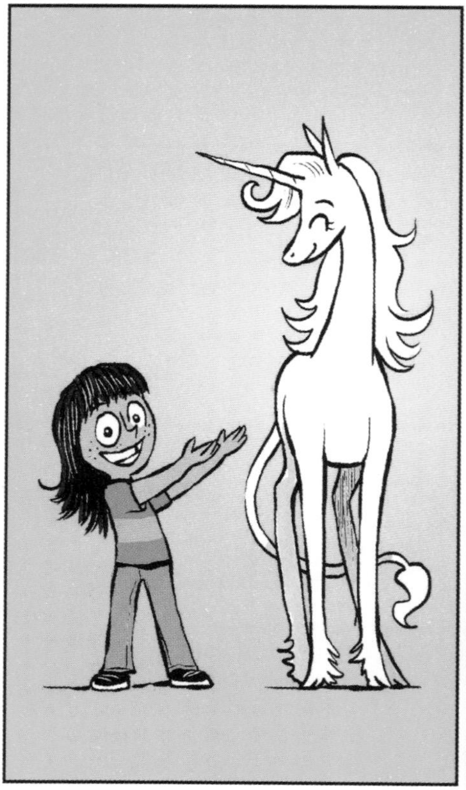

She's jealous of my fingers
I'm jealous of her tail

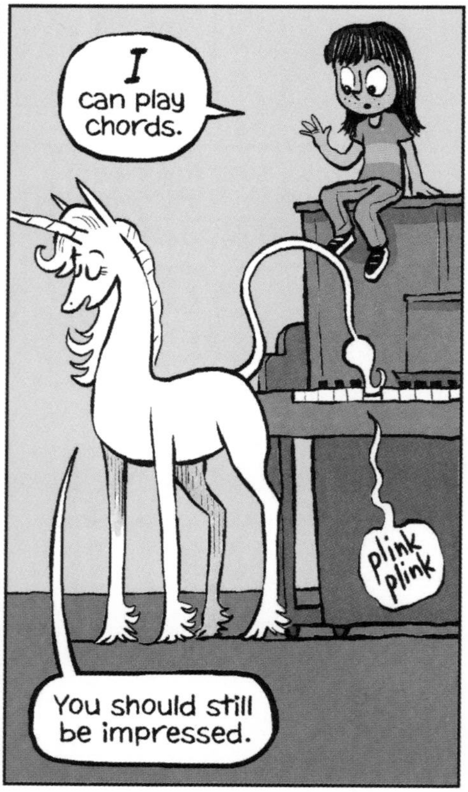
I can play chords.
plink plink
You should still be impressed.

I wish I had a magic horn
She envies me my pants

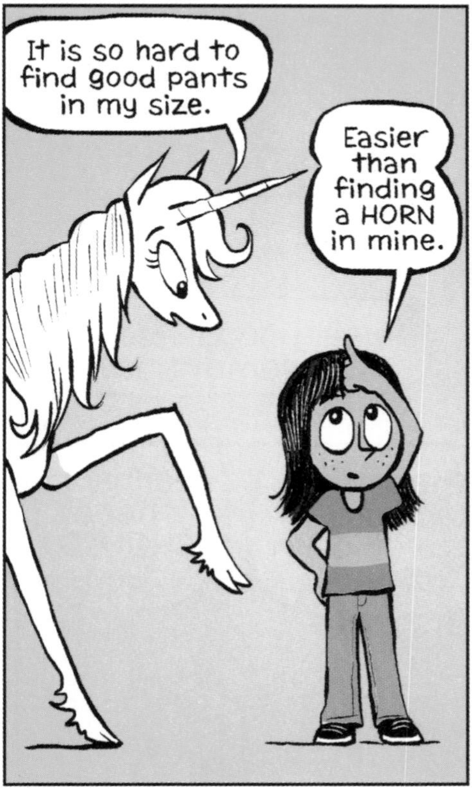
It is so hard to find good pants in my size.
Easier than finding a HORN in mine.

But when we get together
There's nothing that we can't.

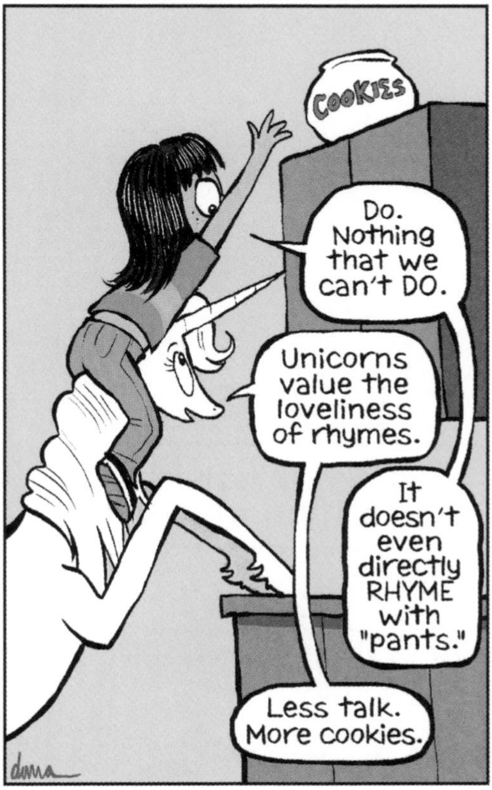
COOKIES
Do. Nothing that we can't DO.
Unicorns value the loveliness of rhymes.
It doesn't even directly RHYME with "pants."
Less talk. More cookies.

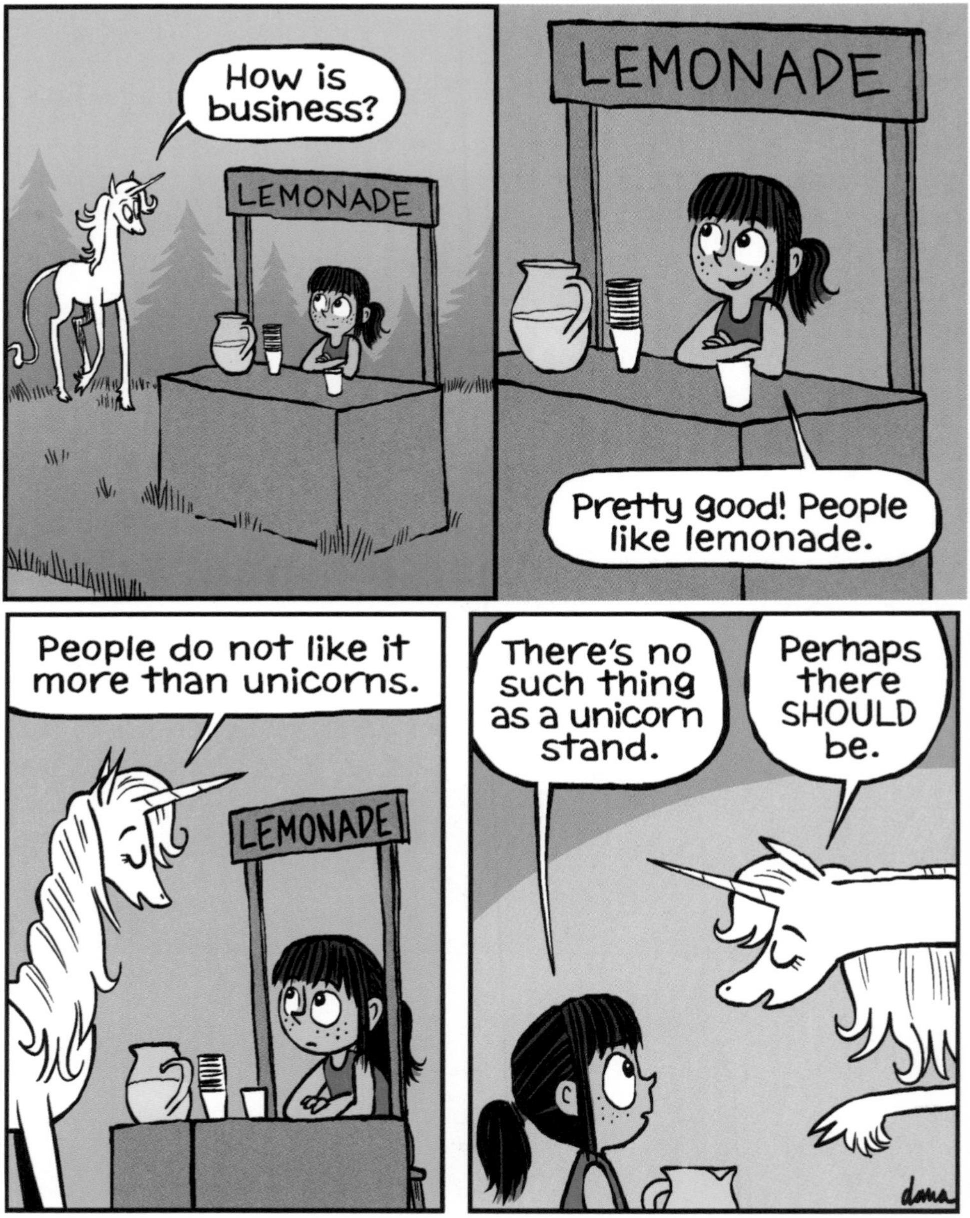
How is business?
LEMONADE
LEMONADE
Pretty good! People like lemonade.
People do not like it more than unicorns.
LEMONADE
There's no such thing as a unicorn stand.
Perhaps there SHOULD be.

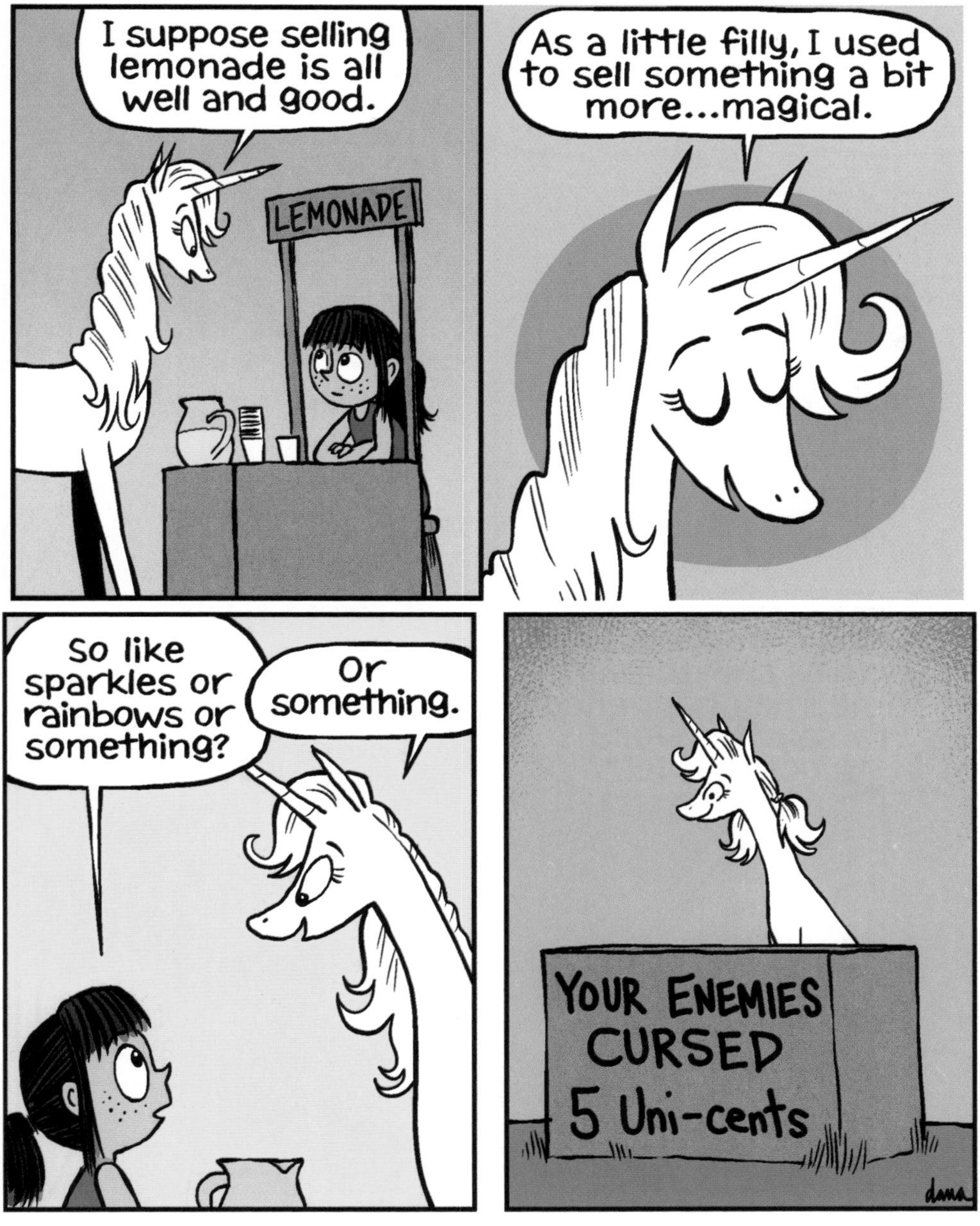
I suppose selling lemonade is all well and good.
LEMONADE
As a little filly, I used to sell something a bit more...magical.
So like sparkles or rainbows or something?
Or something.
YOUR ENEMIES CURSED 5 Uni-cents
dana

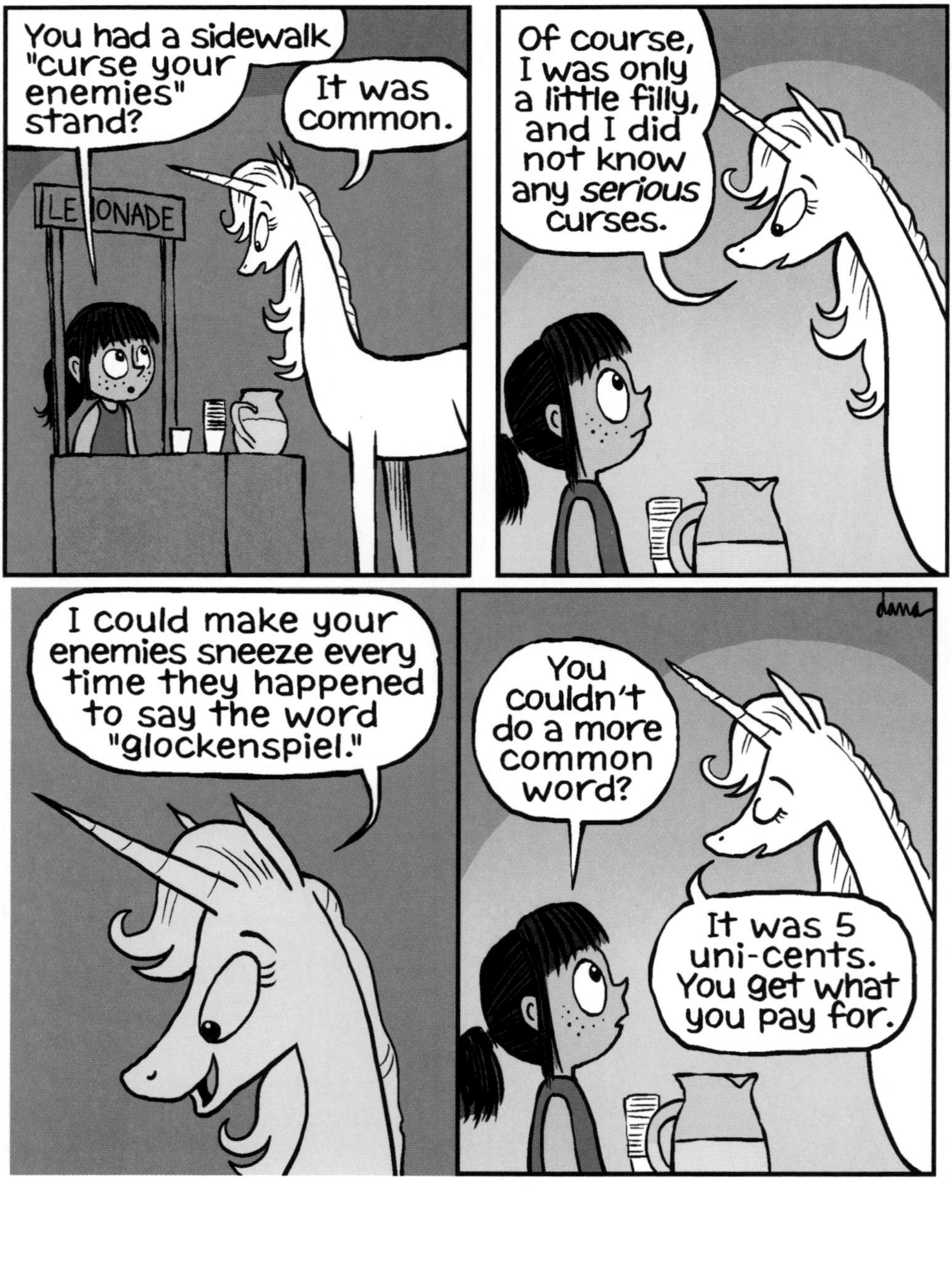
You had a sidewalk "curse your enemies" stand?
It was common.
LE ONADE
Of course, I was only a little filly, and I did not know any *serious* curses.
I could make your enemies sneeze every time they happened to say the word "glockenspiel."
dana
You couldn't do a more common word?
It was 5 uni-cents. You get what you pay for.

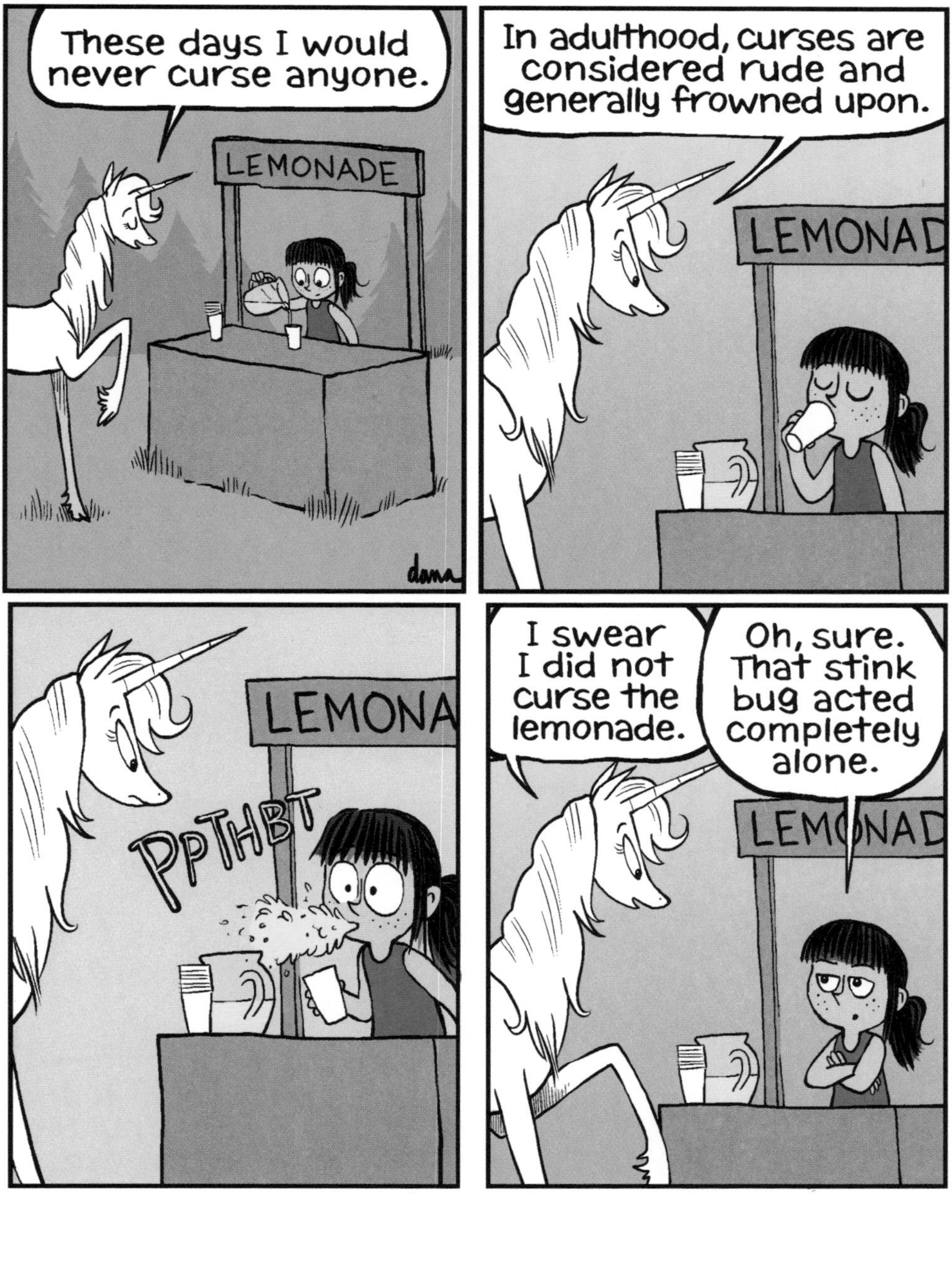
These days I would never curse anyone.
LEMONADE
dana
In adulthood, curses are considered rude and generally frowned upon.
LEMONAD
LEMONA
PPTHBT
I swear I did not curse the lemonade.
Oh, sure. That stink bug acted completely alone.
LEMONAD

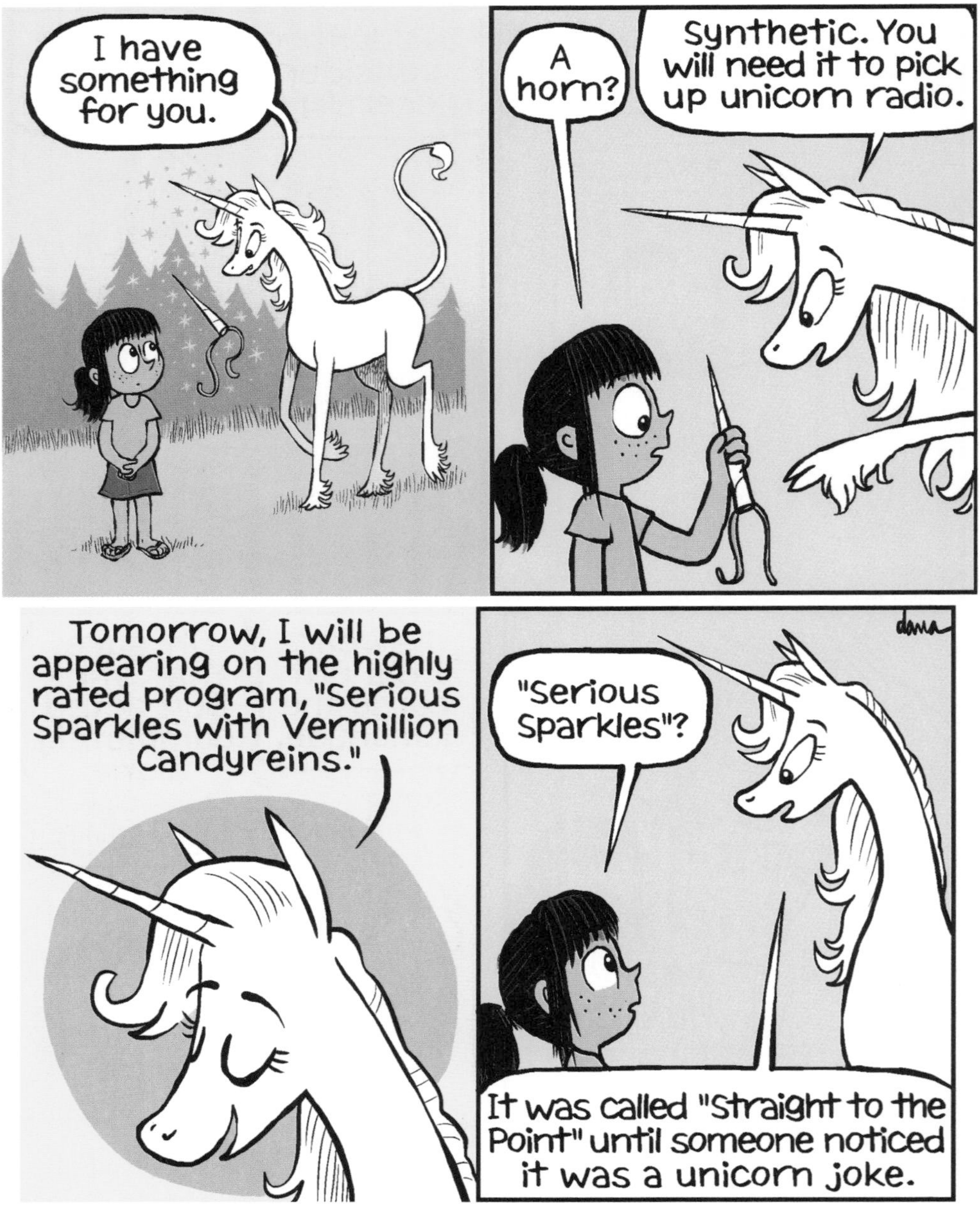
I have something for you.
A horn?
Synthetic. You will need it to pick up unicorn radio.
Tomorrow, I will be appearing on the highly rated program, "Serious Sparkles with Vermillion Candyreins."
"Serious Sparkles"?
It was called "Straight to the Point" until someone noticed it was a unicorn joke.

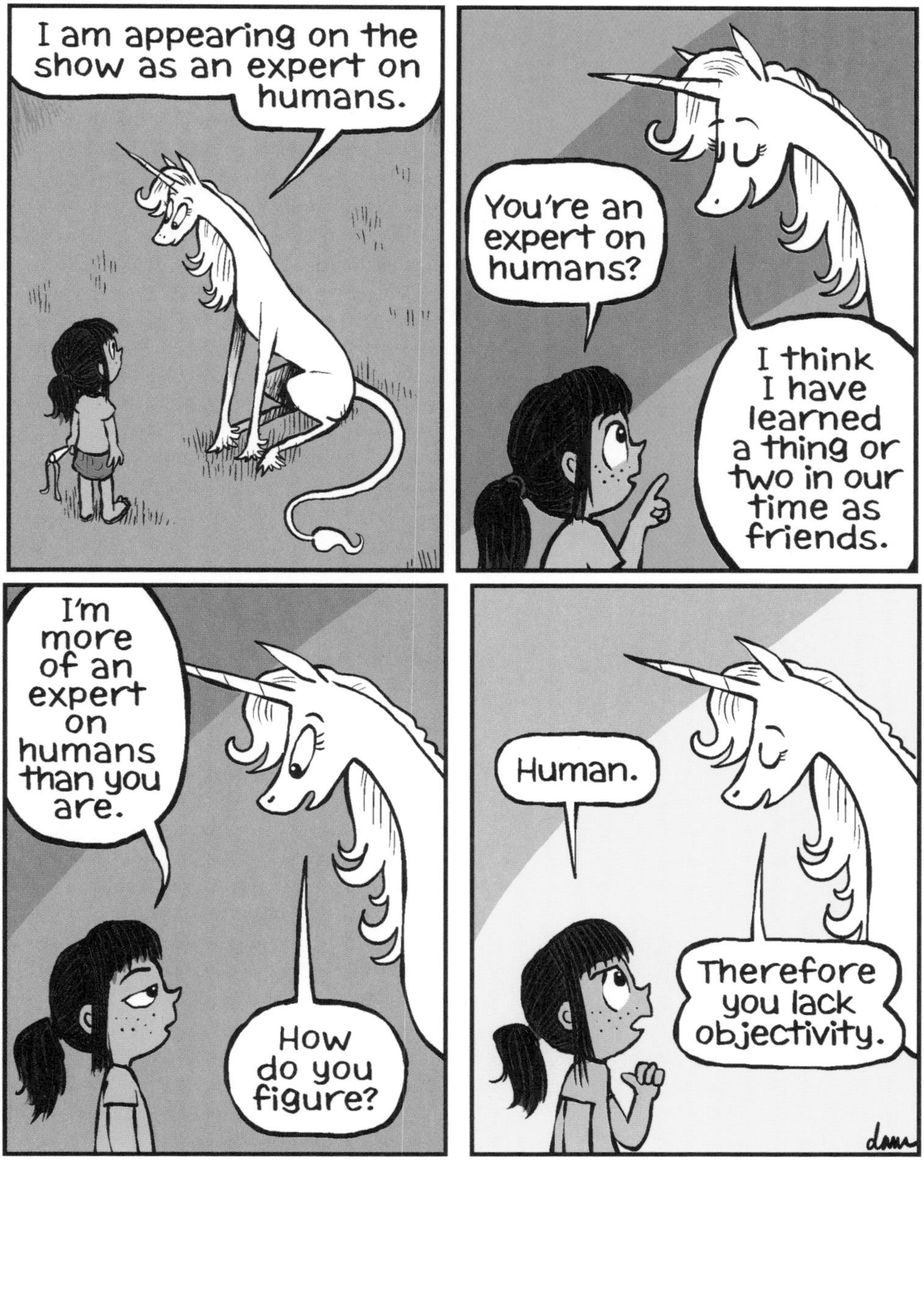
I am appearing on the show as an expert on humans.
You're an expert on humans?
I think I have learned a thing or two in our time as friends.
I'm more of an expert on humans than you are.
How do you figure?
Human.
Therefore you lack objectivity.

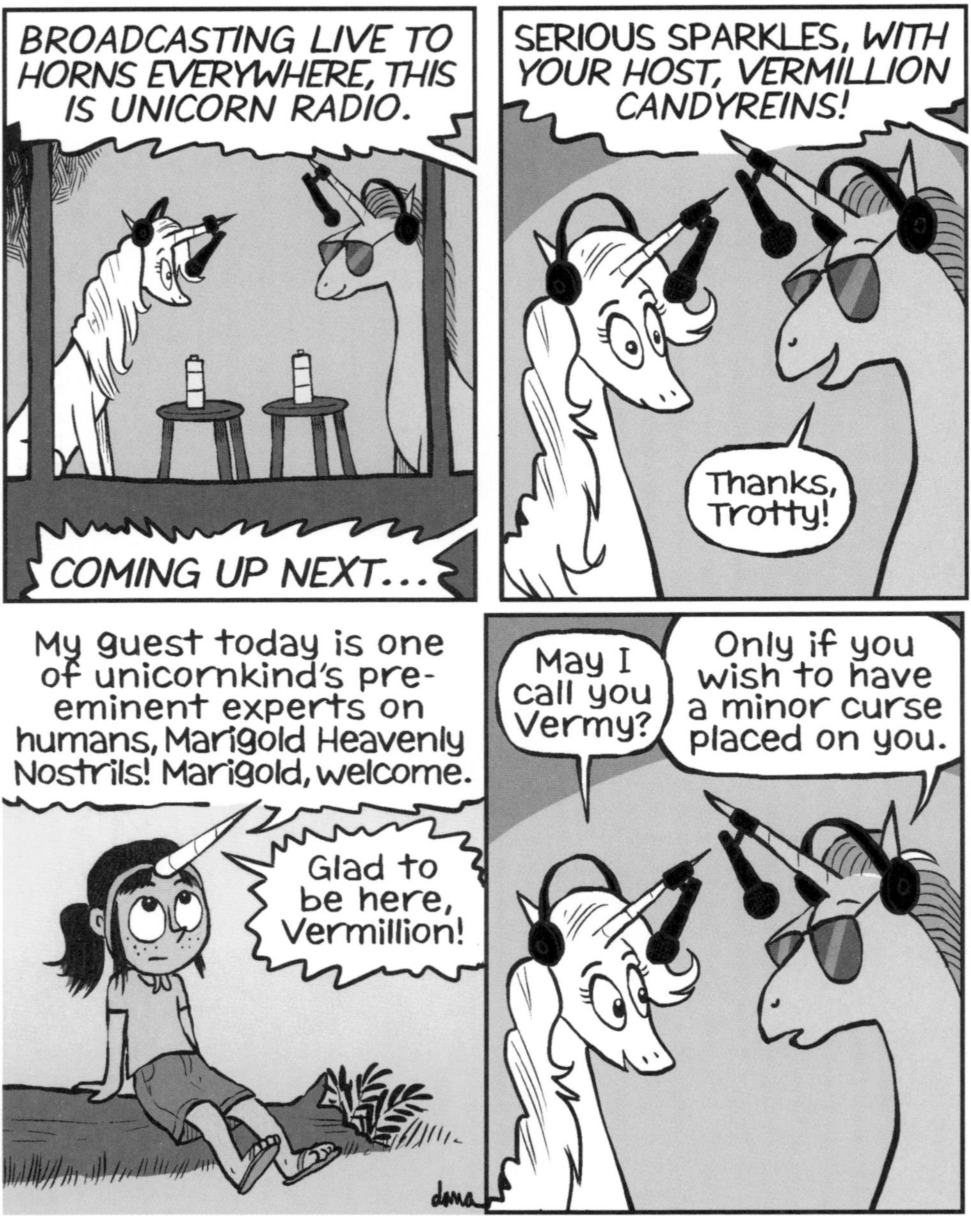
BROADCASTING LIVE TO HORNS EVERYWHERE, THIS IS UNICORN RADIO.
COMING UP NEXT...
SERIOUS SPARKLES, WITH YOUR HOST, VERMILLION CANDYREINS!
Thanks, Trotty!
My guest today is one of unicornkind's pre-eminent experts on humans, Marigold Heavenly Nostrils! Marigold, welcome.
Glad to be here, Vermillion!
May I call you Vermy?
Only if you wish to have a minor curse placed on you.
dana

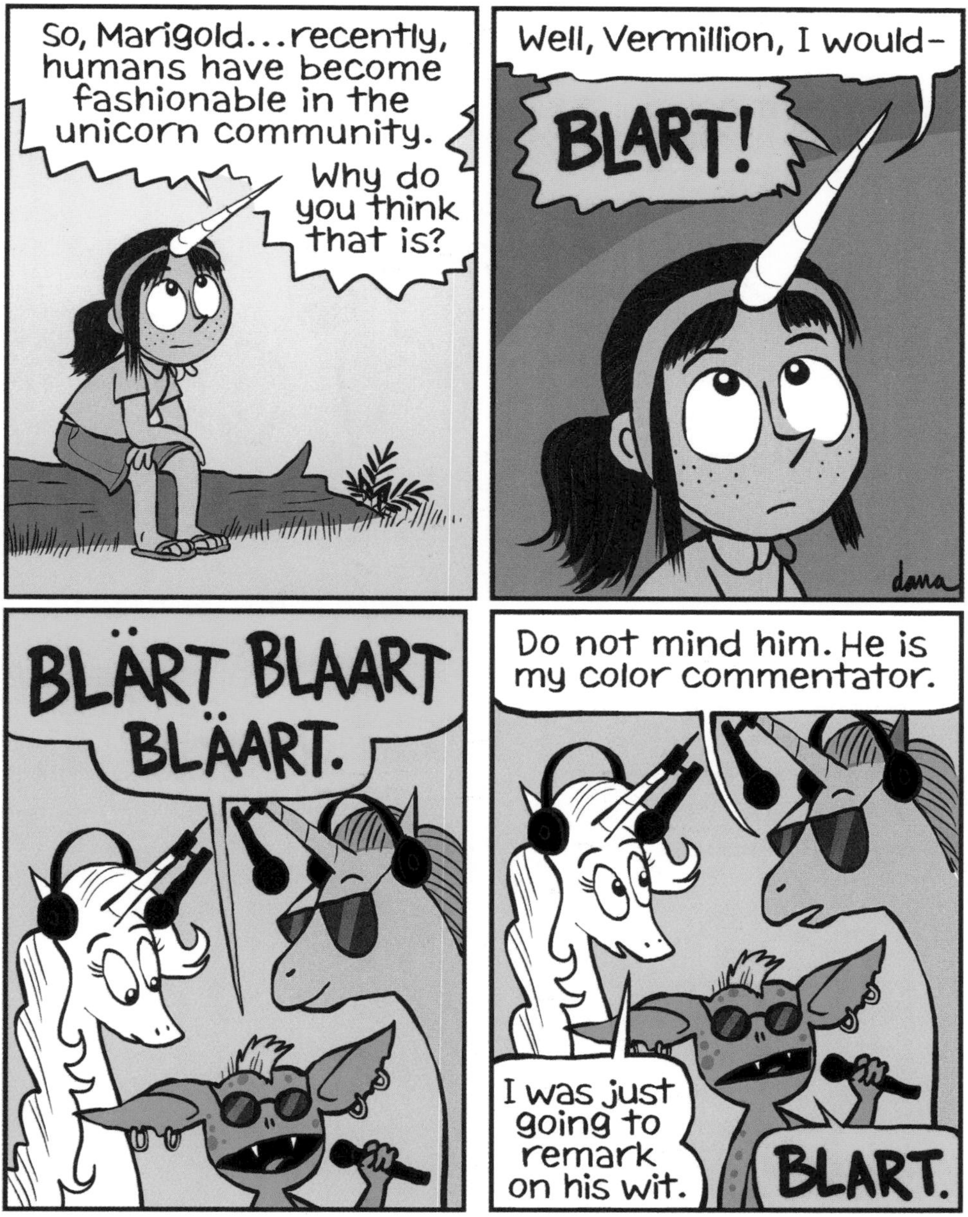

So, Marigold...recently, humans have become fashionable in the unicorn community.
Why do you think that is?
Well, Vermillion, I would-
BLART!
BLÄRT BLAART BLÄART.
Do not mind him. He is my color commentator.
I was just going to remark on his wit.
BLART.
dana

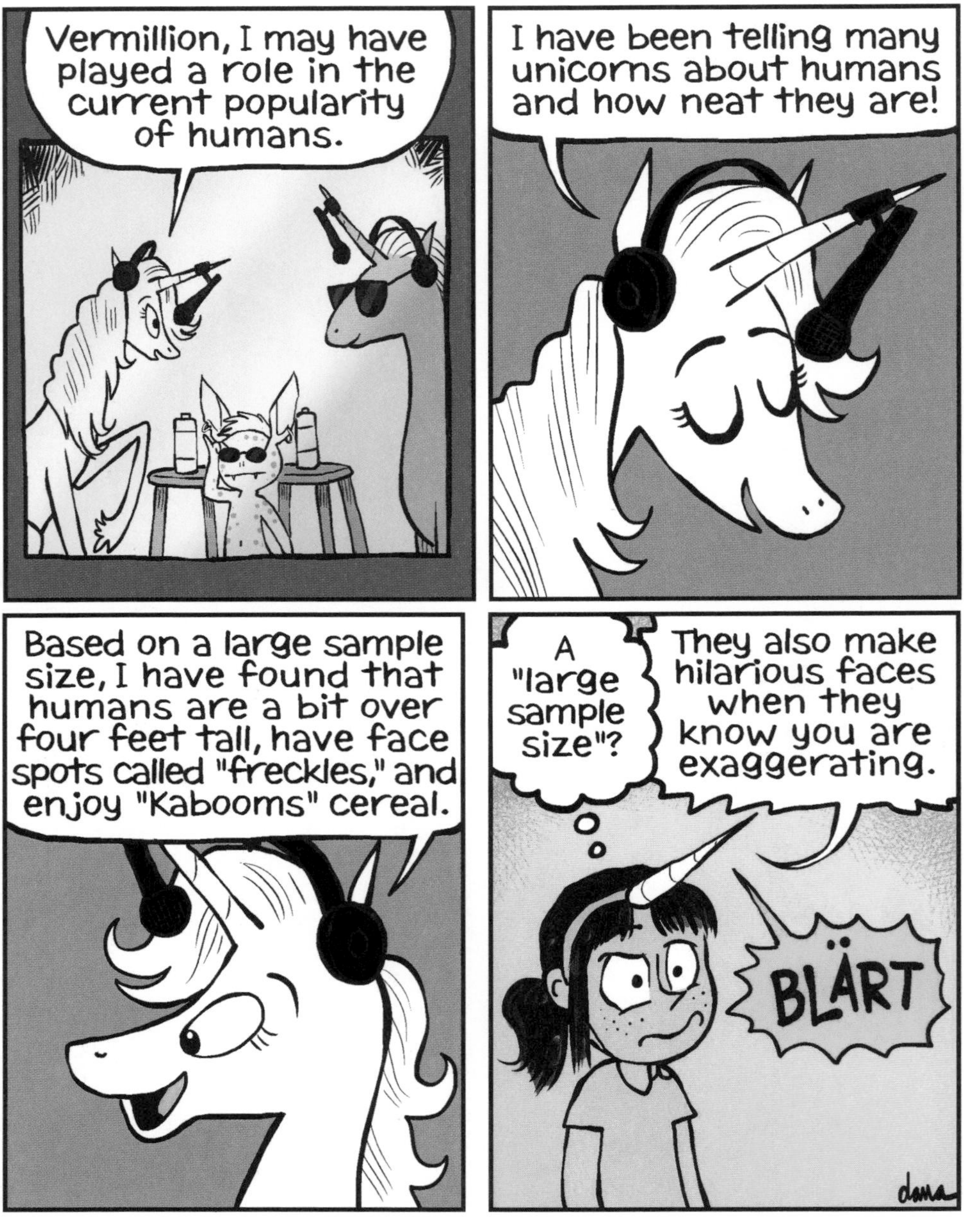
Vermillion, I may have played a role in the current popularity of humans.
I have been telling many unicorns about humans and how neat they are!
Based on a large sample size, I have found that humans are a bit over four feet tall, have face spots called "freckles," and enjoy "Kabooms" cereal.
A "large sample size"?
They also make hilarious faces when they know you are exaggerating.
BLÄRT
dana

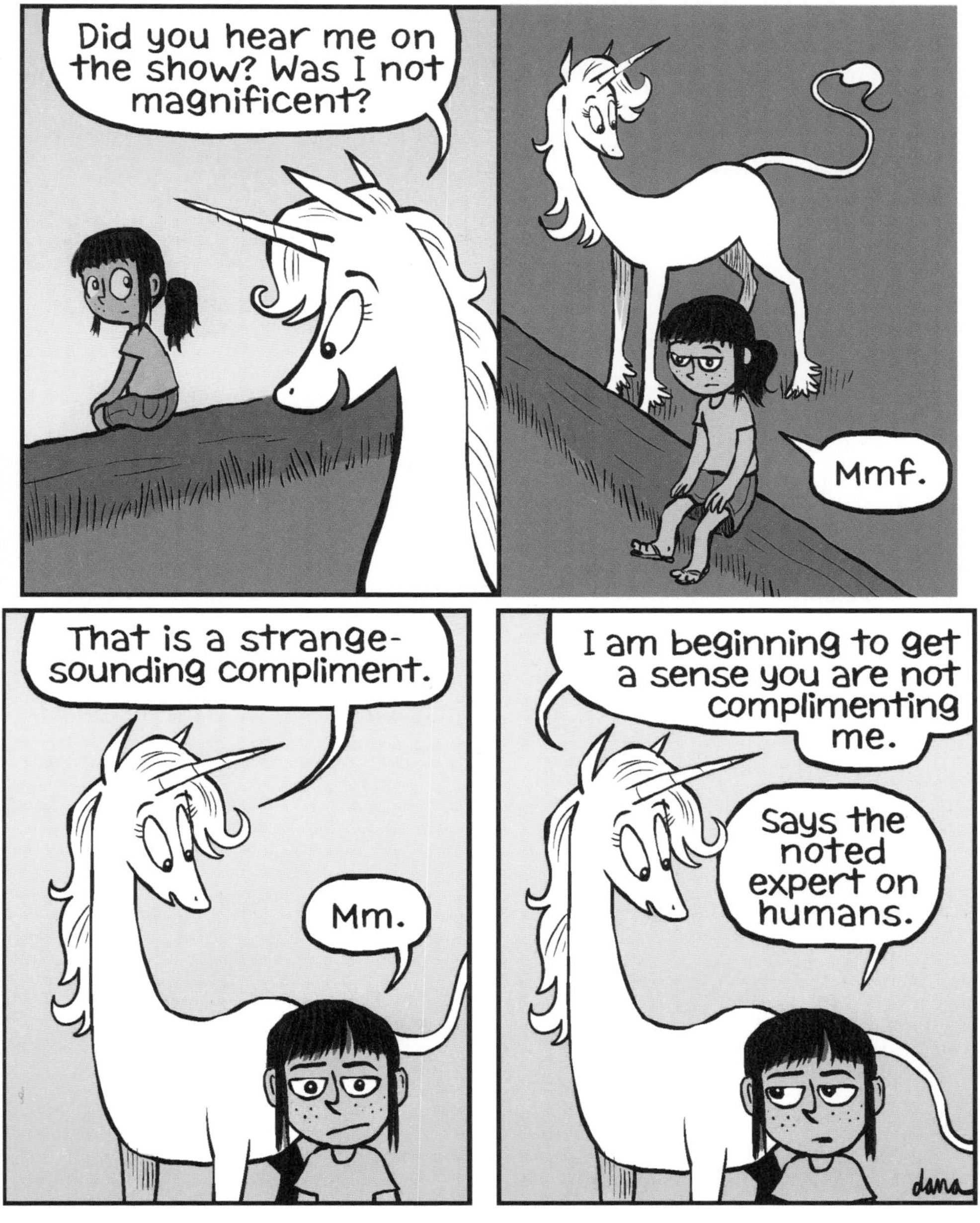
Did you hear me on the show? Was I not magnificent?
Mmf.
That is a strange-sounding compliment.
Mm.
I am beginning to get a sense you are not complimenting me.
Says the noted expert on humans.
dana

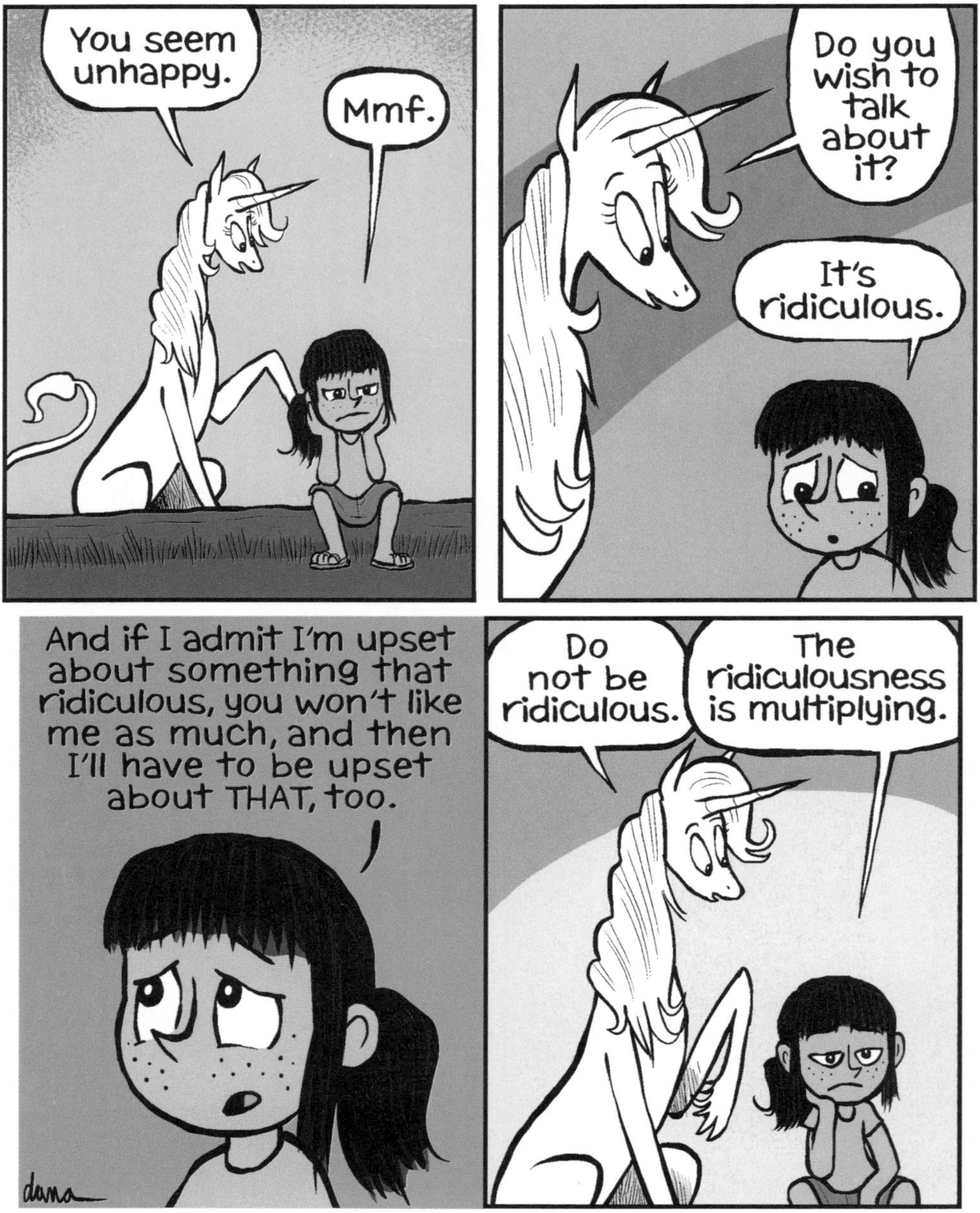
You seem unhappy.
Mmf.
Do you wish to talk about it?
It's ridiculous.
And if I admit I'm upset about something that ridiculous, you won't like me as much, and then I'll have to be upset about THAT, too.
Do not be ridiculous.
The ridiculousness is multiplying.
dana

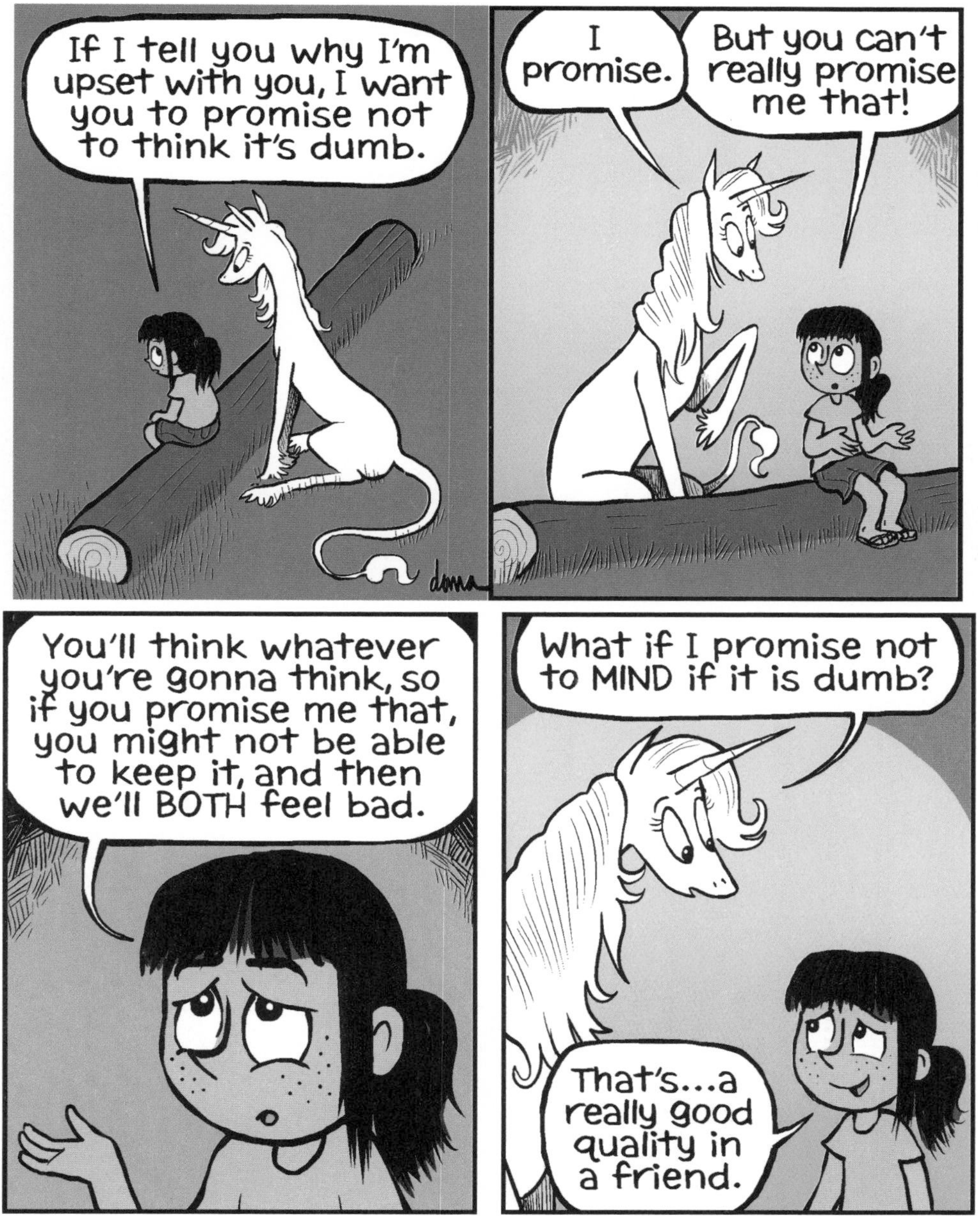
If I tell you why I'm upset with you, I want you to promise not to think it's dumb.
I promise.
But you can't really promise me that!
You'll think whatever you're gonna think, so if you promise me that, you might not be able to keep it, and then we'll BOTH feel bad.
What if I promise not to MIND if it is dumb?
That's...a really good quality in a friend.

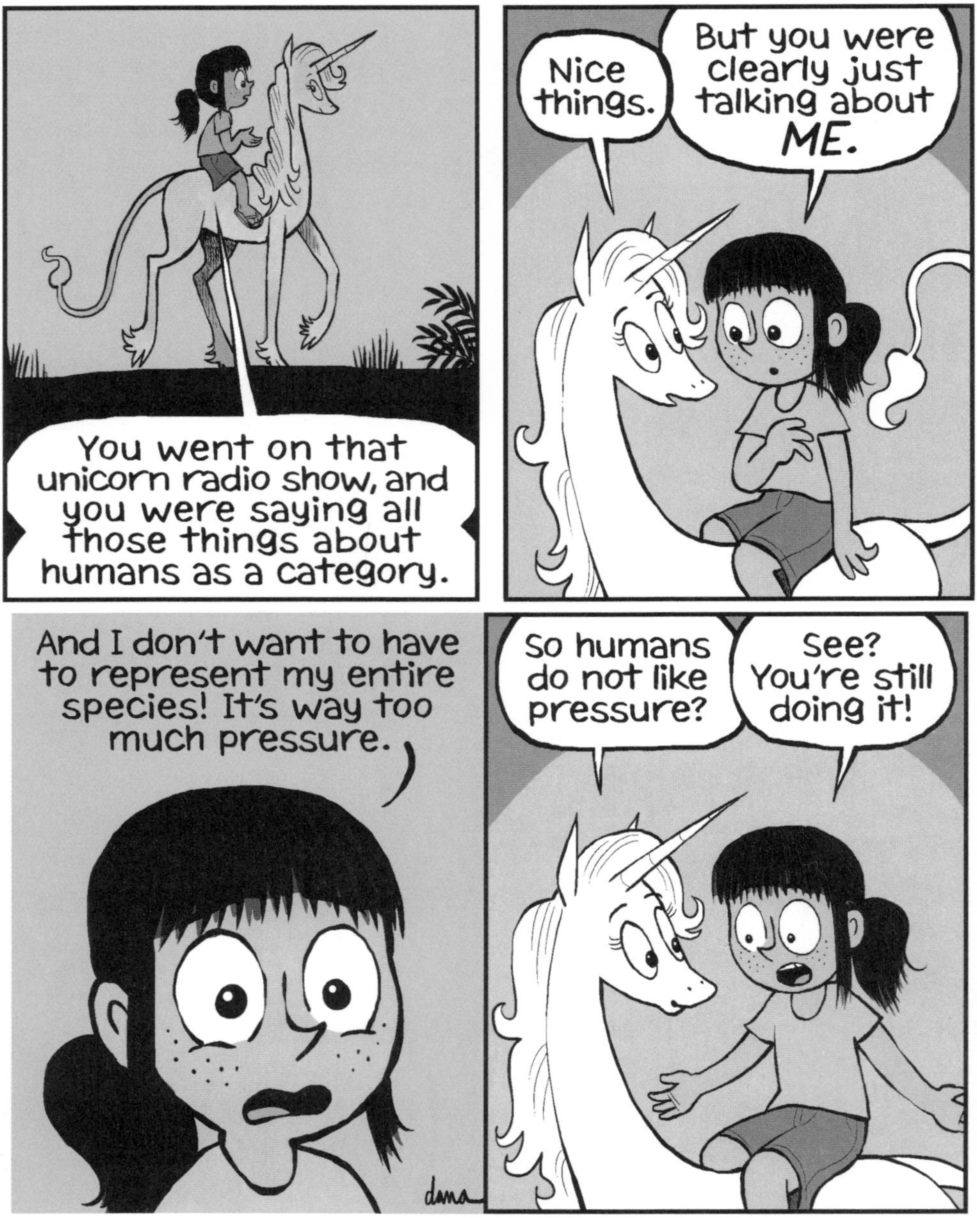
You went on that unicorn radio show, and you were saying all those things about humans as a category.
Nice things.
But you were clearly just talking about ME.
And I don't want to have to represent my entire species! It's way too much pressure.
So humans do not like pressure?
See? You're still doing it!
dana

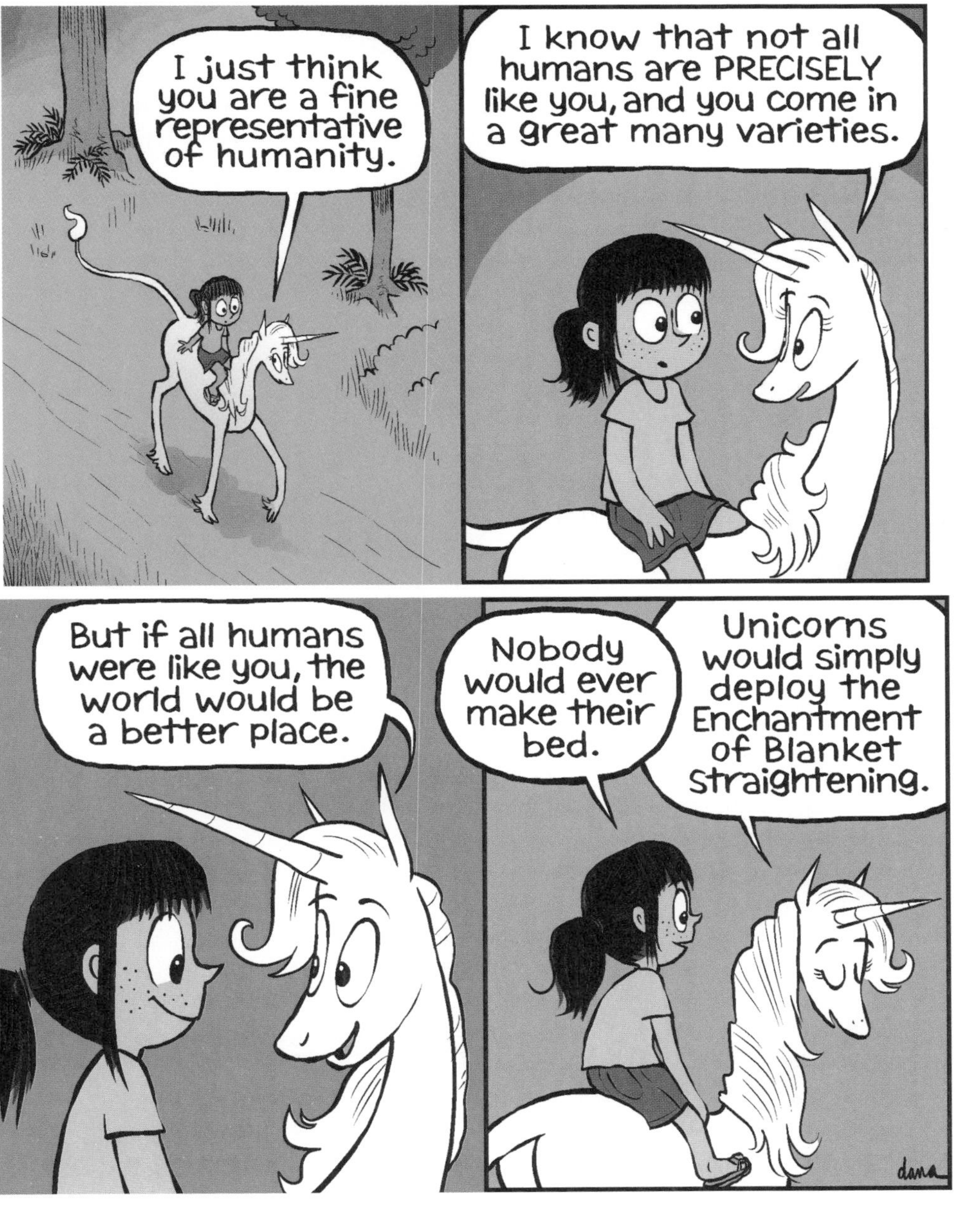
I just think you are a fine representative of humanity.
I know that not all humans are PRECISELY like you, and you come in a great many varieties.
But if all humans were like you, the world would be a better place.
Nobody would ever make their bed.
Unicorns would simply deploy the Enchantment of Blanket Straightening.
dana

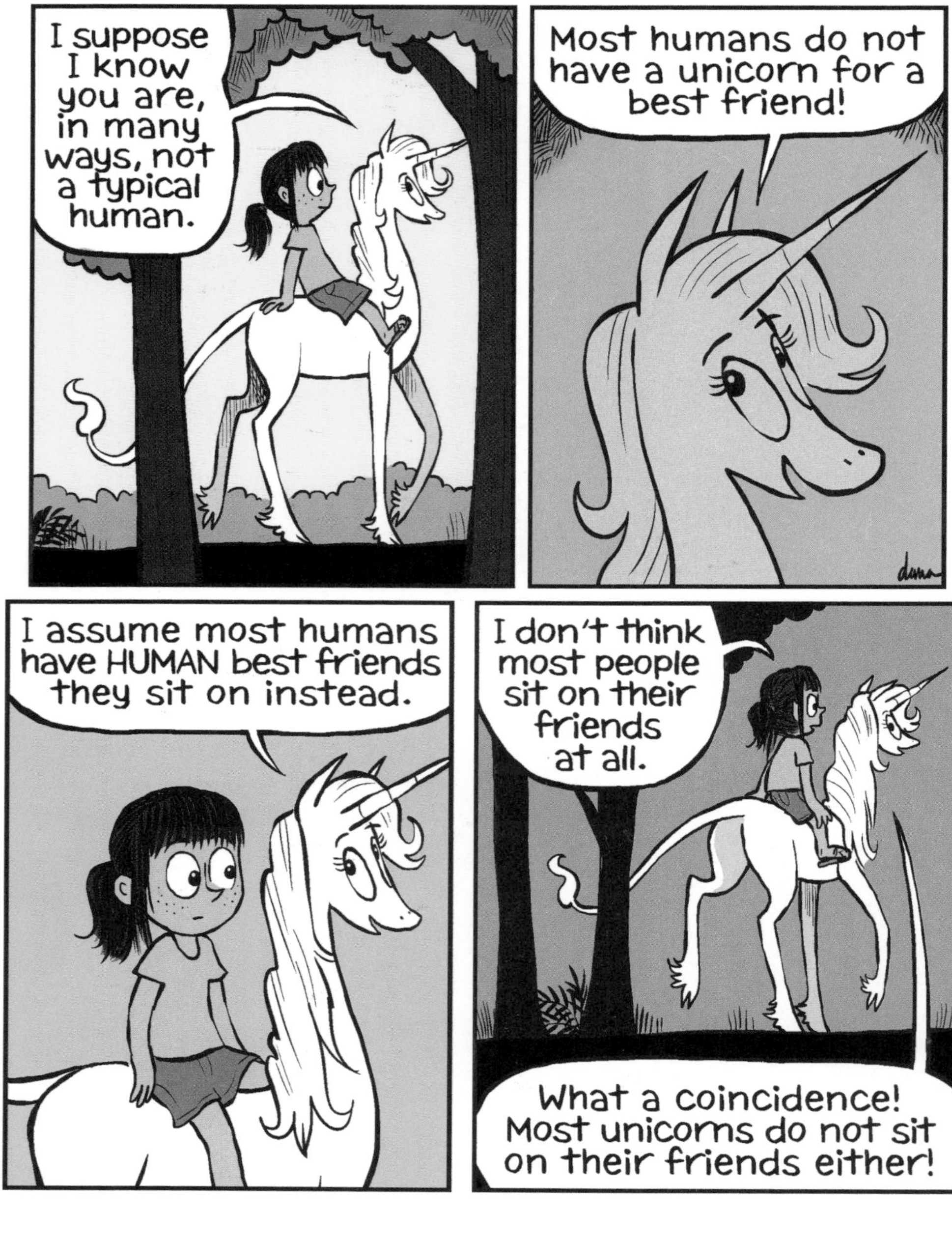
I suppose I know you are, in many ways, not a typical human.
Most humans do not have a unicorn for a best friend!
I assume most humans have HUMAN best friends they sit on instead.
I don't think most people sit on their friends at all.
What a coincidence! Most unicorns do not sit on their friends either!

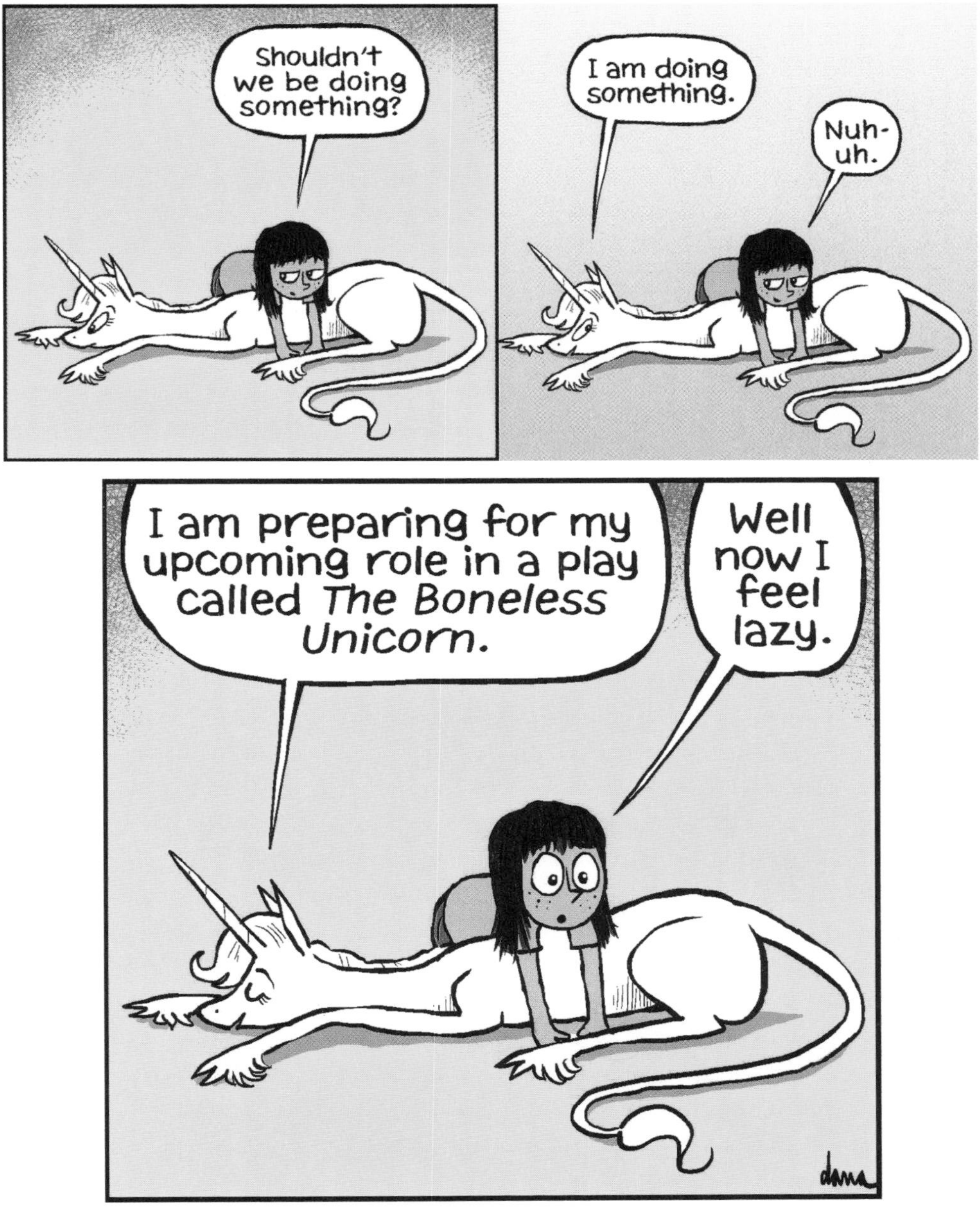
Shouldn't we be doing something?
I am doing something.
Nuh-uh.
I am preparing for my upcoming role in a play called *The Boneless Unicorn.*
Well now I feel lazy.
dana

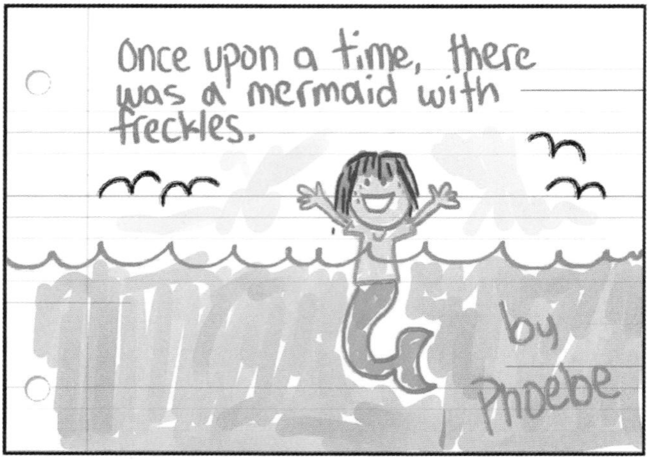
Once upon a time, there was a mermaid with freckles.
by Phoebe

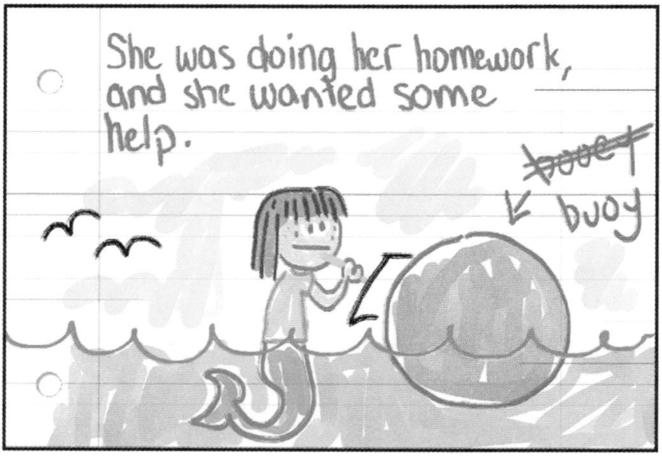
She was doing her homework, and she wanted some help.
~~booey~~
buoy

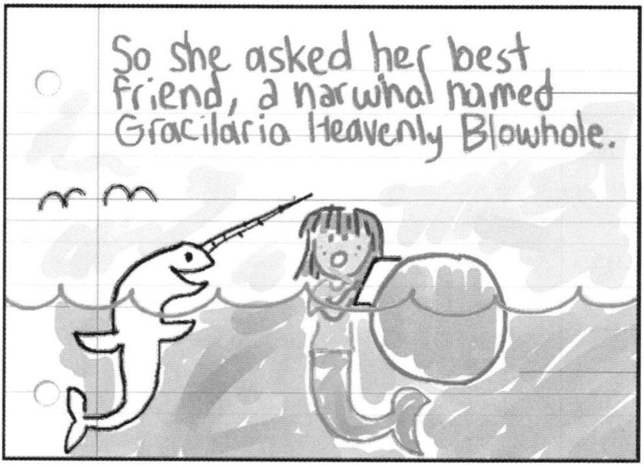
So she asked her best friend, a narwhal named Graciláría Heavenly Blowhole.

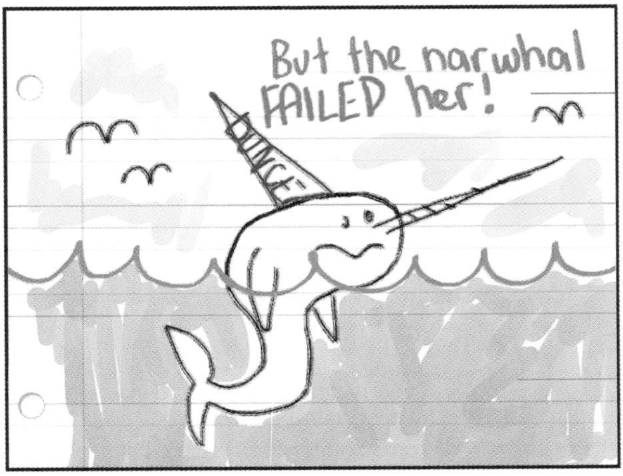
But the narwhal FAILED her!
DUNCE

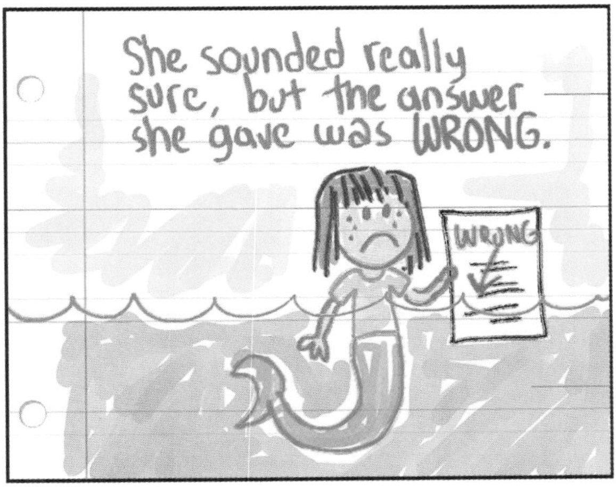
She sounded really sure, but the answer she gave was WRONG.
WRONG

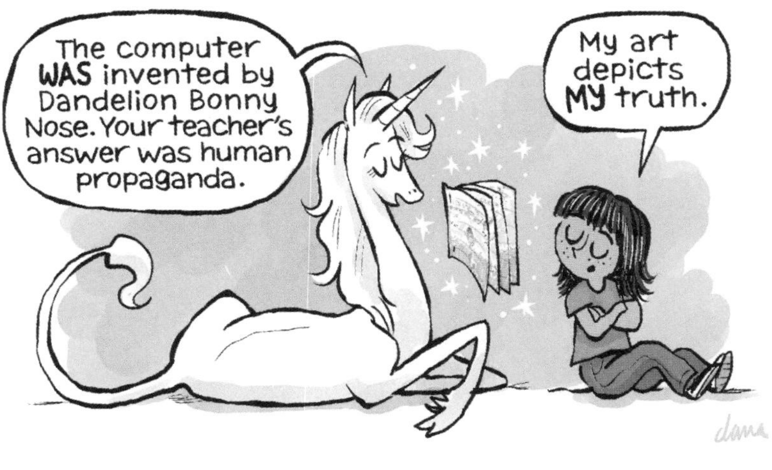
The computer **WAS** invented by Dandelion Bonny Nose. Your teacher's answer was human propaganda.
My art depicts **MY** truth.
dana

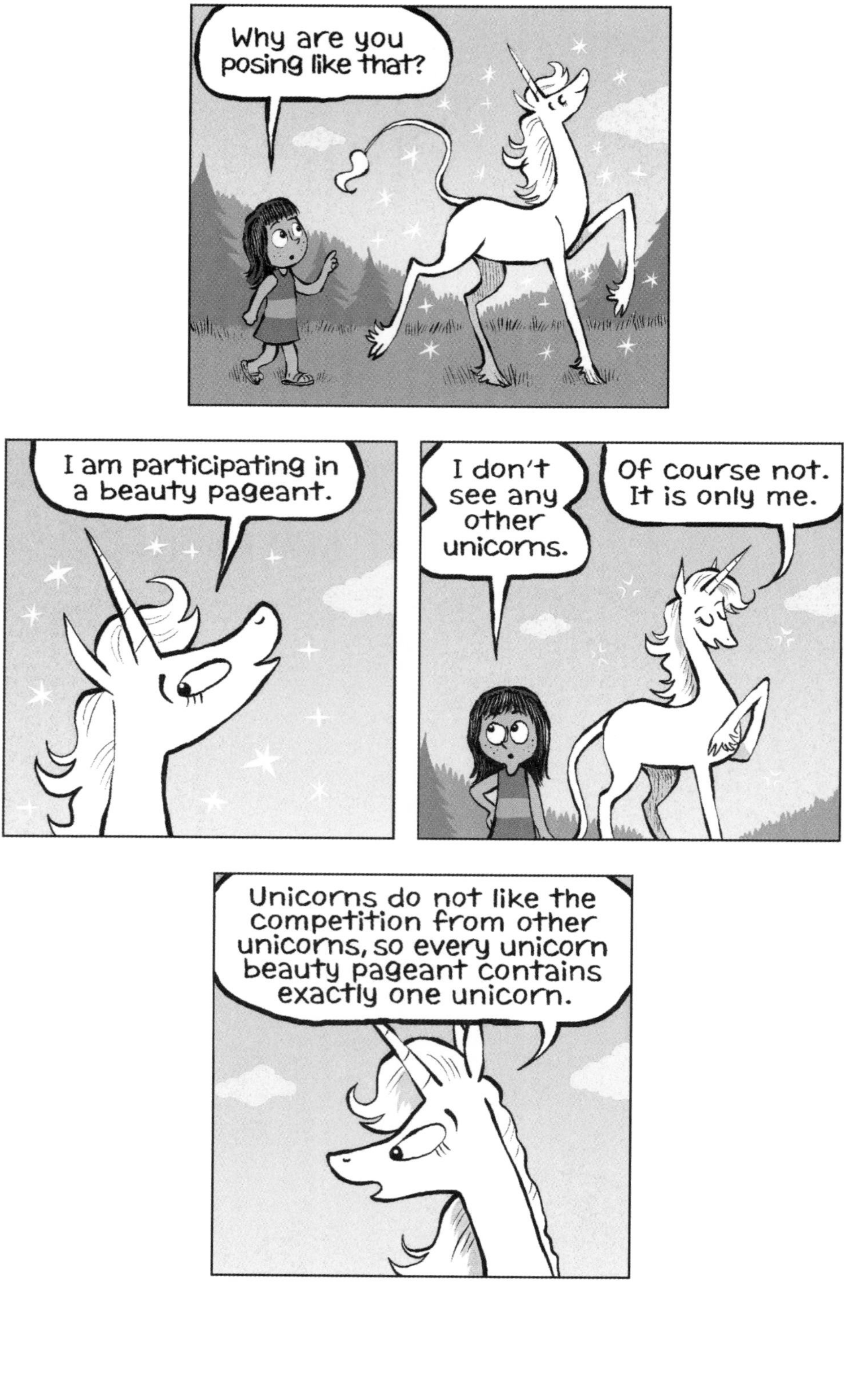
Why are you posing like that?
I am participating in a beauty pageant.
I don't see any other unicorns.
Of course not. It is only me.
Unicorns do not like the competition from other unicorns, so every unicorn beauty pageant contains exactly one unicorn.

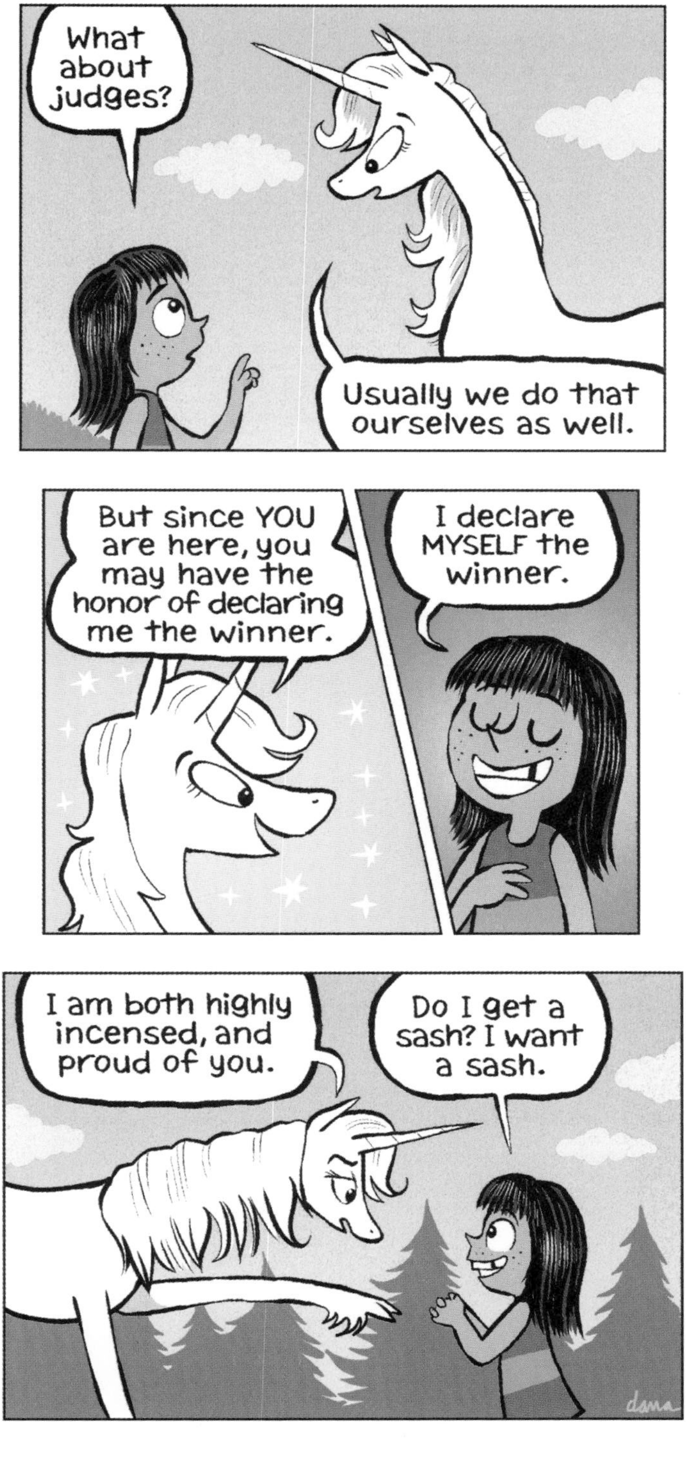
What about judges?
Usually we do that ourselves as well.
But since YOU are here, you may have the honor of declaring me the winner.
I declare MYSELF the winner.
I am both highly incensed, and proud of you.
Do I get a sash? I want a sash.
dana

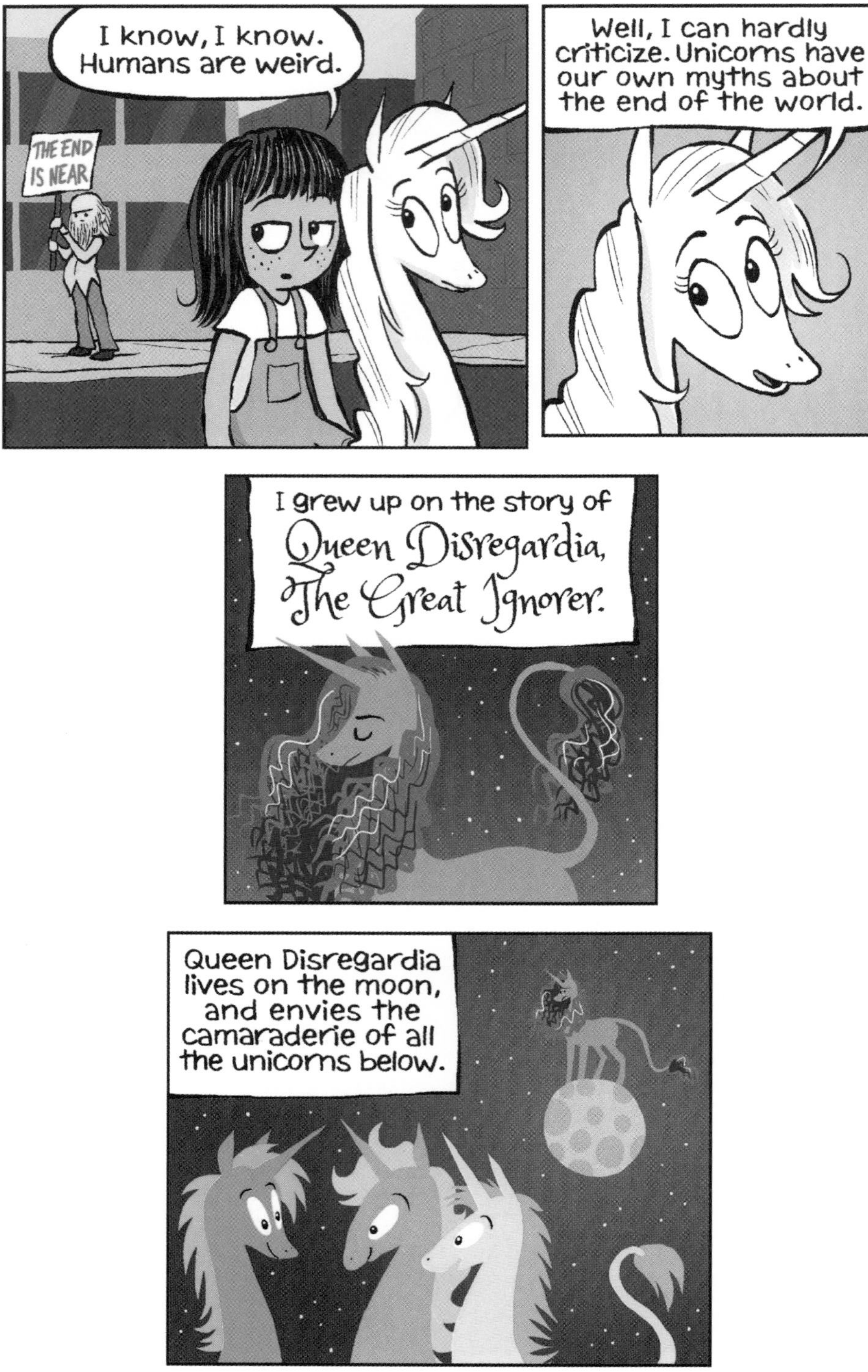
I know, I know. Humans are weird.
THE END IS NEAR
Well, I can hardly criticize. Unicorns have our own myths about the end of the world.
I grew up on the story of Queen Disregardia, The Great Ignorer.
Queen Disregardia lives on the moon, and envies the camaraderie of all the unicorns below.

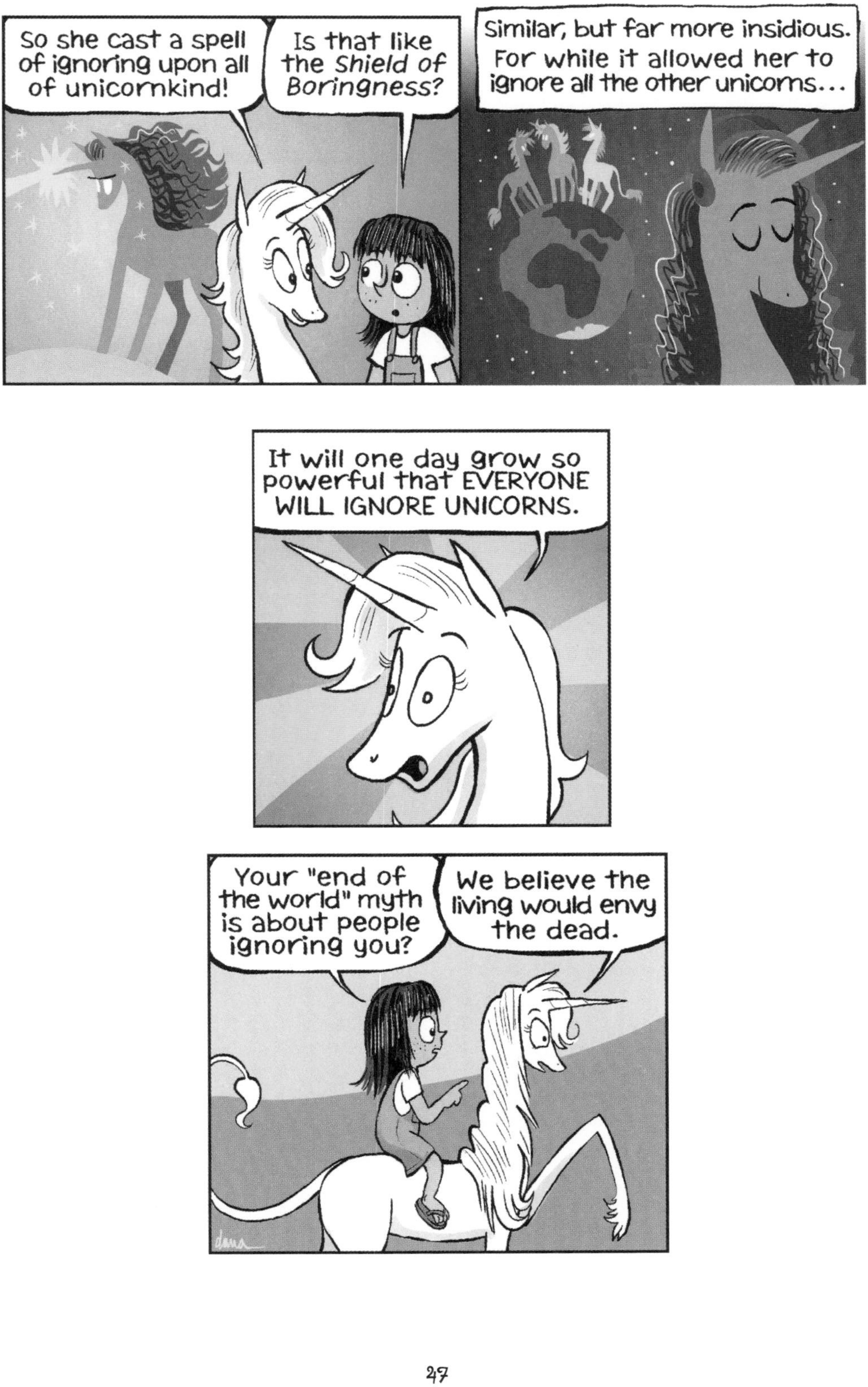
So she cast a spell of ignoring upon all of unicornkind!
Is that like the *Shield of Boringness?*
Similar, but far more insidious. For while it allowed her to ignore all the other unicorns...
It will one day grow so powerful that EVERYONE WILL IGNORE UNICORNS.
Your "end of the world" myth is about people ignoring you?
We believe the living would envy the dead.

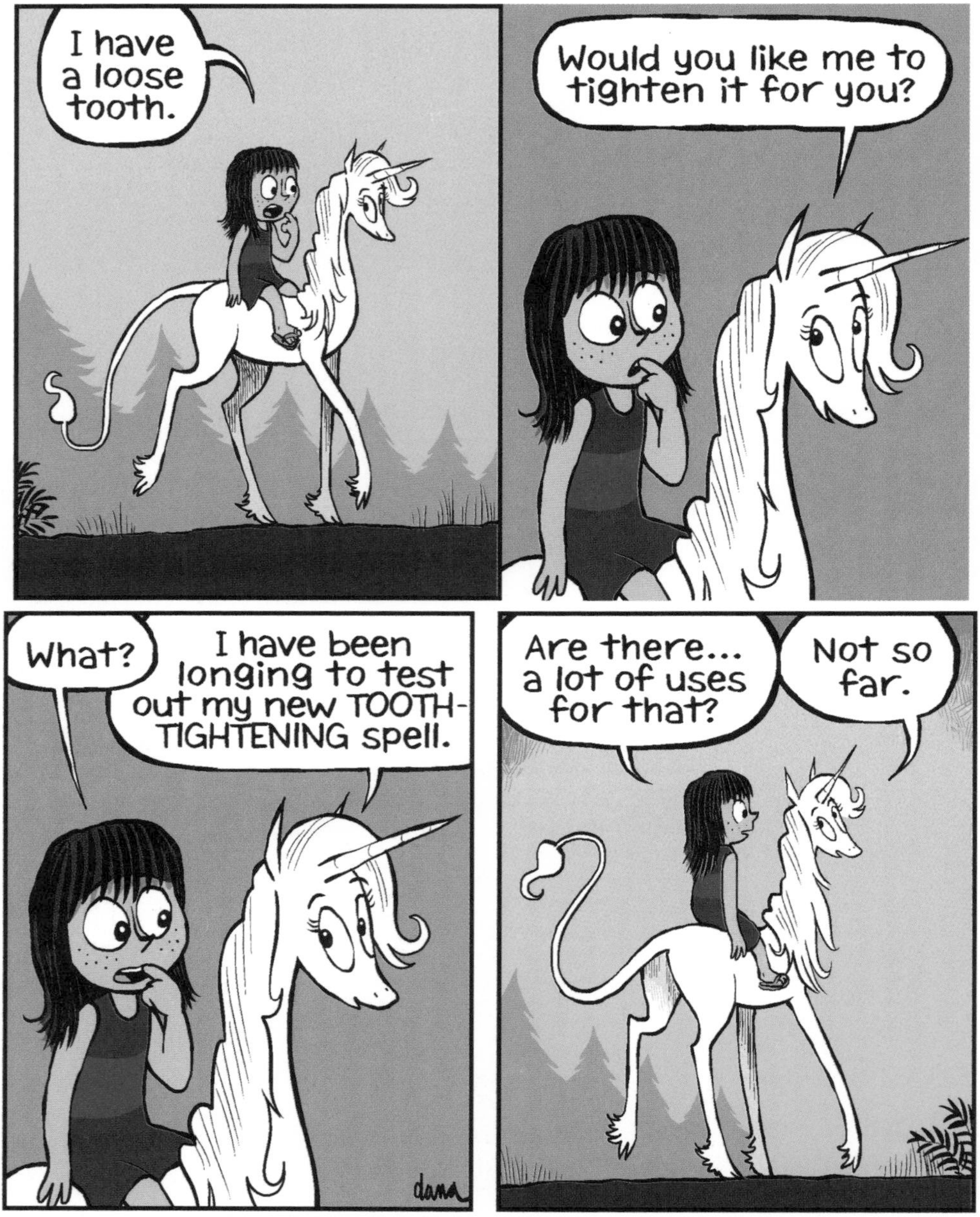
I have a loose tooth.
Would you like me to tighten it for you?
What?
I have been longing to test out my new TOOTH-TIGHTENING spell.
Are there... a lot of uses for that?
Not so far.
dana

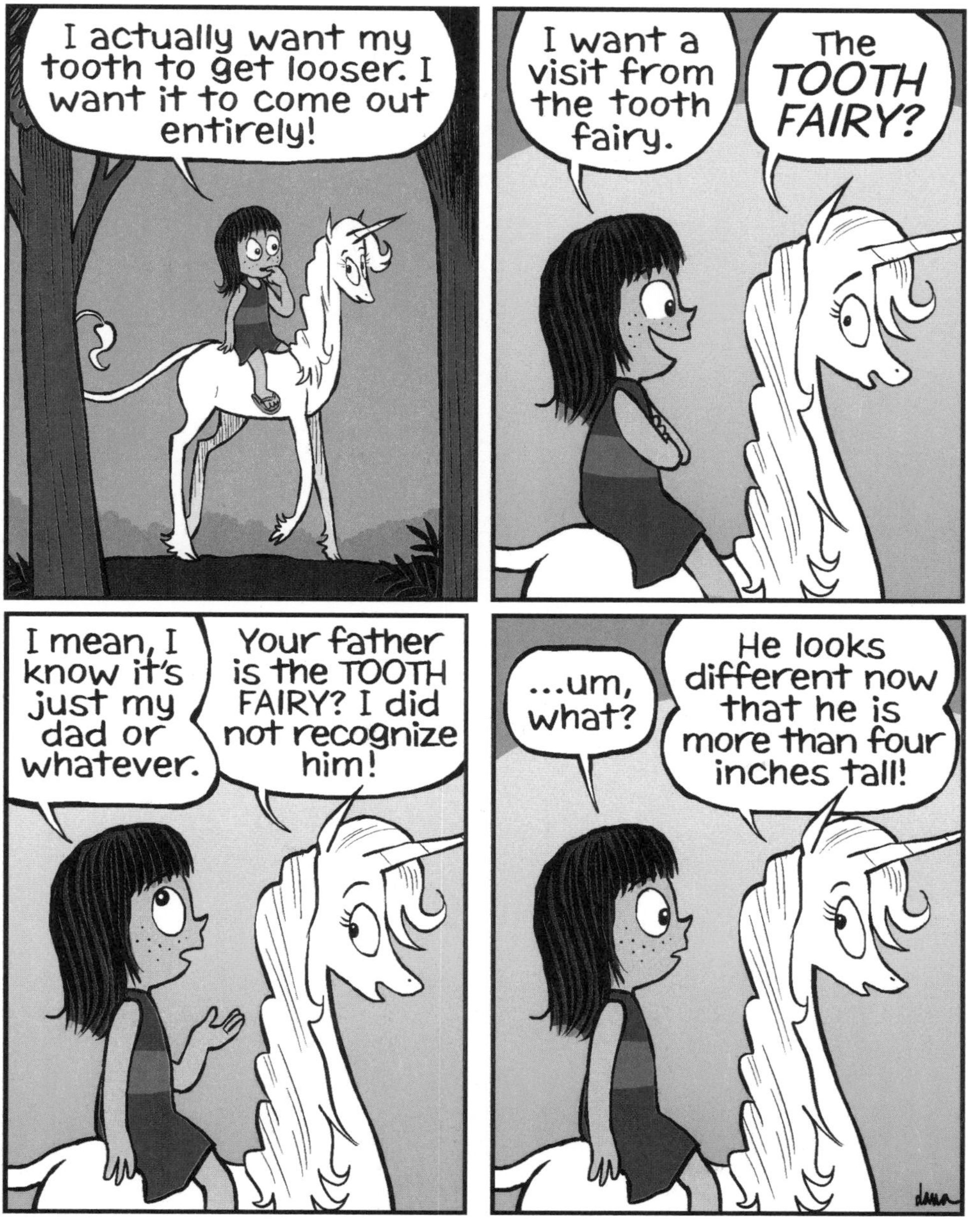
I actually want my tooth to get looser. I want it to come out entirely!
I want a visit from the tooth fairy.
The TOOTH FAIRY?
I mean, I know it's just my dad or whatever.
Your father is the TOOTH FAIRY? I did not recognize him!
...um, what?
He looks different now that he is more than four inches tall!

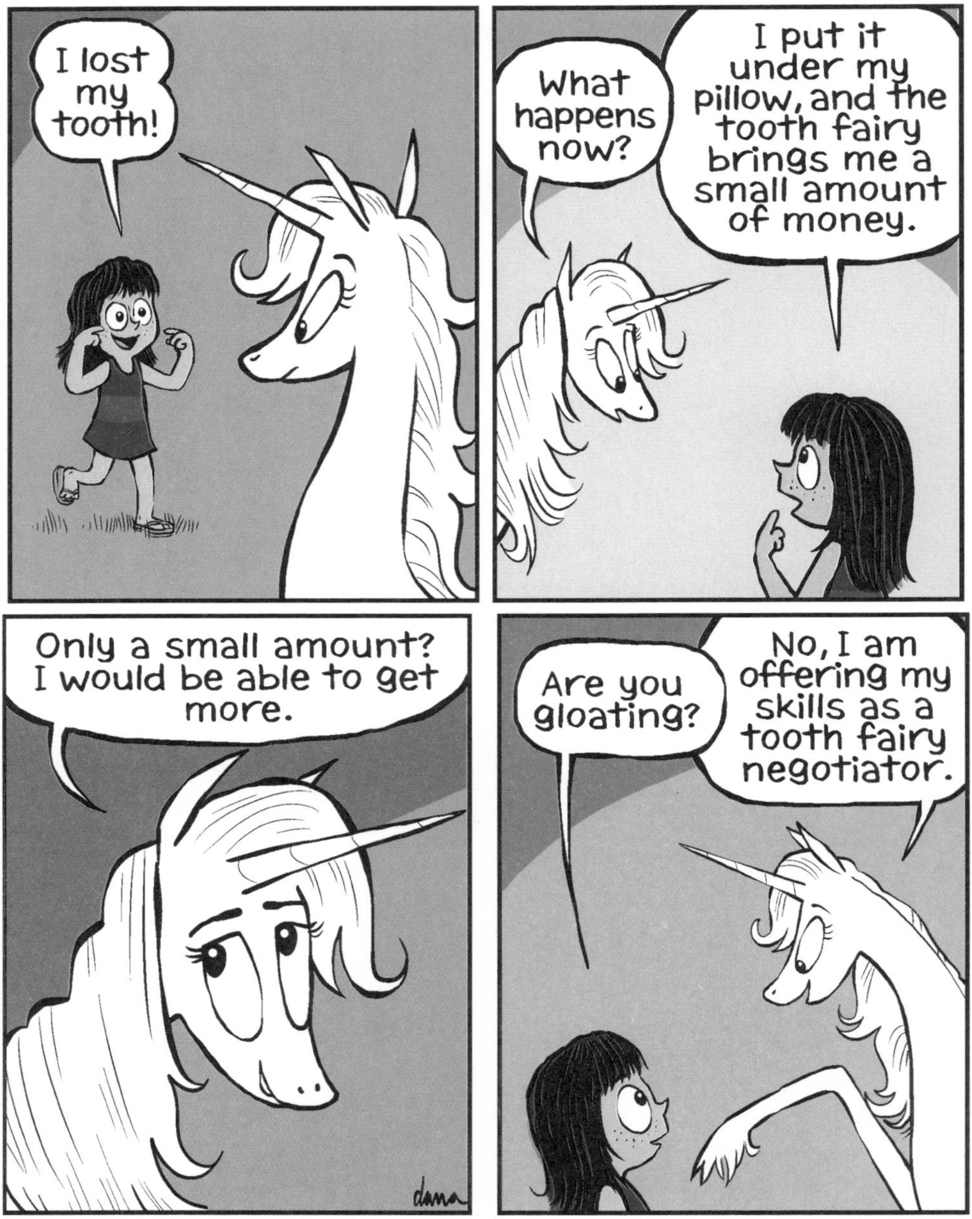
I lost my tooth!
What happens now?
I put it under my pillow, and the tooth fairy brings me a small amount of money.
Only a small amount? I would be able to get more.
Are you gloating?
No, I am offering my skills as a tooth fairy negotiator.
dana

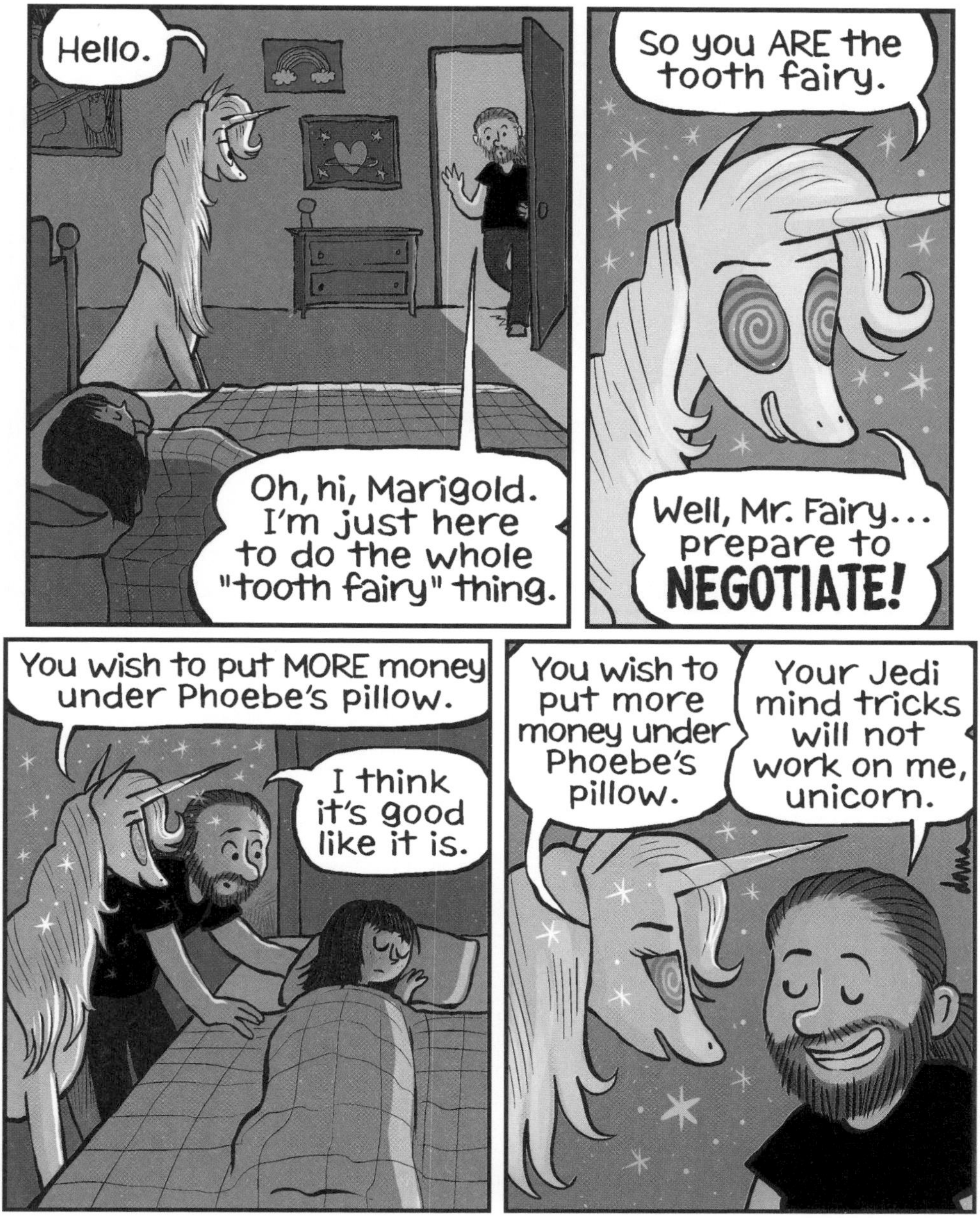
Hello.
Oh, hi, Marigold. I'm just here to do the whole "tooth fairy" thing.
So you ARE the tooth fairy.
Well, Mr. Fairy... prepare to NEGOTIATE!
You wish to put MORE money under Phoebe's pillow.
I think it's good like it is.
You wish to put more money under Phoebe's pillow.
Your Jedi mind tricks will not work on me, unicorn.

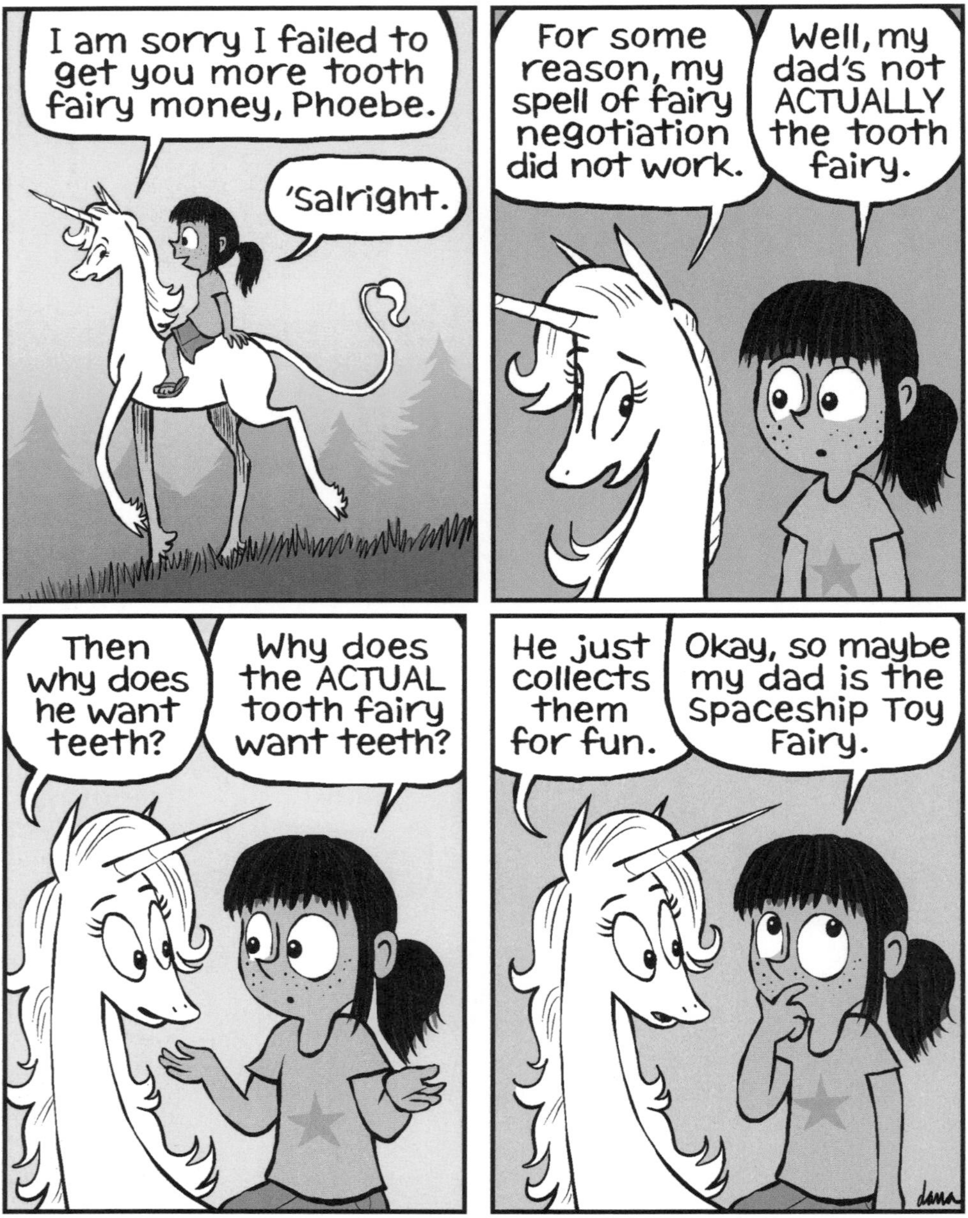
I am sorry I failed to get you more tooth fairy money, Phoebe.
'Salright.
For some reason, my spell of fairy negotiation did not work.
Well, my dad's not ACTUALLY the tooth fairy.
Then why does he want teeth?
Why does the ACTUAL tooth fairy want teeth?
He just collects them for fun.
Okay, so maybe my dad is the Spaceship Toy Fairy.
dana

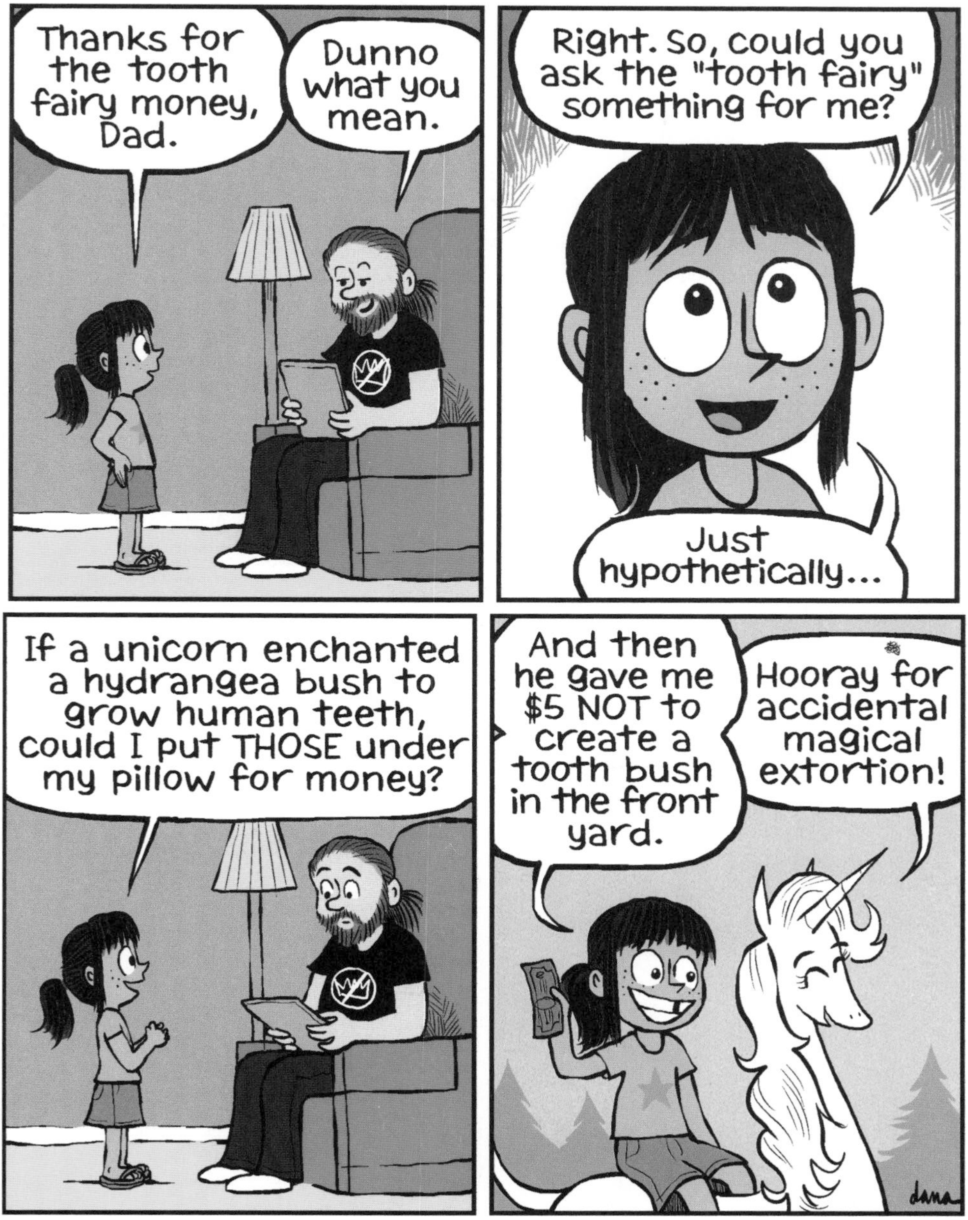
Thanks for the tooth fairy money, Dad.
Dunno what you mean.
Right. So, could you ask the "tooth fairy" something for me?
Just hypothetically...
If a unicorn enchanted a hydrangea bush to grow human teeth, could I put THOSE under my pillow for money?
And then he gave me $5 NOT to create a tooth bush in the front yard.
Hooray for accidental magical extortion!
dana

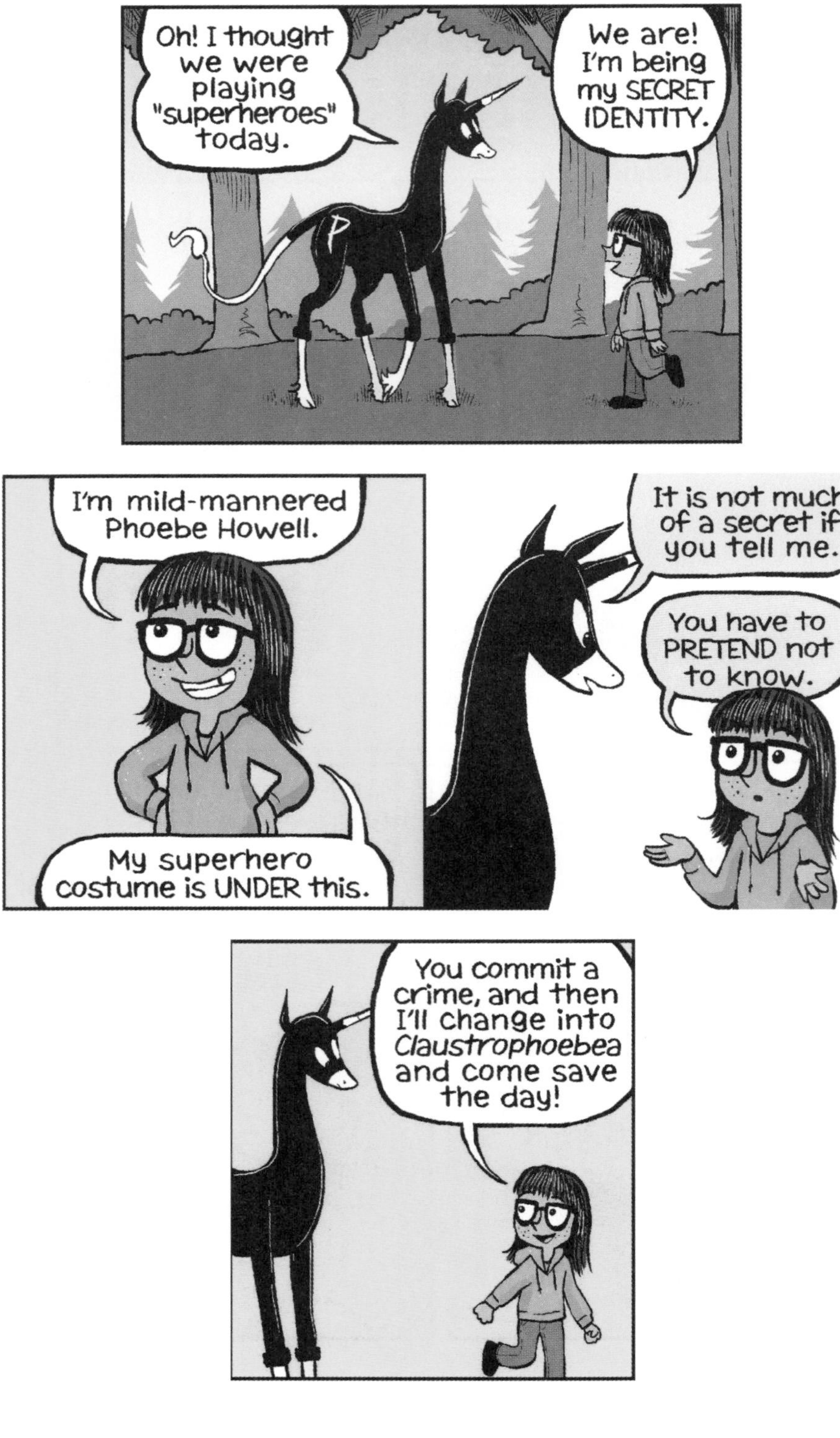
Oh! I thought we were playing "superheroes" today.
We are! I'm being my SECRET IDENTITY.
I'm mild-mannered Phoebe Howell.
My superhero costume is UNDER this.
It is not much of a secret if you tell me.
You have to PRETEND not to know.
You commit a crime, and then I'll change into *Claustrophoebea* and come save the day!

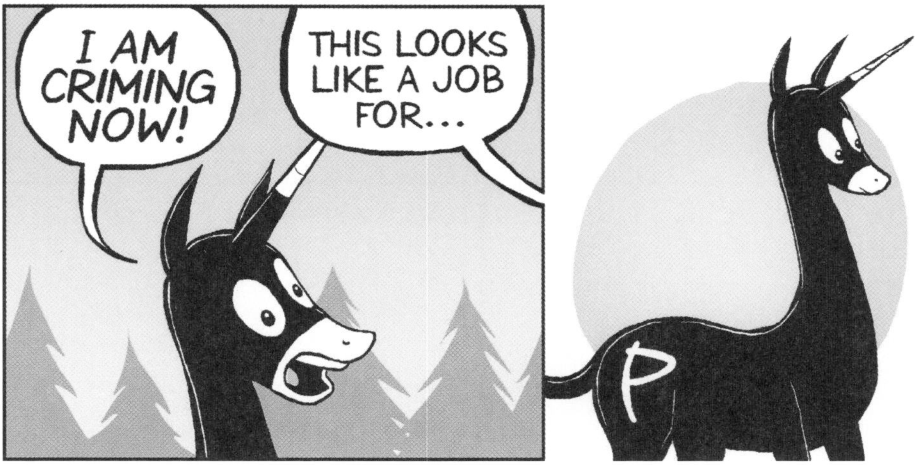
I AM CRIMING NOW!
THIS LOOKS LIKE A JOB FOR...

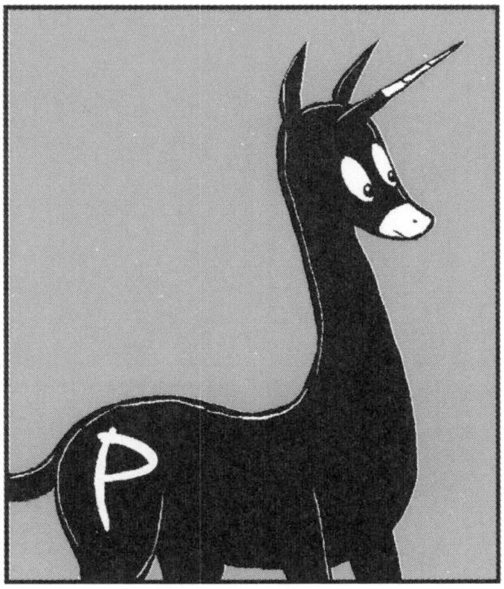

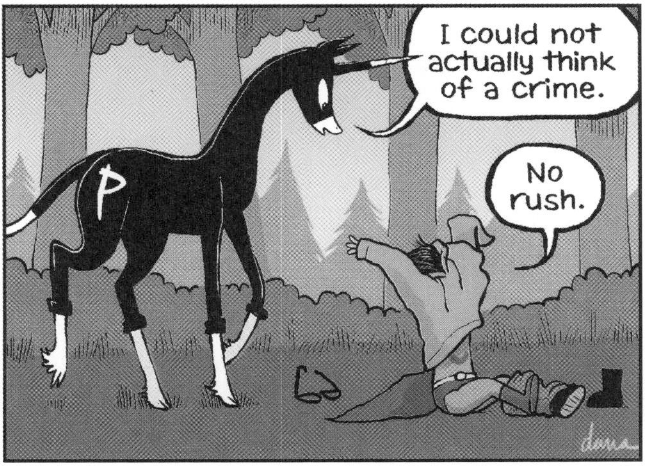
I could not actually think of a crime.
No rush.

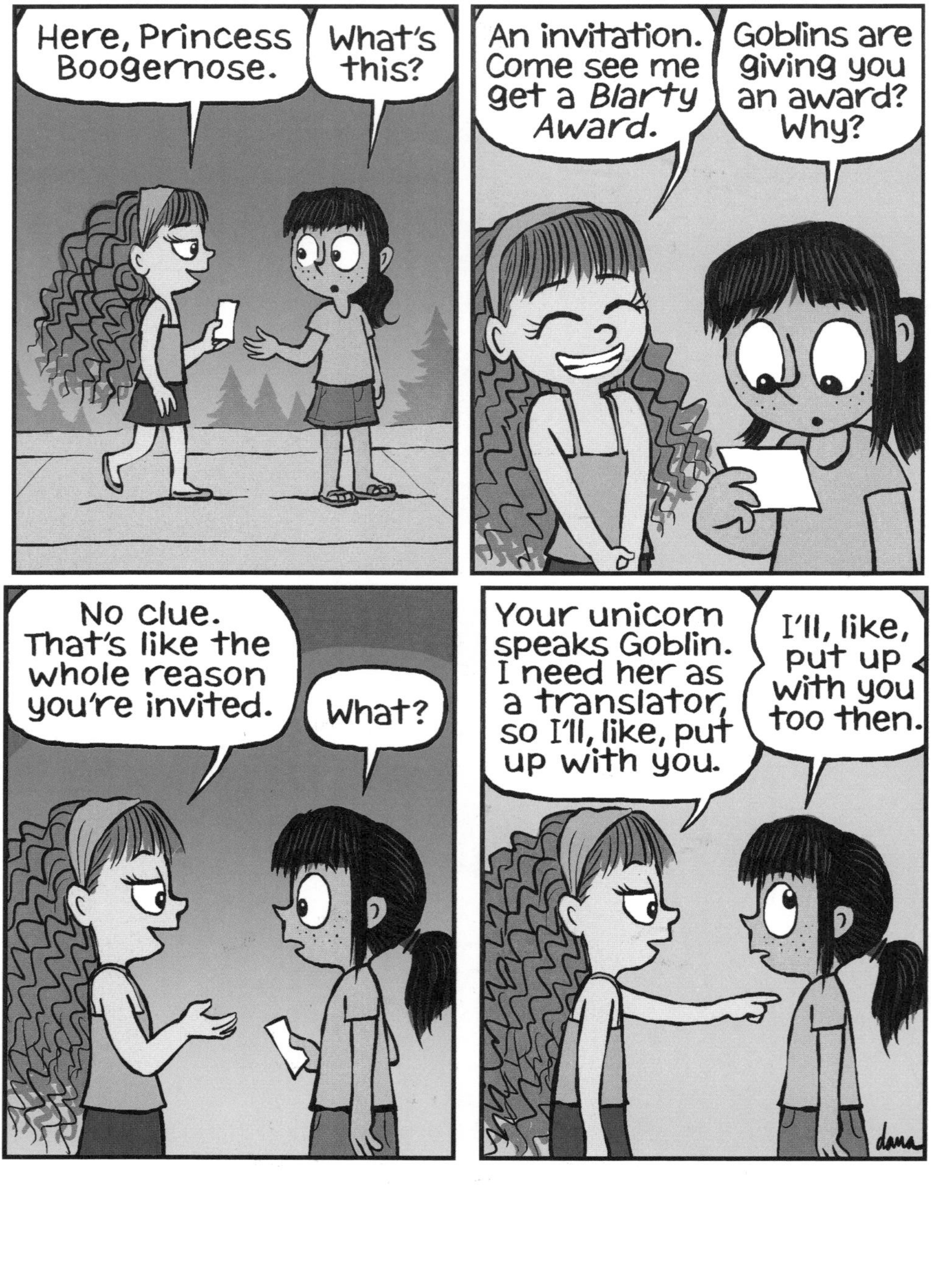
Here, Princess Boogernose.
What's this?
An invitation. Come see me get a *Blarty Award.*
Goblins are giving you an award? Why?
No clue. That's like the whole reason you're invited.
What?
Your unicorn speaks Goblin. I need her as a translator, so I'll, like, put up with you.
I'll, like, put up with you too then.
dana

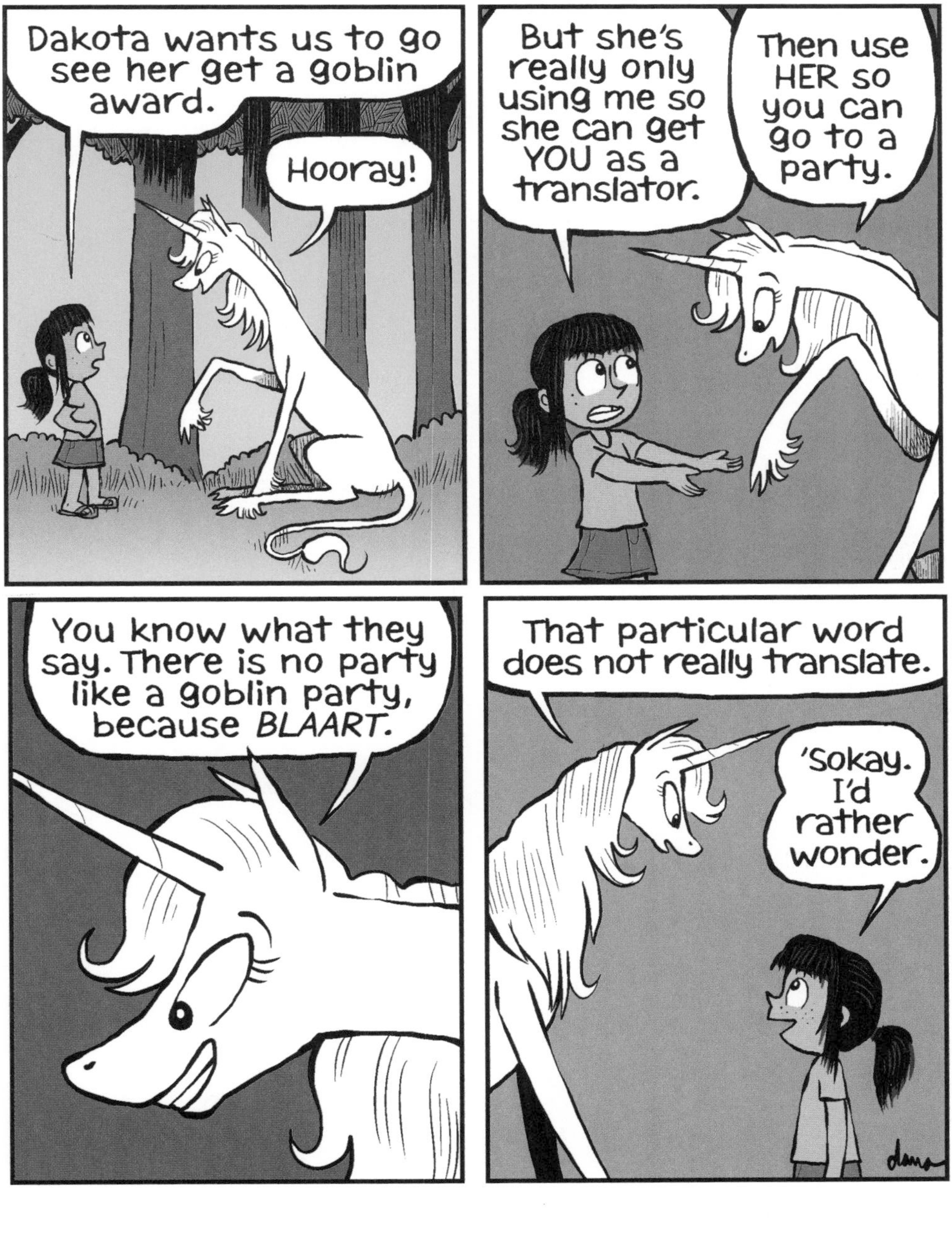
Dakota wants us to go see her get a goblin award.
Hooray!
But she's really only using me so she can get YOU as a translator.
Then use HER so you can go to a party.
You know what they say. There is no party like a goblin party, because *BLAART*.
That particular word does not really translate.
'Sokay. I'd rather wonder.
dana

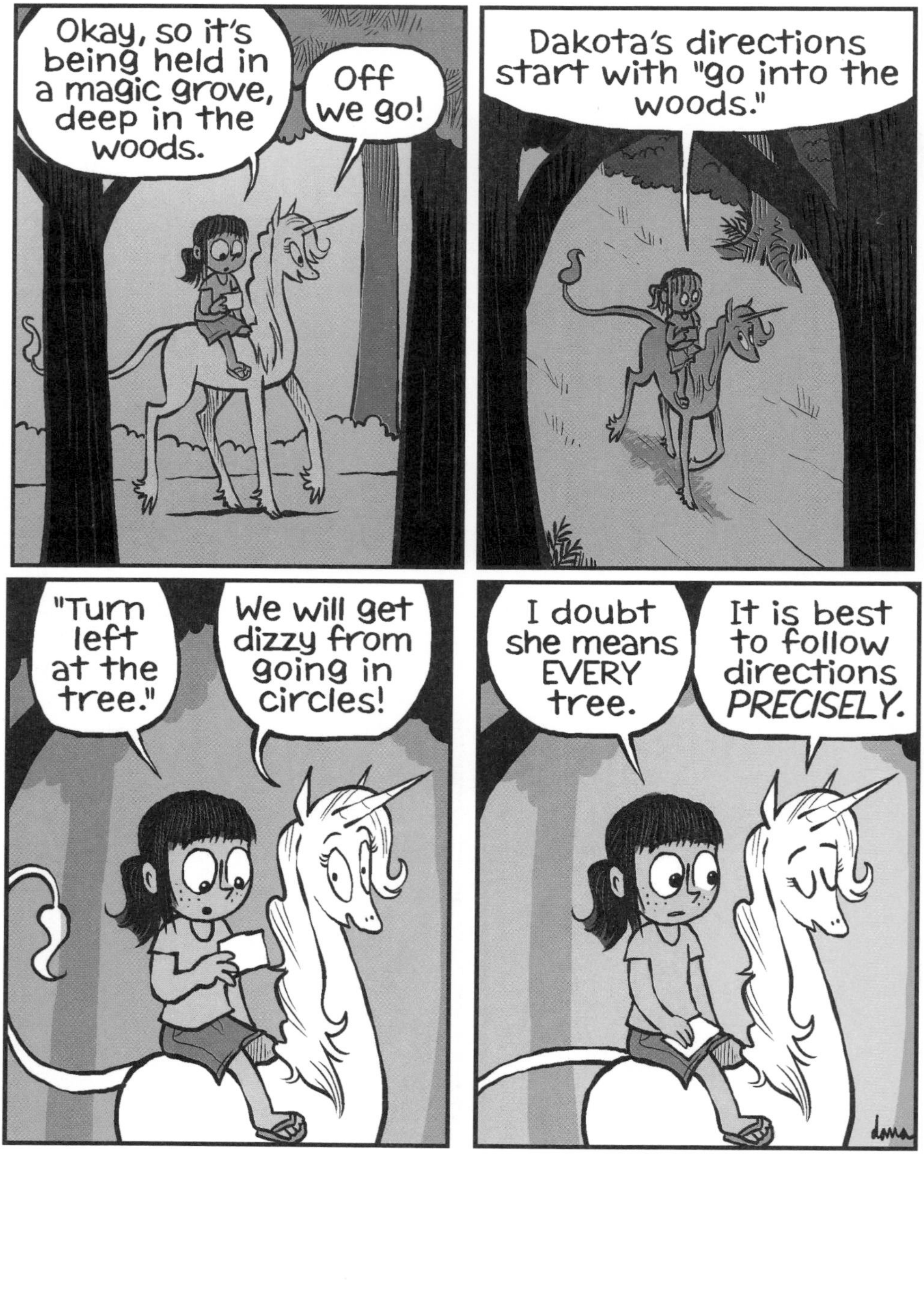
Okay, so it's being held in a magic grove, deep in the woods.
Off we go!
Dakota's directions start with "go into the woods."
"Turn left at the tree."
We will get dizzy from going in circles!
I doubt she means EVERY tree.
It is best to follow directions *PRECISELY*.
dana

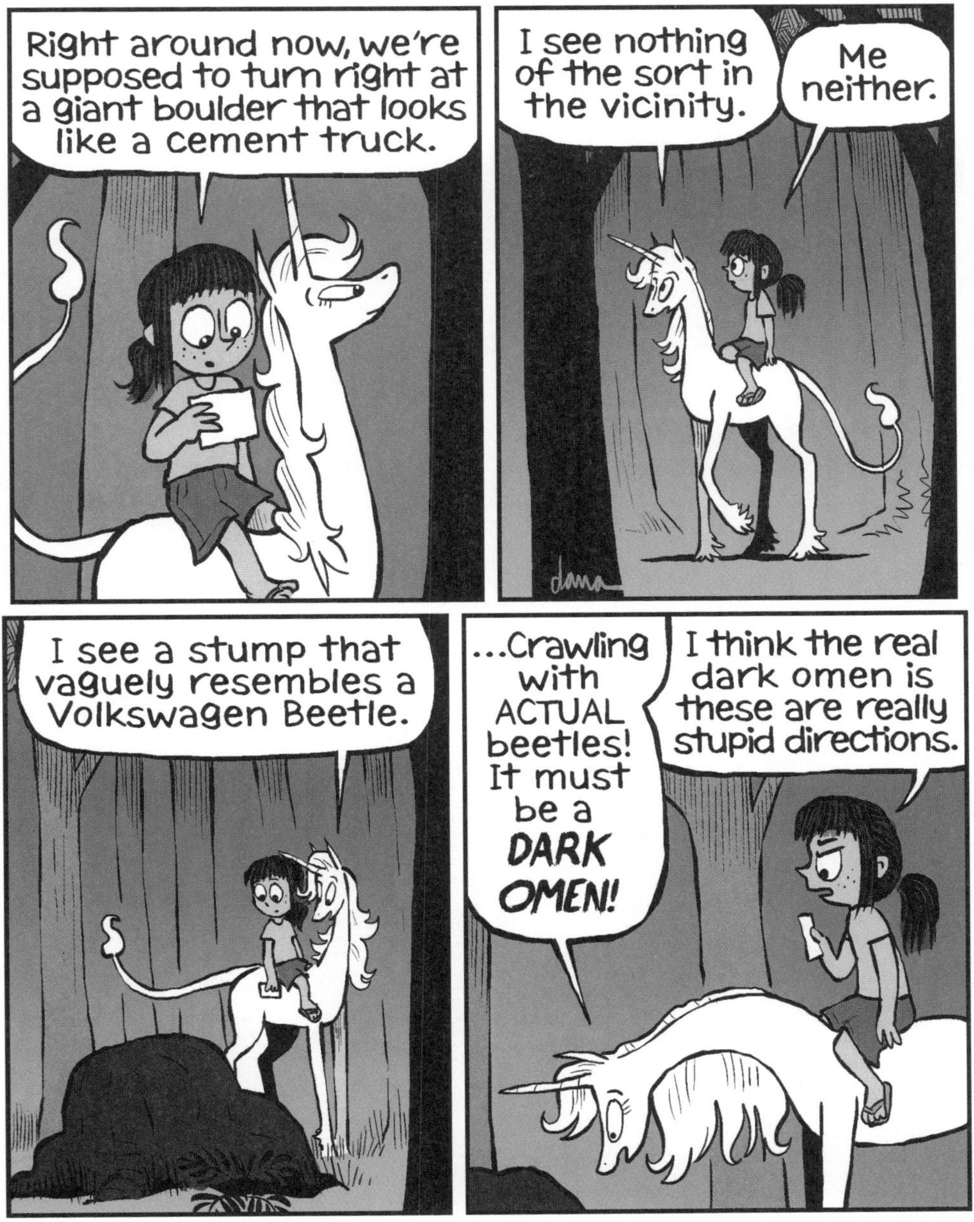
Right around now, we're supposed to turn right at a giant boulder that looks like a cement truck.
I see nothing of the sort in the vicinity.
Me neither.
dana
I see a stump that vaguely resembles a Volkswagen Beetle.
...Crawling with ACTUAL beetles! It must be a DARK OMEN!
I think the real dark omen is these are really stupid directions.

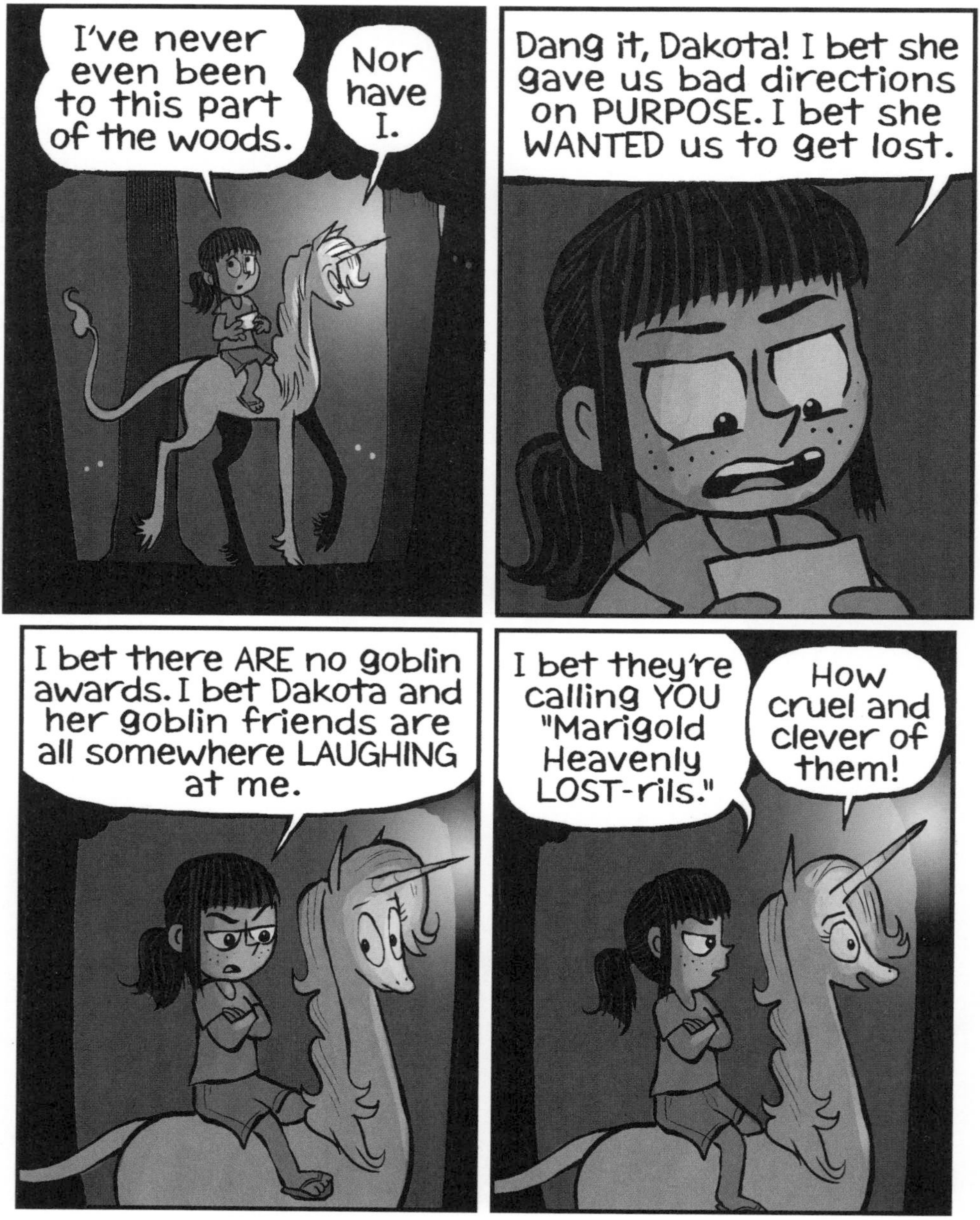
I've never even been to this part of the woods.
Nor have I.
Dang it, Dakota! I bet she gave us bad directions on PURPOSE. I bet she WANTED us to get lost.
I bet there ARE no goblin awards. I bet Dakota and her goblin friends are all somewhere LAUGHING at me.
I bet they're calling YOU "Marigold Heavenly LOST-rils."
How cruel and clever of them!

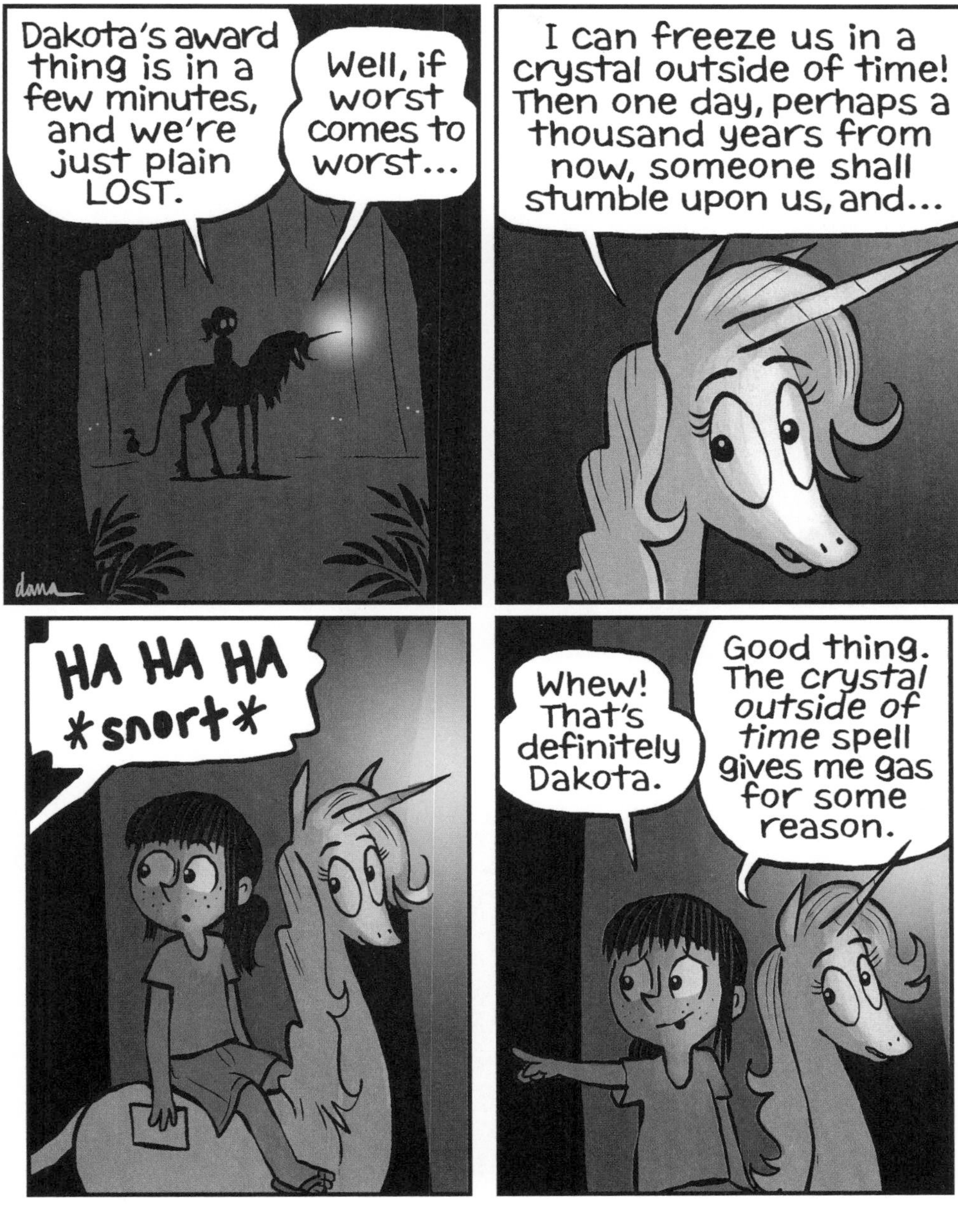
Dakota's award thing is in a few minutes, and we're just plain LOST.
Well, if worst comes to worst...
I can freeze us in a crystal outside of time! Then one day, perhaps a thousand years from now, someone shall stumble upon us, and...
HA HA HA *snort*
Whew! That's definitely Dakota.
Good thing. The *crystal outside of time* spell gives me gas for some reason.

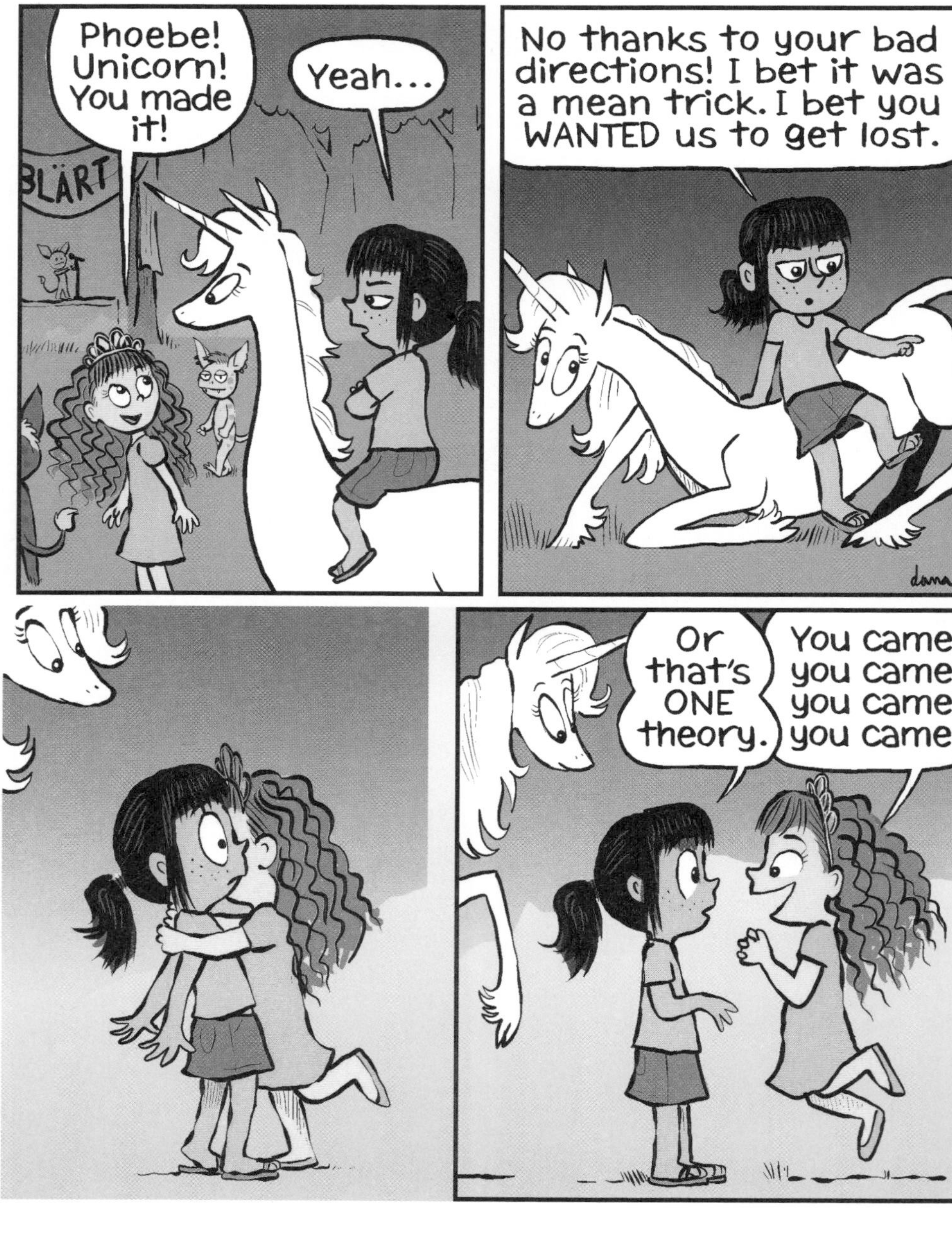

Phoebe! Unicorn! You made it!
Yeah...
BLÄRT
No thanks to your bad directions! I bet it was a mean trick. I bet you WANTED us to get lost.
Or that's ONE theory.
You came you came you came you came

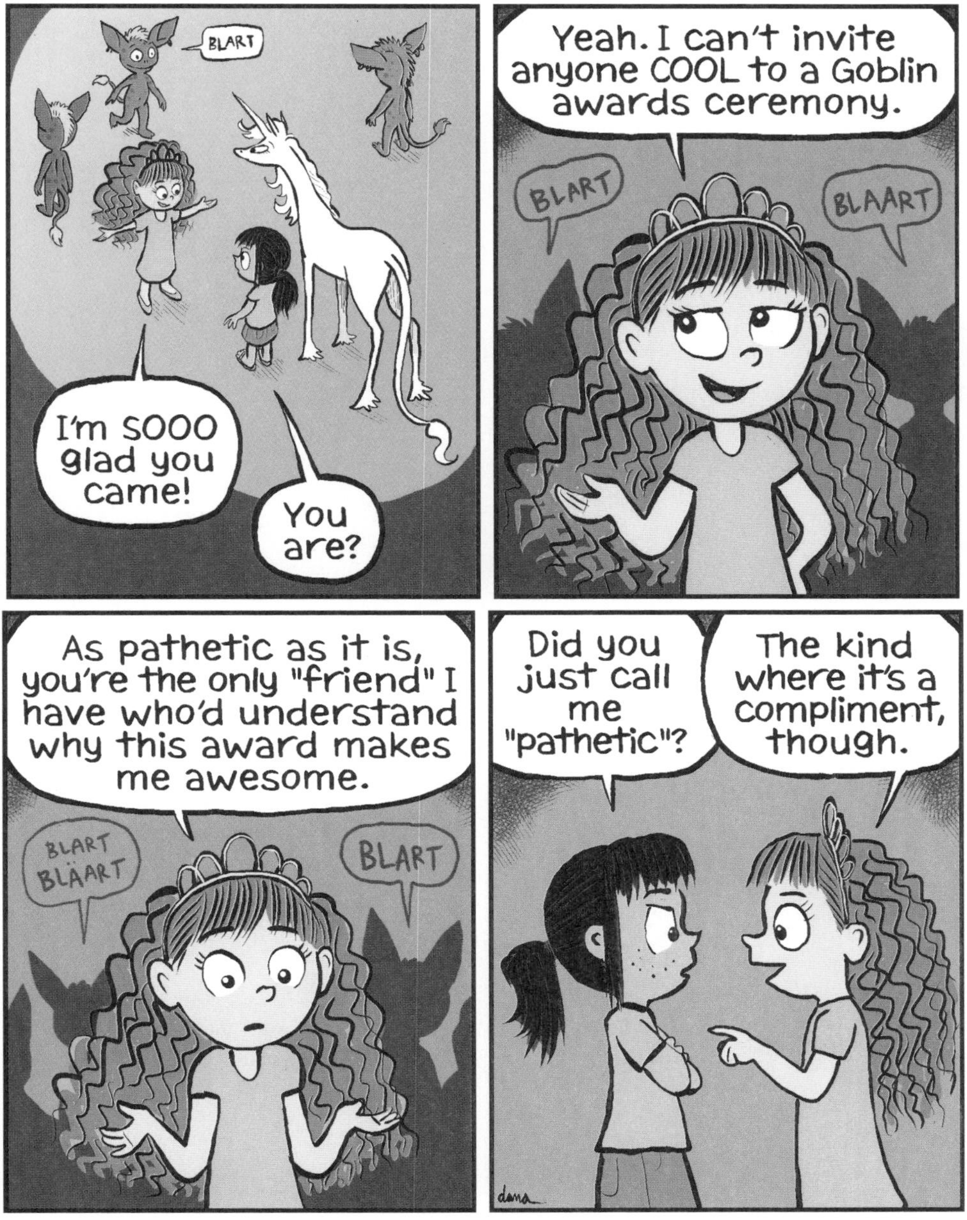
BLART
I'm SOOO glad you came!
You are?
Yeah. I can't invite anyone COOL to a Goblin awards ceremony.
BLART
BLAART
As pathetic as it is, you're the only "friend" I have who'd understand why this award makes me awesome.
BLART BLÄART
BLART
Did you just call me "pathetic"?
The kind where it's a compliment, though.
dana

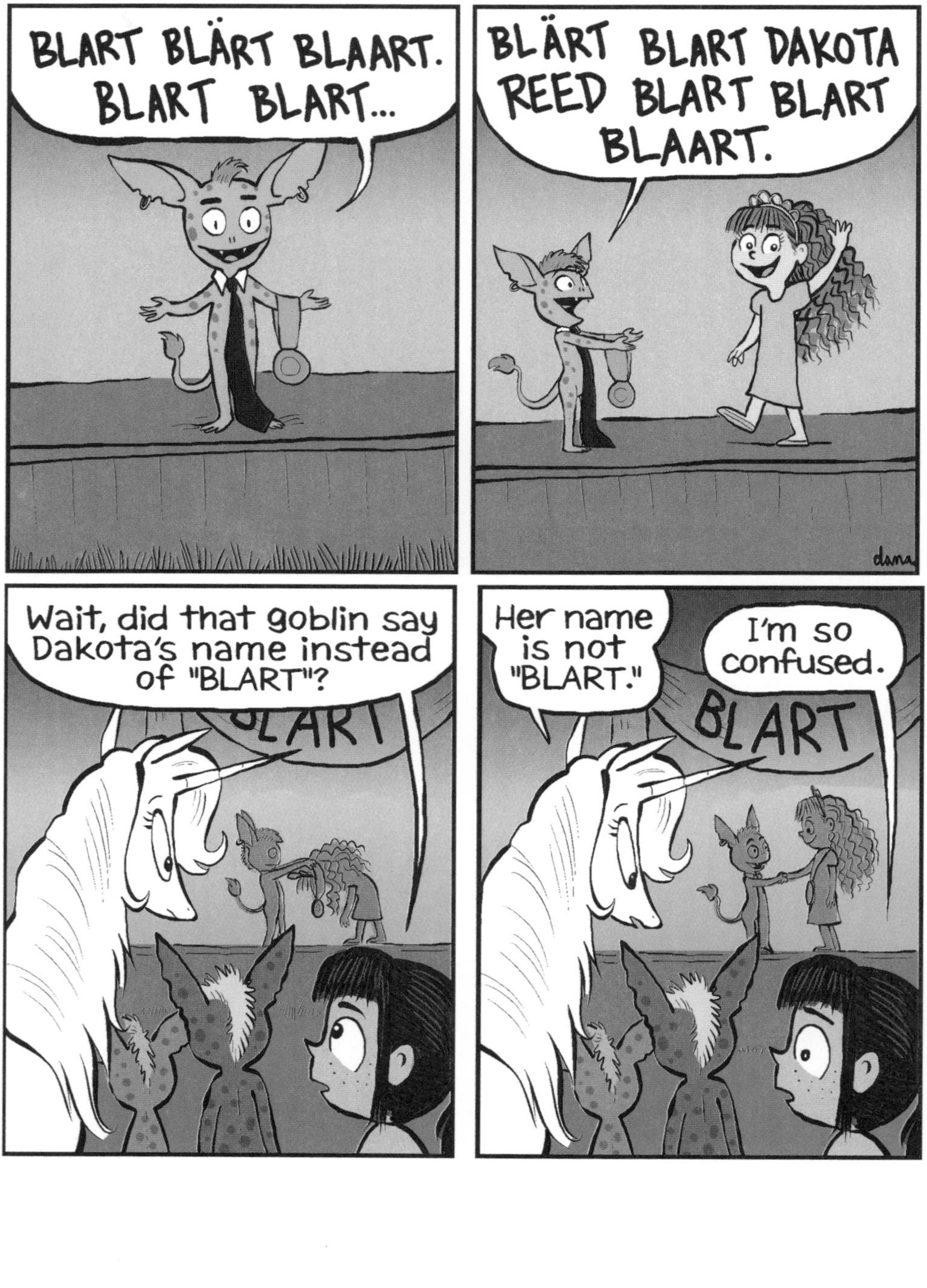
BLART BLÄRT BLAART.
BLART BLART...
BLÄRT BLART DAKOTA REED BLART BLART BLAART.
dana
Wait, did that goblin say Dakota's name instead of "BLART"?
BLART
Her name is not "BLART."
I'm so confused.
BLART

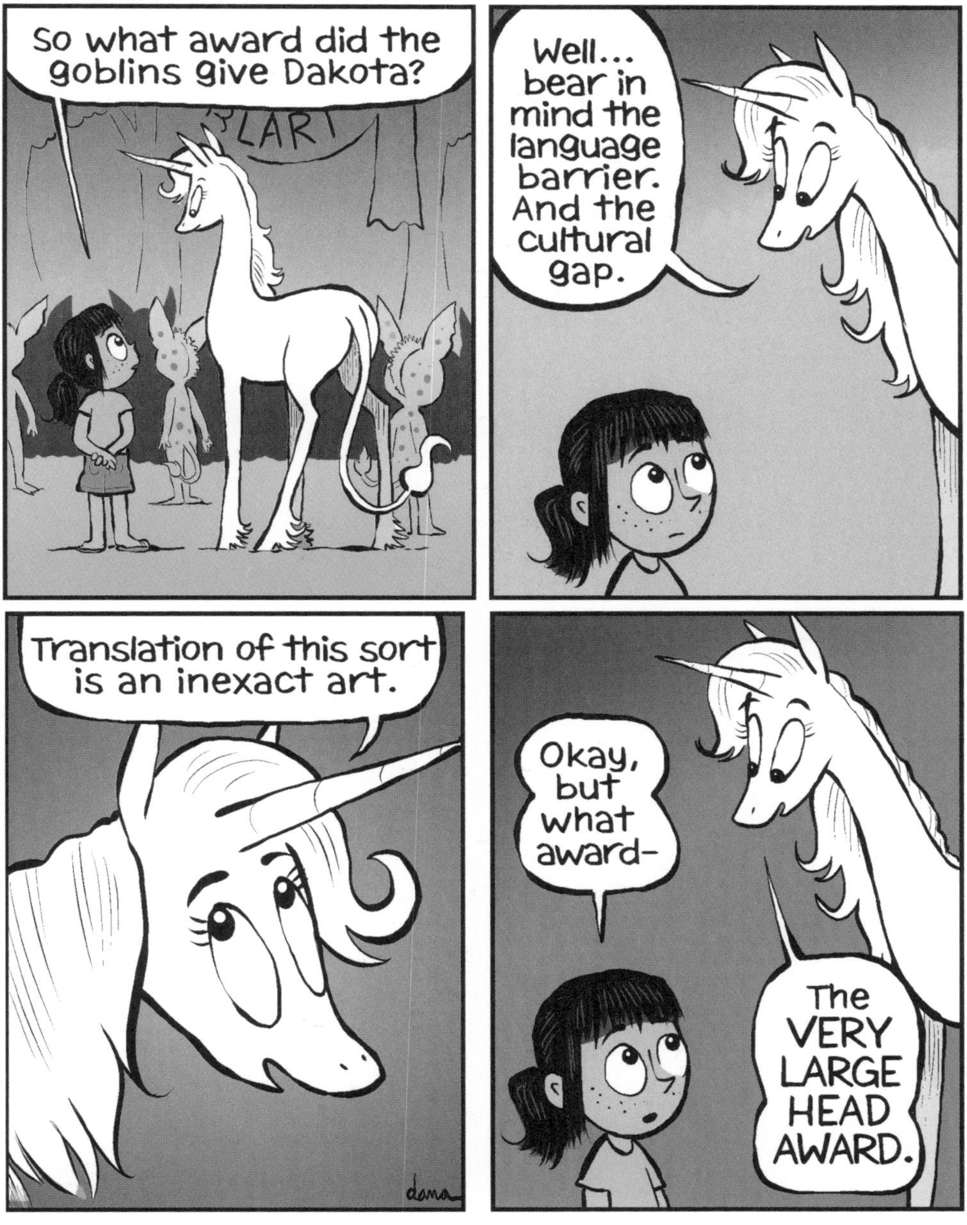
So what award did the goblins give Dakota?
BLART
Well... bear in mind the language barrier. And the cultural gap.
Translation of this sort is an inexact art.
Okay, but what award-
The VERY LARGE HEAD AWARD.
dana

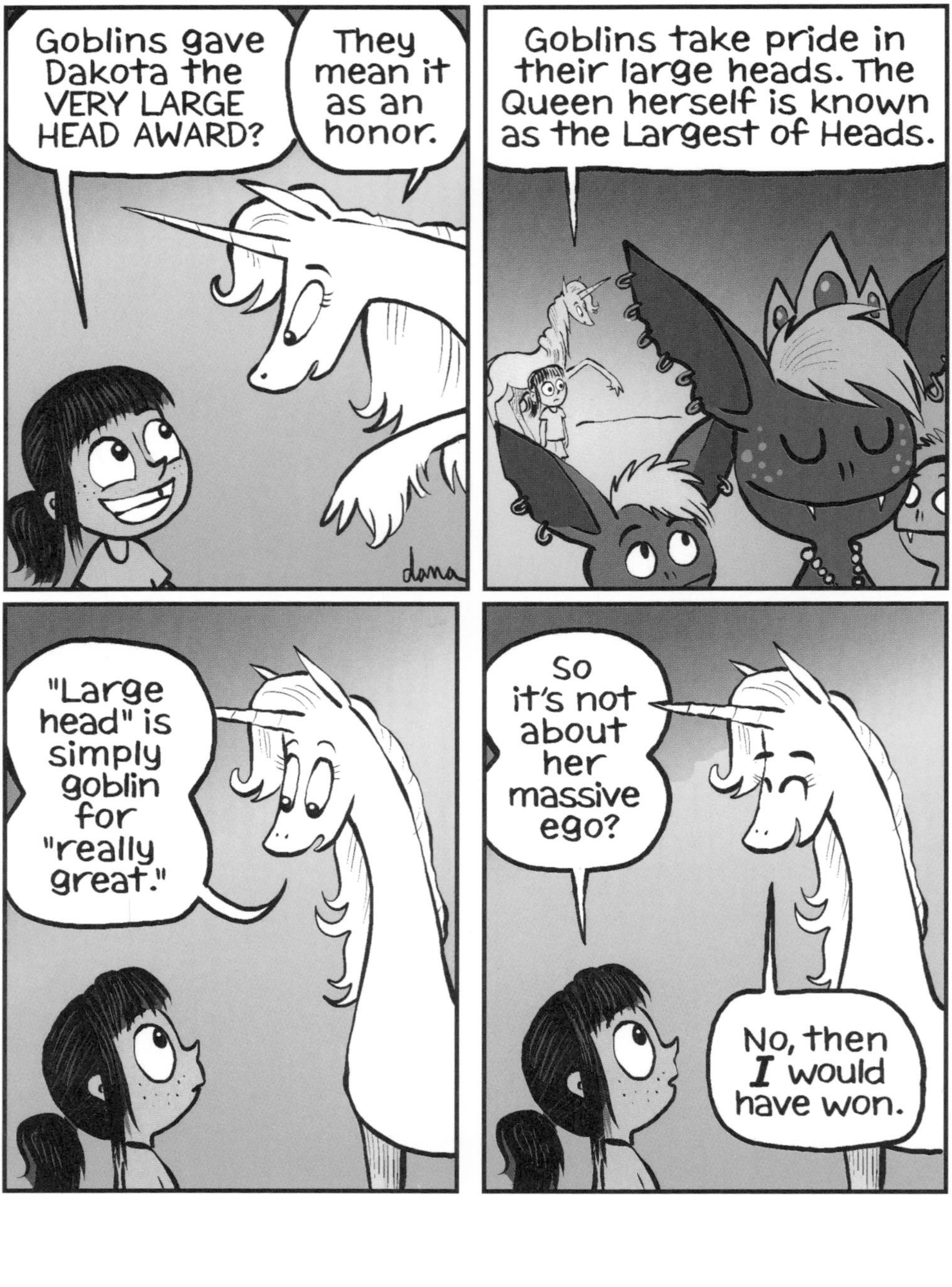
Goblins gave Dakota the VERY LARGE HEAD AWARD?
They mean it as an honor.
Goblins take pride in their large heads. The Queen herself is known as the Largest of Heads.
"Large head" is simply goblin for "really great."
So it's not about her massive ego?
No, then *I* would have won.

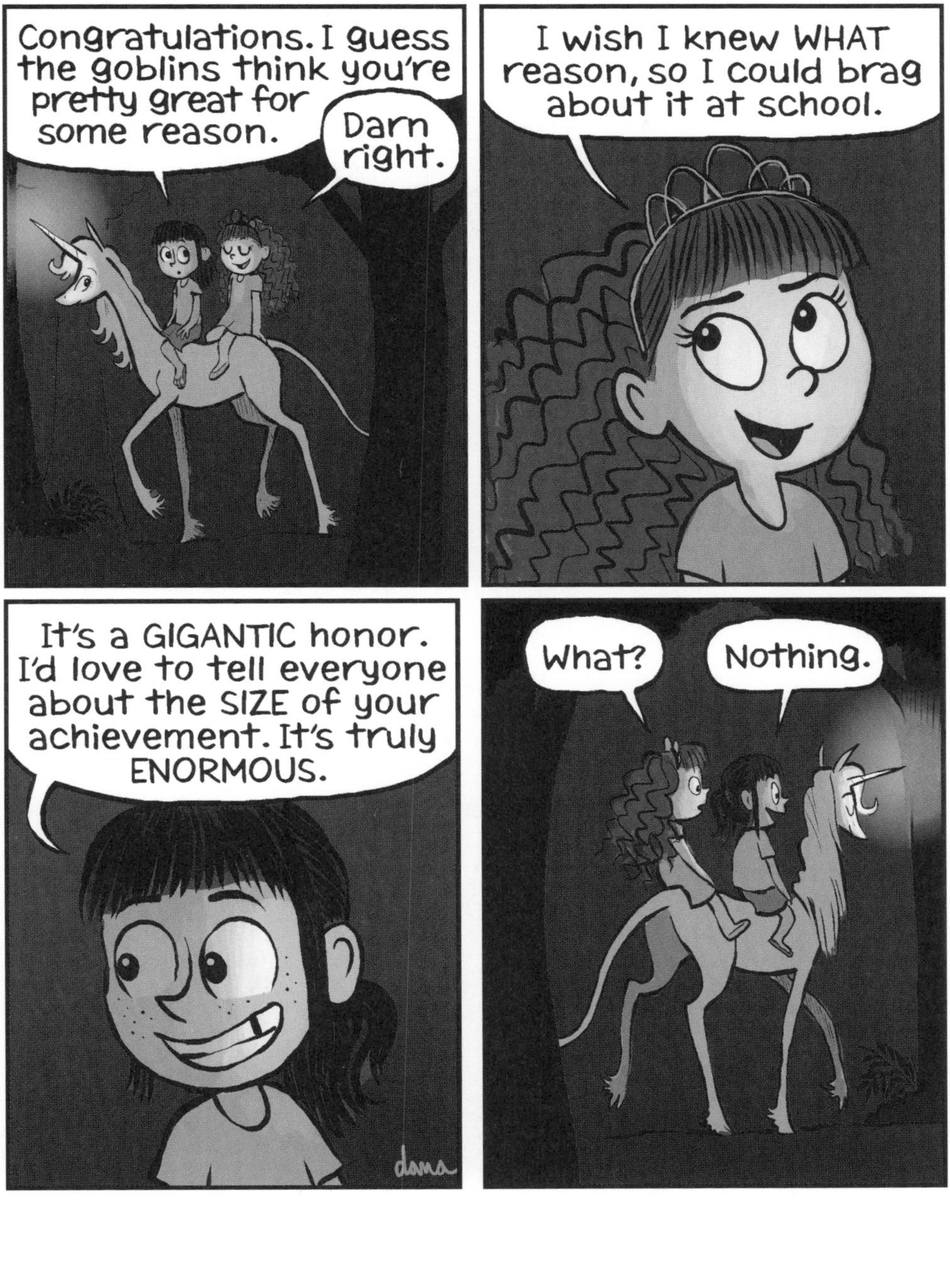
Congratulations. I guess the goblins think you're pretty great for some reason.
Darn right.
I wish I knew WHAT reason, so I could brag about it at school.
It's a GIGANTIC honor. I'd love to tell everyone about the SIZE of your achievement. It's truly ENORMOUS.
What?
Nothing.
dana

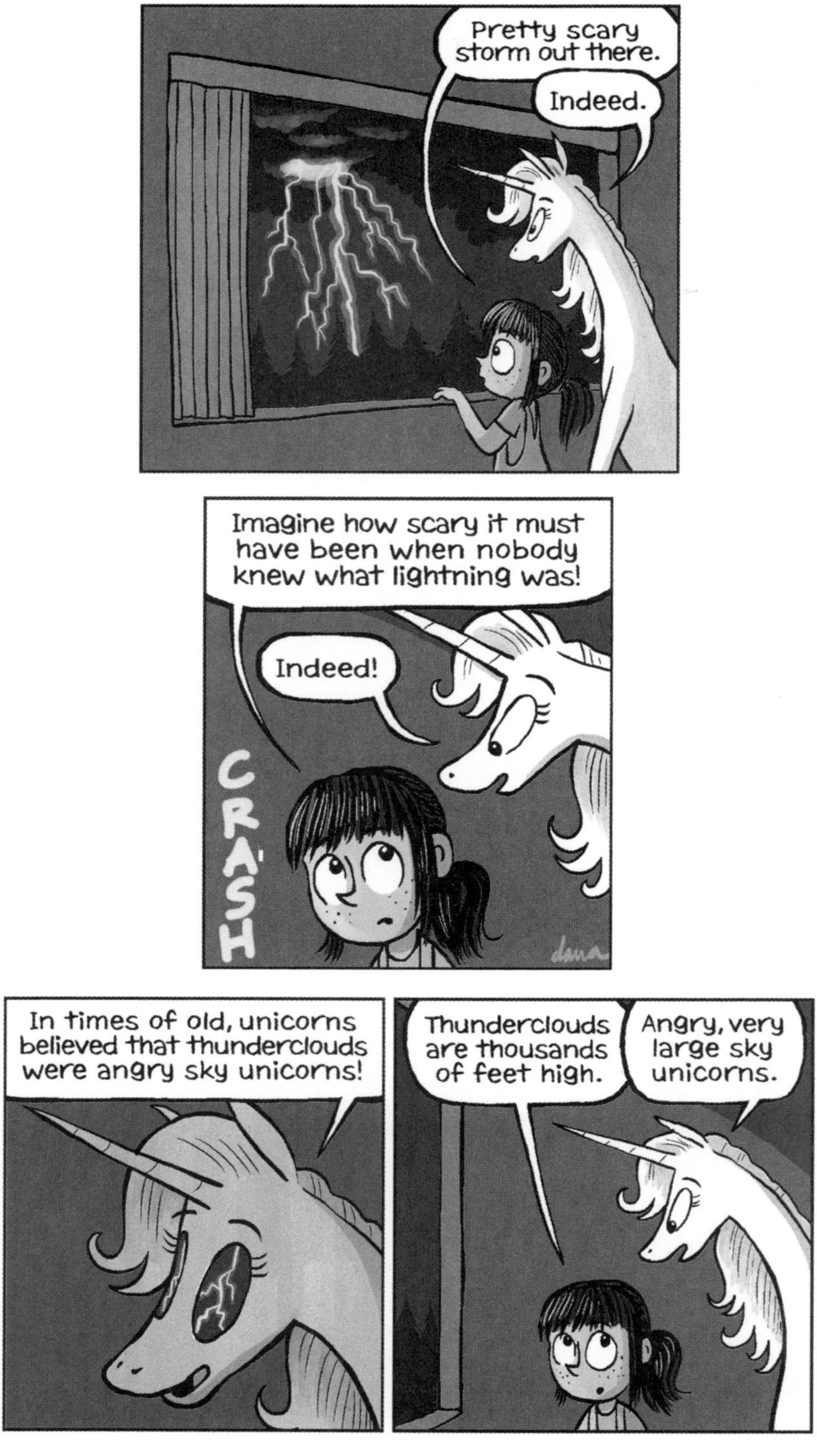
Pretty scary storm out there.
Indeed.
Imagine how scary it must have been when nobody knew what lightning was!
Indeed!
CRASH
dana
In times of old, unicorns believed that thunderclouds were angry sky unicorns!
Thunderclouds are thousands of feet high.
Angry, very large sky unicorns.

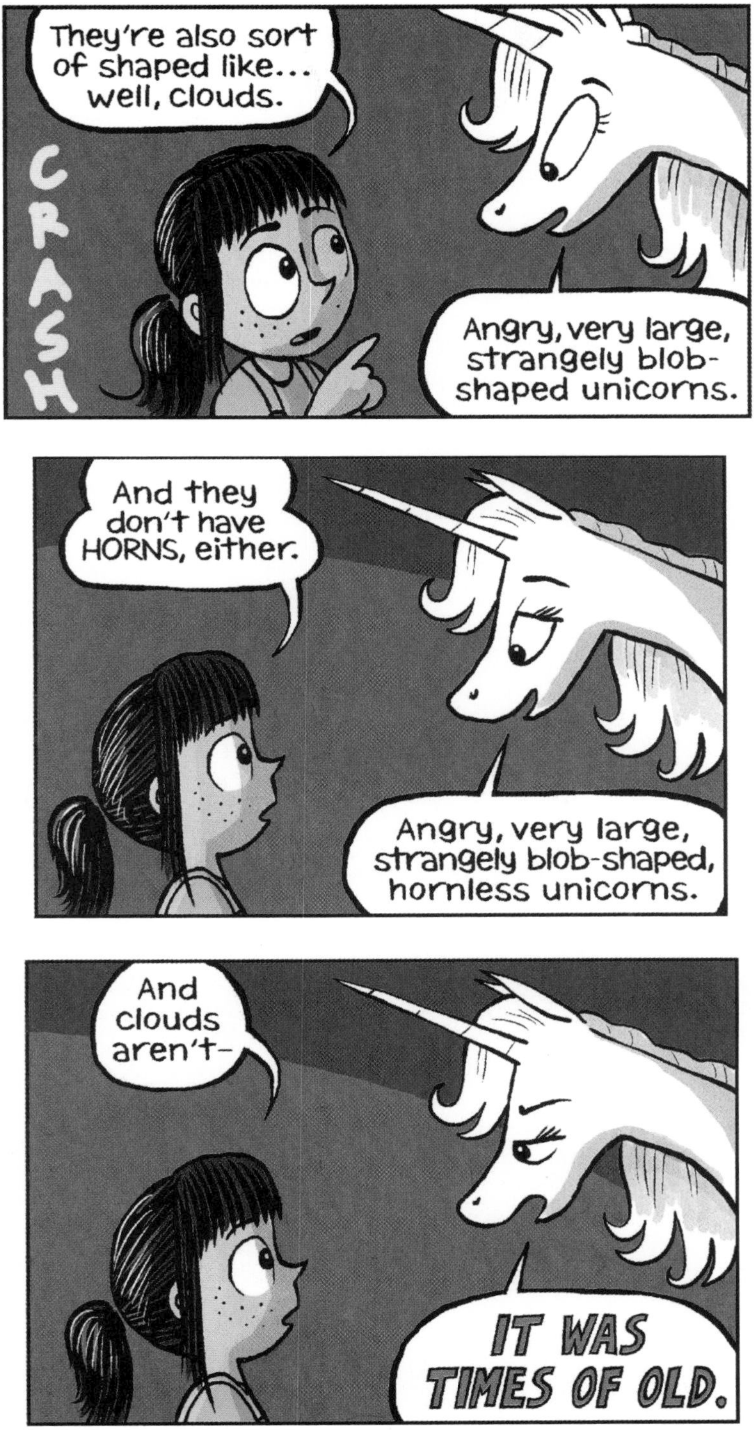
They're also sort of shaped like... well, clouds.
CRASH
Angry, very large, strangely blob-shaped unicorns.
And they don't have HORNS, either.
Angry, very large, strangely blob-shaped, hornless unicorns.
And clouds aren't-
IT WAS TIMES OF OLD.

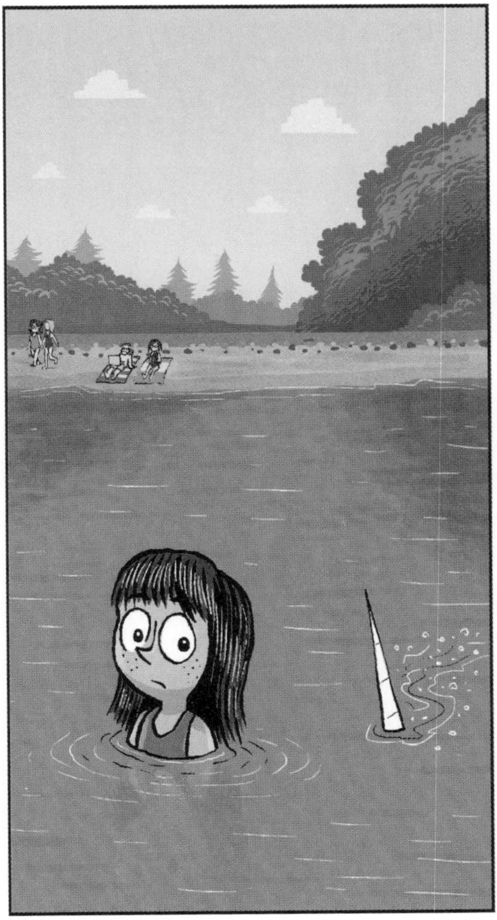

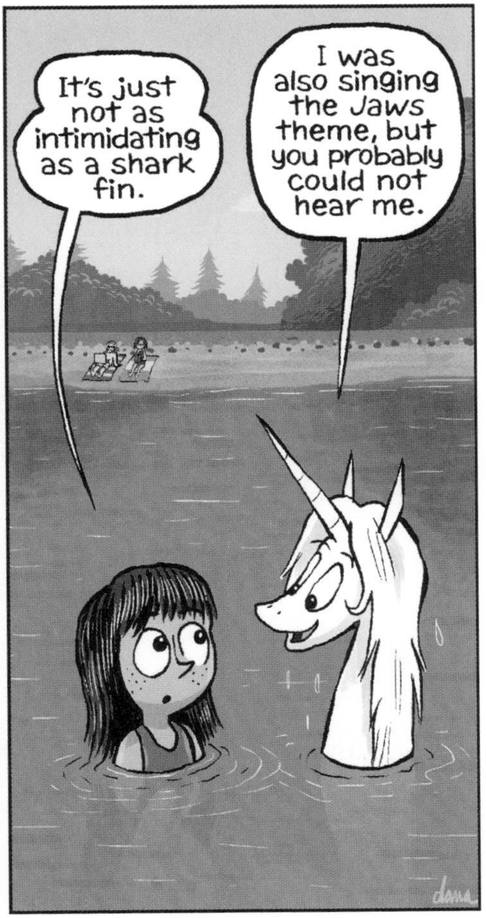
It's just not as intimidating as a shark fin.
I was also singing the *Jaws* theme, but you probably could not hear me.
dana

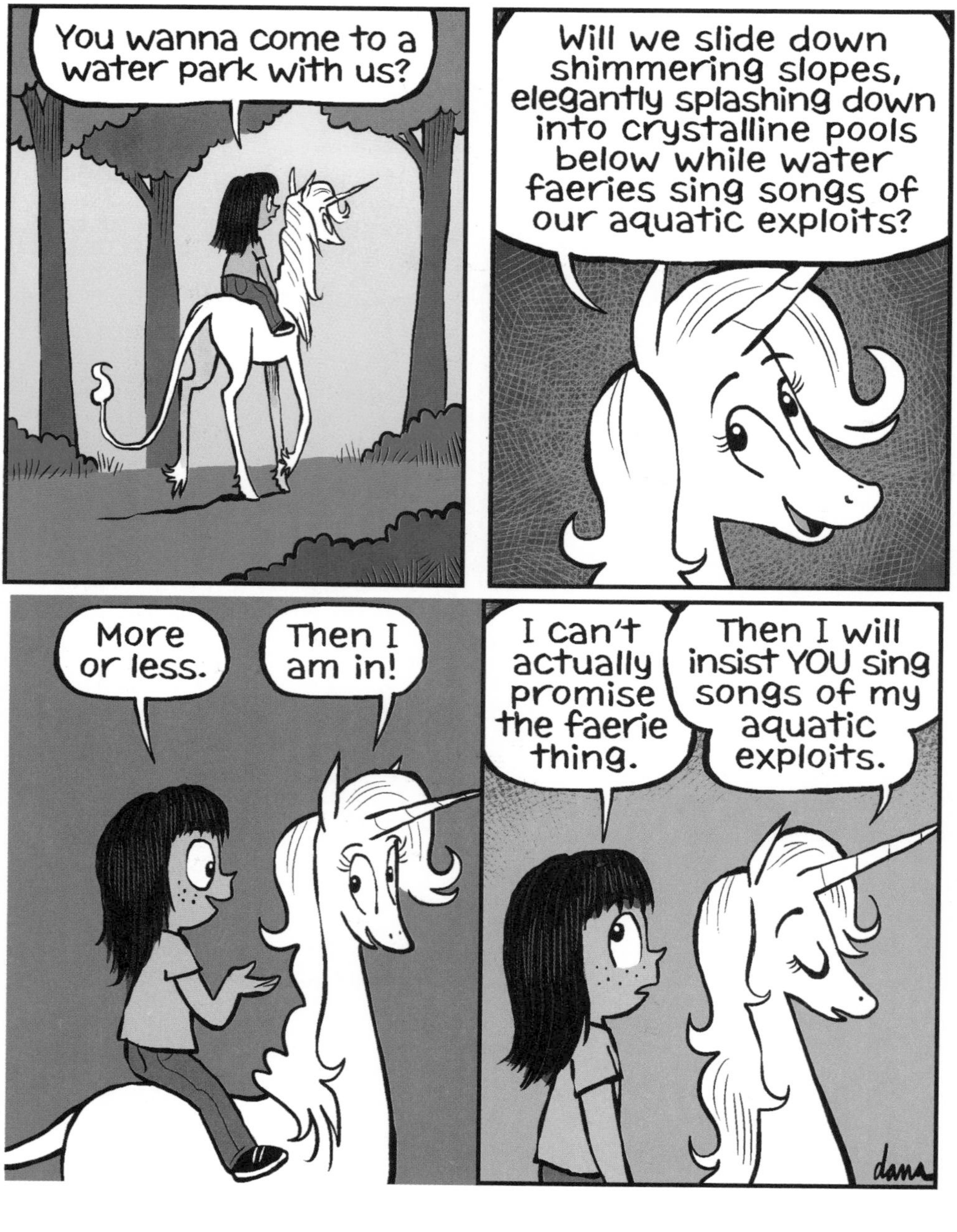
You wanna come to a water park with us?
Will we slide down shimmering slopes, elegantly splashing down into crystalline pools below while water faeries sing songs of our aquatic exploits?
More or less.
Then I am in!
I can't actually promise the faerie thing.
Then I will insist YOU sing songs of my aquatic exploits.
dana

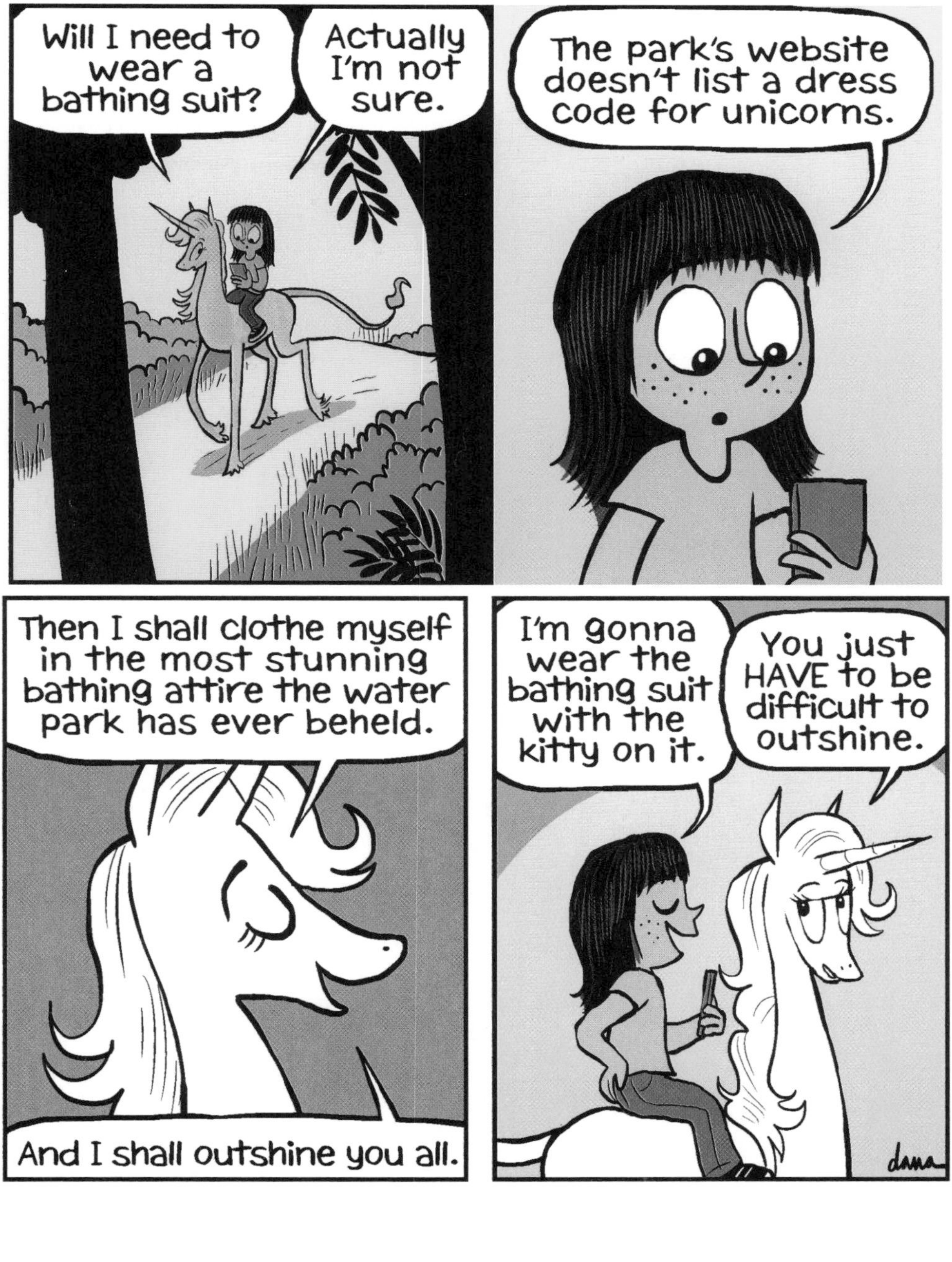
Will I need to wear a bathing suit?
Actually I'm not sure.
The park's website doesn't list a dress code for unicorns.
Then I shall clothe myself in the most stunning bathing attire the water park has ever beheld.
And I shall outshine you all.
I'm gonna wear the bathing suit with the kitty on it.
You just HAVE to be difficult to outshine.
dana

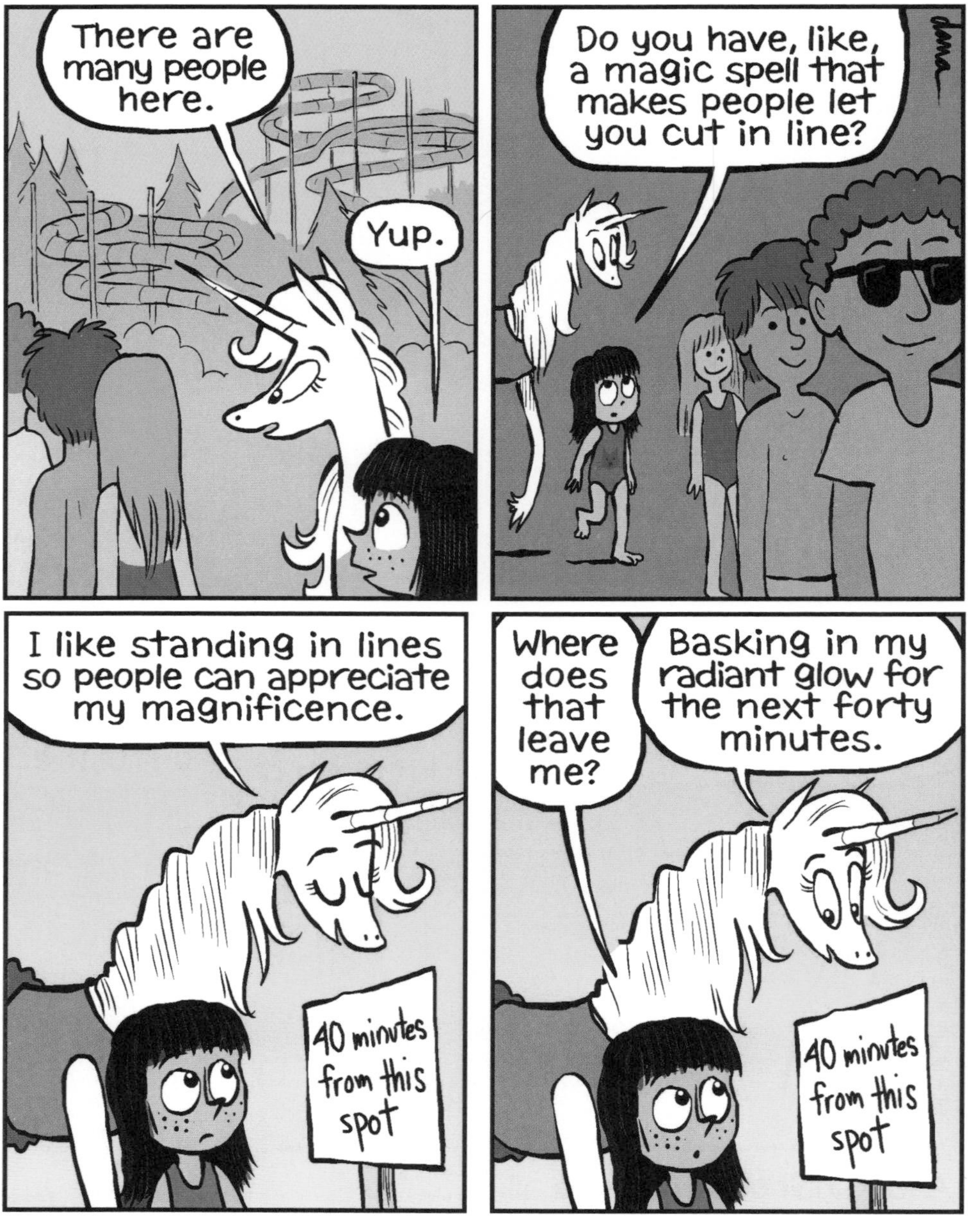
There are many people here.
Yup.
Do you have, like, a magic spell that makes people let you cut in line?
dana
I like standing in lines so people can appreciate my magnificence.
40 minutes from this spot
Where does that leave me?
Basking in my radiant glow for the next forty minutes.
40 minutes from this spot

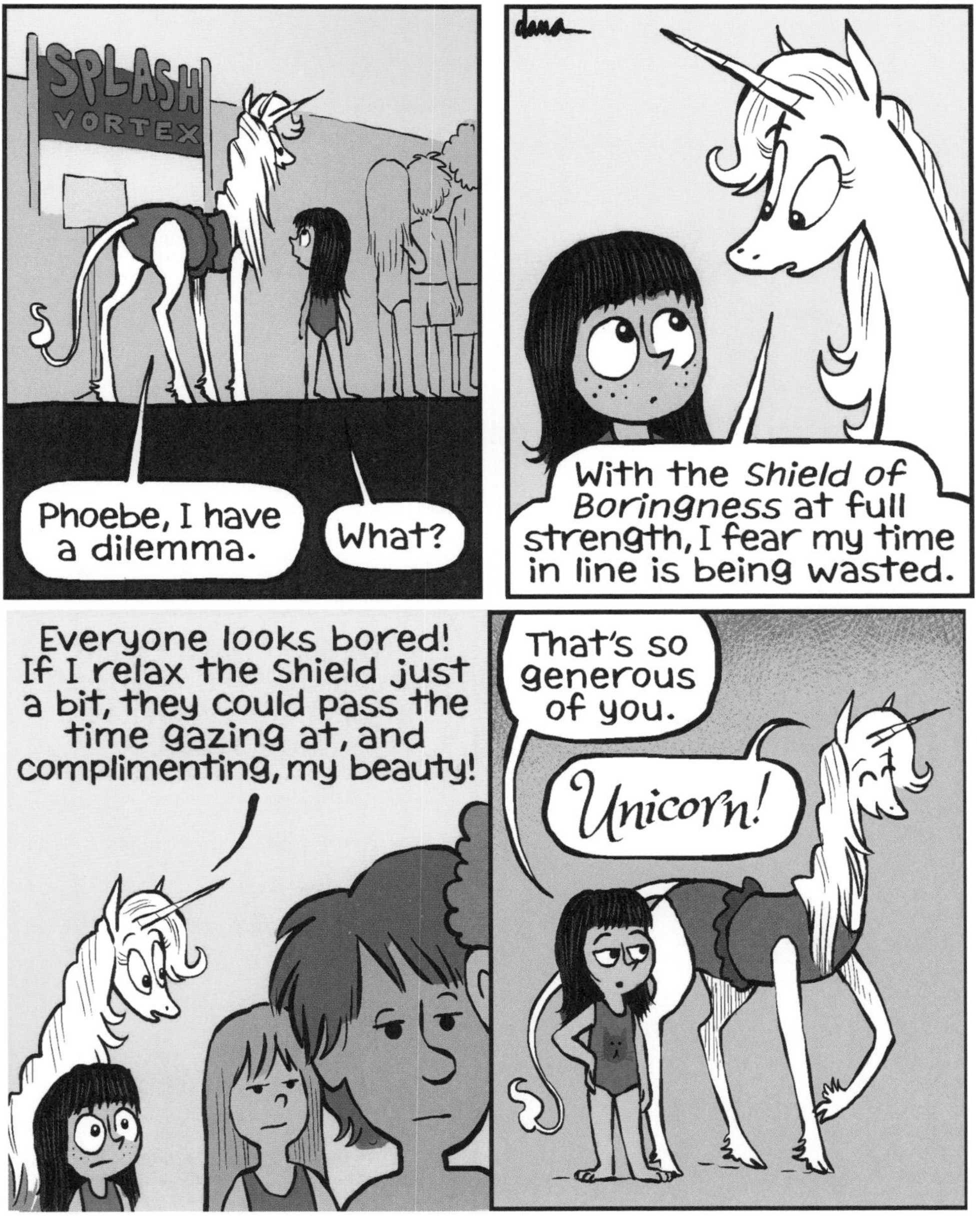
SPLASH
VORTEX
Phoebe, I have a dilemma.
What?
dana
With the *Shield of Boringness* at full strength, I fear my time in line is being wasted.
Everyone looks bored! If I relax the Shield just a bit, they could pass the time gazing at, and complimenting, my beauty!
That's so generous of you.
Unicorn!

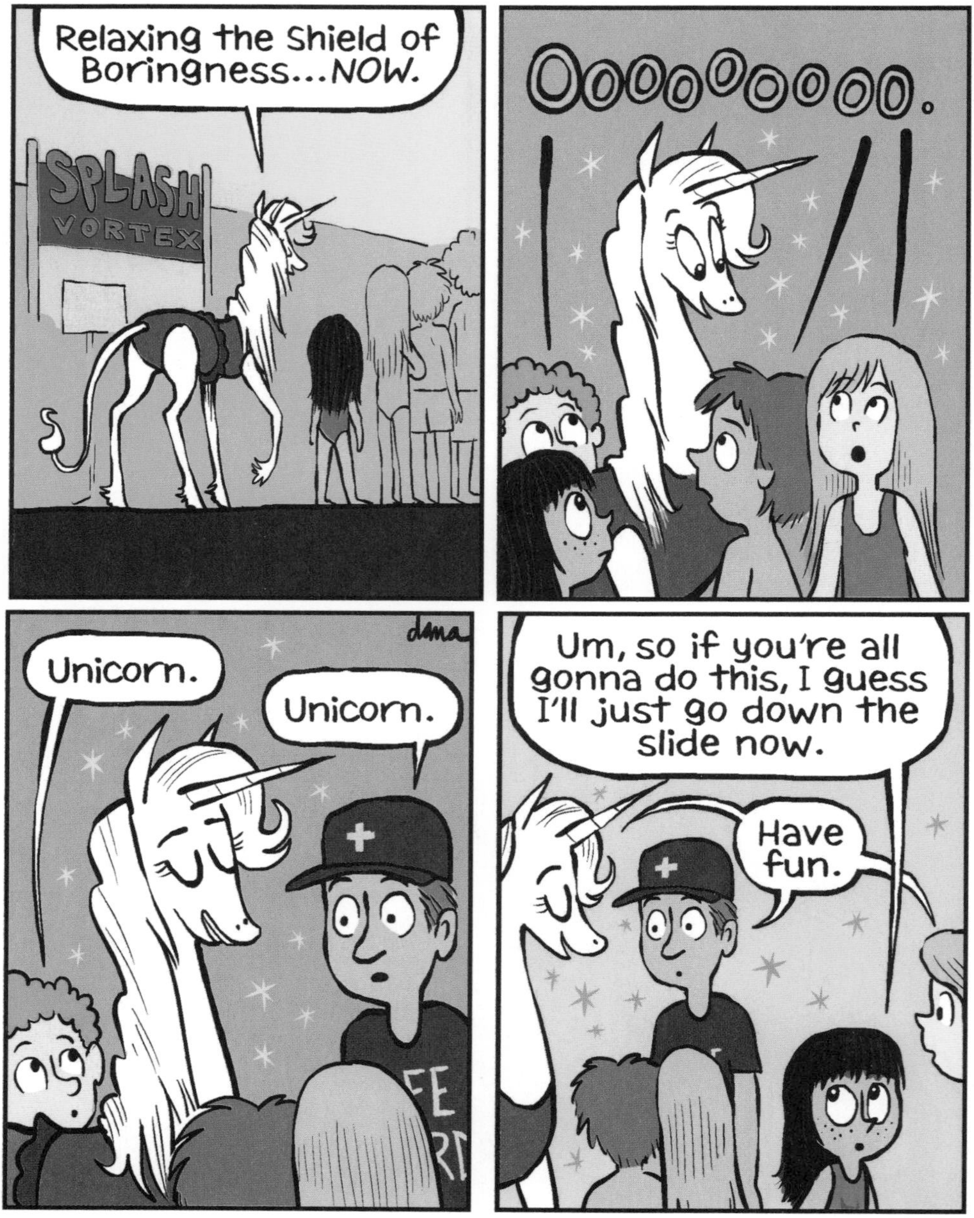
Relaxing the Shield of Boringness...NOW.
SPLASH VORTEX
Ooooooooo.
Unicorn.
Unicorn.
Um, so if you're all gonna do this, I guess I'll just go down the slide now.
Have fun.

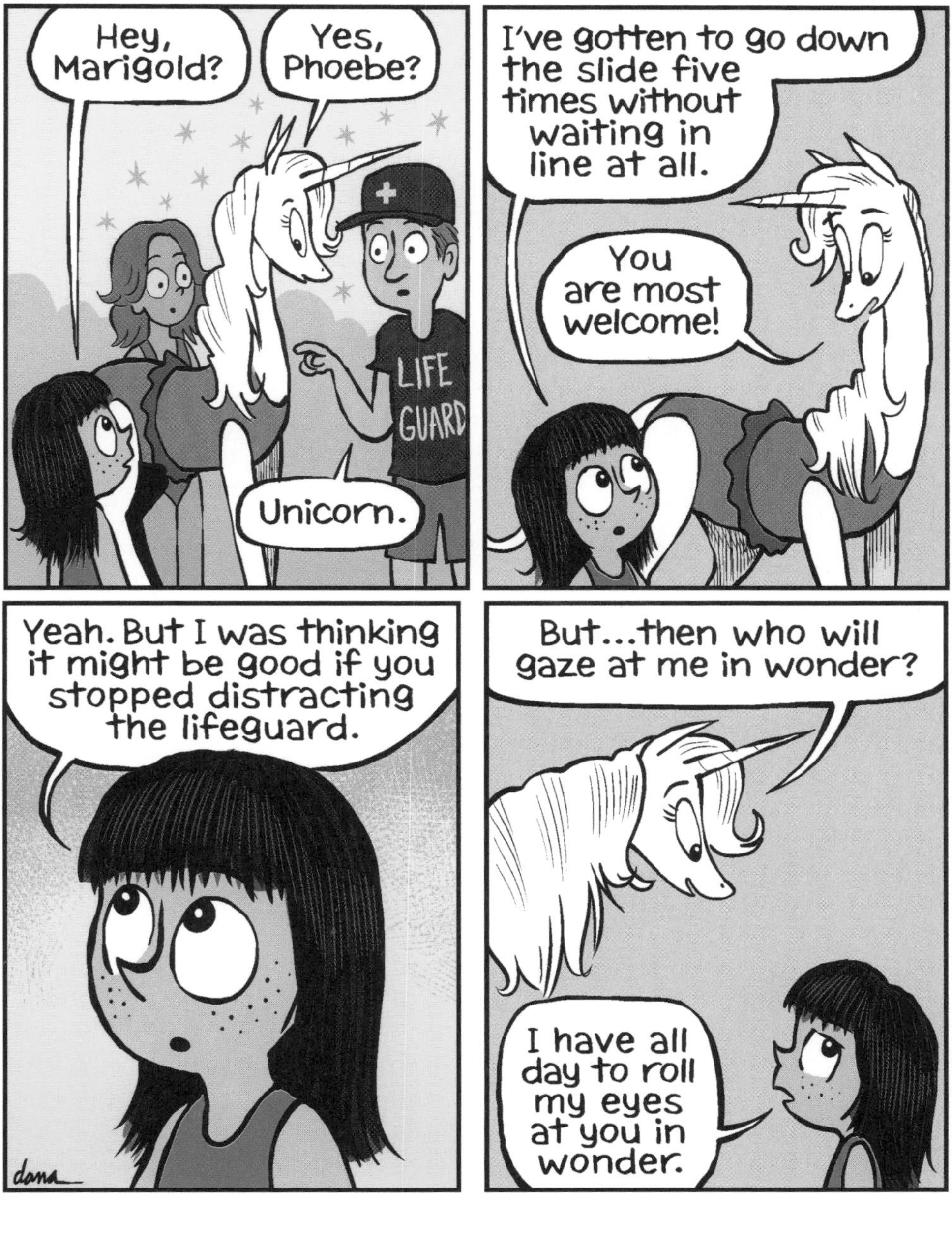
Hey, Marigold?
Yes, Phoebe?
LIFE GUARD
Unicorn.
I've gotten to go down the slide five times without waiting in line at all.
You are most welcome!
Yeah. But I was thinking it might be good if you stopped distracting the lifeguard.
dana
But...then who will gaze at me in wonder?
I have all day to roll my eyes at you in wonder.

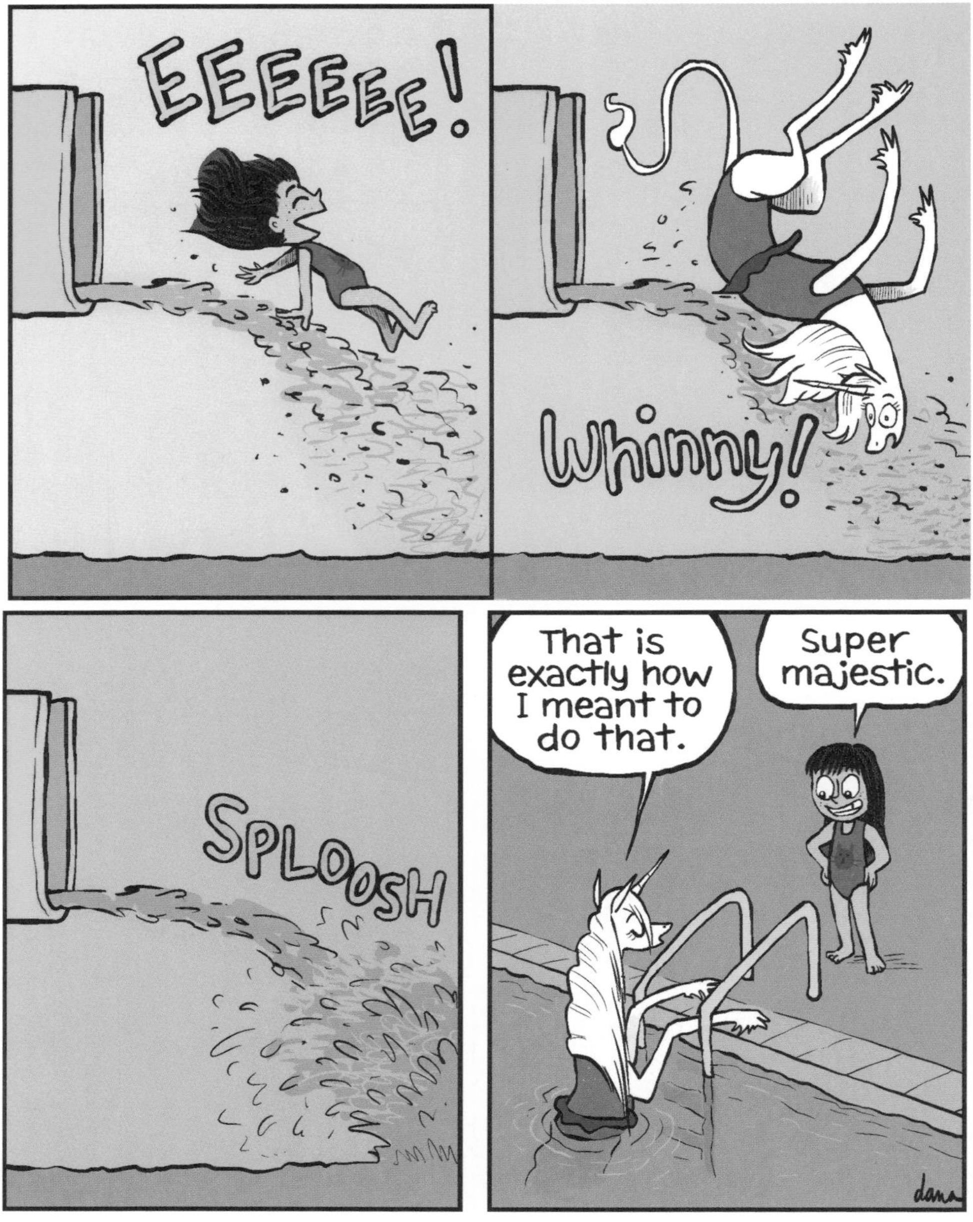
EEEEEE!
Whinny!
SPLOOSH
That is exactly how I meant to do that.
Super majestic.
dana

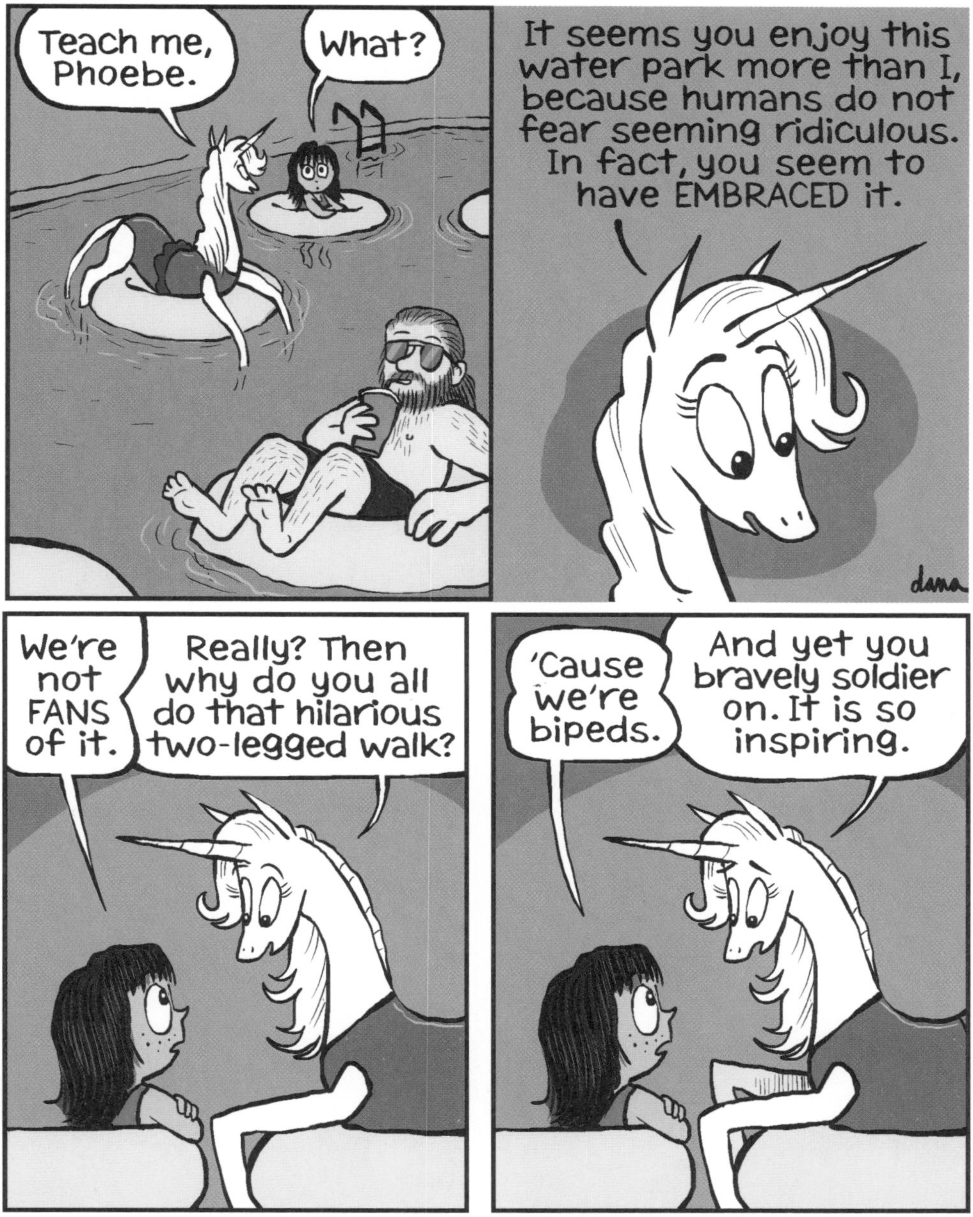
Teach me, Phoebe.
What?
It seems you enjoy this water park more than I, because humans do not fear seeming ridiculous. In fact, you seem to have EMBRACED it.
dana
We're not FANS of it.
Really? Then why do you all do that hilarious two-legged walk?
'Cause we're bipeds.
And yet you bravely soldier on. It is so inspiring.

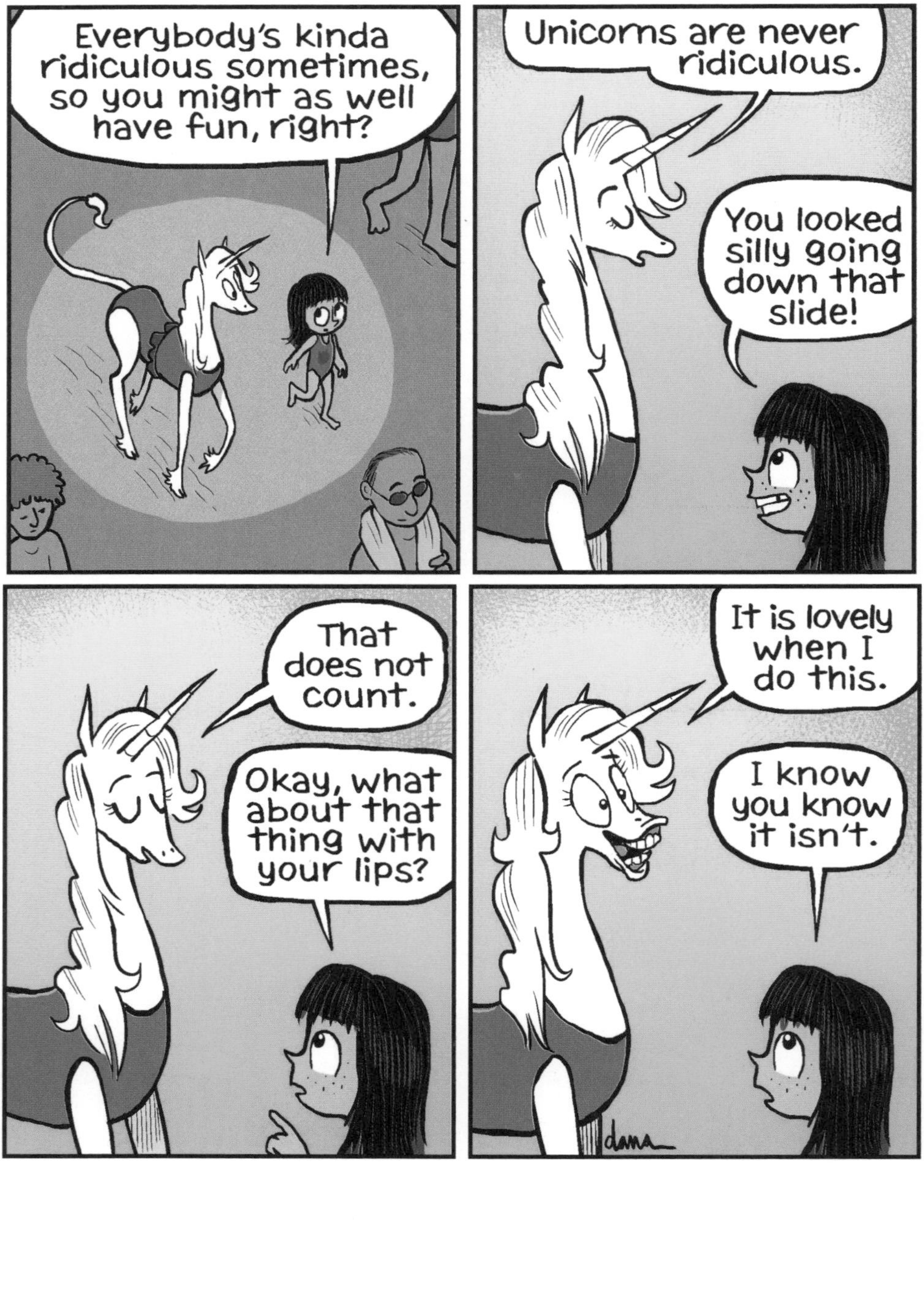
Everybody's kinda ridiculous sometimes, so you might as well have fun, right?
Unicorns are never ridiculous.
You looked silly going down that slide!
That does not count.
Okay, what about that thing with your lips?
It is lovely when I do this.
I know you know it isn't.
dana

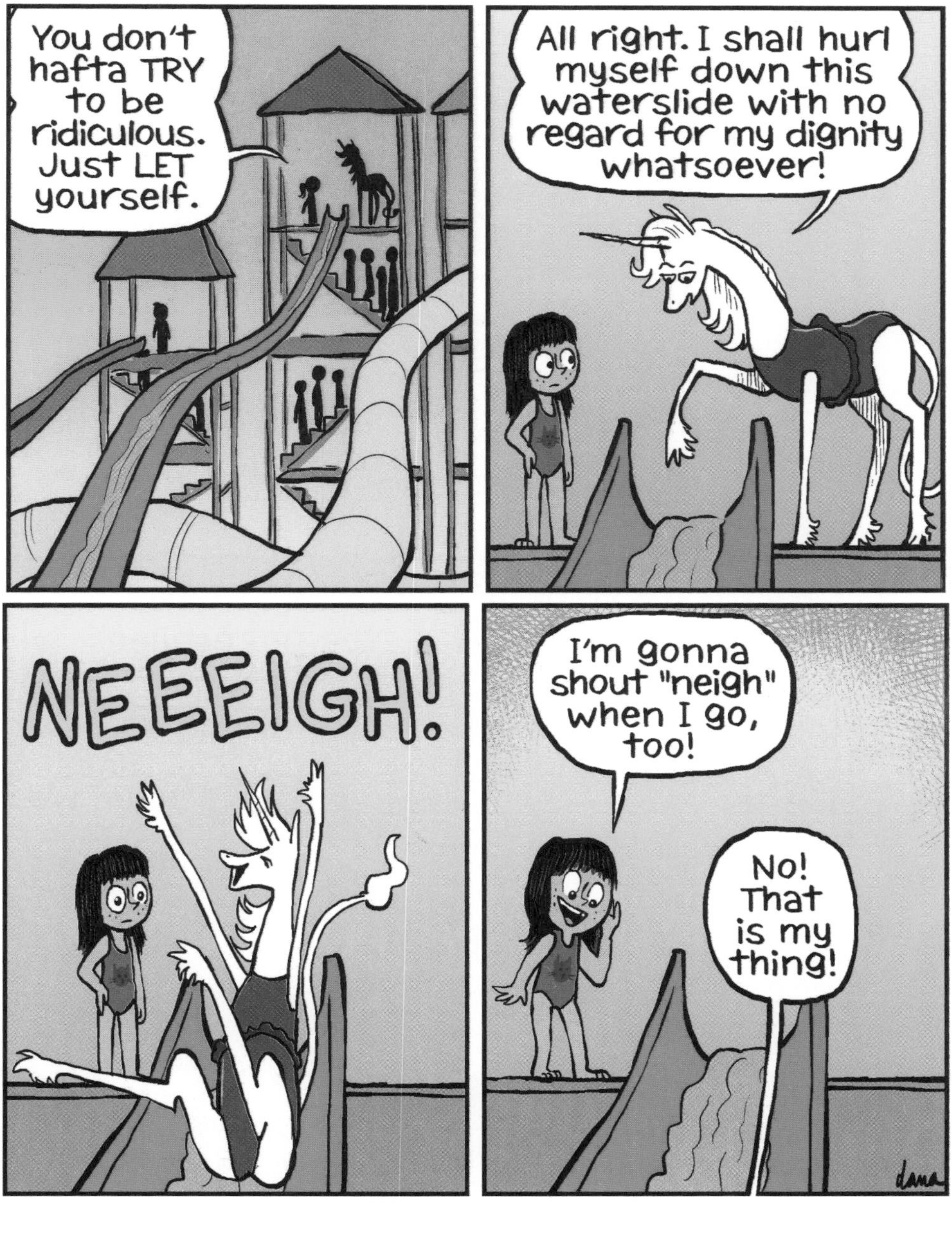
You don't hafta TRY to be ridiculous. Just LET yourself.
All right. I shall hurl myself down this waterslide with no regard for my dignity whatsoever!
NEEEIGH!
I'm gonna shout "neigh" when I go, too!
No! That is my thing!
dana

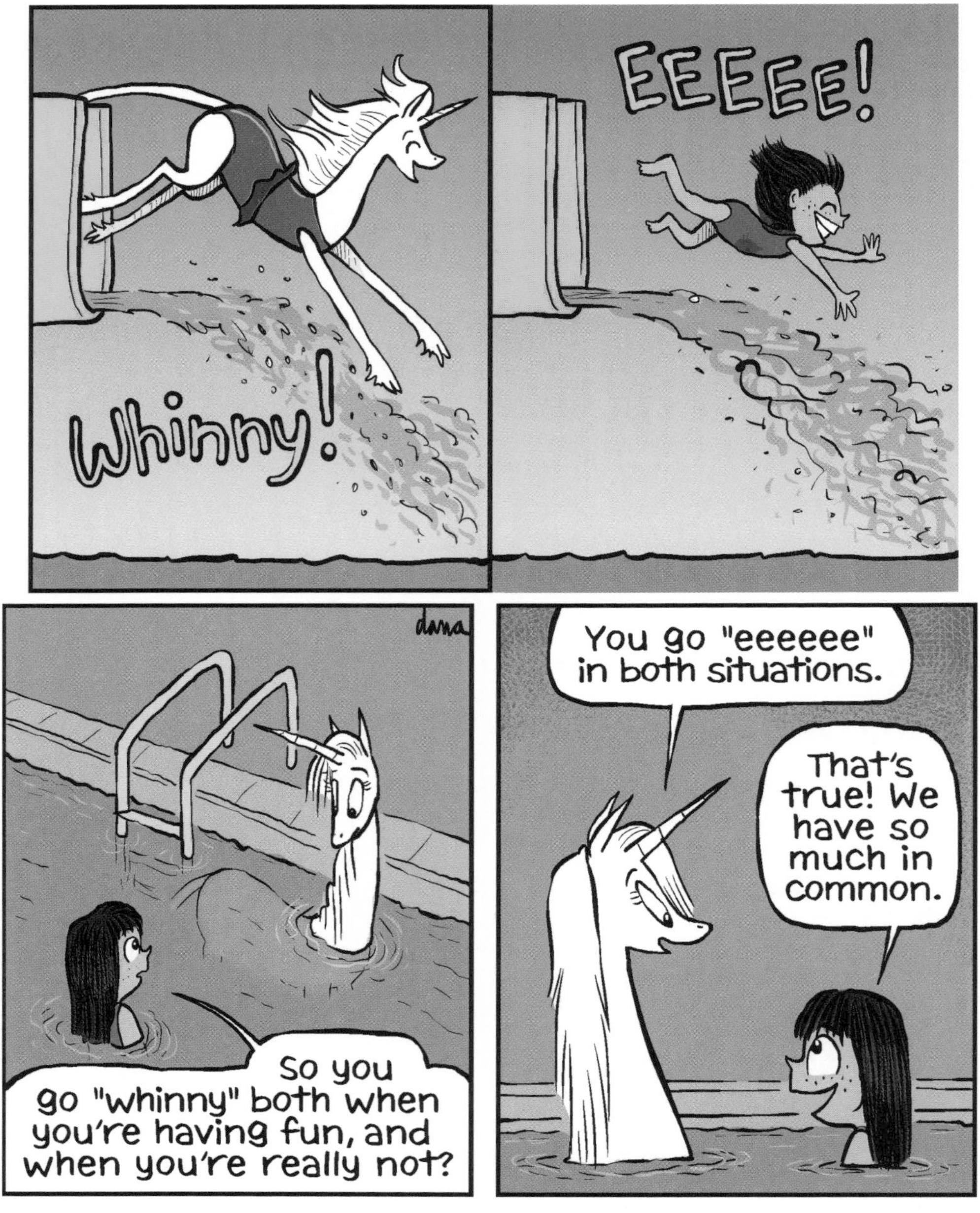
Whinny!
EEEEE!
dana
So you go "whinny" both when you're having fun, and when you're really not?
You go "eeeeee" in both situations.
That's true! We have so much in common.

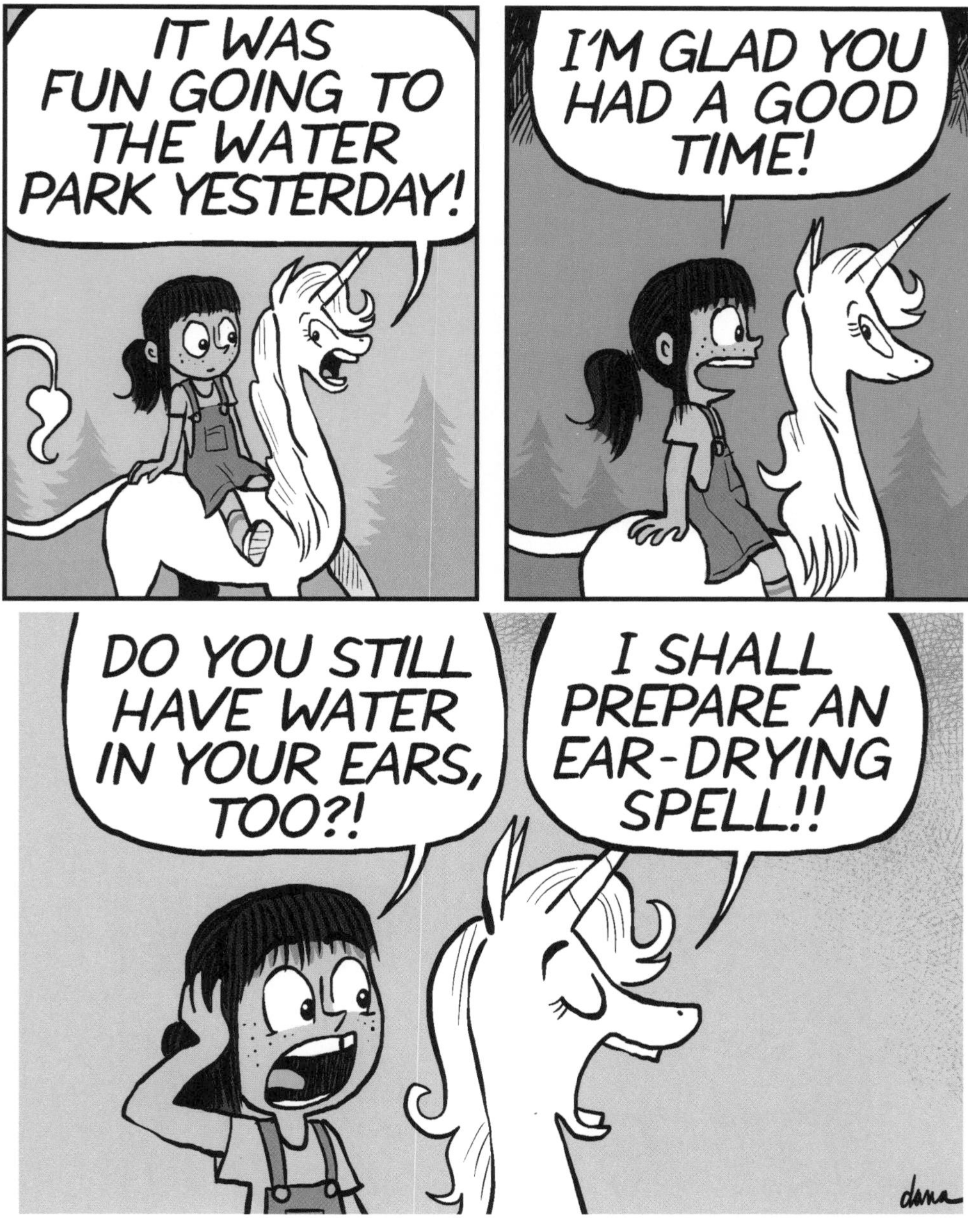
IT WAS FUN GOING TO THE WATER PARK YESTERDAY!
I'M GLAD YOU HAD A GOOD TIME!
DO YOU STILL HAVE WATER IN YOUR EARS, TOO?!
I SHALL PREPARE AN EAR-DRYING SPELL!!
dana

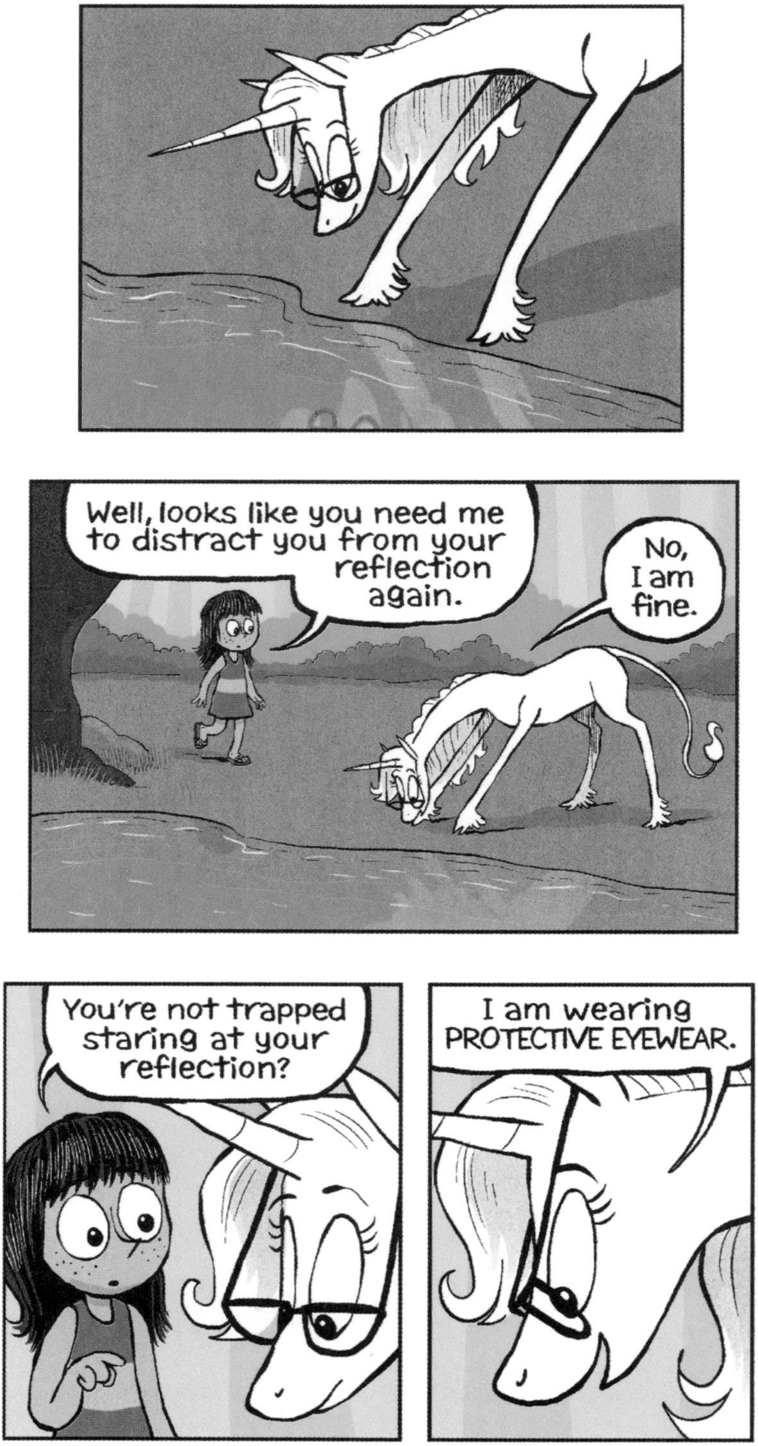
Well, looks like you need me to distract you from your reflection again.
No, I am fine.
You're not trapped staring at your reflection?
I am wearing PROTECTIVE EYEWEAR.

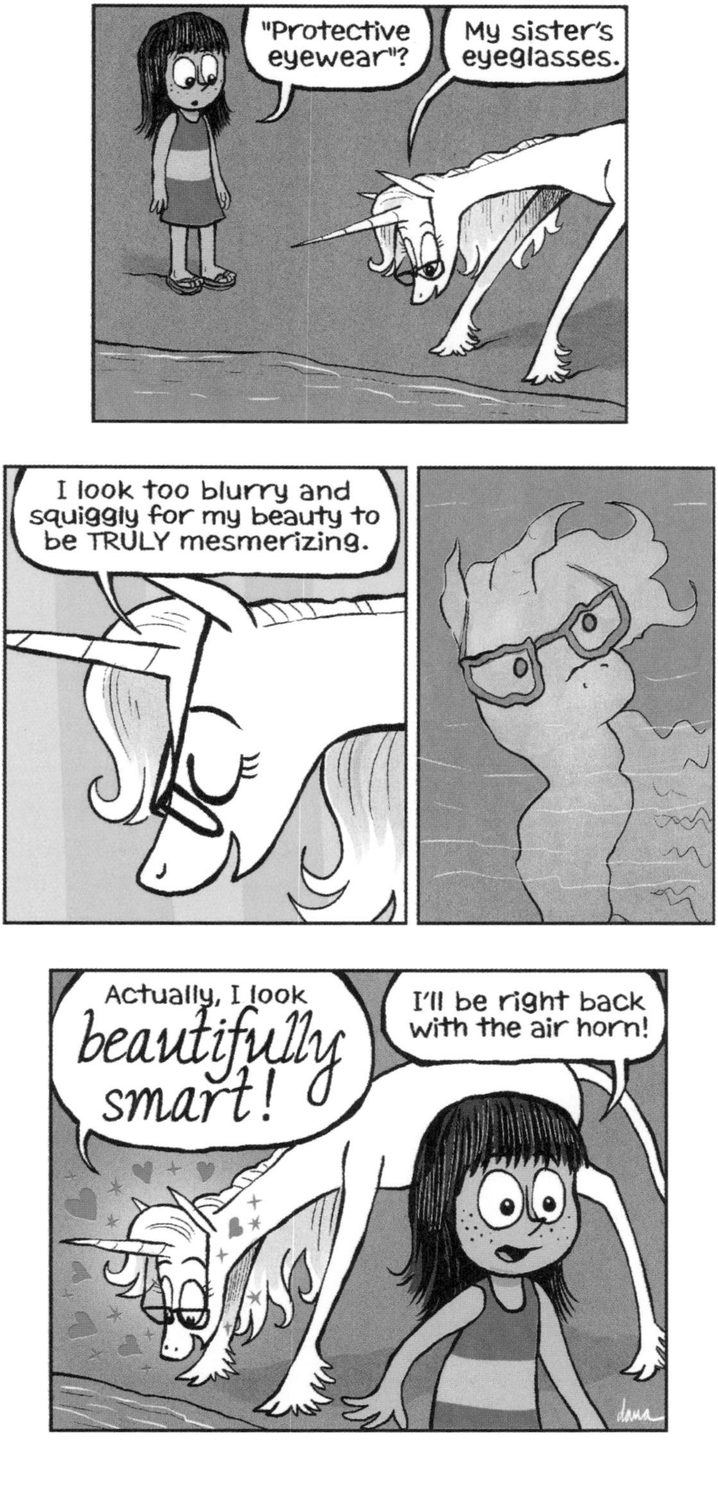
"Protective eyewear"?
My sister's eyeglasses.
I look too blurry and squiggly for my beauty to be TRULY mesmerizing.
Actually, I look *beautifully smart!*
I'll be right back with the air horn!
dana

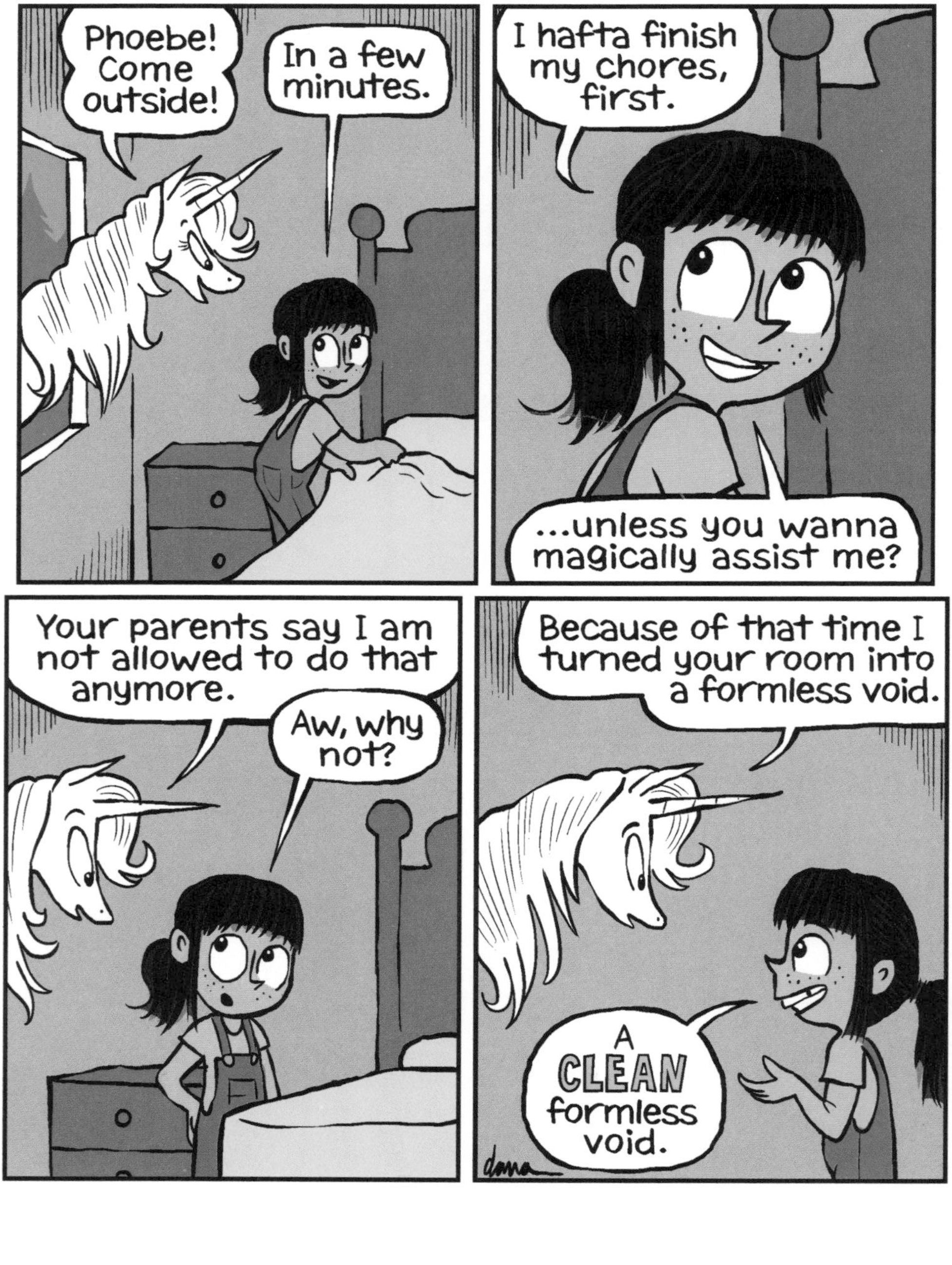
Phoebe! Come outside!
In a few minutes.
I hafta finish my chores, first.
...unless you wanna magically assist me?
Your parents say I am not allowed to do that anymore.
Aw, why not?
Because of that time I turned your room into a formless void.
A CLEAN formless void.

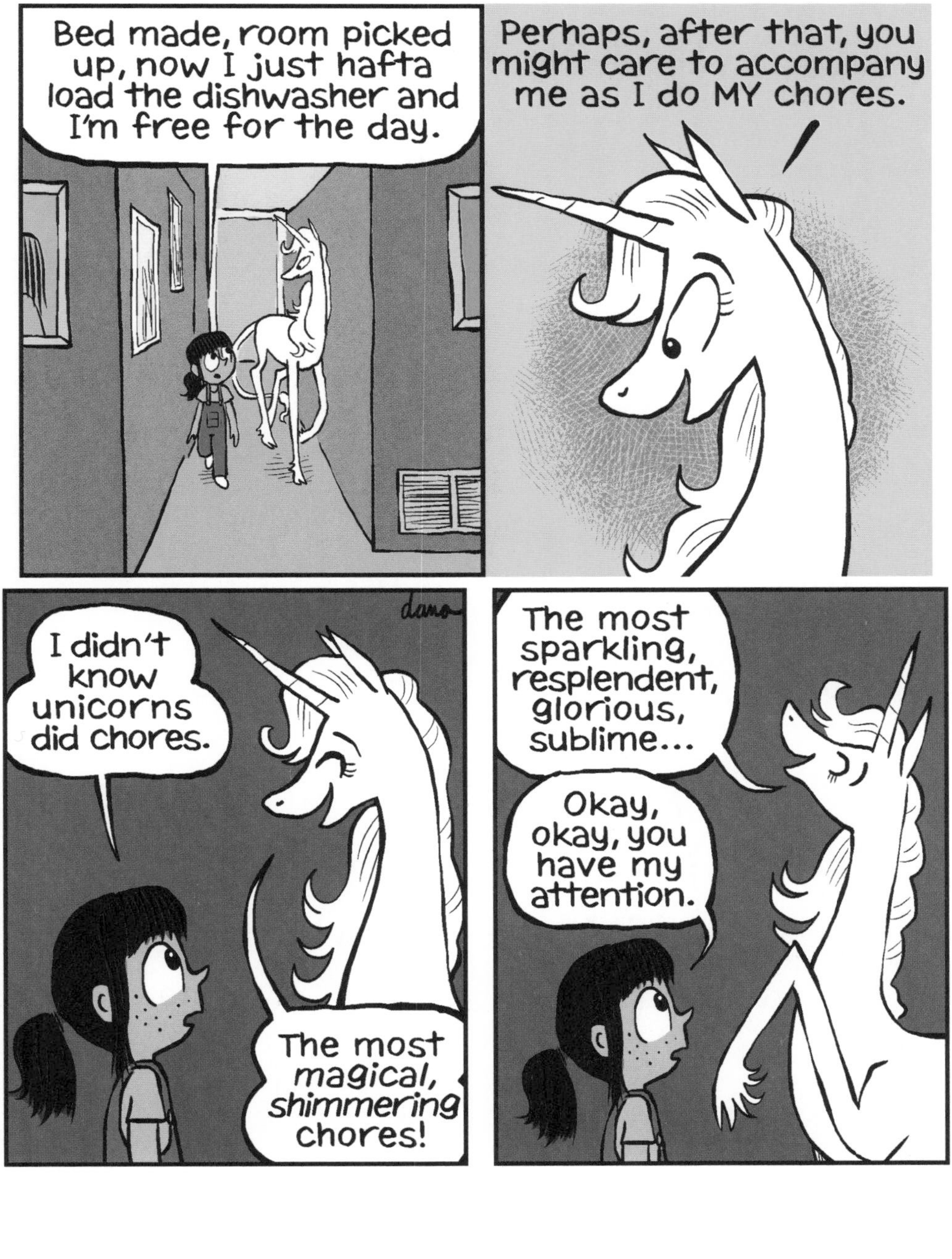
Bed made, room picked up, now I just hafta load the dishwasher and I'm free for the day.
Perhaps, after that, you might care to accompany me as I do MY chores.
I didn't know unicorns did chores.
The most *magical, shimmering* chores!
The most sparkling, resplendent, glorious, sublime...
Okay, okay, you have my attention.

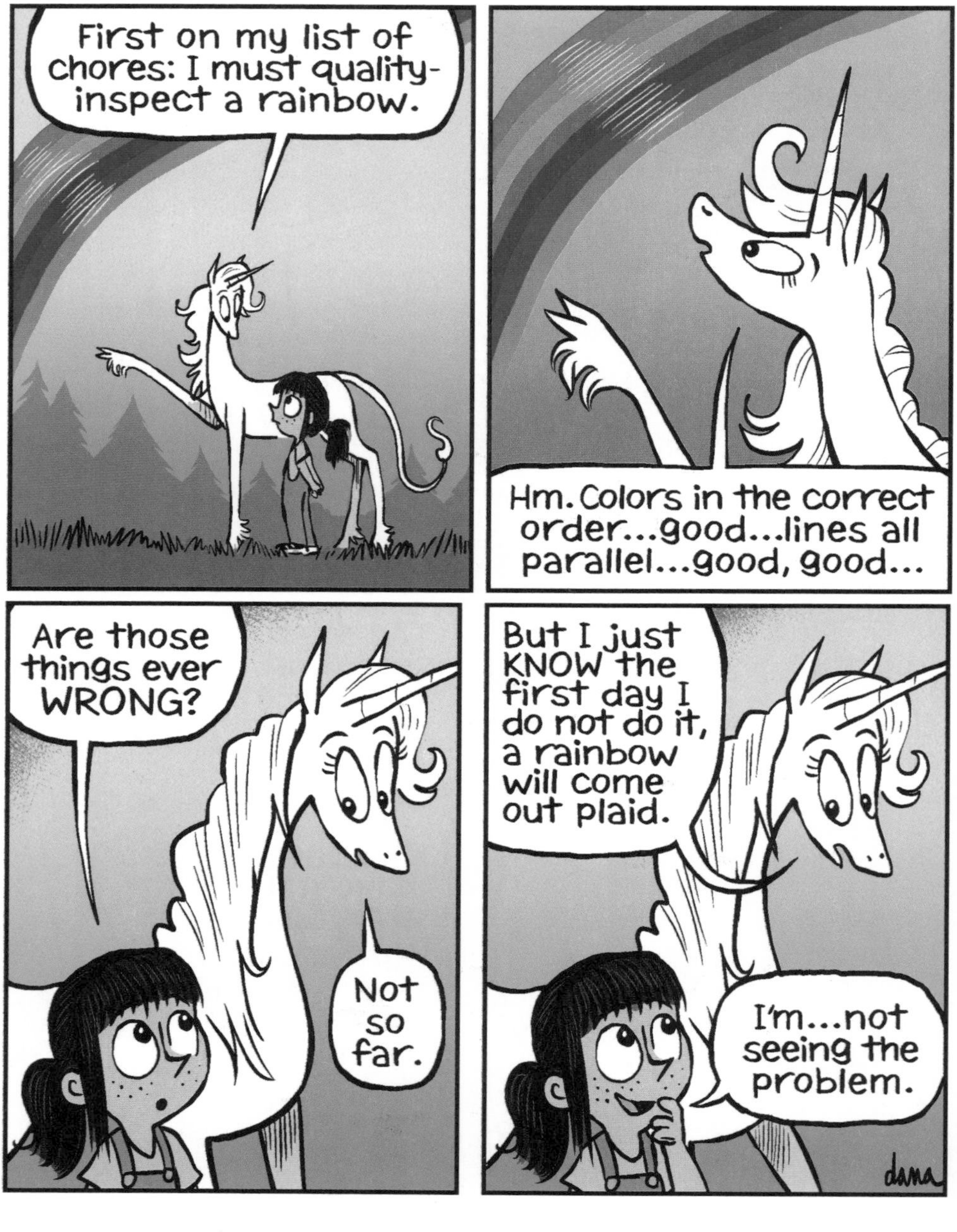
First on my list of chores: I must quality-inspect a rainbow.
Hm. Colors in the correct order...good...lines all parallel...good, good...
Are those things ever WRONG?
Not so far.
But I just KNOW the first day I do not do it, a rainbow will come out plaid.
I'm...not seeing the problem.
dana

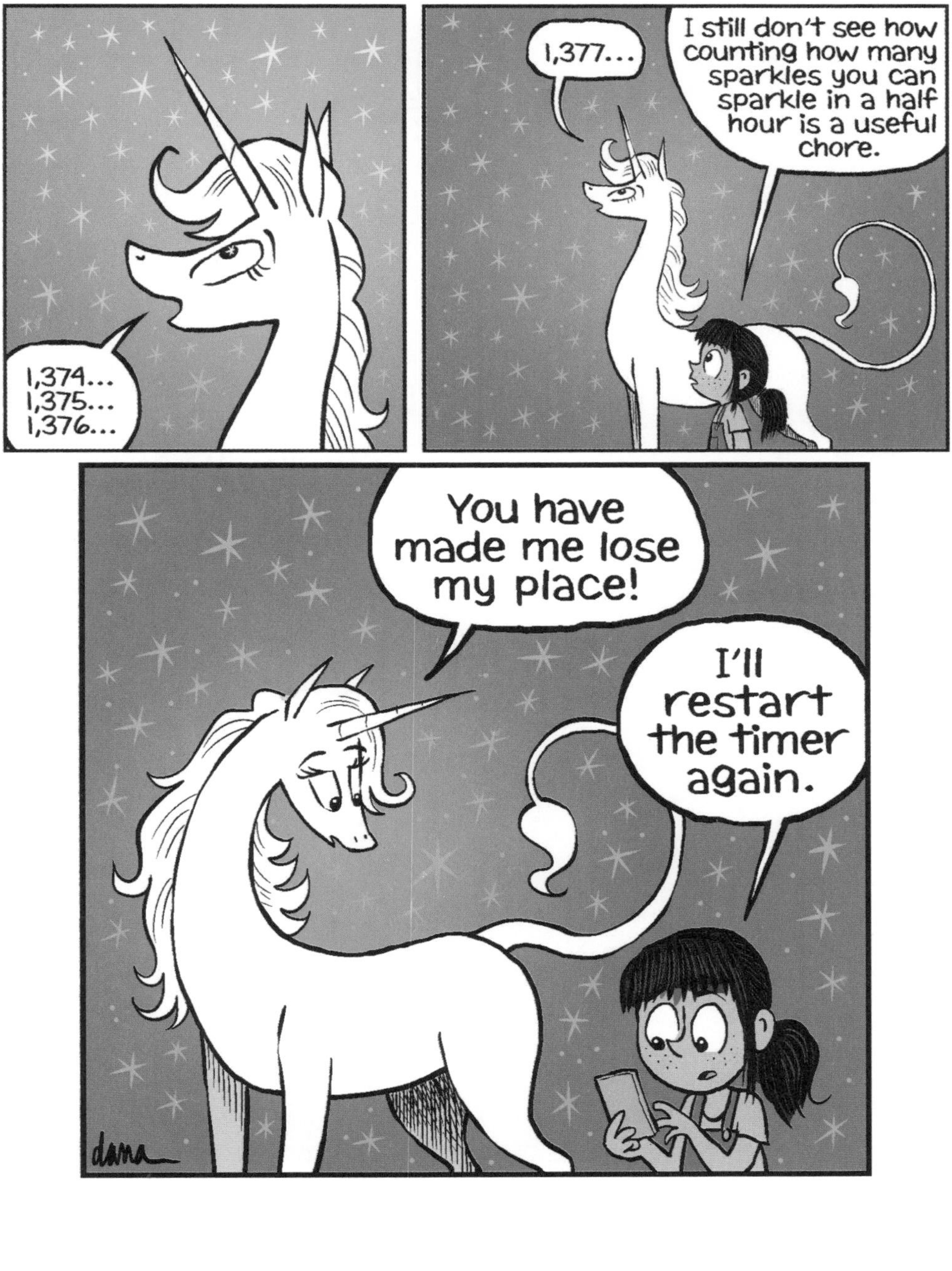
1,374...
1,375...
1,376...
1,377...
I still don't see how counting how many sparkles you can sparkle in a half hour is a useful chore.
You have made me lose my place!
I'll restart the timer again.
dana

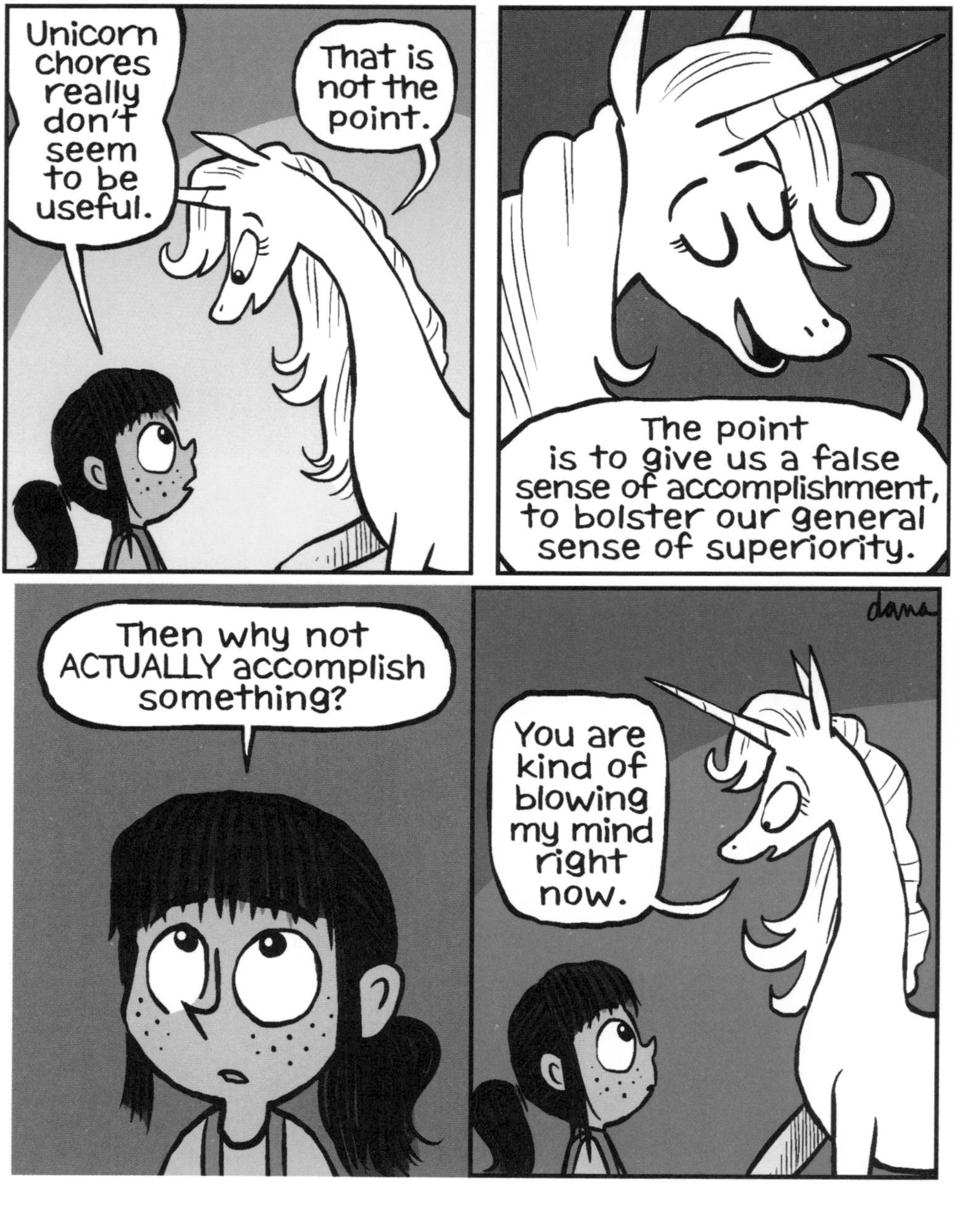
Unicorn chores really don't seem to be useful.
That is not the point.
The point is to give us a false sense of accomplishment, to bolster our general sense of superiority.
Then why not ACTUALLY accomplish something?
dana
You are kind of blowing my mind right now.

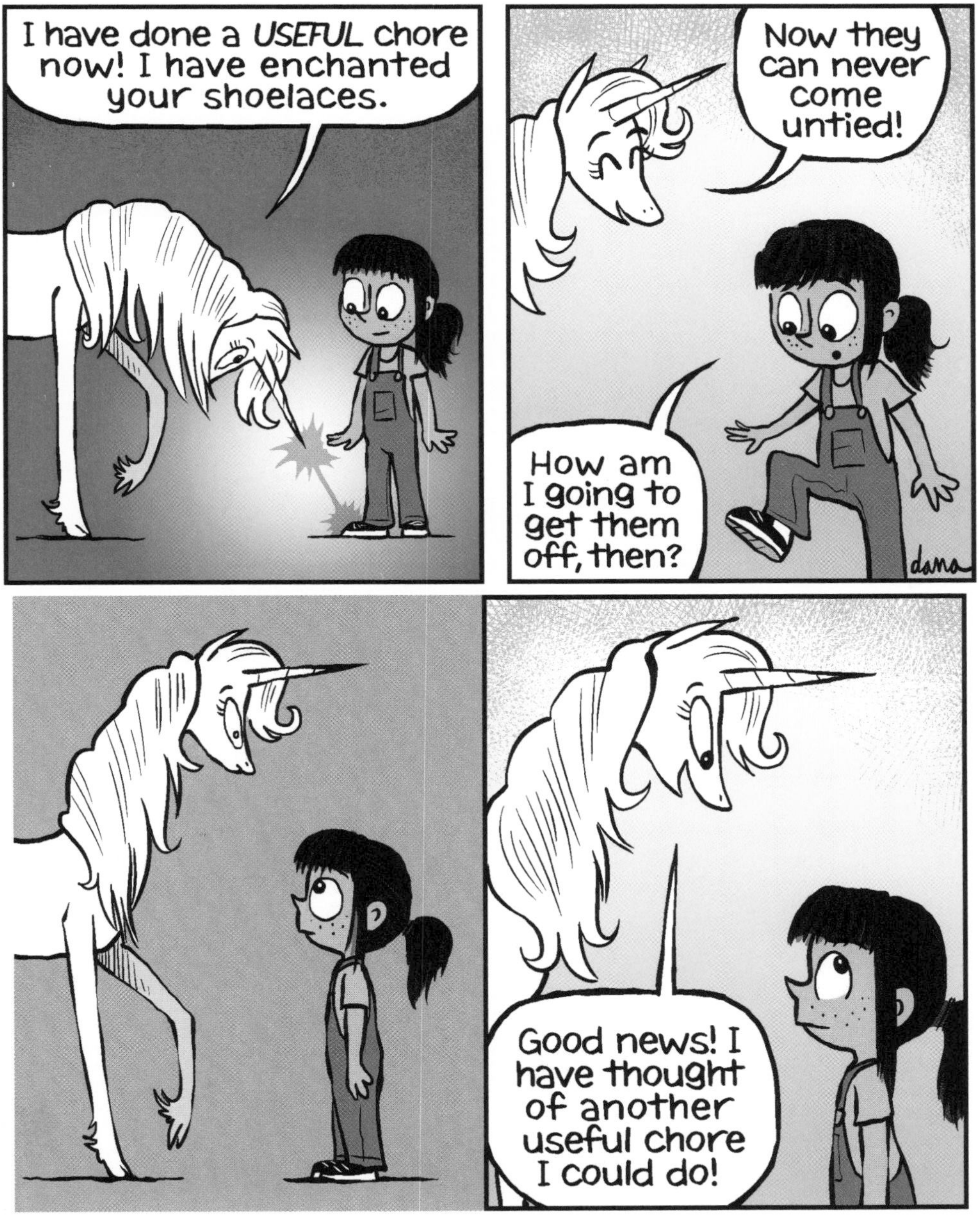
I have done a USEFUL chore now! I have enchanted your shoelaces.
Now they can never come untied!
How am I going to get them off, then?
dana
Good news! I have thought of another useful chore I could do!

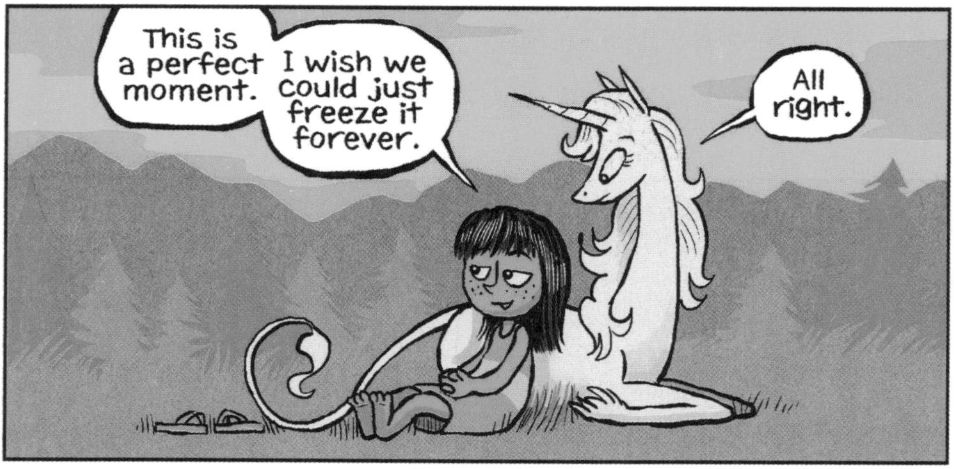
This is a perfect moment.
I wish we could just freeze it forever.
All right.

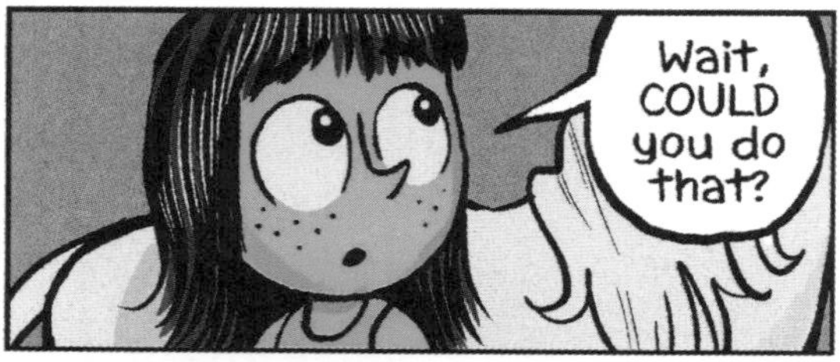
Wait, COULD you do that?

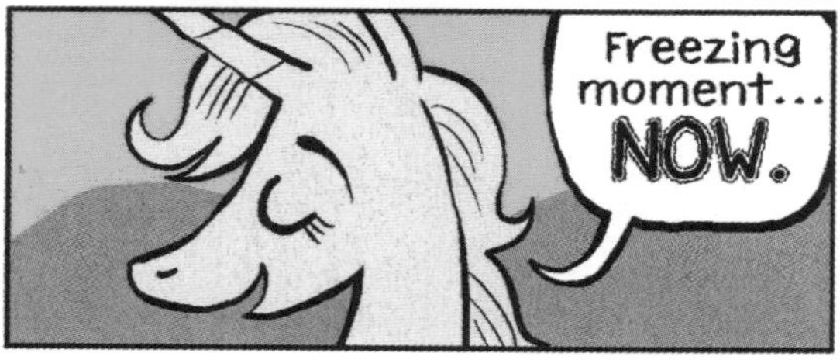
Freezing moment... NOW.

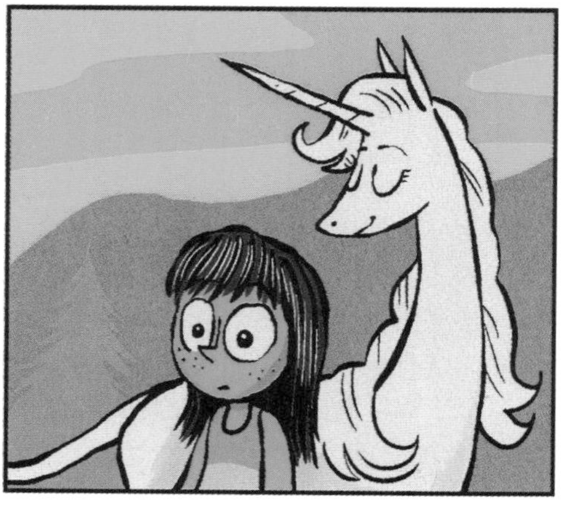

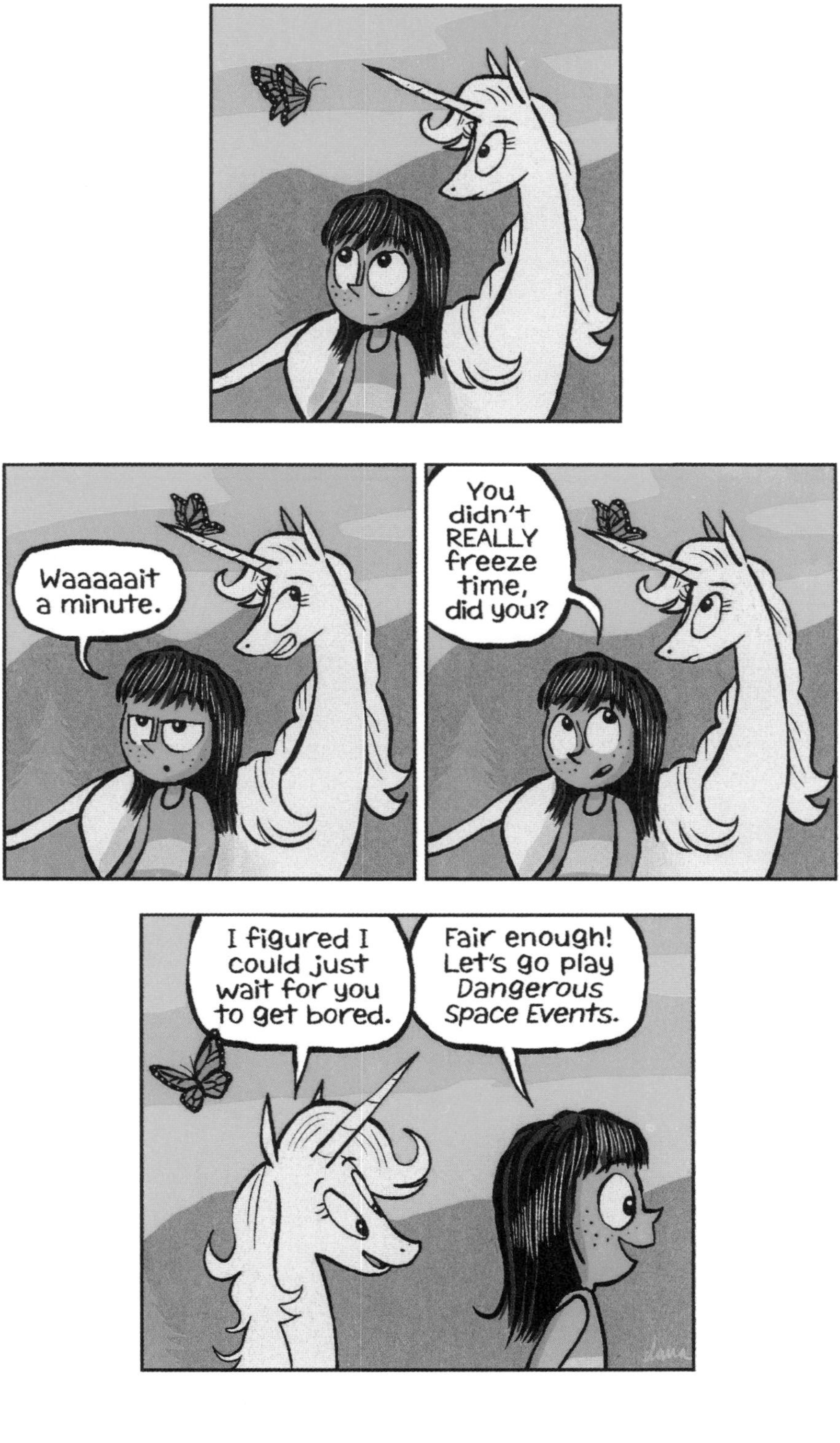
Waaaaait a minute.
You didn't REALLY freeze time, did you?
I figured I could just wait for you to get bored.
Fair enough! Let's go play *Dangerous Space Events.*

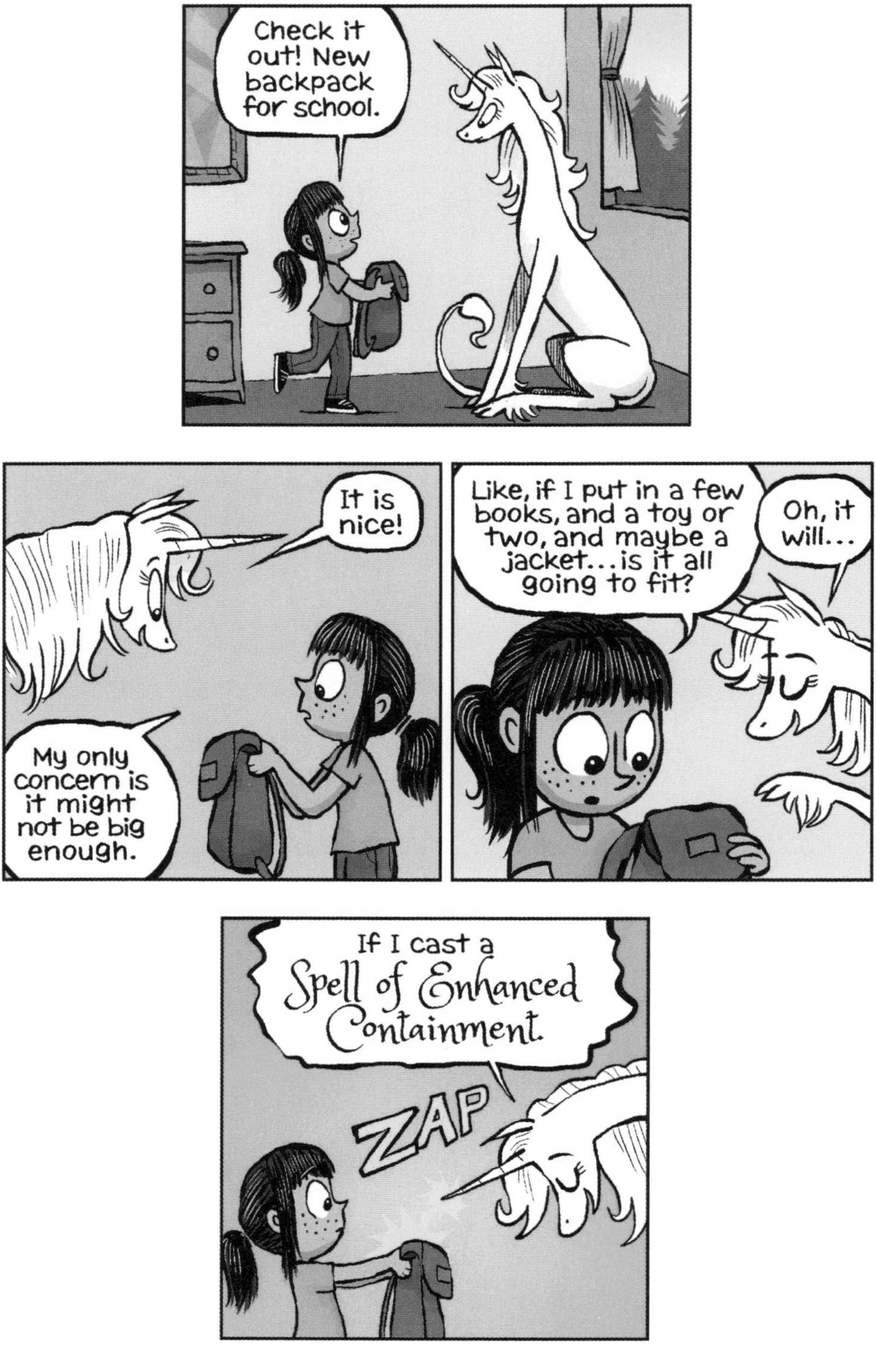
Check it out! New backpack for school.
It is nice!
My only concern is it might not be big enough.
Like, if I put in a few books, and a toy or two, and maybe a jacket...is it all going to fit?
Oh, it will...
If I cast a Spell of Enhanced Containment.
ZAP

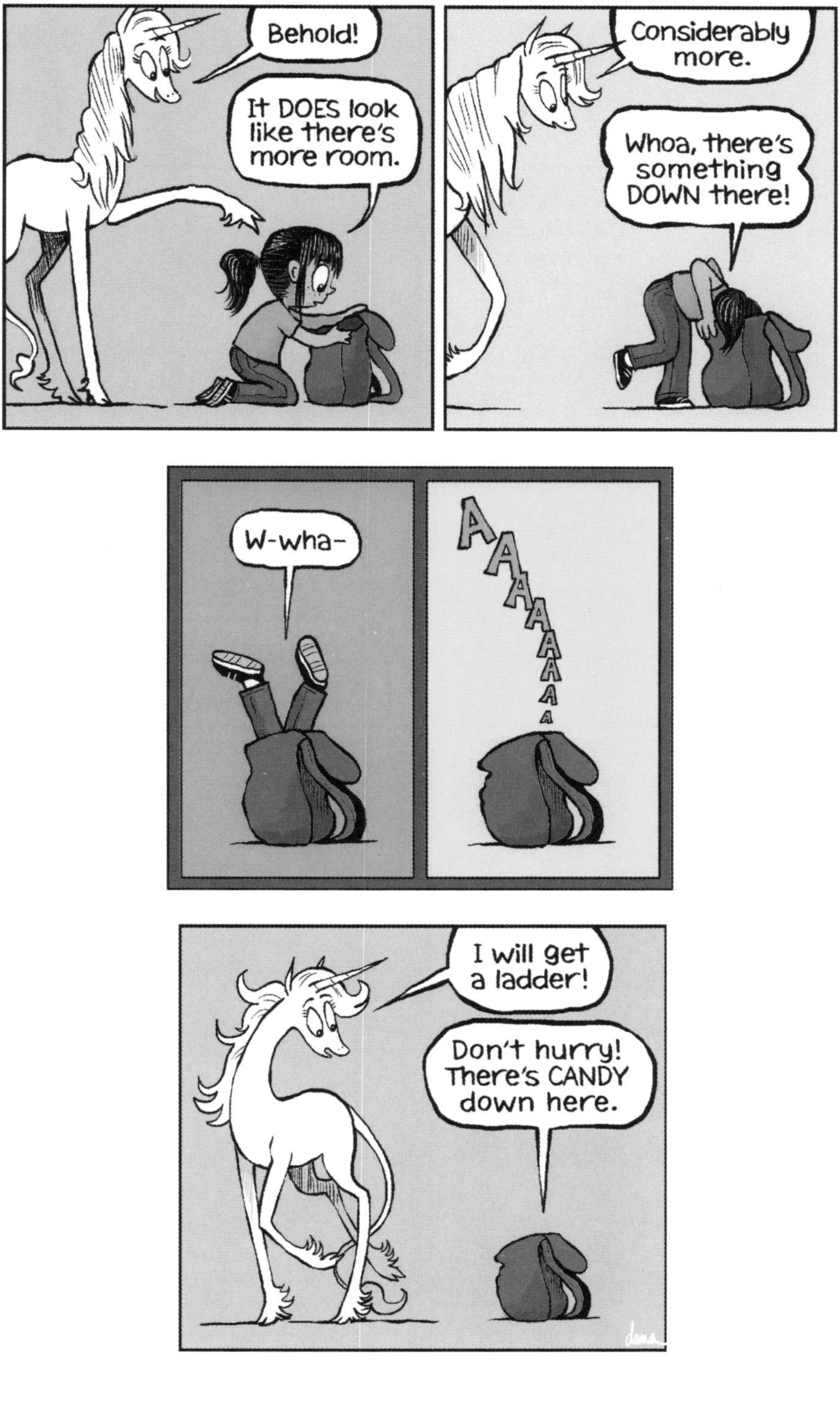
Behold!
It DOES look like there's more room.
Considerably more.
Whoa, there's something DOWN there!
W-wha-
AAAAAAAAAA
I will get a ladder!
Don't hurry! There's CANDY down here.

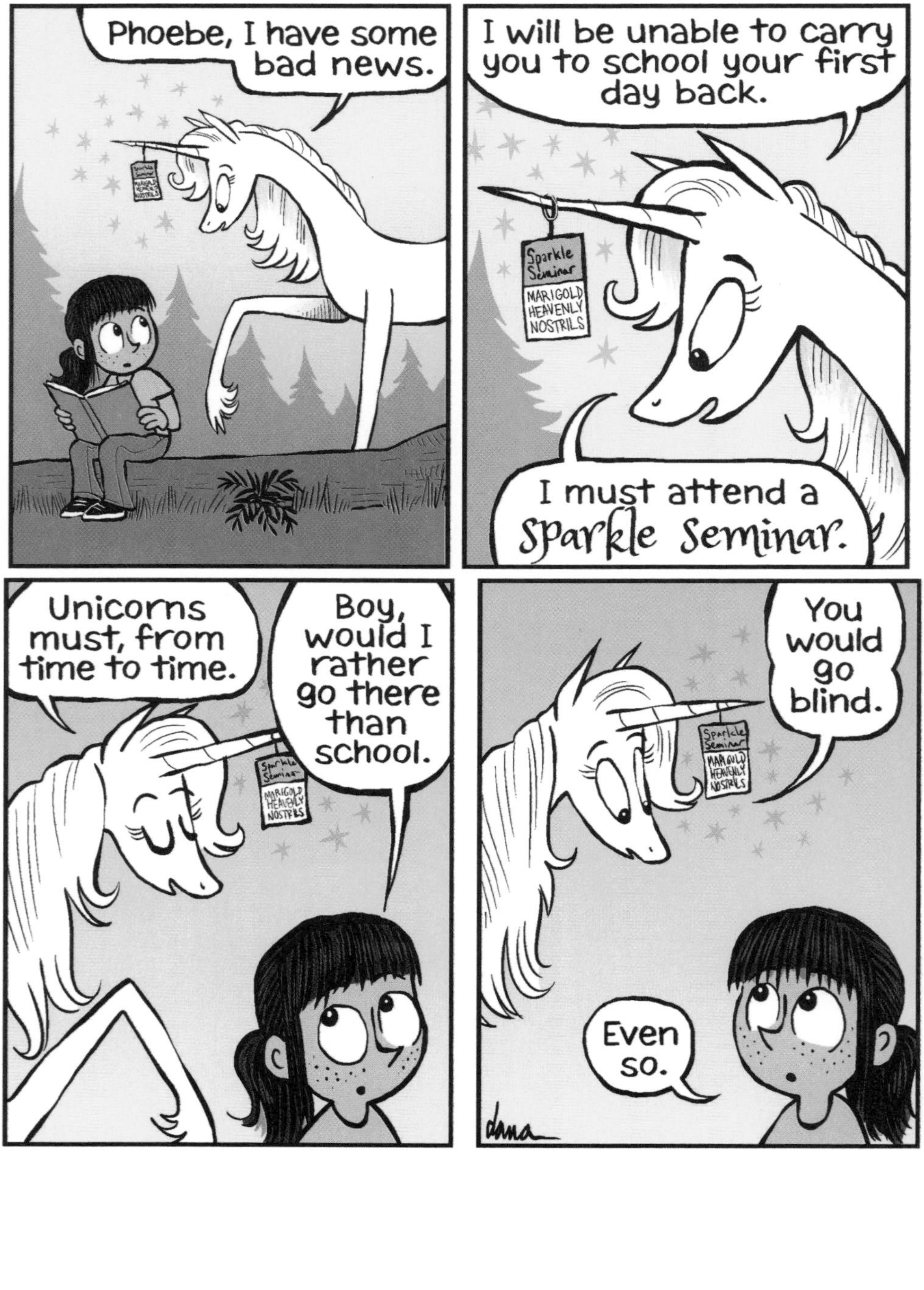
Phoebe, I have some bad news.
Sparkle Seminar
MARIGOLD HEAVENLY NOSTRILS
I will be unable to carry you to school your first day back.
I must attend a Sparkle Seminar.
Unicorns must, from time to time.
Boy, would I rather go there than school.
You would go blind.
Even so.
dana

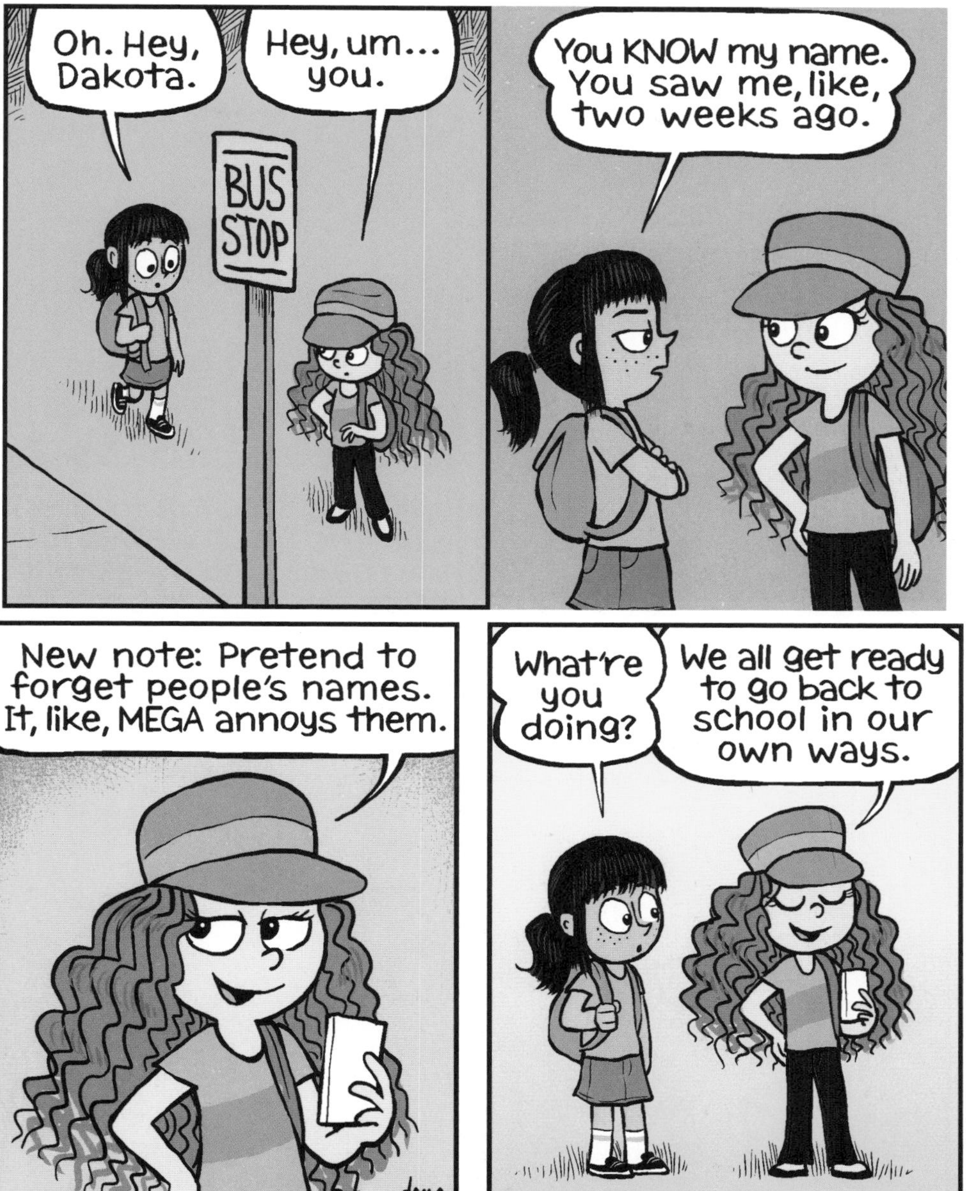
Oh. Hey, Dakota.
Hey, um... you.
BUS STOP
You KNOW my name. You saw me, like, two weeks ago.
New note: Pretend to forget people's names. It, like, MEGA annoys them.
dana
What're you doing?
We all get ready to go back to school in our own ways.

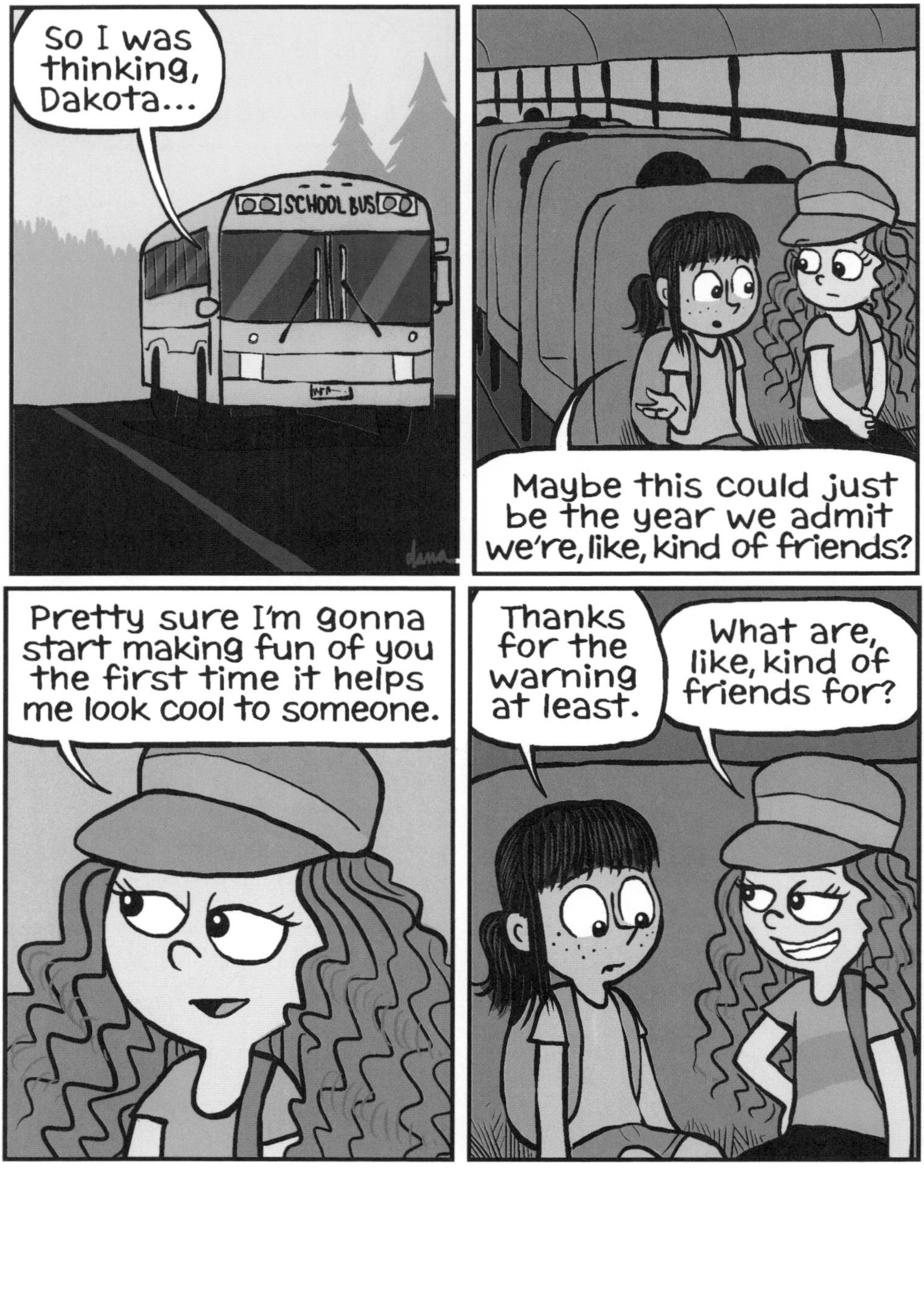
So I was thinking, Dakota...
SCHOOL BUS
Maybe this could just be the year we admit we're, like, kind of friends?
Pretty sure I'm gonna start making fun of you the first time it helps me look cool to someone.
Thanks for the warning at least.
What are, like, kind of friends for?

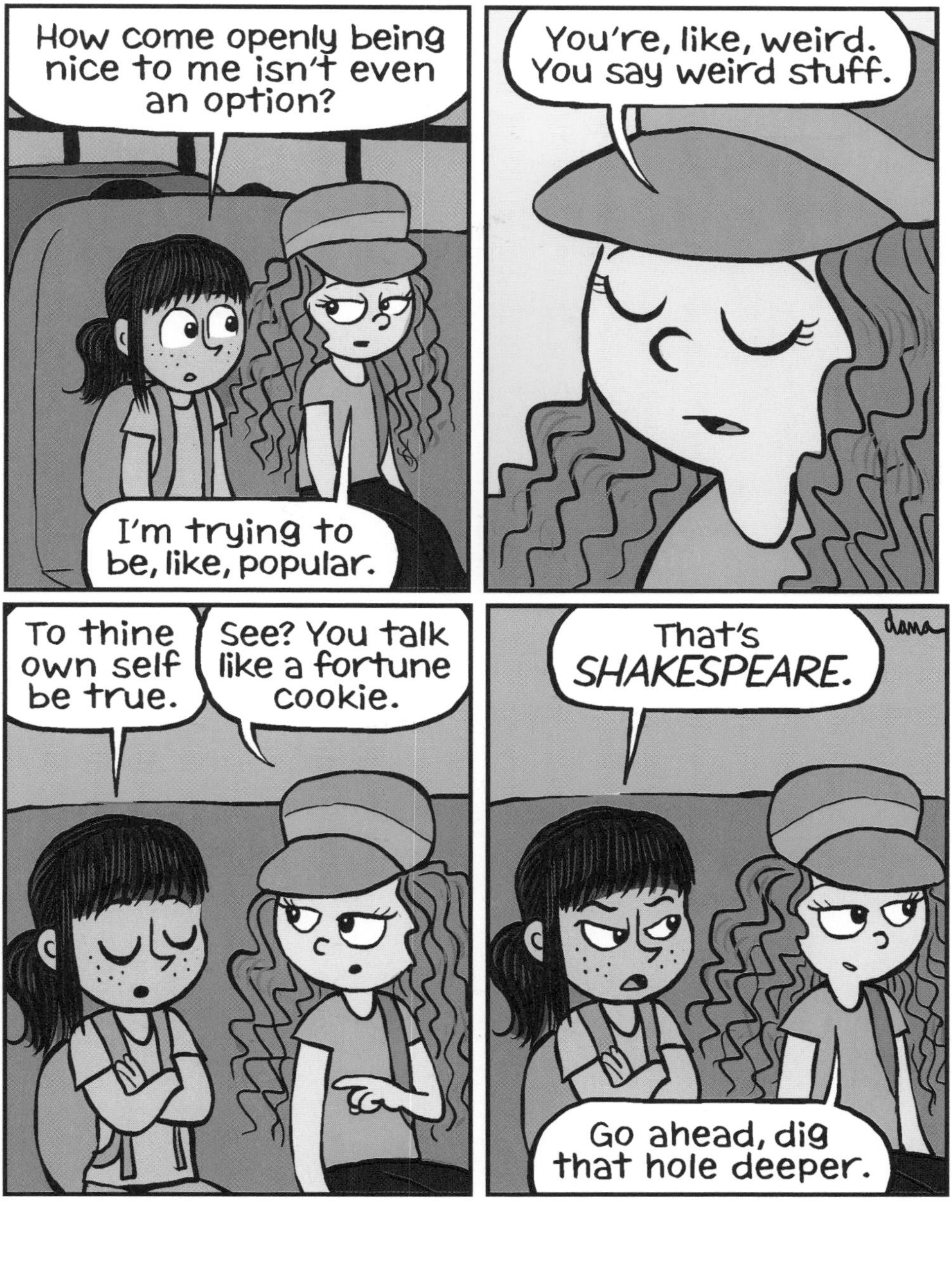
How come openly being nice to me isn't even an option?
I'm trying to be, like, popular.
You're, like, weird. You say weird stuff.
To thine own self be true.
See? You talk like a fortune cookie.
That's *SHAKESPEARE.*
Go ahead, dig that hole deeper.
dana

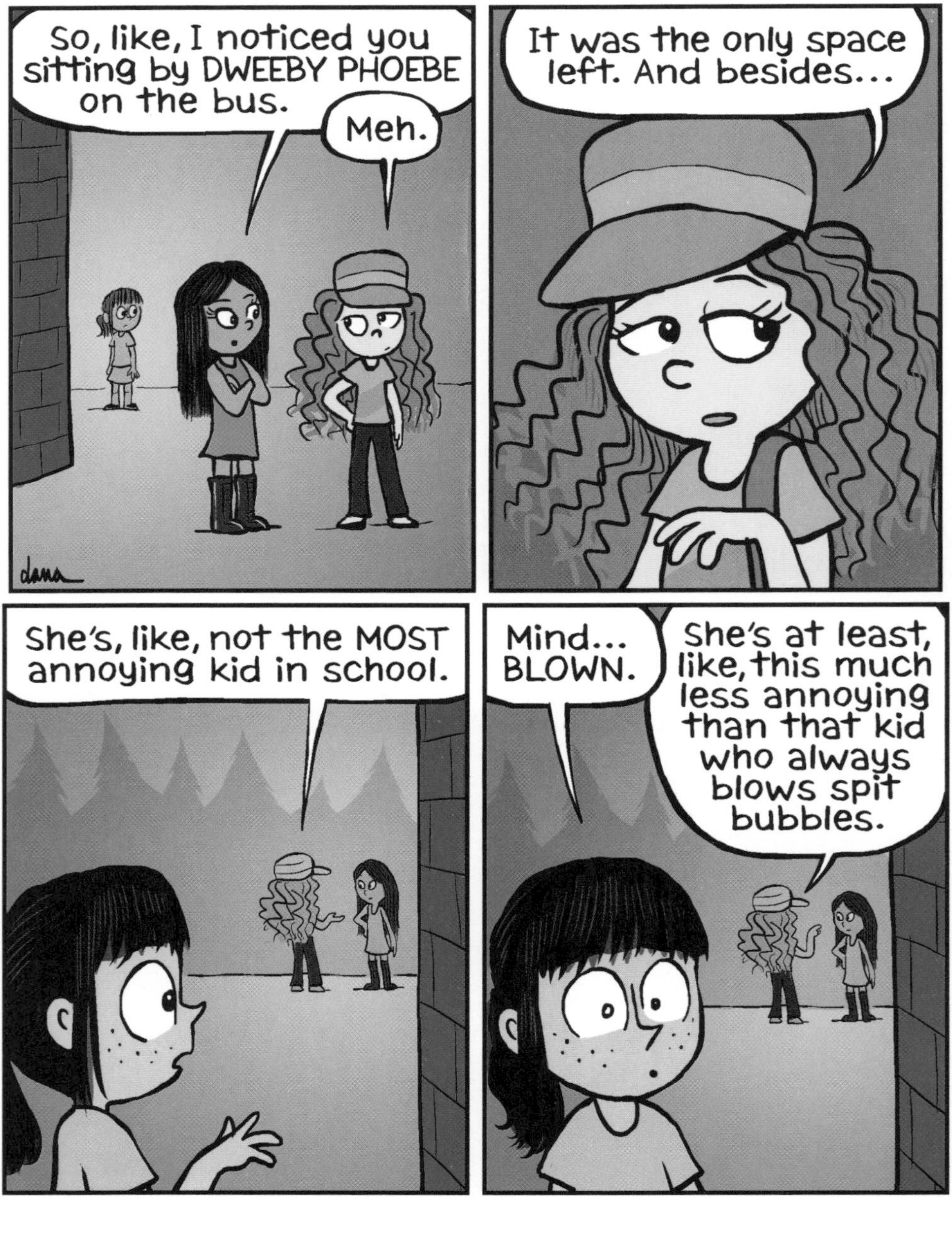
So, like, I noticed you sitting by DWEEBY PHOEBE on the bus.
Meh.
dana
It was the only space left. And besides...
She's, like, not the MOST annoying kid in school.
Mind... BLOWN.
She's at least, like, this much less annoying than that kid who always blows spit bubbles.

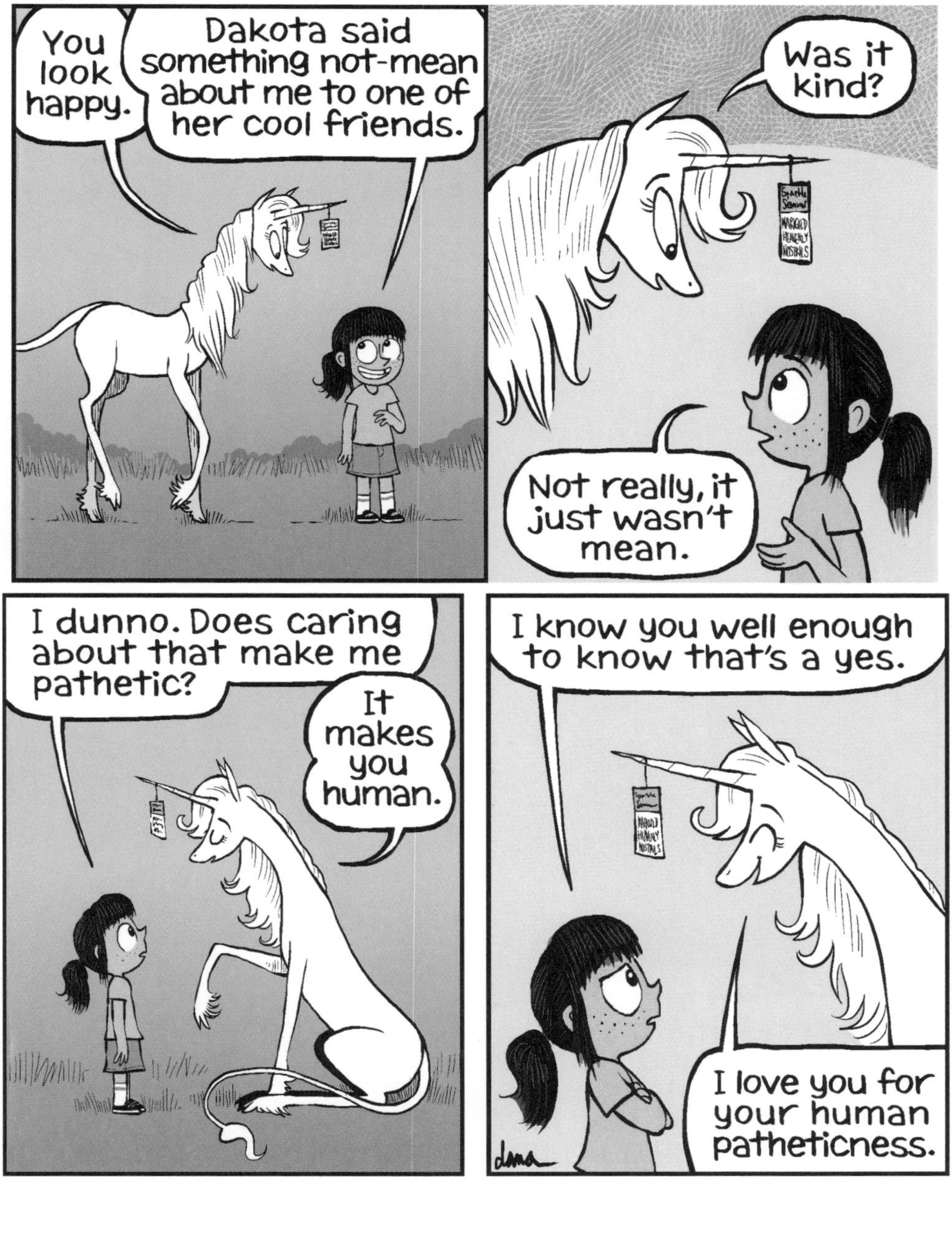
You look happy.
Dakota said something not-mean about me to one of her cool friends.
Was it kind?
Not really, it just wasn't mean.
I dunno. Does caring about that make me pathetic?
It makes you human.
I know you well enough to know that's a yes.
I love you for your human patheticness.

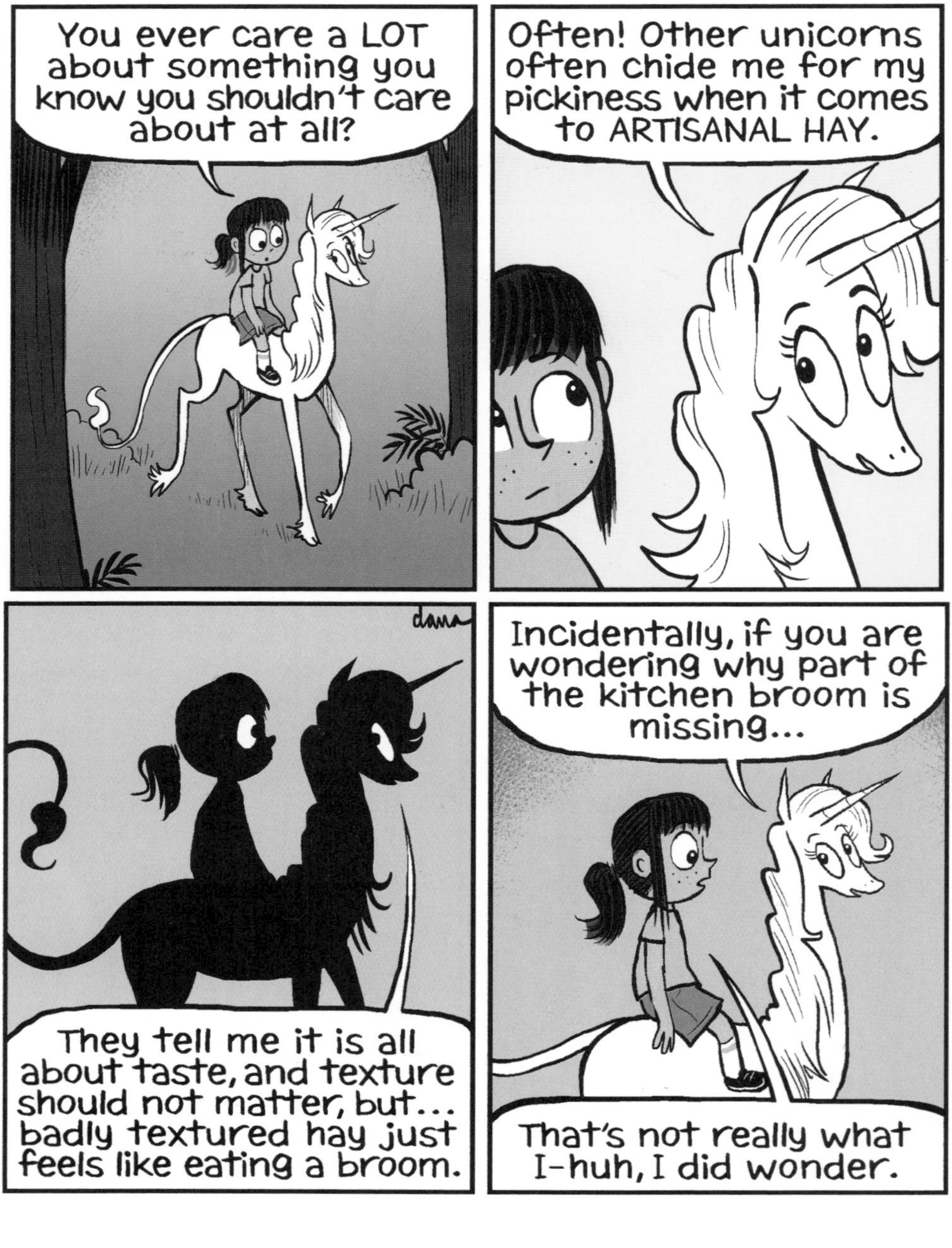
You ever care a LOT about something you know you shouldn't care about at all?
Often! Other unicorns often chide me for my pickiness when it comes to ARTISANAL HAY.
dana
They tell me it is all about taste, and texture should not matter, but... badly textured hay just feels like eating a broom.
Incidentally, if you are wondering why part of the kitchen broom is missing...
That's not really what I-huh, I did wonder.

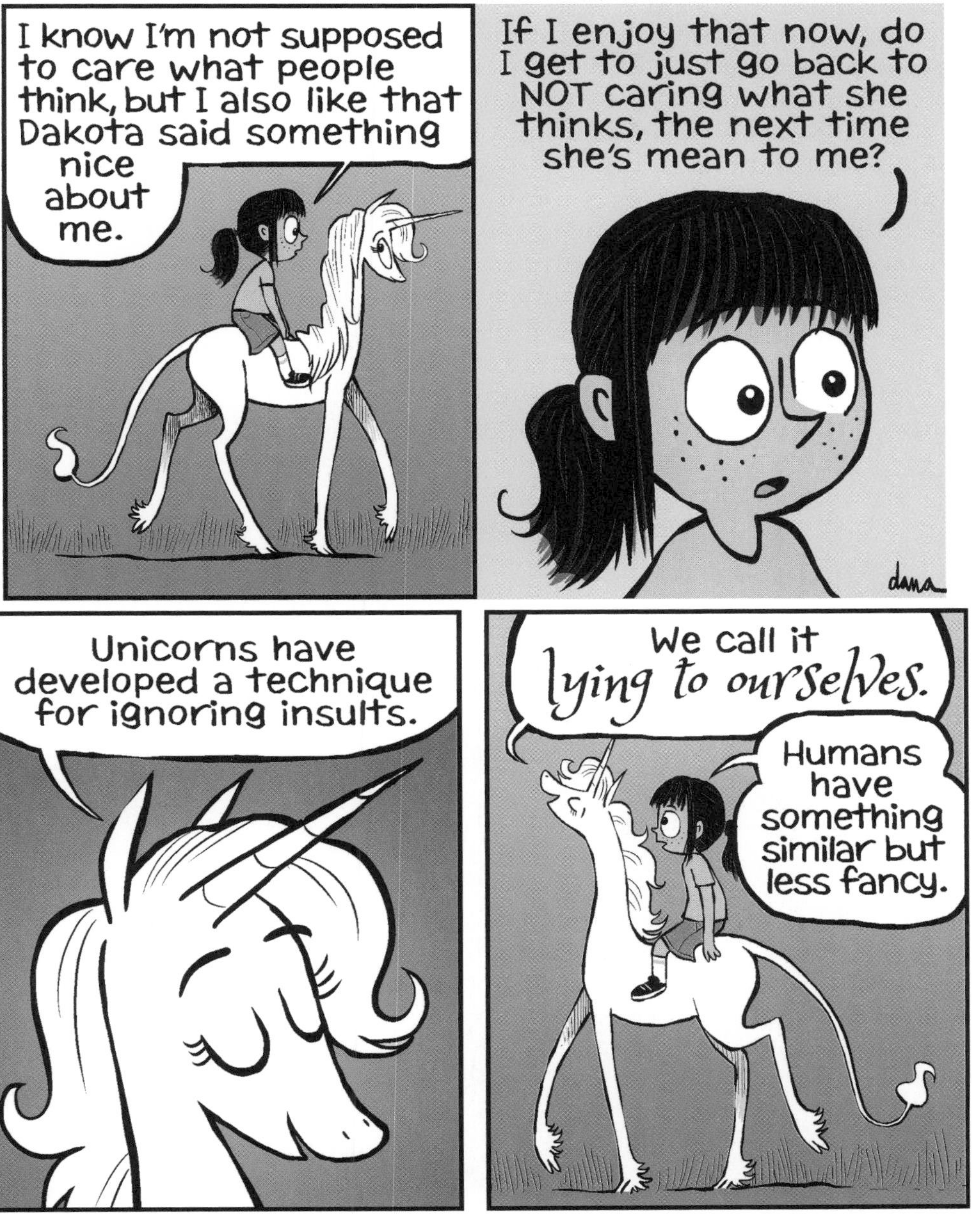
I know I'm not supposed to care what people think, but I also like that Dakota said something nice about me.
If I enjoy that now, do I get to just go back to NOT caring what she thinks, the next time she's mean to me?
dana
Unicorns have developed a technique for ignoring insults.
We call it *lying to ourselves.*
Humans have something similar but less fancy.

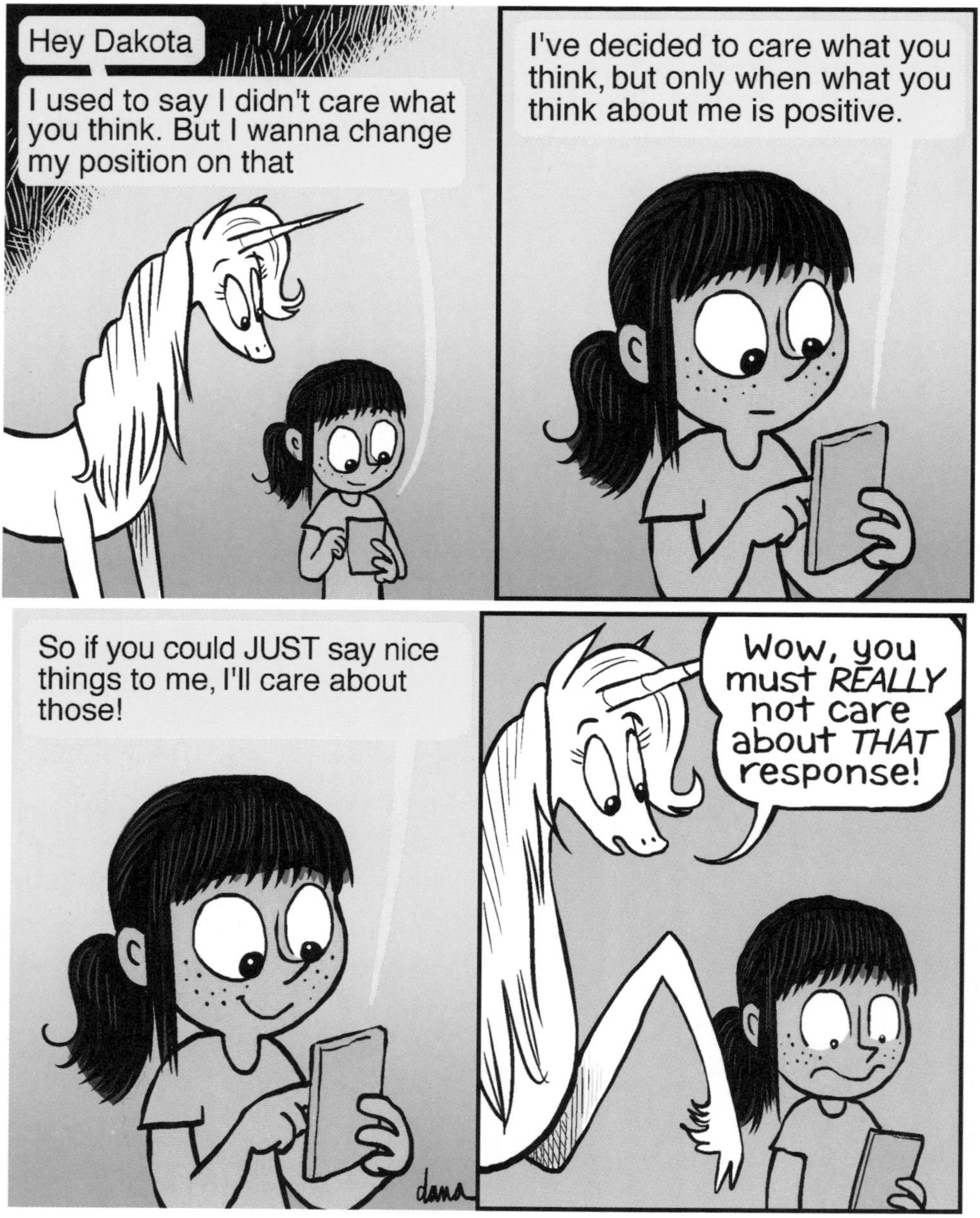
Hey Dakota
I used to say I didn't care what you think. But I wanna change my position on that
I've decided to care what you think, but only when what you think about me is positive.
So if you could JUST say nice things to me, I'll care about those!
Wow, you must REALLY not care about THAT response!
dana

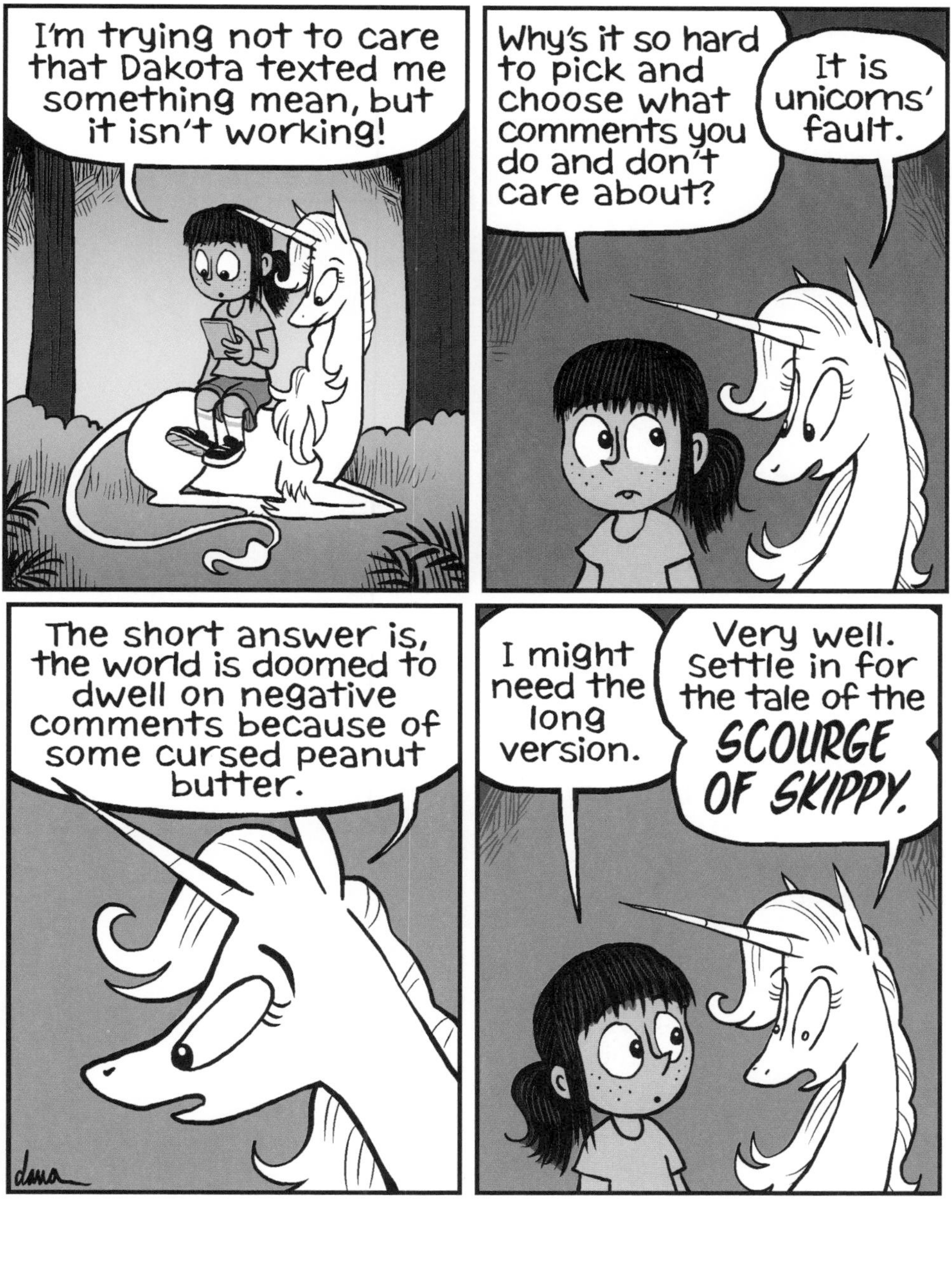
I'm trying not to care that Dakota texted me something mean, but it isn't working!
Why's it so hard to pick and choose what comments you do and don't care about?
It is unicorns' fault.
The short answer is, the world is doomed to dwell on negative comments because of some cursed peanut butter.
I might need the long version.
Very well. Settle in for the tale of the SCOURGE OF SKIPPY.
dana

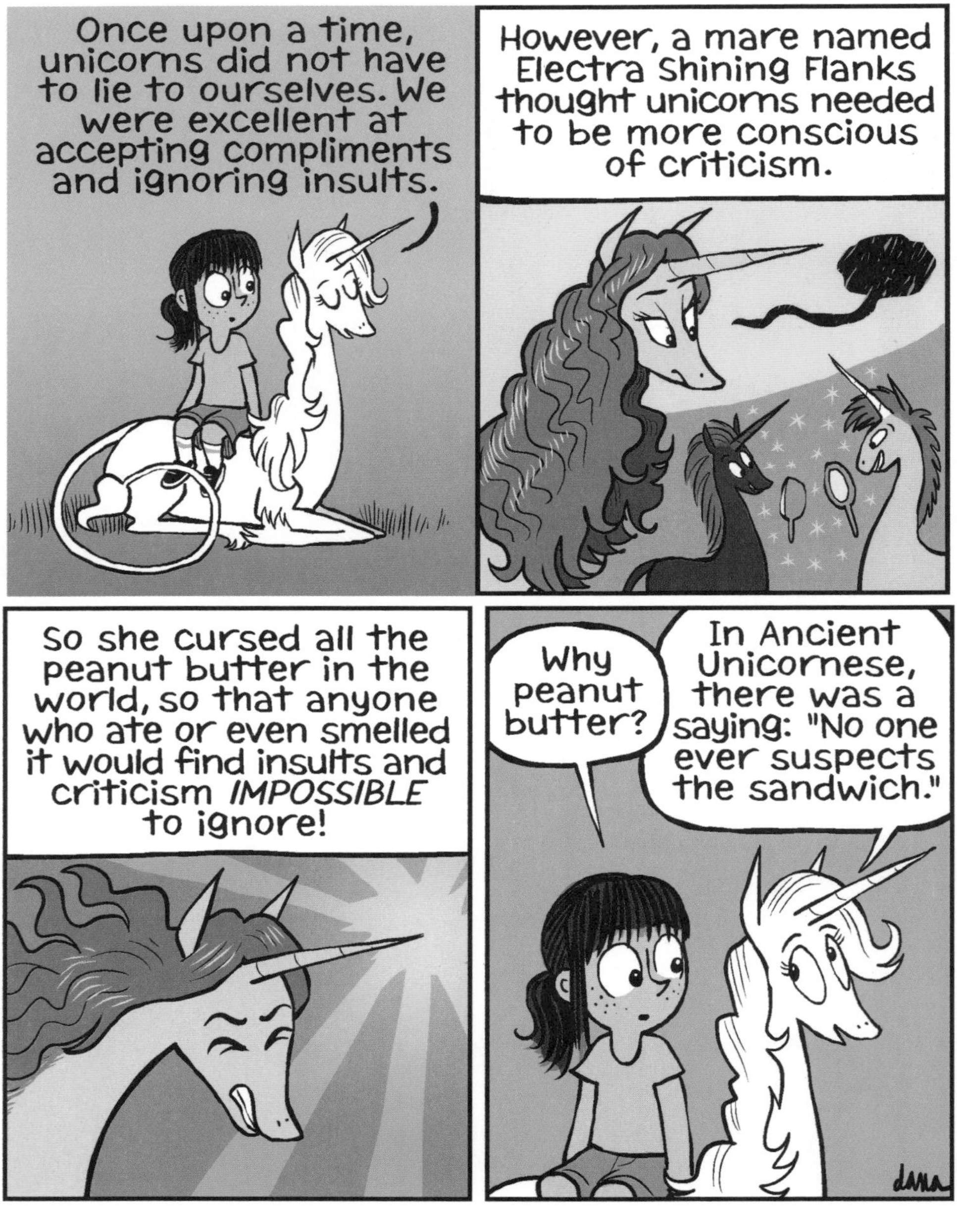
Once upon a time, unicorns did not have to lie to ourselves. We were excellent at accepting compliments and ignoring insults.
However, a mare named Electra Shining Flanks thought unicorns needed to be more conscious of criticism.
So she cursed all the peanut butter in the world, so that anyone who ate or even smelled it would find insults and criticism *IMPOSSIBLE* to ignore!
Why peanut butter?
In Ancient Unicornese, there was a saying: "No one ever suspects the sandwich."
dana

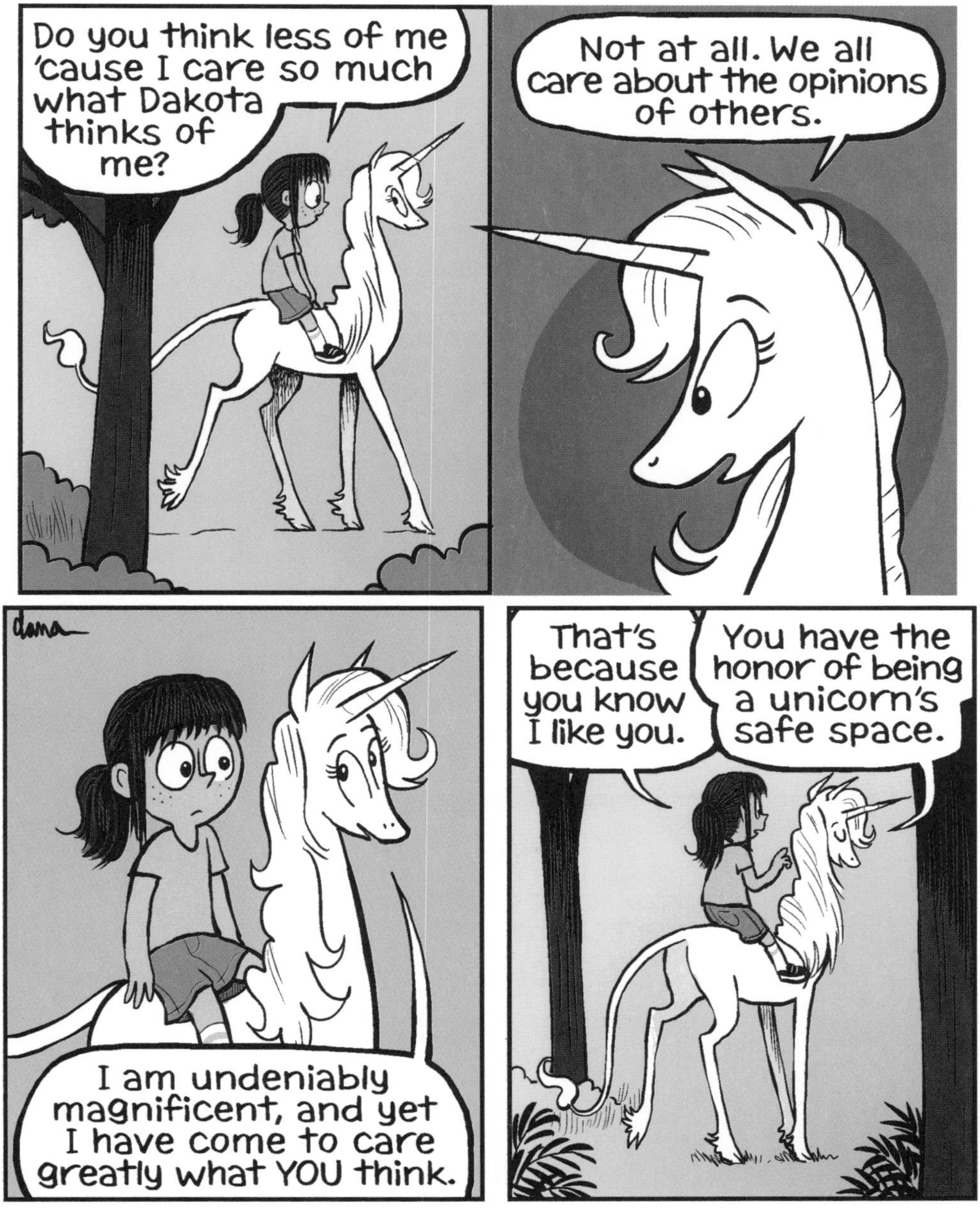
Do you think less of me 'cause I care so much what Dakota thinks of me?
Not at all. We all care about the opinions of others.
dana
I am undeniably magnificent, and yet I have come to care greatly what YOU think.
That's because you know I like you.
You have the honor of being a unicorn's safe space.

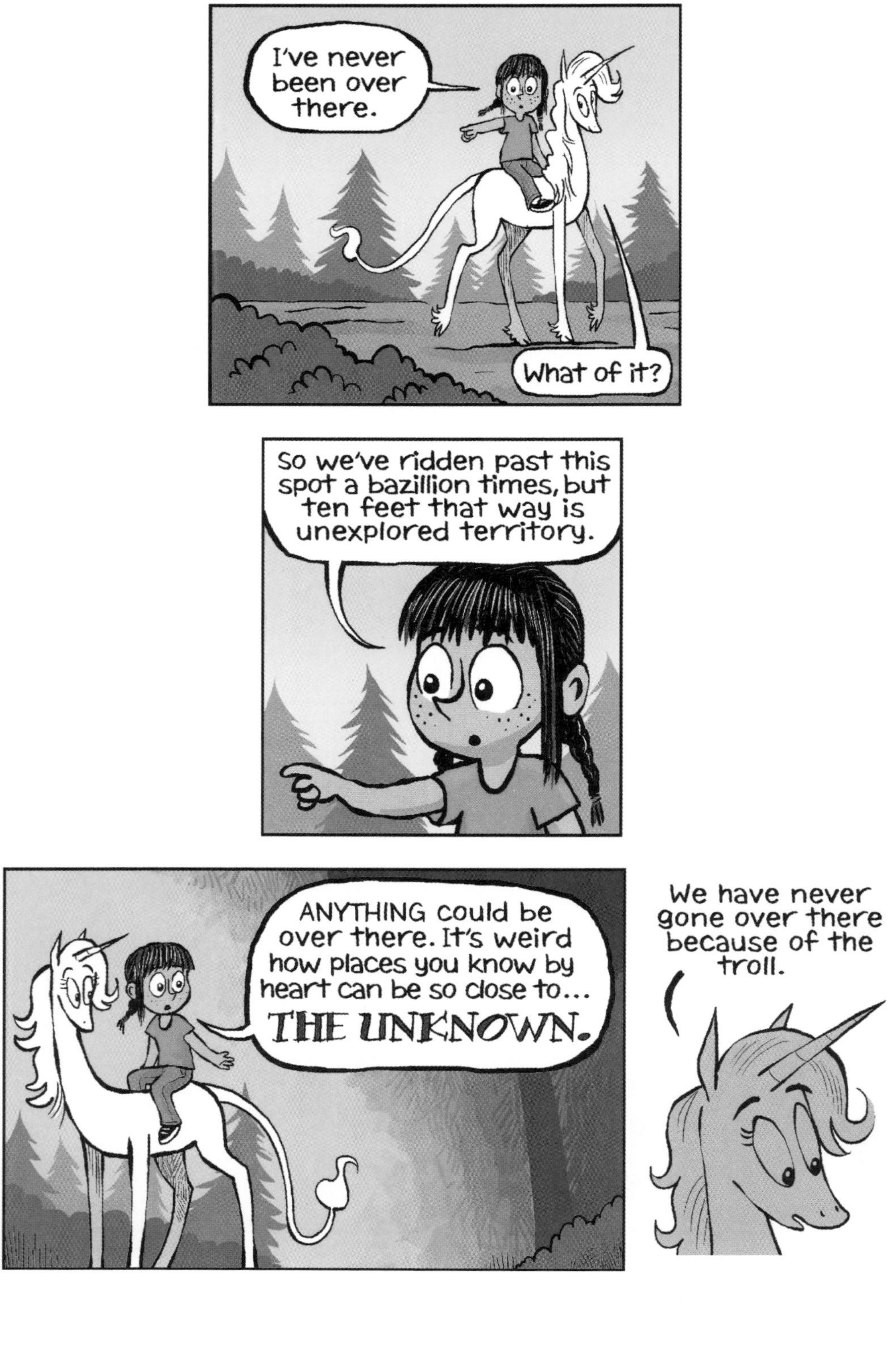
I've never been over there.
What of it?
So we've ridden past this spot a bazillion times, but ten feet that way is unexplored territory.
ANYTHING could be over there. It's weird how places you know by heart can be so close to... THE UNKNOWN.
We have never gone over there because of the troll.

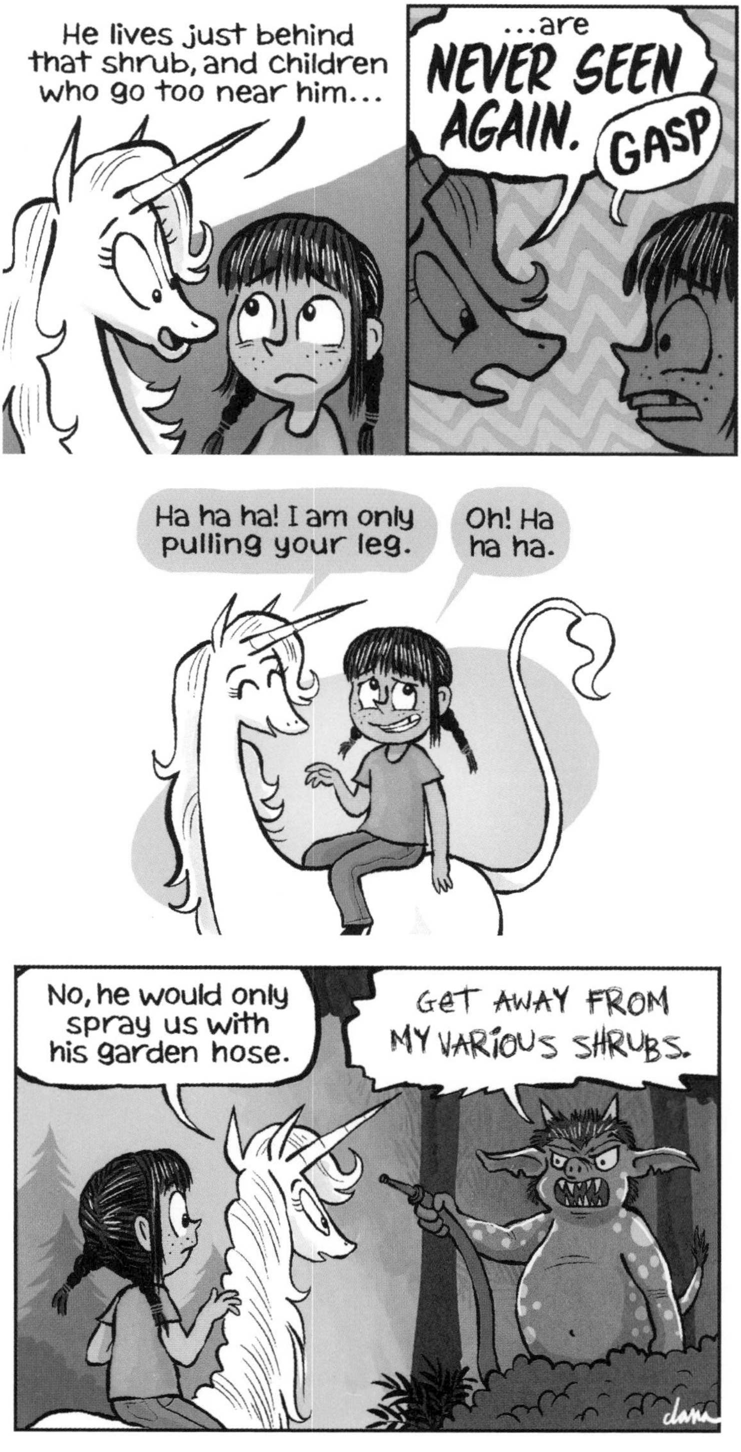
He lives just behind that shrub, and children who go too near him...
...are NEVER SEEN AGAIN.
GASP
Ha ha ha! I am only pulling your leg.
Oh! Ha ha ha.
No, he would only spray us with his garden hose.
GET AWAY FROM MY VARIOUS SHRUBS.
dana

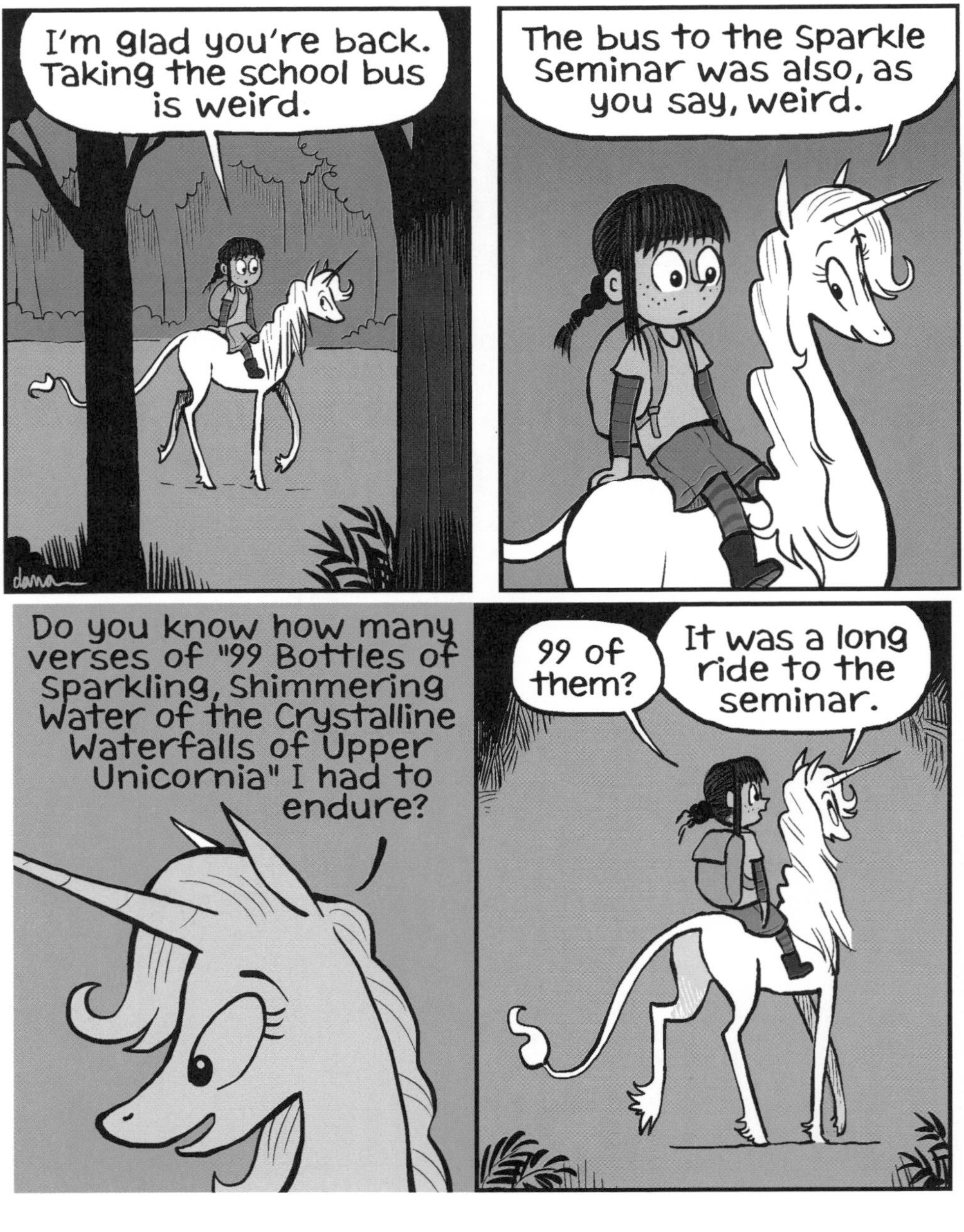
I'm glad you're back. Taking the school bus is weird.
The bus to the Sparkle Seminar was also, as you say, weird.
Do you know how many verses of "99 Bottles of Sparkling, Shimmering Water of the Crystalline Waterfalls of Upper Unicornia" I had to endure?
99 of them?
It was a long ride to the seminar.

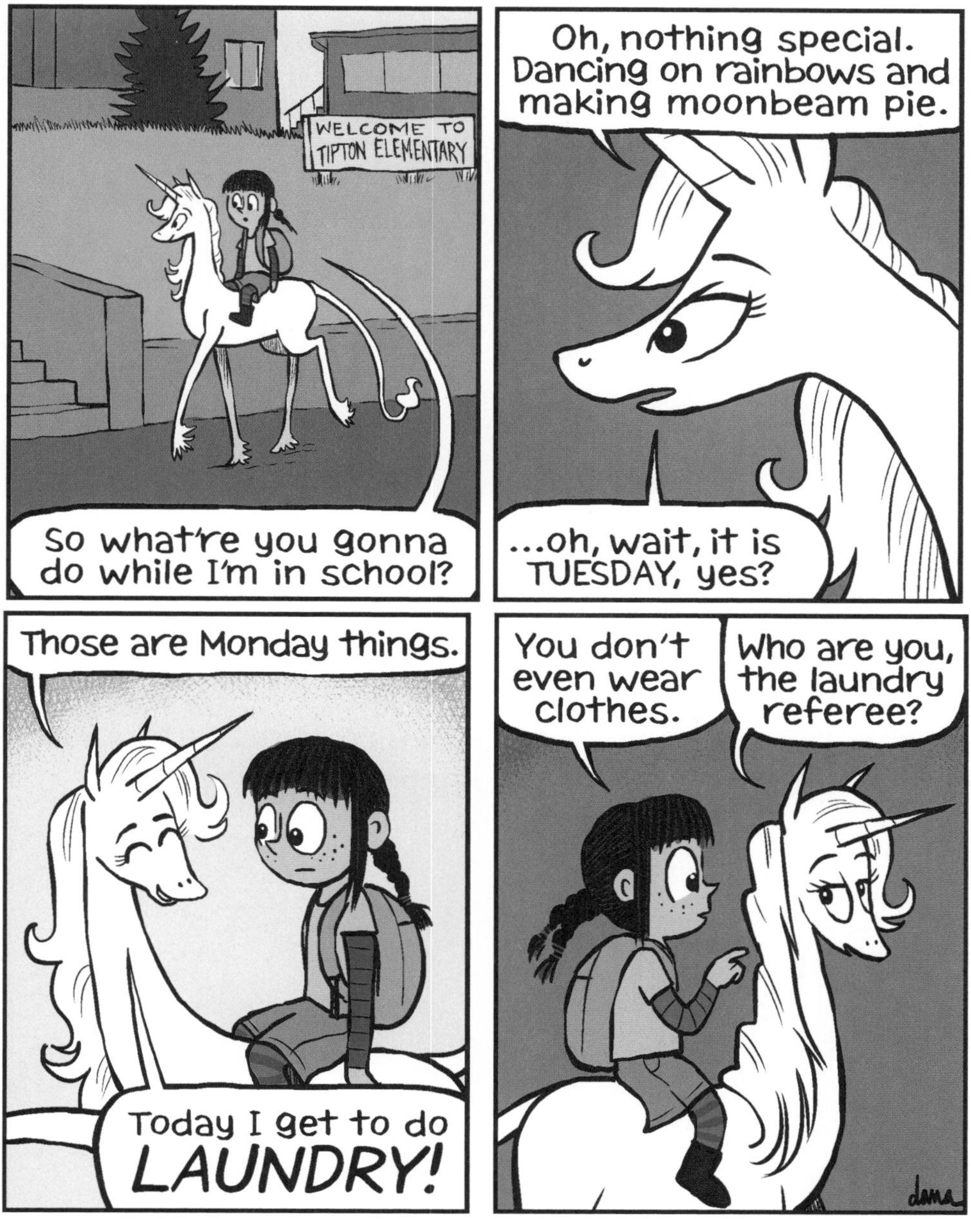
WELCOME TO
TIPTON ELEMENTARY
So what're you gonna do while I'm in school?
Oh, nothing special. Dancing on rainbows and making moonbeam pie.
...oh, wait, it is TUESDAY, yes?
Those are Monday things.
Today I get to do *LAUNDRY!*
You don't even wear clothes.
Who are you, the laundry referee?
dana

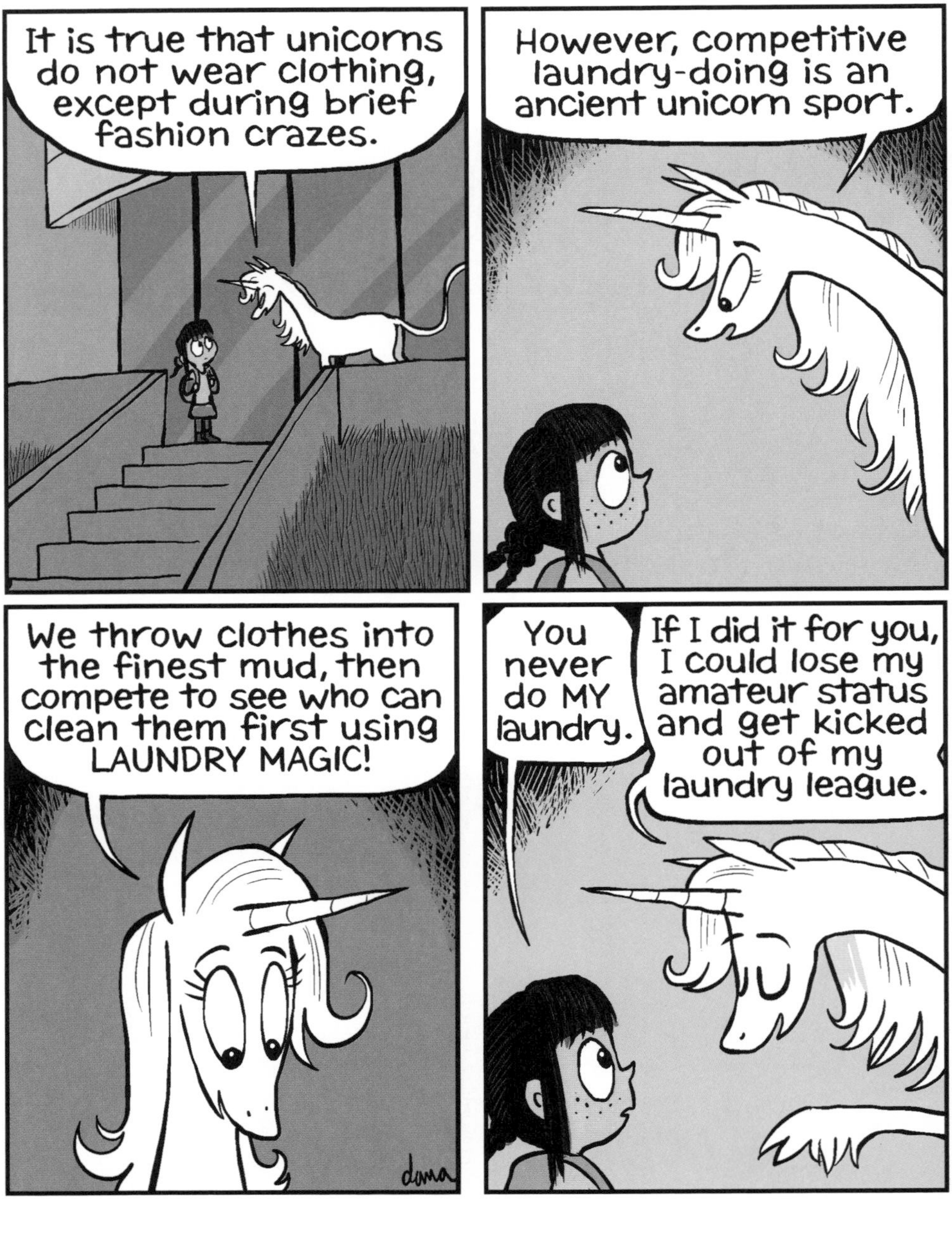
It is true that unicorns do not wear clothing, except during brief fashion crazes.
However, competitive laundry-doing is an ancient unicorn sport.
We throw clothes into the finest mud, then compete to see who can clean them first using LAUNDRY MAGIC!
You never do MY laundry.
If I did it for you, I could lose my amateur status and get kicked out of my laundry league.
dana

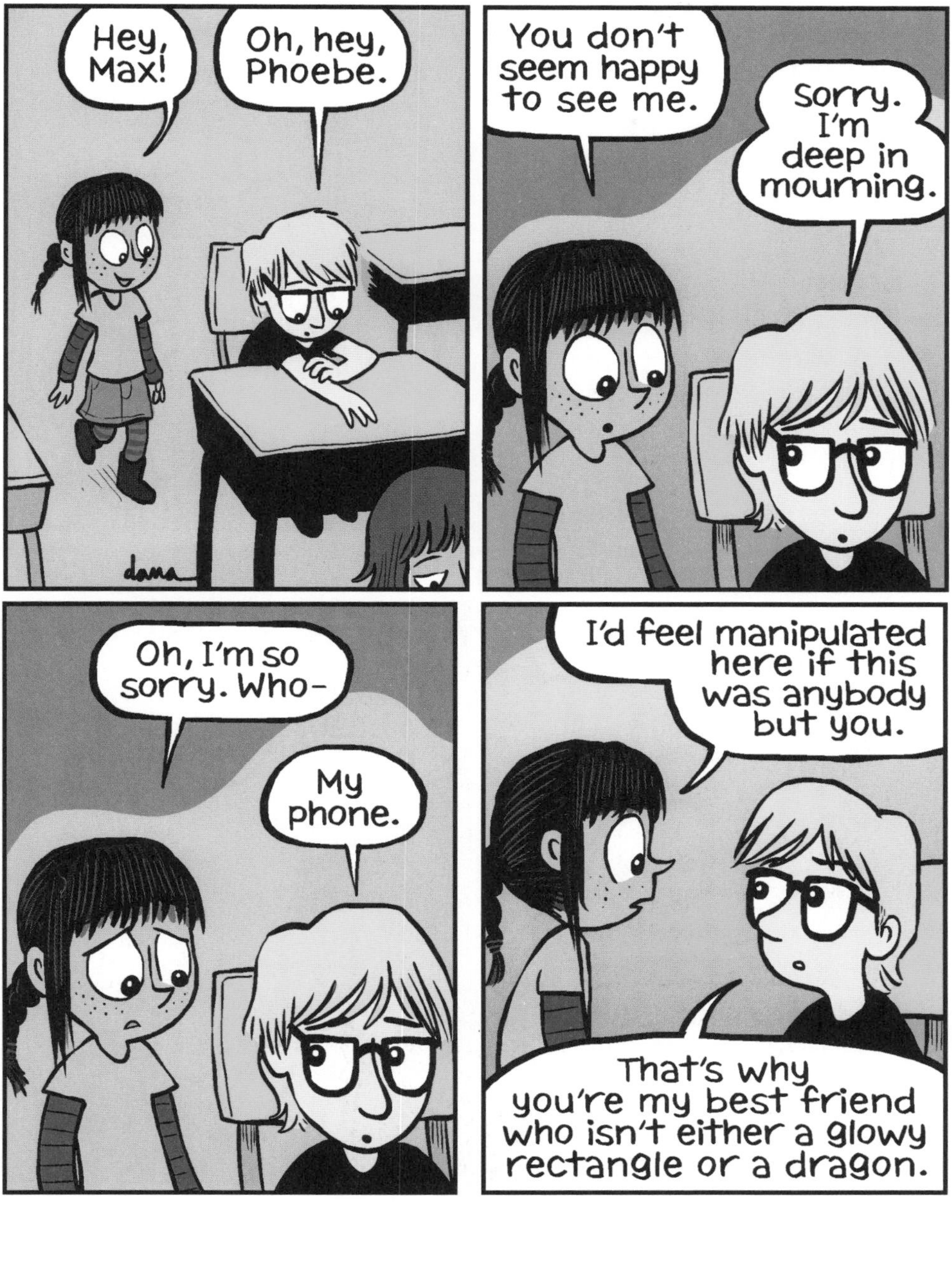
Hey, Max!
Oh, hey, Phoebe.
dana
You don't seem happy to see me.
Sorry. I'm deep in mourning.
Oh, I'm so sorry. Who-
My phone.
I'd feel manipulated here if this was anybody but you.
That's why you're my best friend who isn't either a glowy rectangle or a dragon.

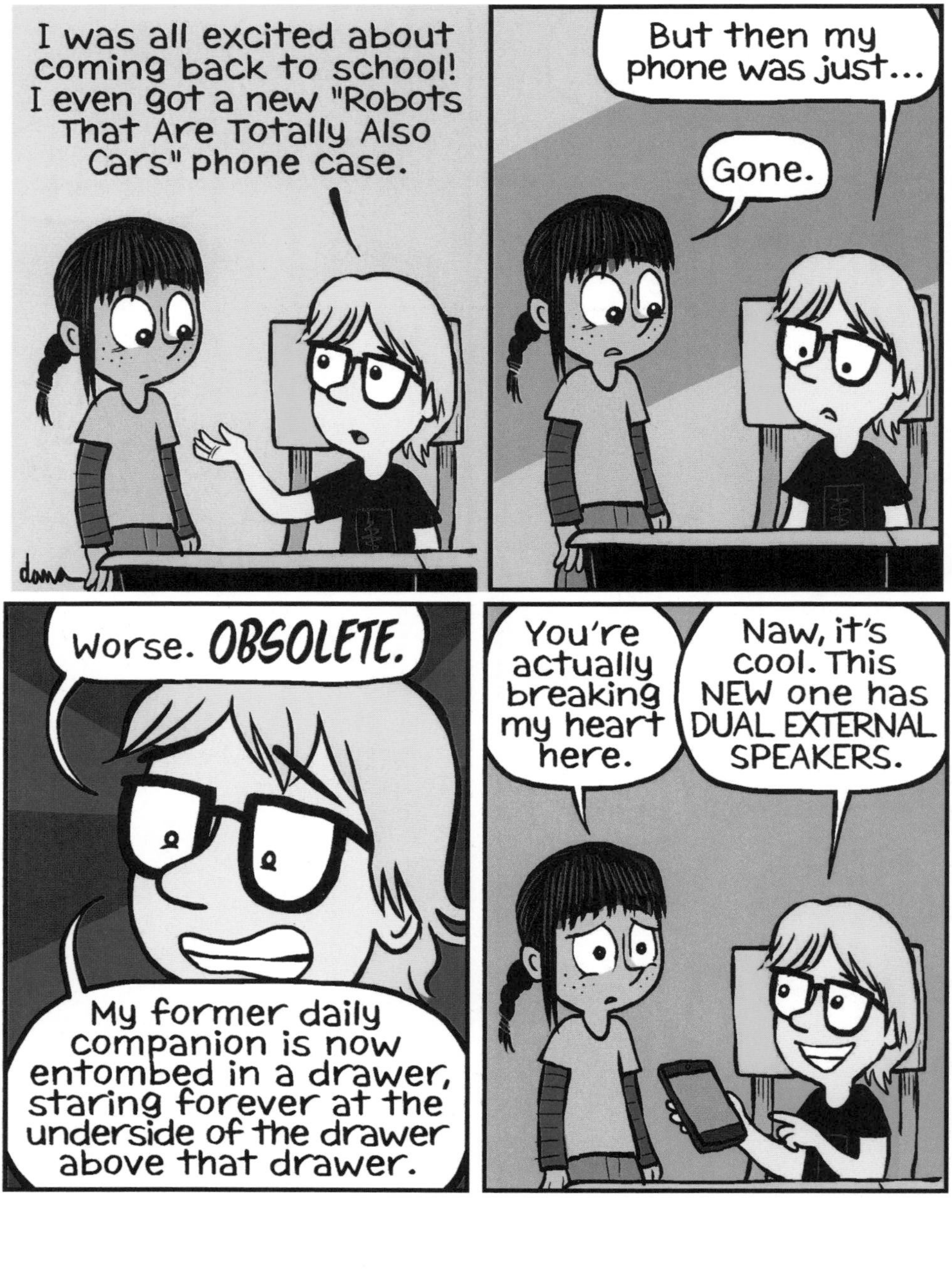
I was all excited about coming back to school! I even got a new "Robots That Are Totally Also Cars" phone case.
But then my phone was just...
Gone.
Worse. OBSOLETE.
My former daily companion is now entombed in a drawer, staring forever at the underside of the drawer above that drawer.
You're actually breaking my heart here.
Naw, it's cool. This NEW one has DUAL EXTERNAL SPEAKERS.

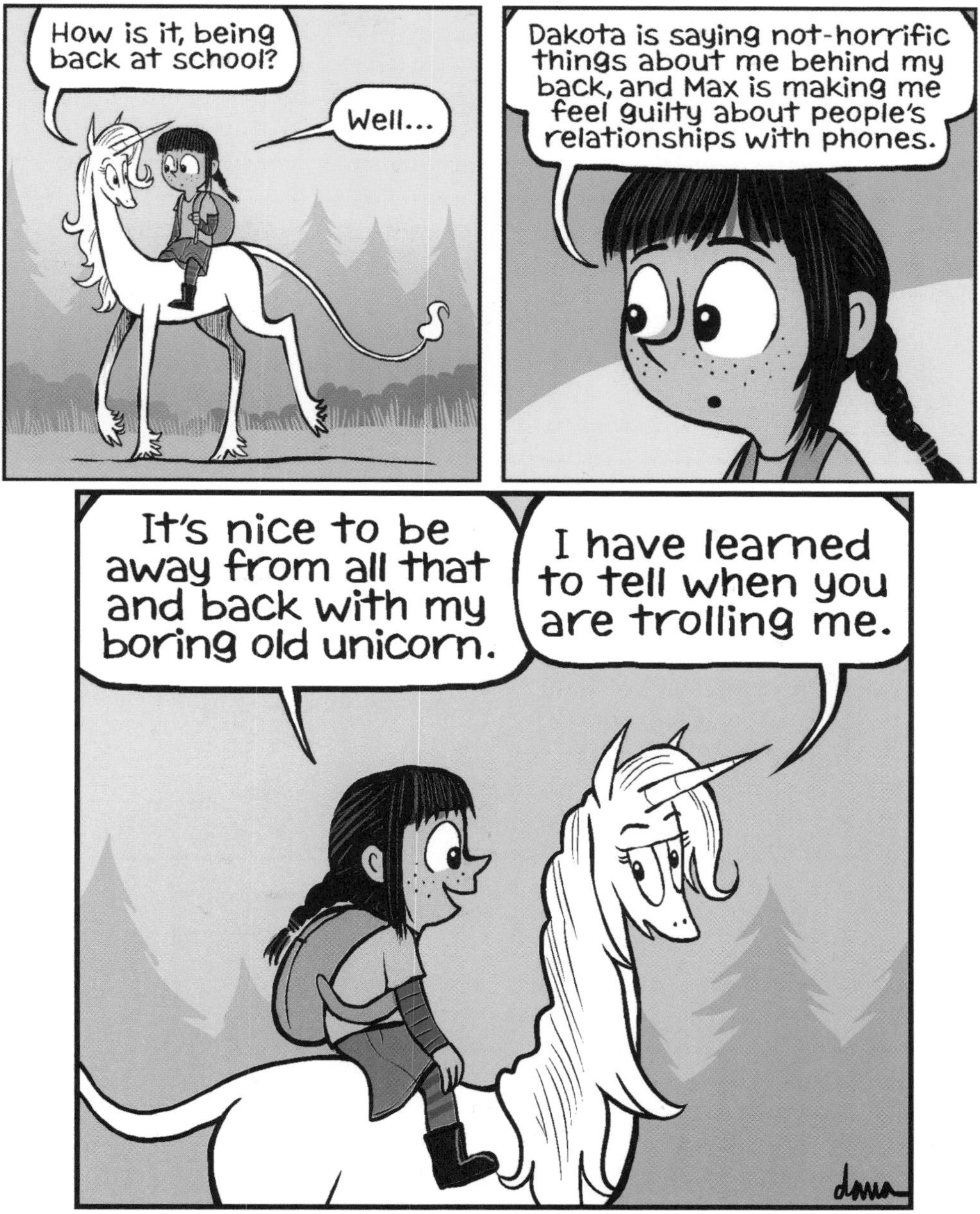
How is it, being back at school?
Well...
Dakota is saying not-horrific things about me behind my back, and Max is making me feel guilty about people's relationships with phones.
It's nice to be away from all that and back with my boring old unicorn.
I have learned to tell when you are trolling me.

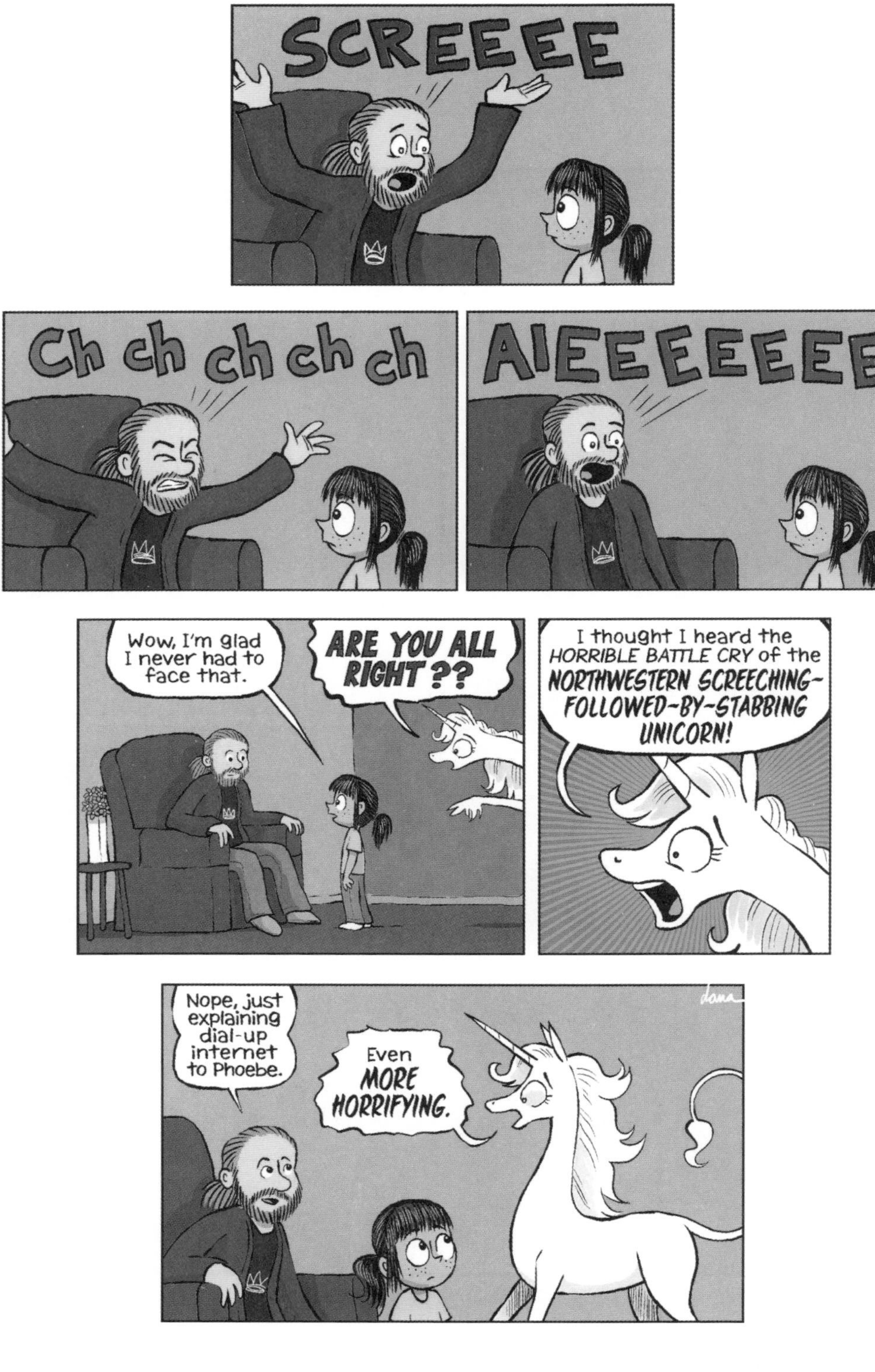
SCREEEE
Ch ch ch ch ch
AIEEEEEEE
Wow, I'm glad I never had to face that.
ARE YOU ALL RIGHT??
I thought I heard the HORRIBLE BATTLE CRY of the NORTHWESTERN SCREECHING-FOLLOWED-BY-STABBING UNICORN!
Nope, just explaining dial-up internet to Phoebe.
Even MORE HORRIFYING.
dana

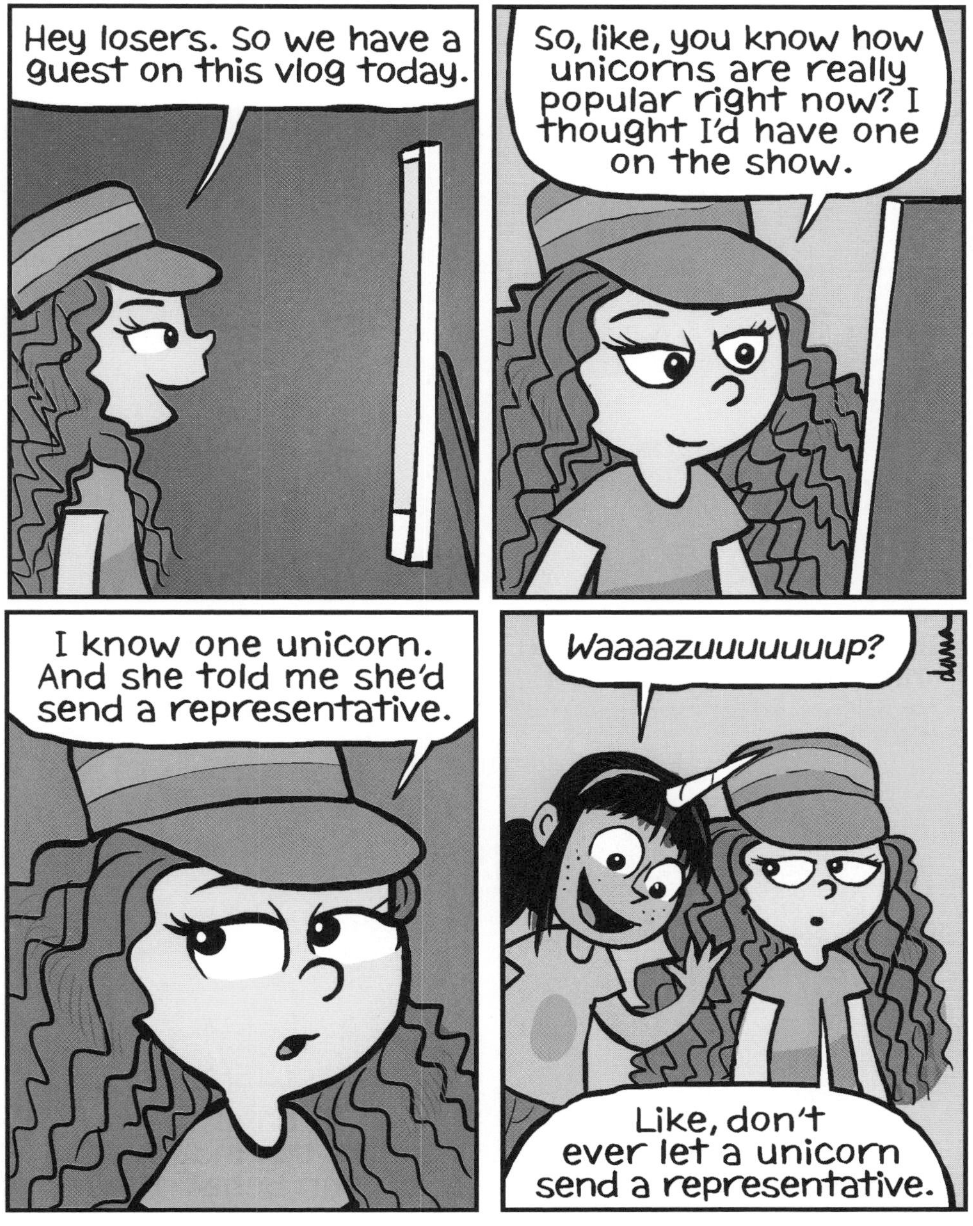
Hey losers. So we have a guest on this vlog today.
So, like, you know how unicorns are really popular right now? I thought I'd have one on the show.
I know one unicorn. And she told me she'd send a representative.
Waaaazuuuuuuup?
Like, don't ever let a unicorn send a representative.

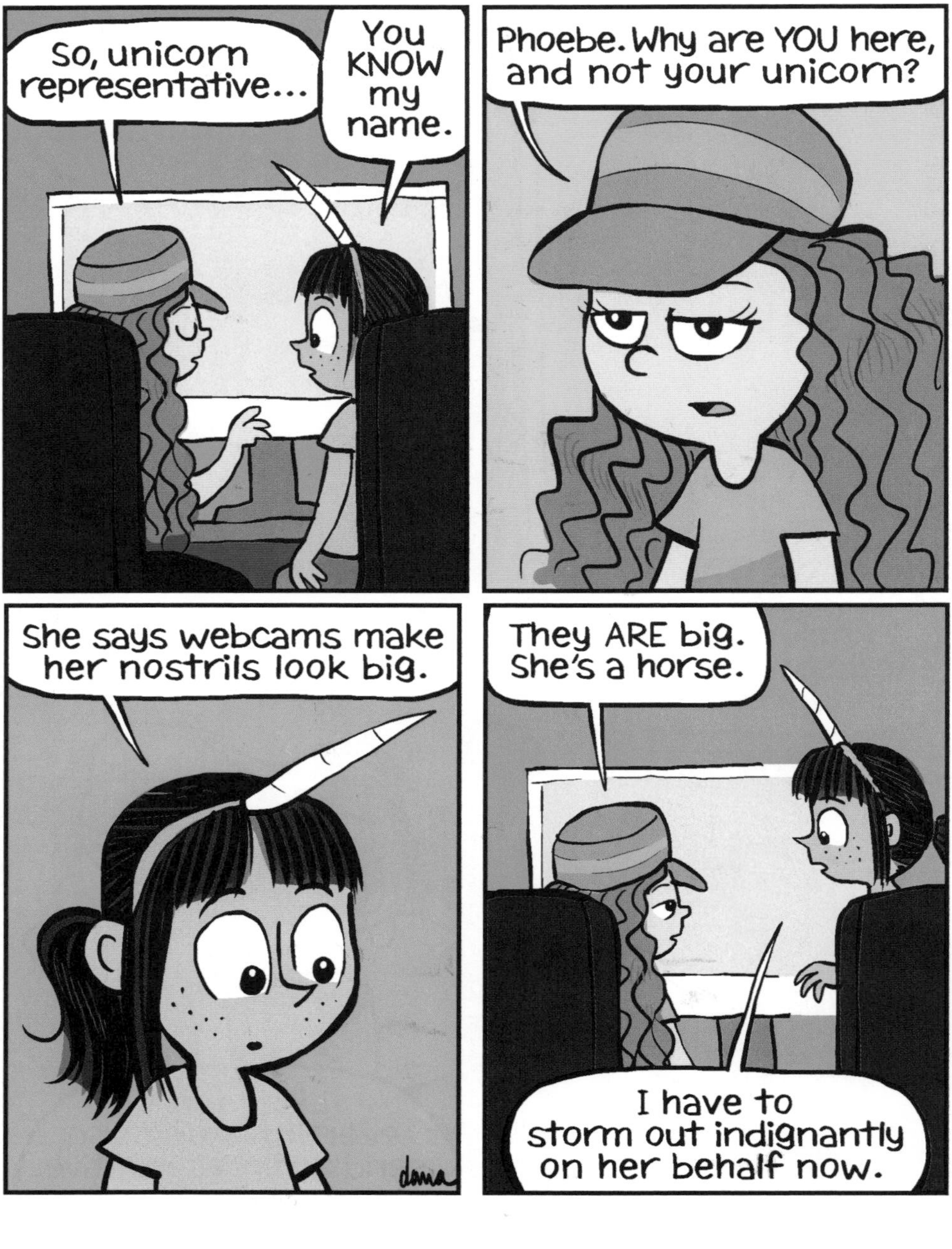
So, unicorn representative...
You KNOW my name.
Phoebe. Why are YOU here, and not your unicorn?
She says webcams make her nostrils look big.
They ARE big. She's a horse.
I have to storm out indignantly on her behalf now.
dana

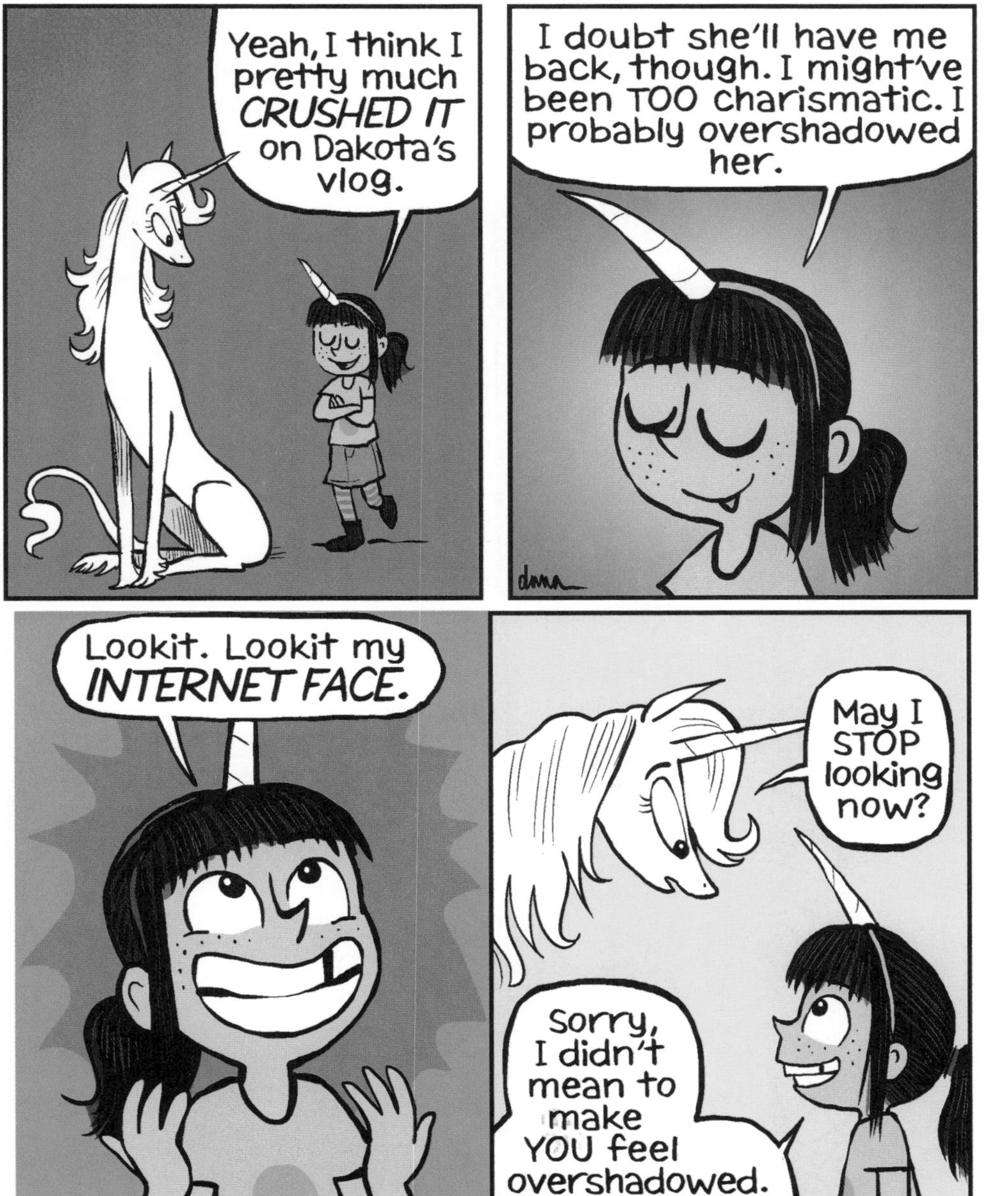
Yeah, I think I pretty much CRUSHED IT on Dakota's vlog.
I doubt she'll have me back, though. I might've been TOO charismatic. I probably overshadowed her.
Lookit. Lookit my INTERNET FACE.
May I STOP looking now?
Sorry, I didn't mean to make YOU feel overshadowed.

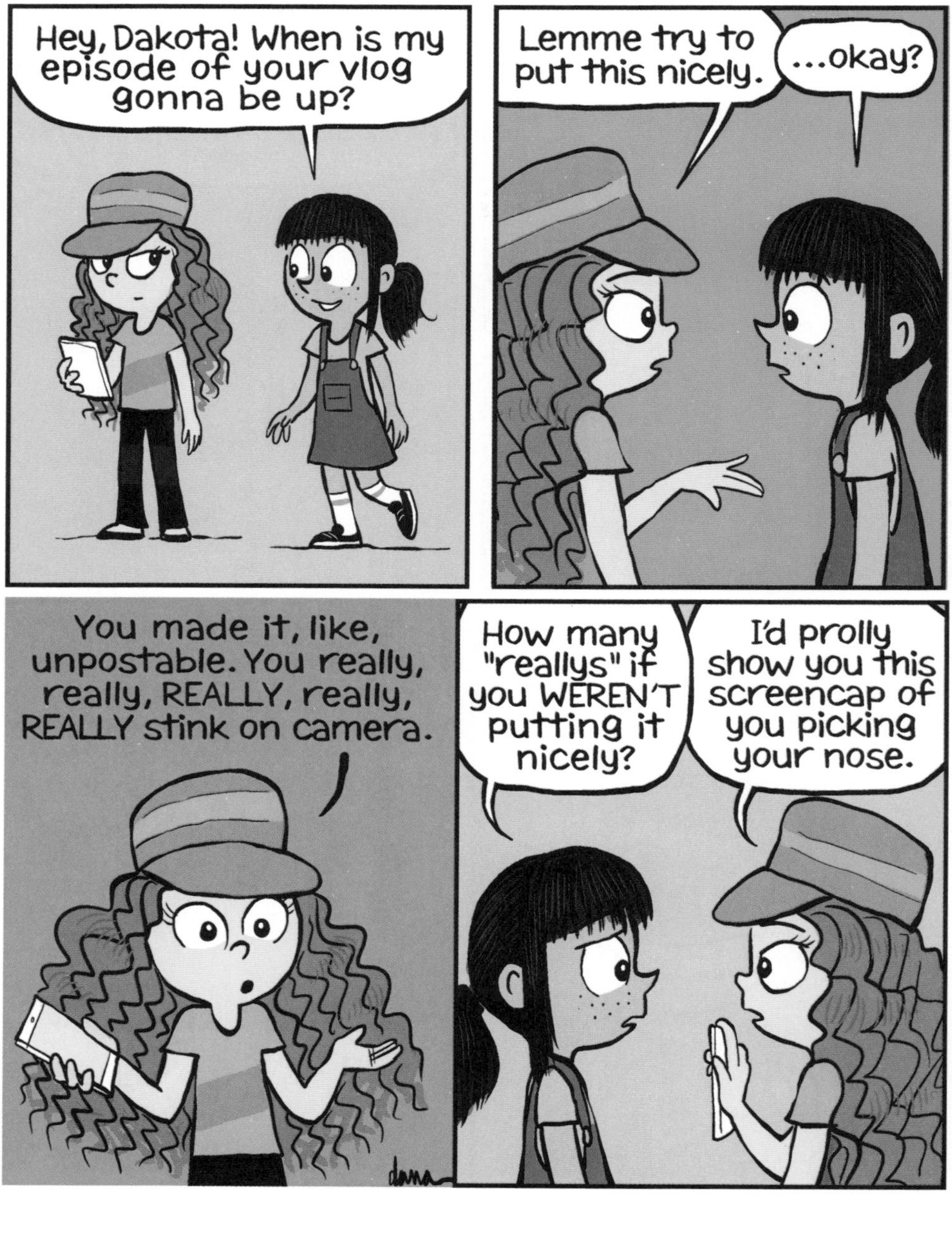
Hey, Dakota! When is my episode of your vlog gonna be up?
Lemme try to put this nicely.
...okay?
You made it, like, unpostable. You really, really, REALLY, really, REALLY stink on camera.
How many "reallys" if you WEREN'T putting it nicely?
I'd prolly show you this screencap of you picking your nose.
dana

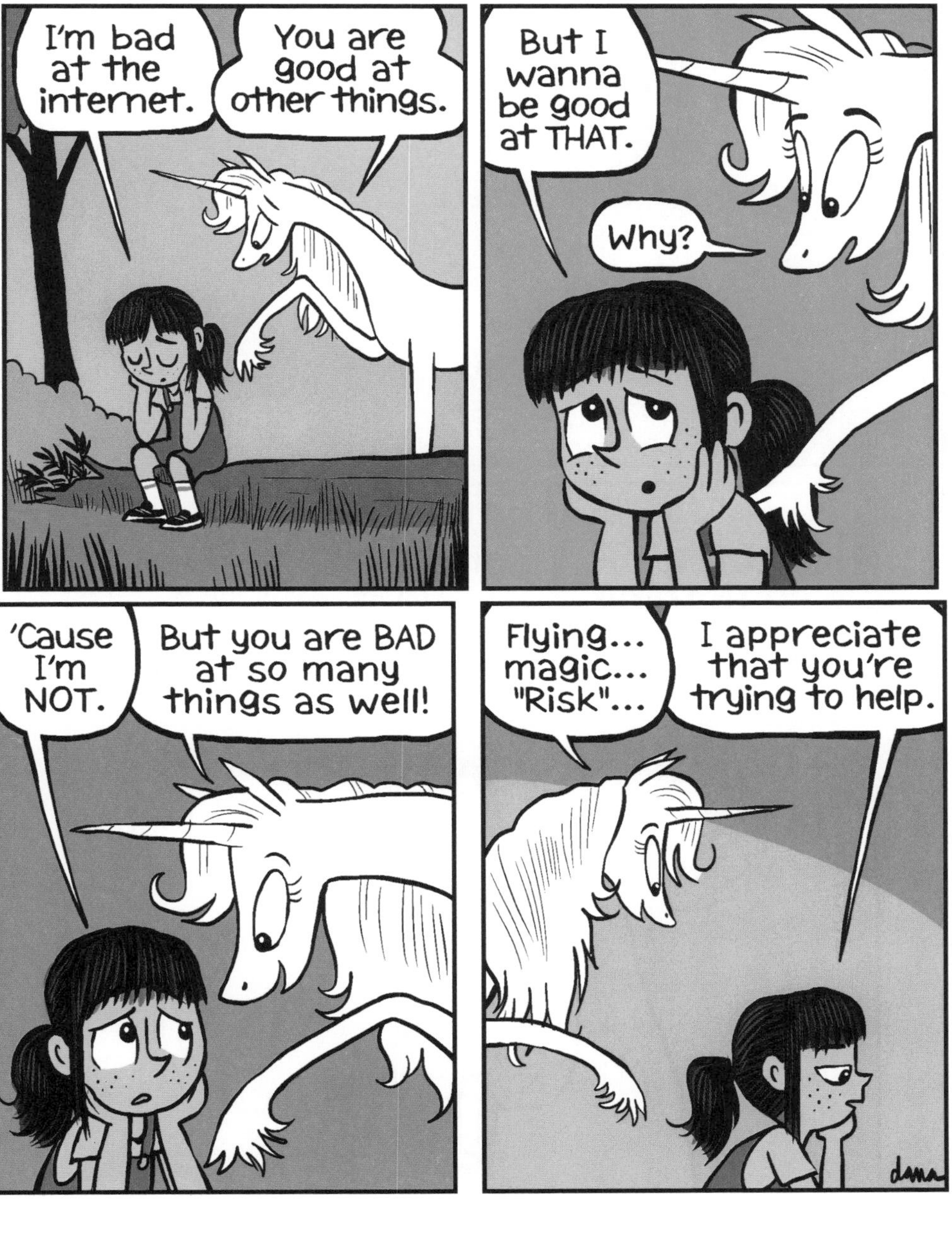
I'm bad at the internet.
You are good at other things.
But I wanna be good at THAT.
Why?
'Cause I'm NOT.
But you are BAD at so many things as well!
Flying... magic... "Risk"...
I appreciate that you're trying to help.
dana

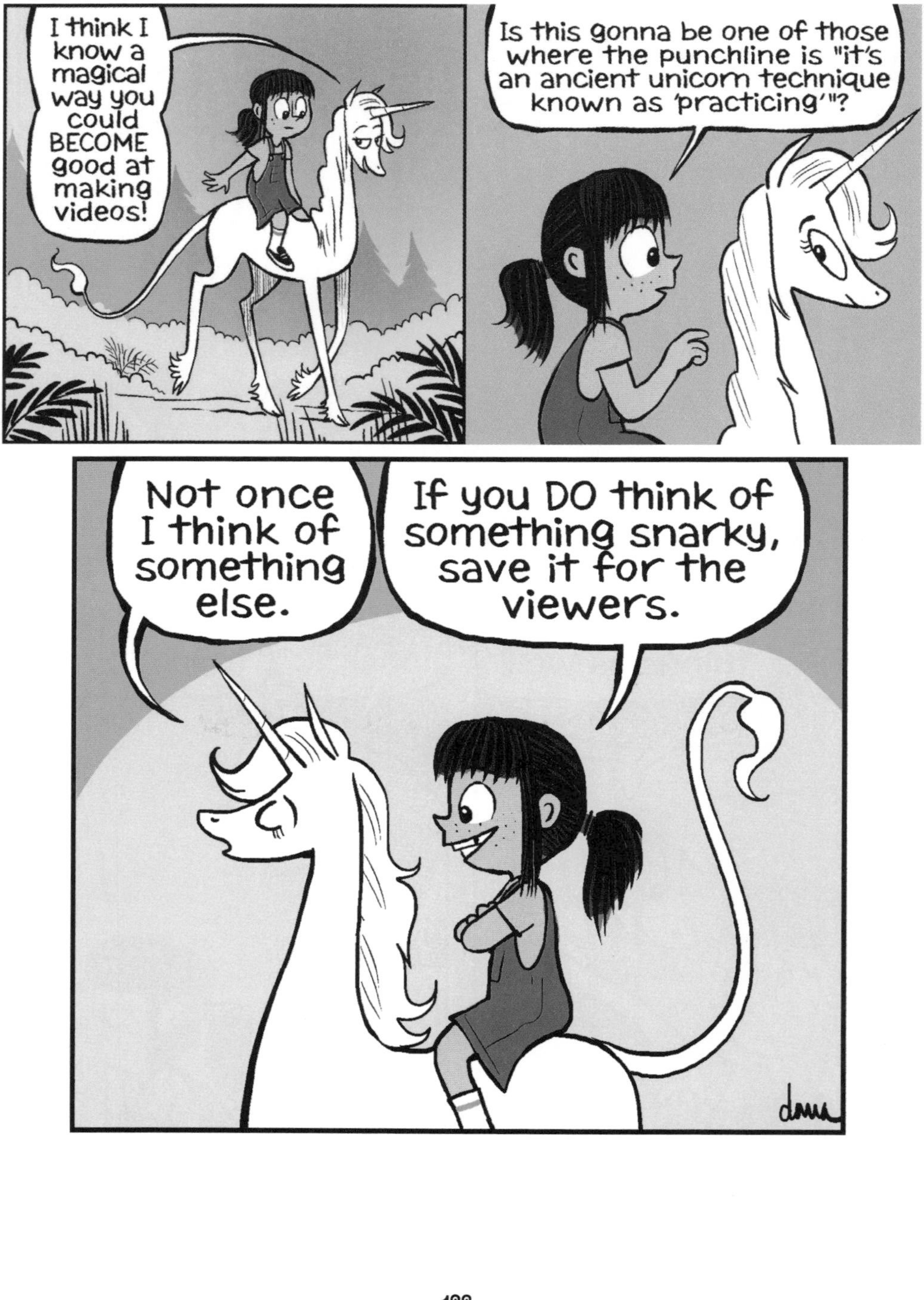
I think I know a magical way you could BECOME good at making videos!
Is this gonna be one of those where the punchline is "it's an ancient unicorn technique known as 'practicing'"?
Not once I think of something else.
If you DO think of something snarky, save it for the viewers.
dana

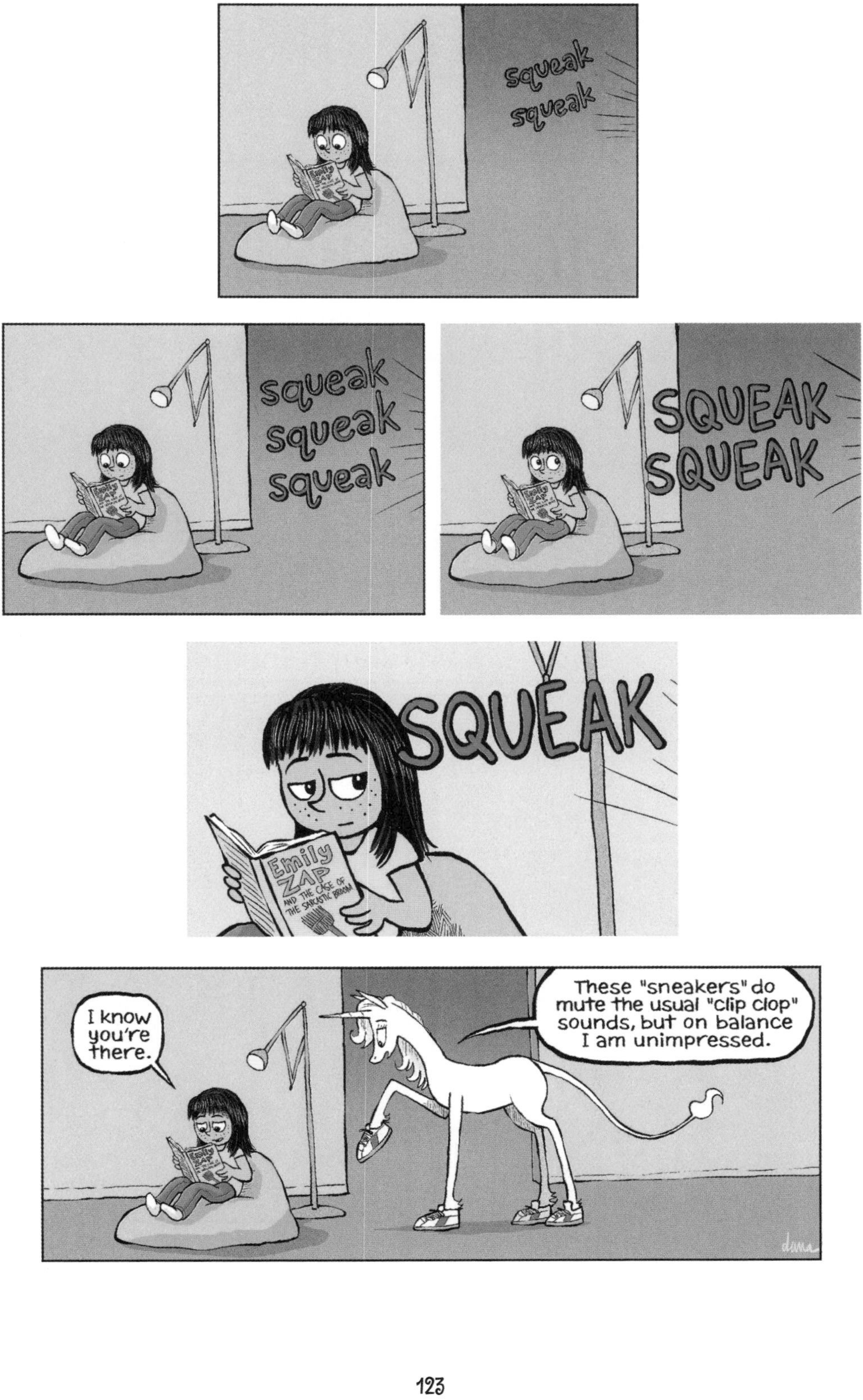

squeak
squeak
squeak
squeak
squeak
SQUEAK
SQUEAK
SQUEAK
Emily ZAP AND THE CASE OF THE SARCASTIC BROOM
I know you're there.
These "sneakers" do mute the usual "clip clop" sounds, but on balance I am unimpressed.

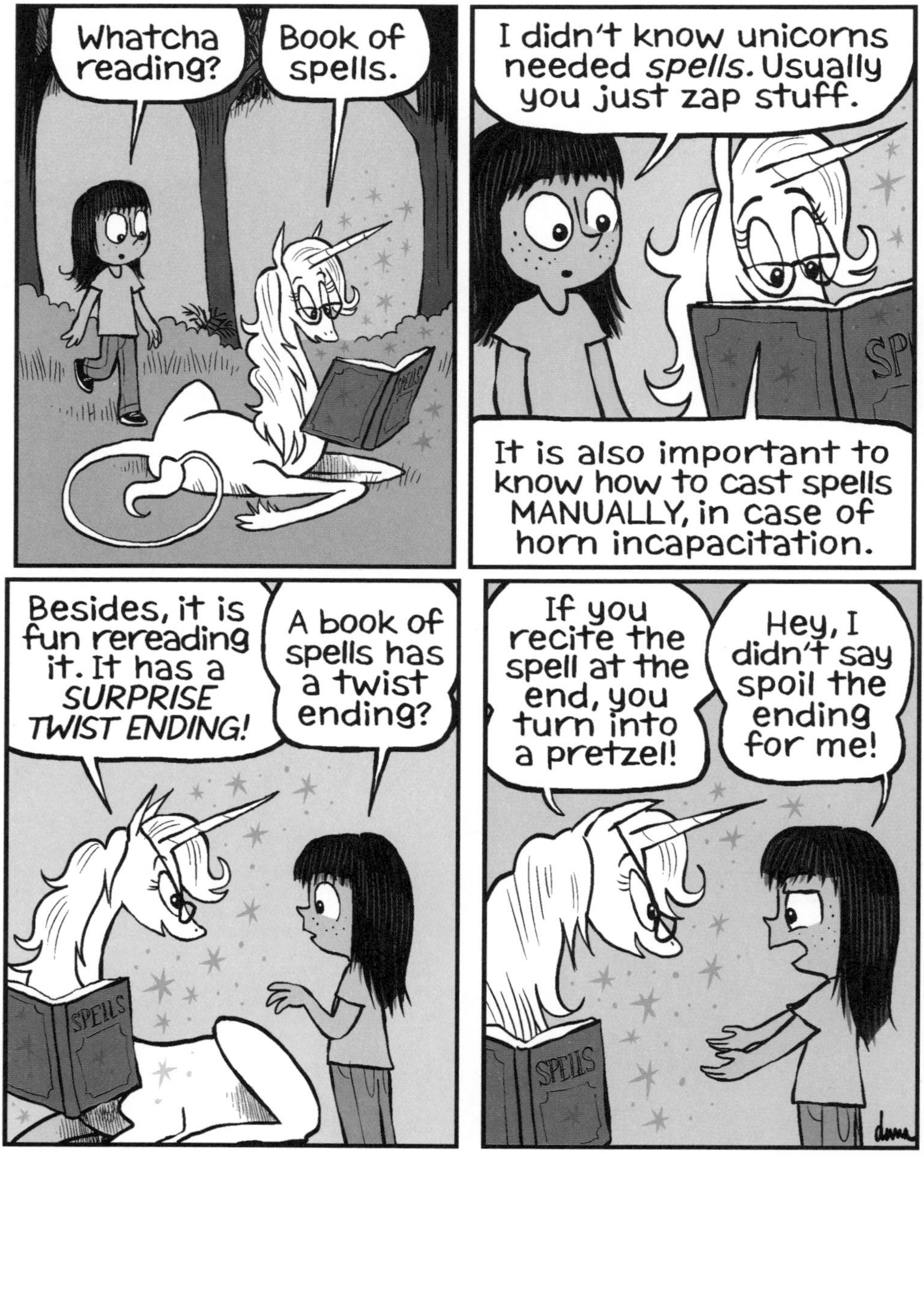
Whatcha reading?
Book of spells.
I didn't know unicorns needed *spells*. Usually you just zap stuff.
It is also important to know how to cast spells MANUALLY, in case of horn incapacitation.
SPELLS
Besides, it is fun rereading it. It has a *SURPRISE TWIST ENDING!*
A book of spells has a twist ending?
SPELLS
If you recite the spell at the end, you turn into a pretzel!
Hey, I didn't say spoil the ending for me!
SPELLS

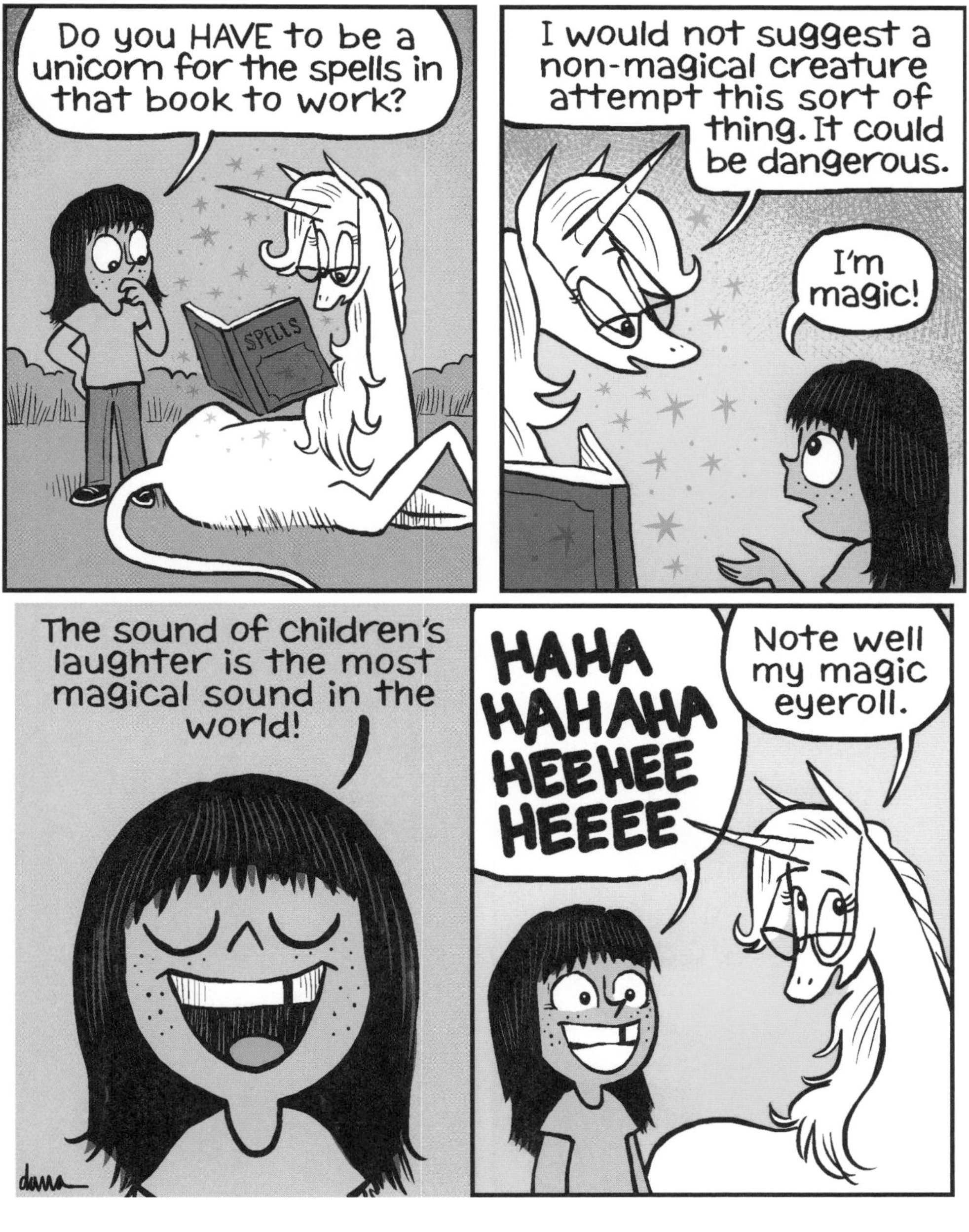
Do you HAVE to be a unicorn for the spells in that book to work?
SPELLS
I would not suggest a non-magical creature attempt this sort of thing. It could be dangerous.
I'm magic!
The sound of children's laughter is the most magical sound in the world!
HAHA HAHAHA HEEHEE HEEEE
Note well my magic eyeroll.
dana

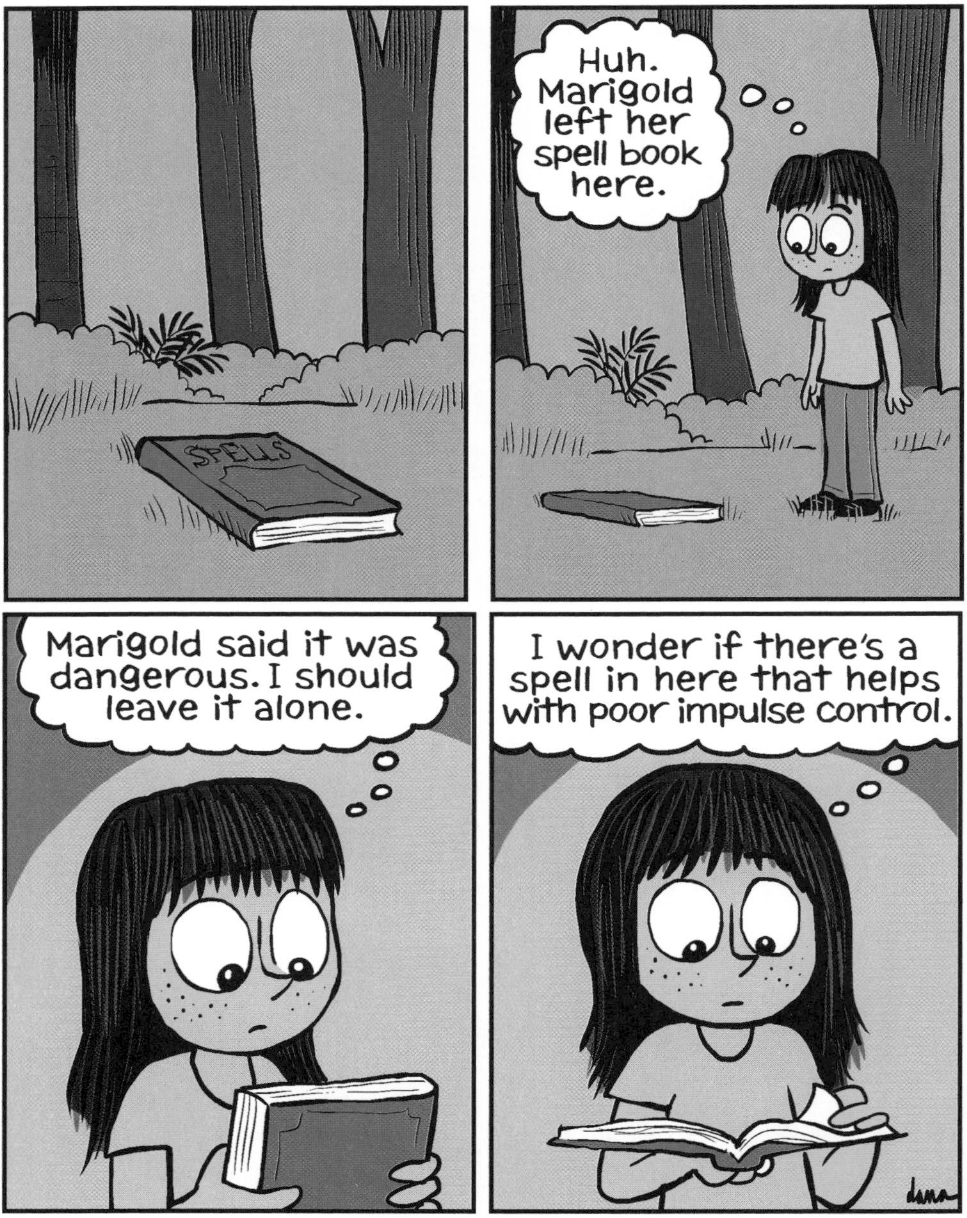
SPELLS
Huh. Marigold left her spell book here.
Marigold said it was dangerous. I should leave it alone.
I wonder if there's a spell in here that helps with poor impulse control.
dana

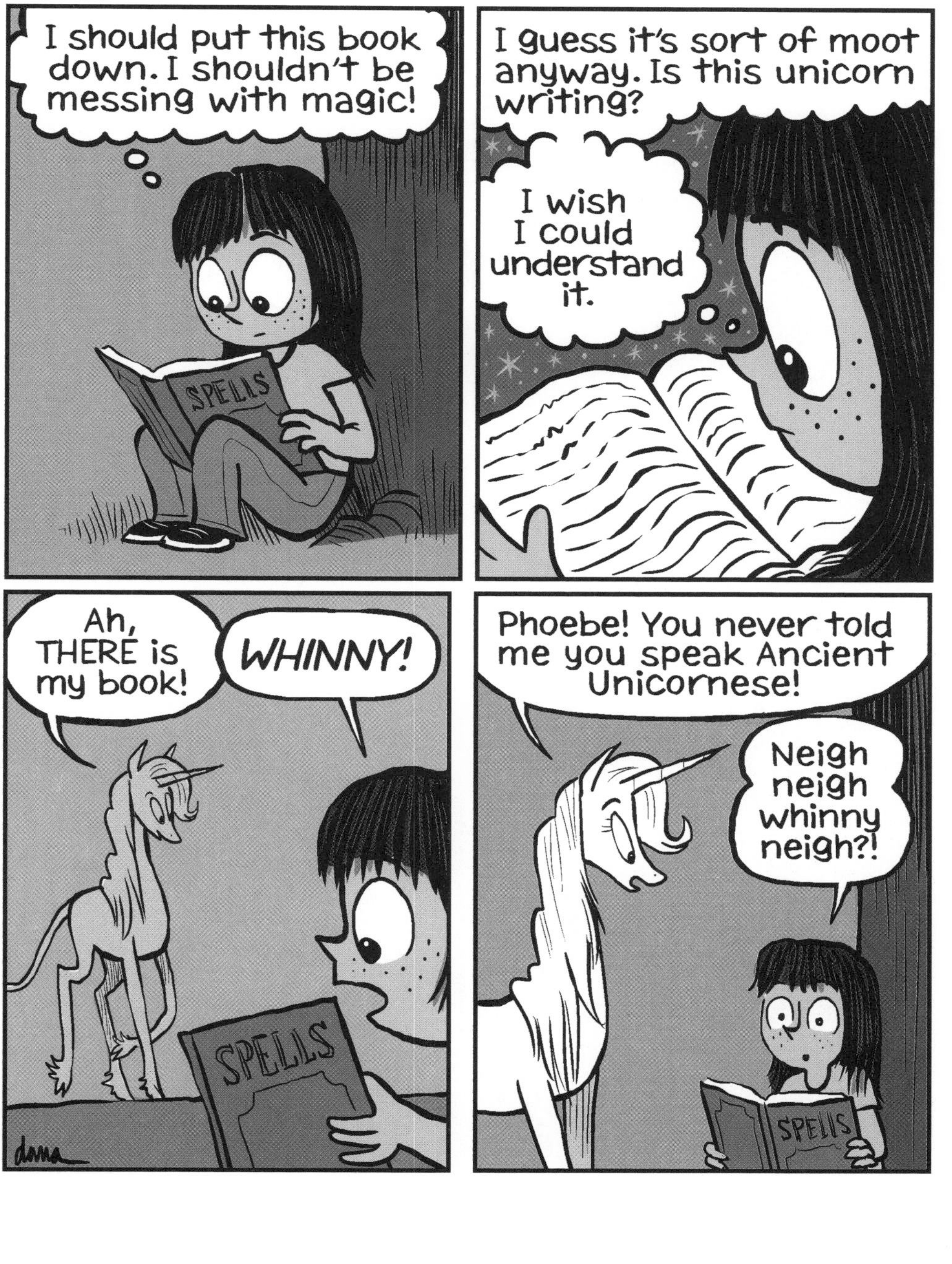

I should put this book down. I shouldn't be messing with magic!
SPELLS
I guess it's sort of moot anyway. Is this unicorn writing?
I wish I could understand it.
Ah, THERE is my book!
WHINNY!
SPELLS
Phoebe! You never told me you speak Ancient Unicornese!
Neigh neigh whinny neigh?!
SPELLS

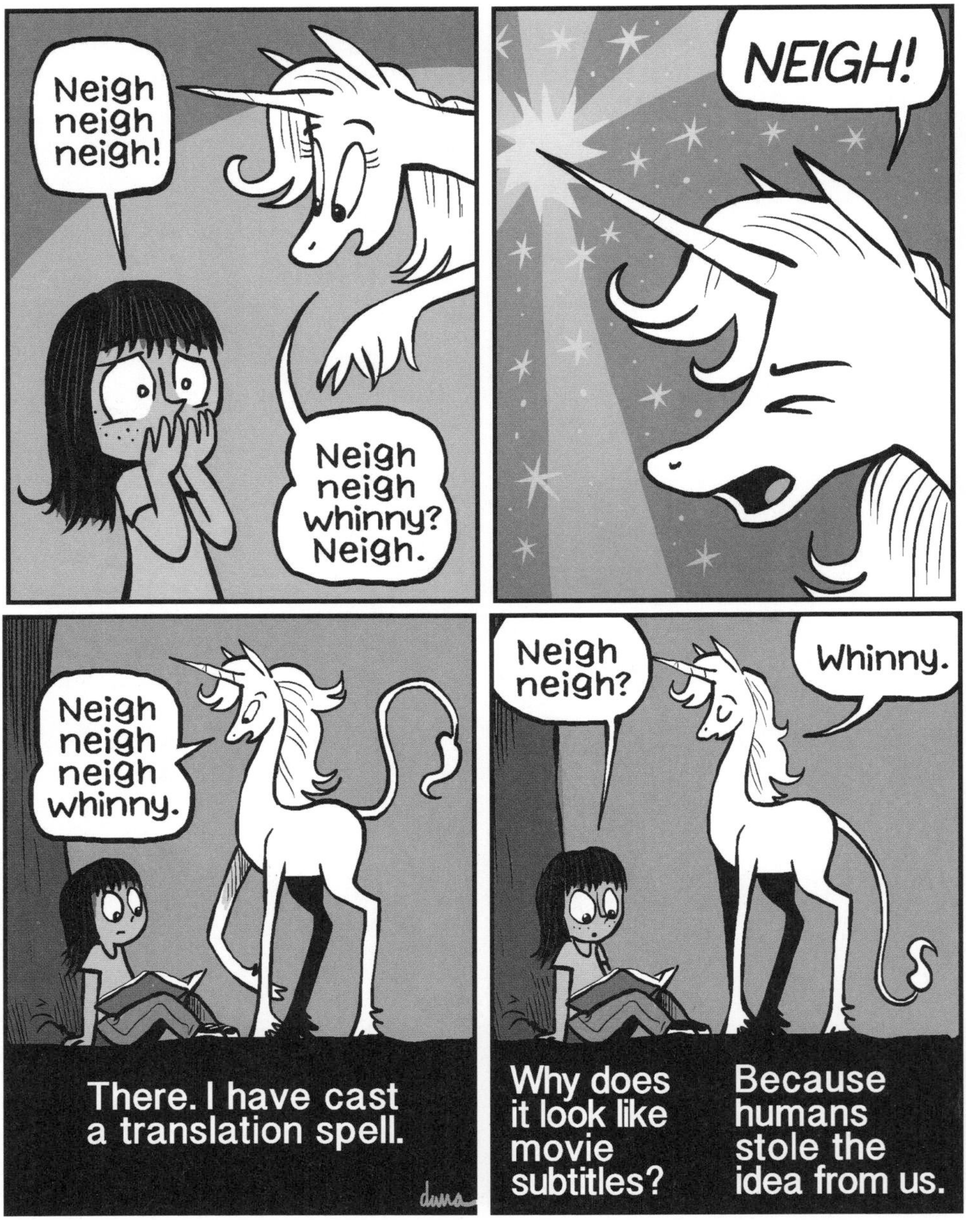
Neigh neigh neigh!
Neigh neigh whinny? Neigh.
NEIGH!
Neigh neigh neigh whinny.
There. I have cast a translation spell.
Neigh neigh?
Whinny.
Why does it look like movie subtitles?
Because humans stole the idea from us.

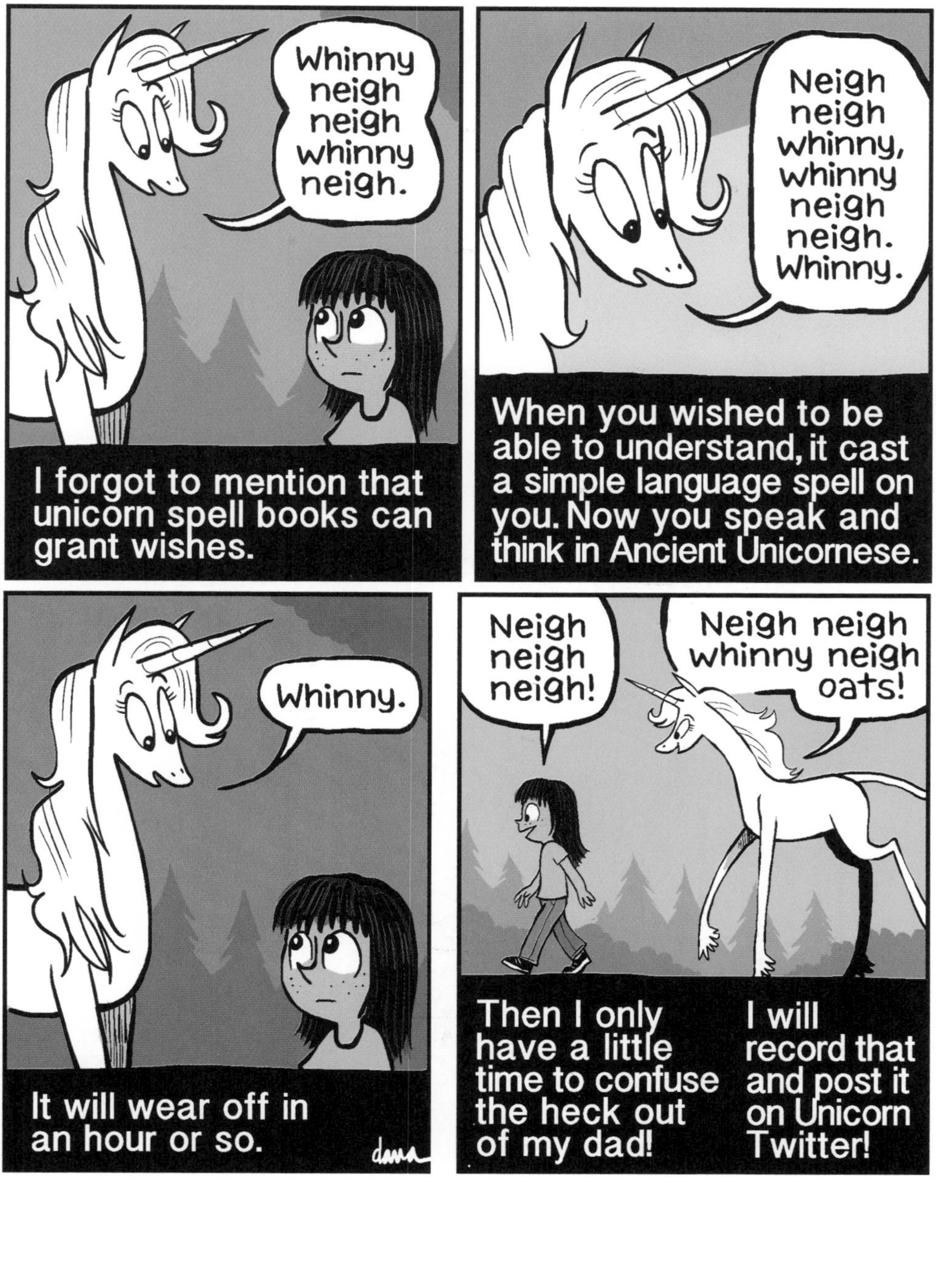
Whinny neigh neigh whinny neigh.
I forgot to mention that unicorn spell books can grant wishes.
Neigh neigh whinny, whinny neigh neigh. Whinny.
When you wished to be able to understand, it cast a simple language spell on you. Now you speak and think in Ancient Unicornese.
Whinny.
It will wear off in an hour or so.
Neigh neigh neigh!
Neigh neigh whinny neigh oats!
Then I only have a little time to confuse the heck out of my dad!
I will record that and post it on Unicorn Twitter!

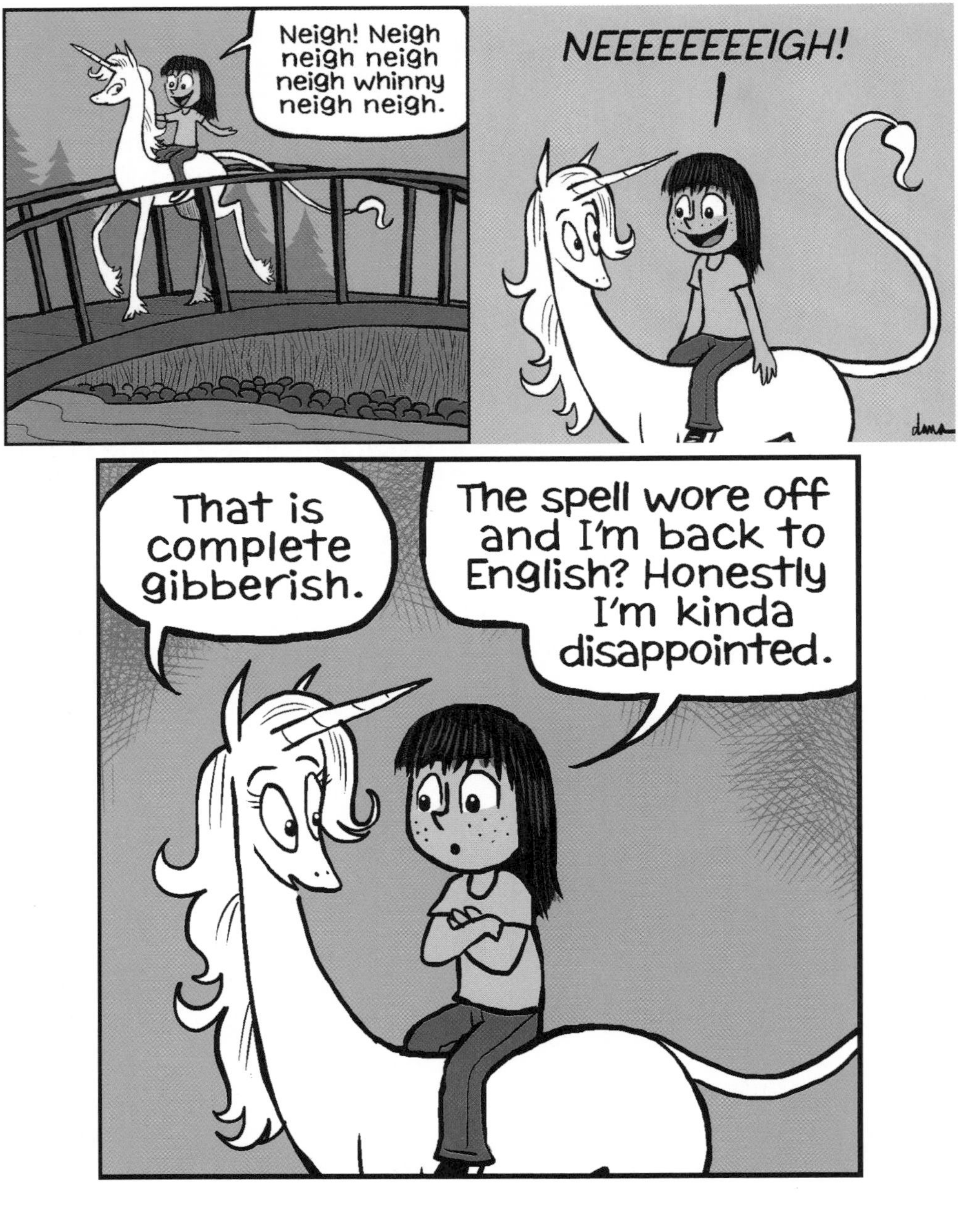
Neigh! Neigh neigh neigh neigh whinny neigh neigh.
NEEEEEEEEEIGH!
That is complete gibberish.
The spell wore off and I'm back to English? Honestly I'm kinda disappointed.

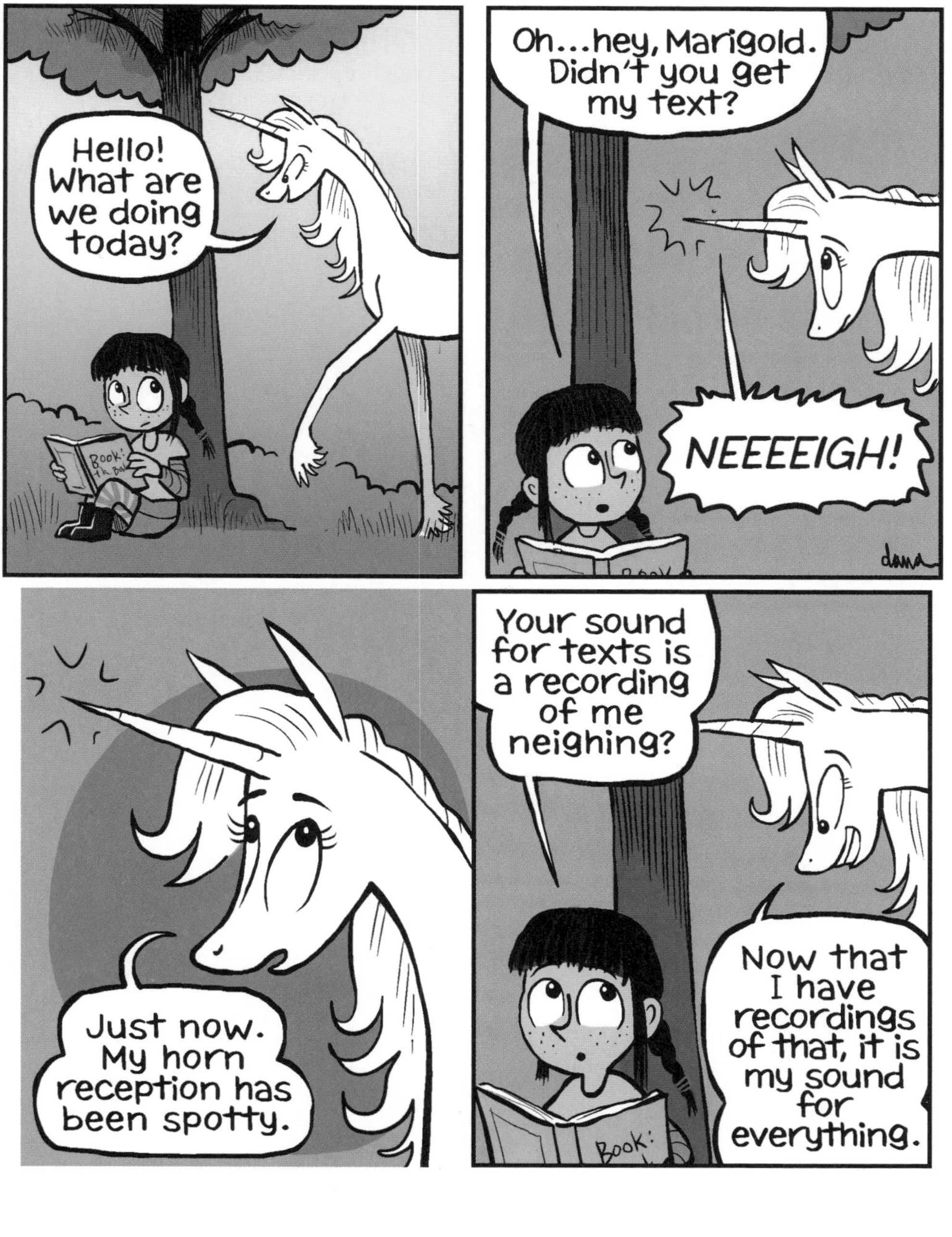
Hello! What are we doing today?
Oh...hey, Marigold. Didn't you get my text?
NEEEEIGH!
Just now. My horn reception has been spotty.
Your sound for texts is a recording of me neighing?
Now that I have recordings of that, it is my sound for everything.

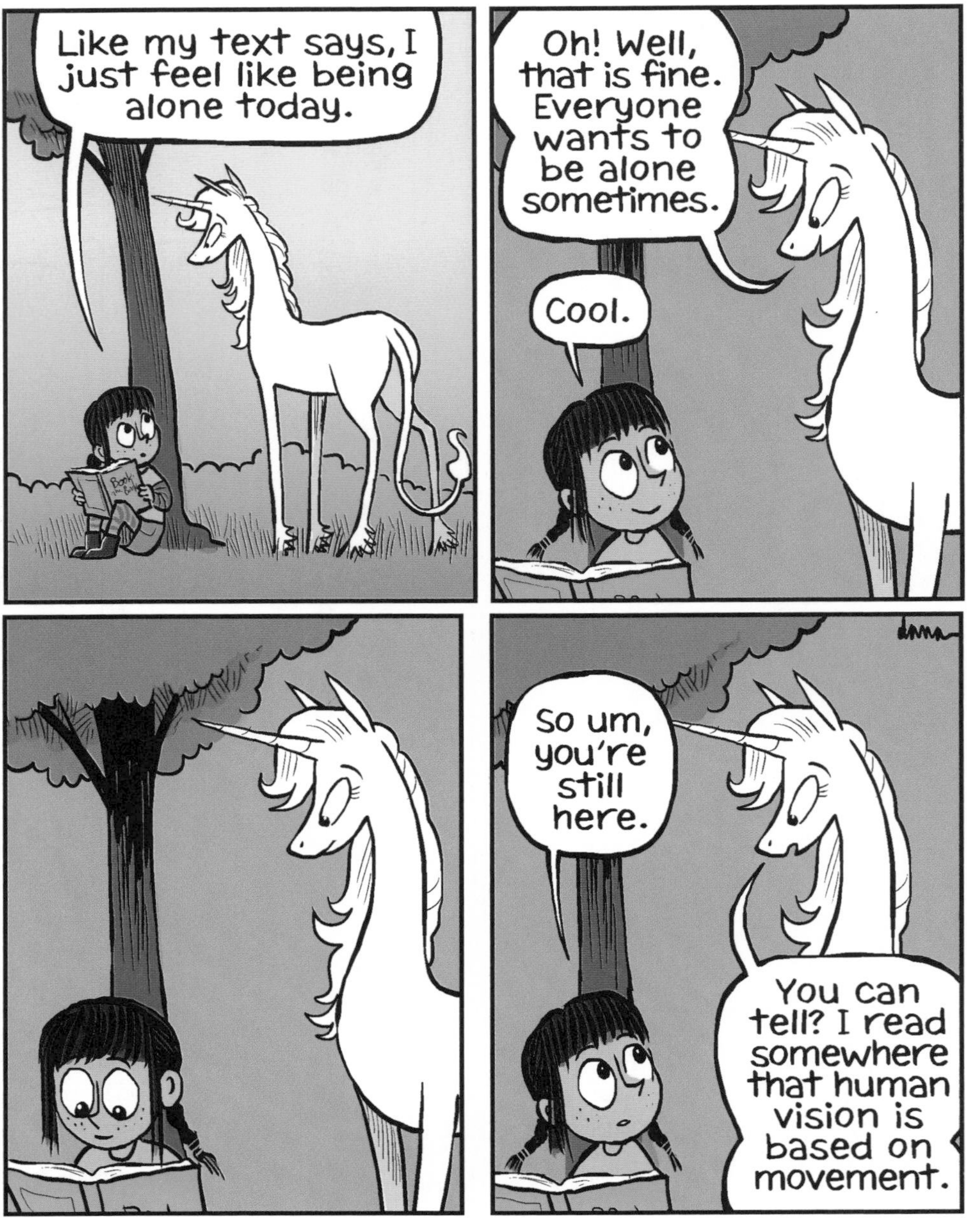
Like my text says, I just feel like being alone today.
Oh! Well, that is fine. Everyone wants to be alone sometimes.
Cool.
So um, you're still here.
You can tell? I read somewhere that human vision is based on movement.

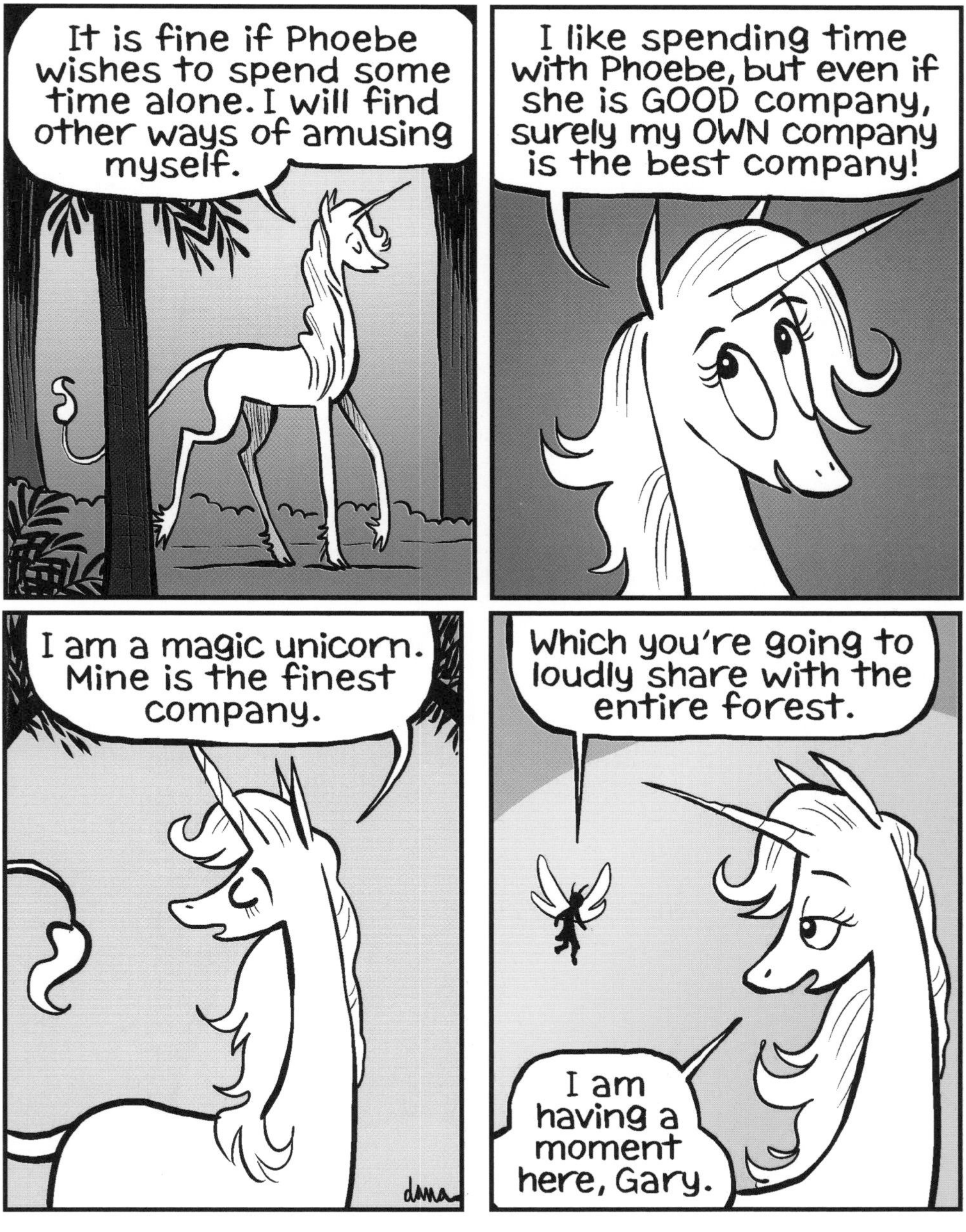
It is fine if Phoebe wishes to spend some time alone. I will find other ways of amusing myself.
I like spending time with Phoebe, but even if she is GOOD company, surely my OWN company is the best company!
I am a magic unicorn. Mine is the finest company.
Which you're going to loudly share with the entire forest.
I am having a moment here, Gary.

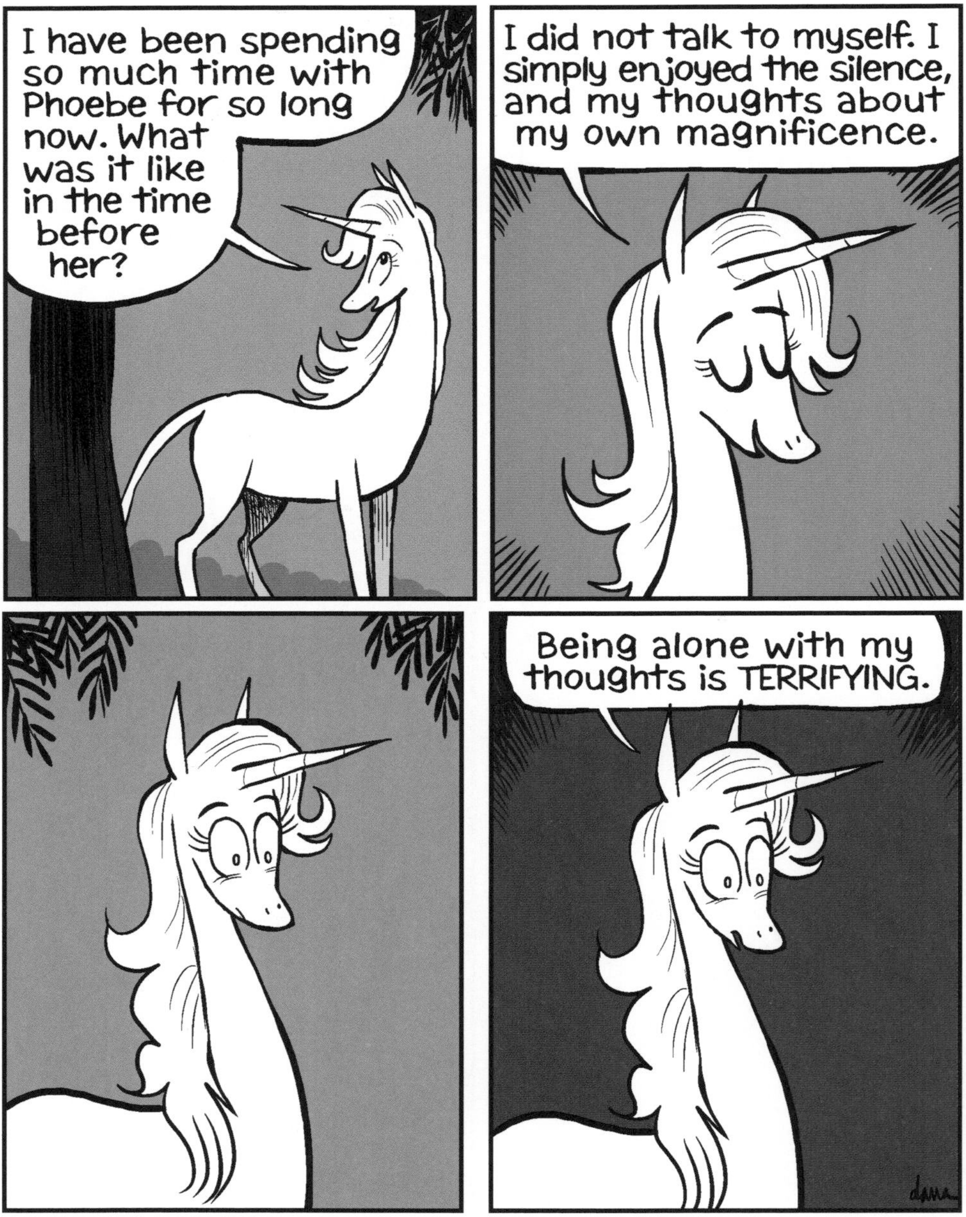
I have been spending so much time with Phoebe for so long now. What was it like in the time before her?
I did not talk to myself. I simply enjoyed the silence, and my thoughts about my own magnificence.
Being alone with my thoughts is TERRIFYING.
dana

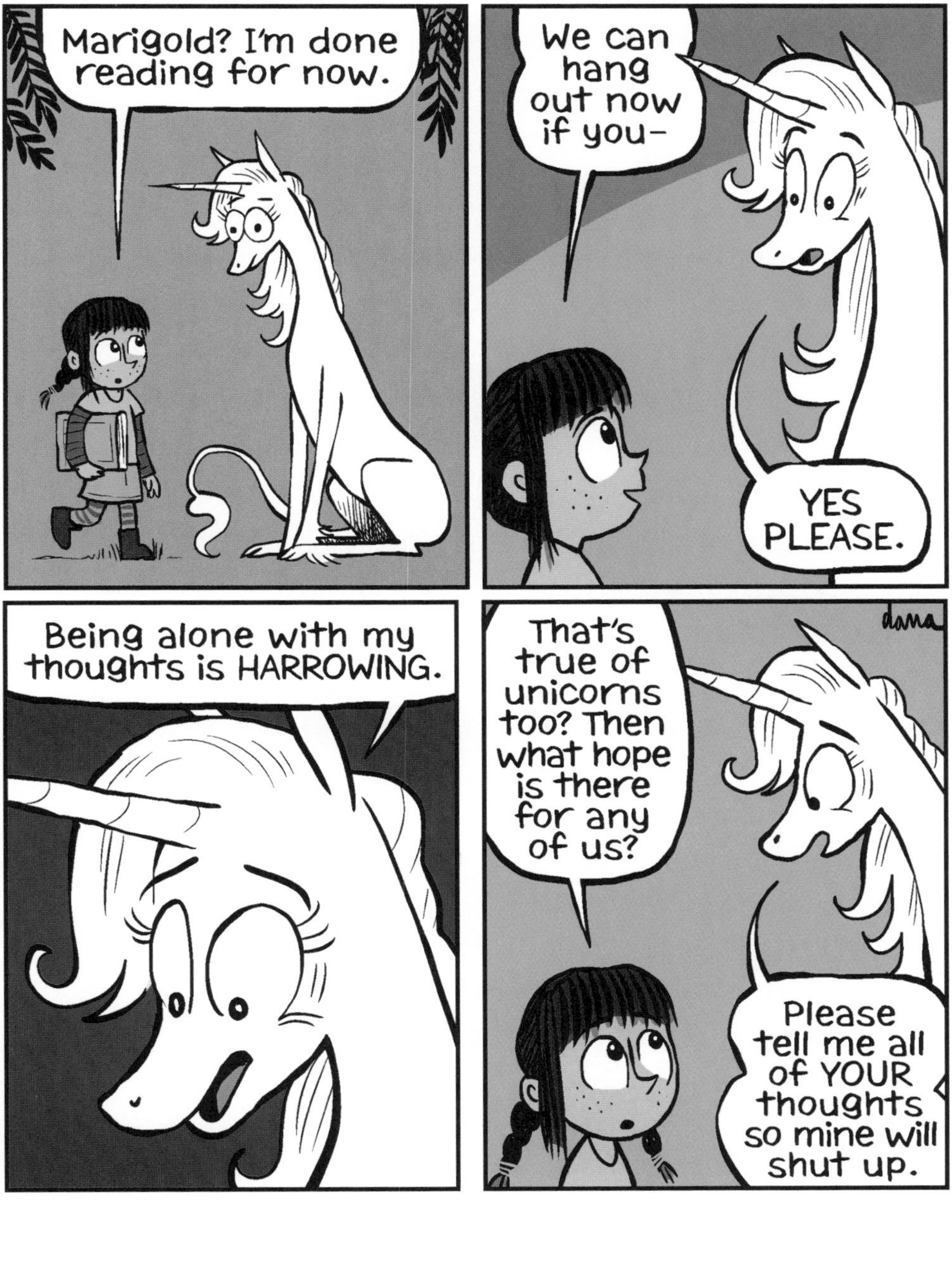

Marigold? I'm done reading for now.
We can hang out now if you-
YES PLEASE.
Being alone with my thoughts is HARROWING.
That's true of unicorns too? Then what hope is there for any of us?
Please tell me all of YOUR thoughts so mine will shut up.
dana

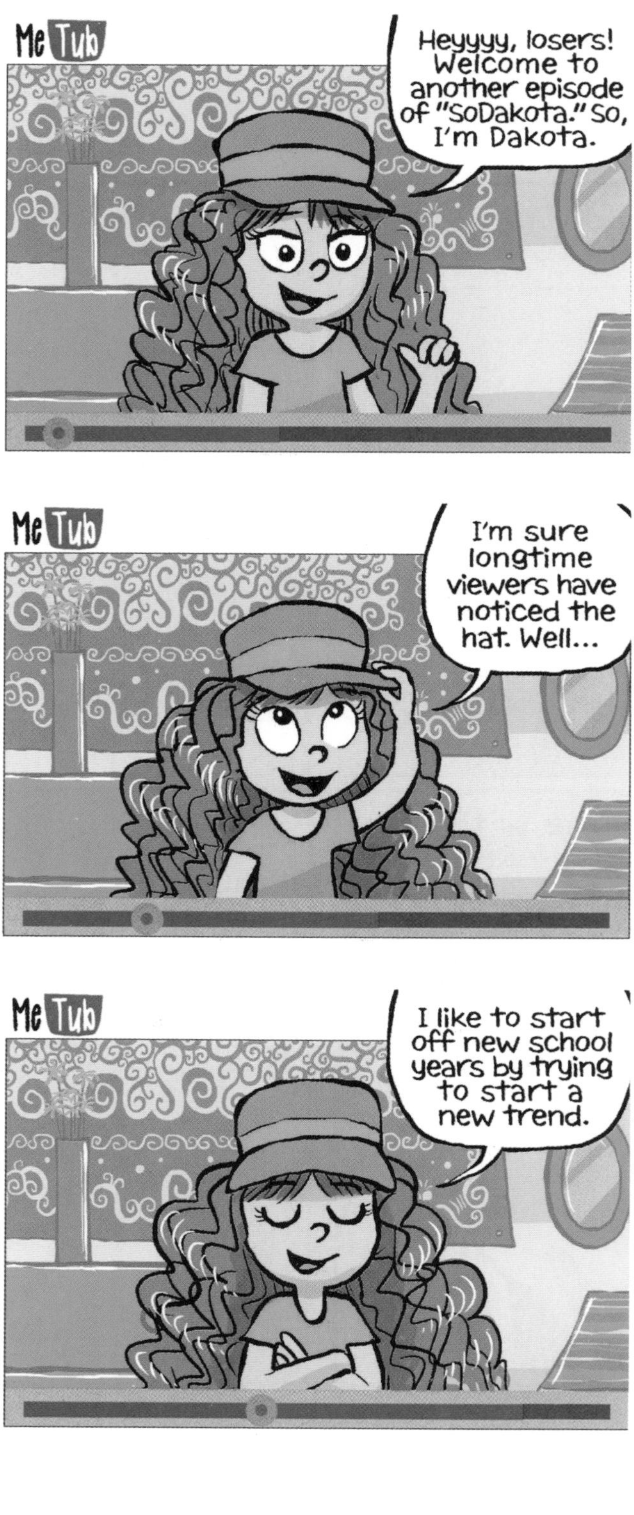
Me Tub
Heyyyy, losers! Welcome to another episode of "SoDakota." So, I'm Dakota.
Me Tub
I'm sure longtime viewers have noticed the hat. Well...
Me Tub
I like to start off new school years by trying to start a new trend.

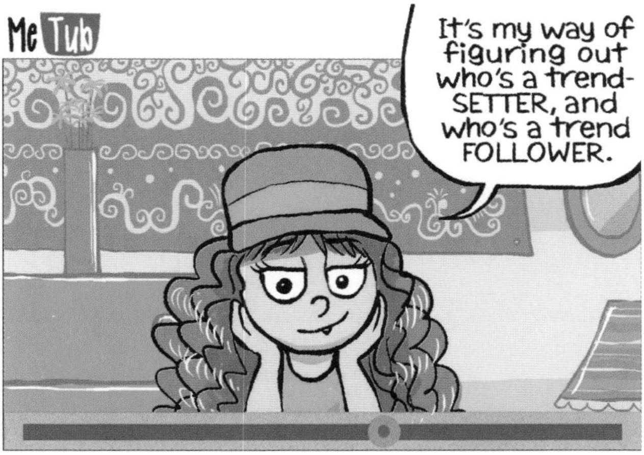
Me Tub
It's my way of figuring out who's a trend-SETTER, and who's a trend FOLLOWER.

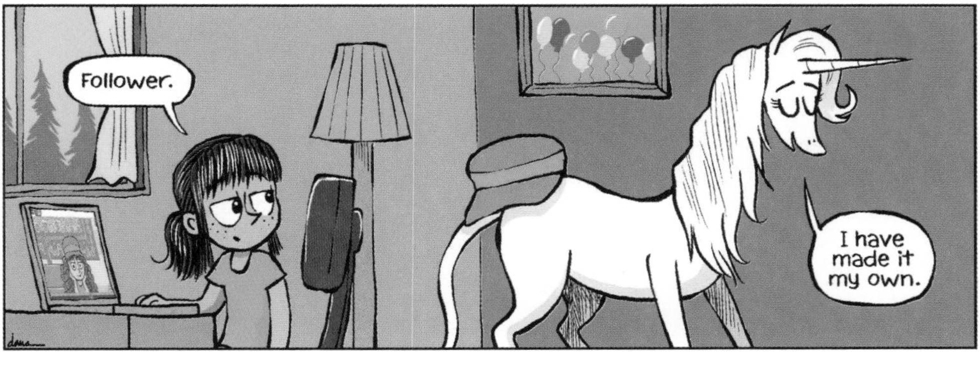
Follower.
I have made it my own.

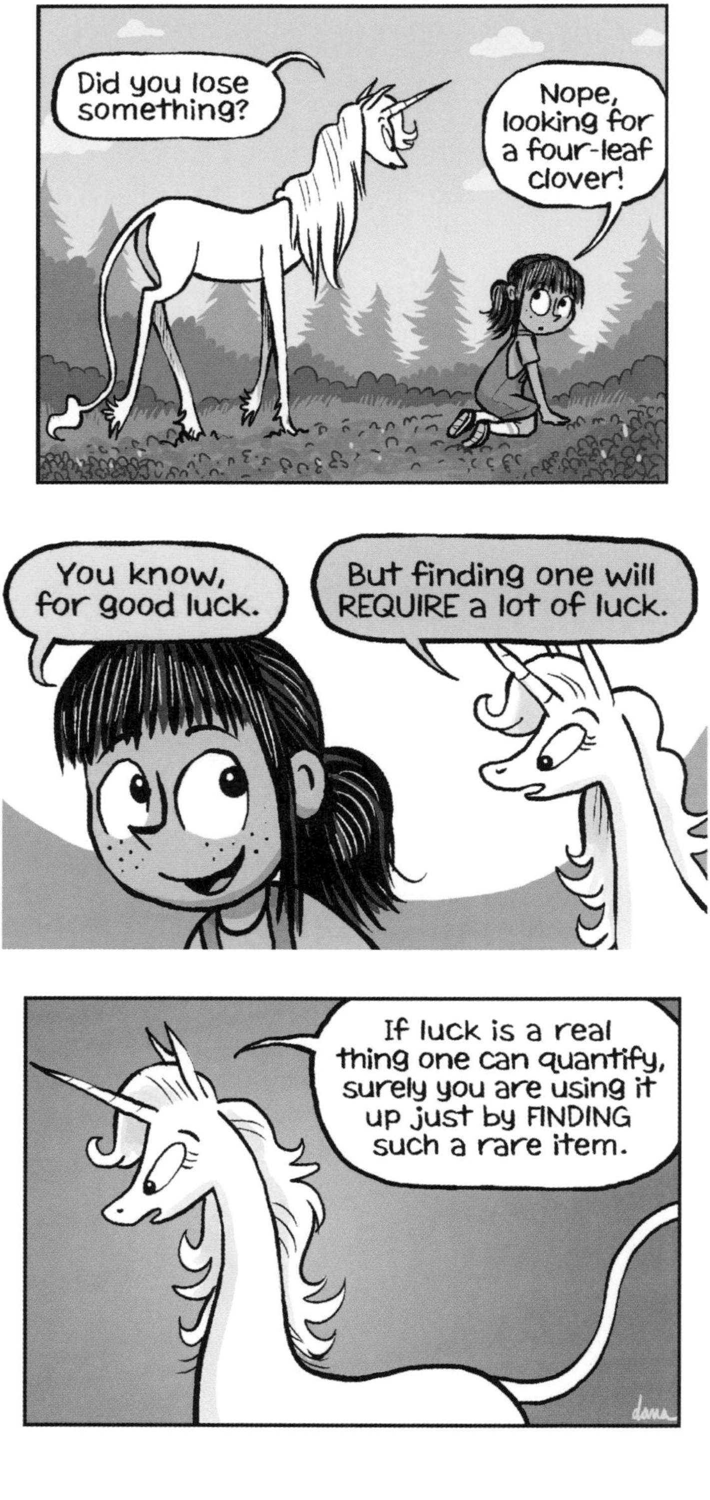
Did you lose something?
Nope, looking for a four-leaf clover!
You know, for good luck.
But finding one will REQUIRE a lot of luck.
If luck is a real thing one can quantify, surely you are using it up just by FINDING such a rare item.
dana

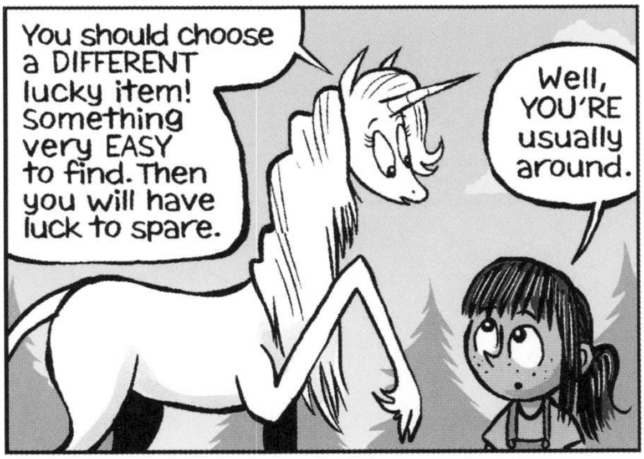
You should choose a DIFFERENT lucky item! Something very EASY to find. Then you will have luck to spare.
Well, YOU'RE usually around.

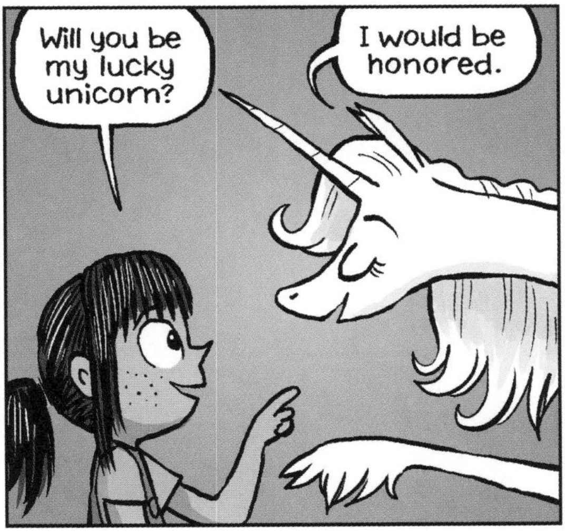
Will you be my lucky unicorn?
I would be honored.

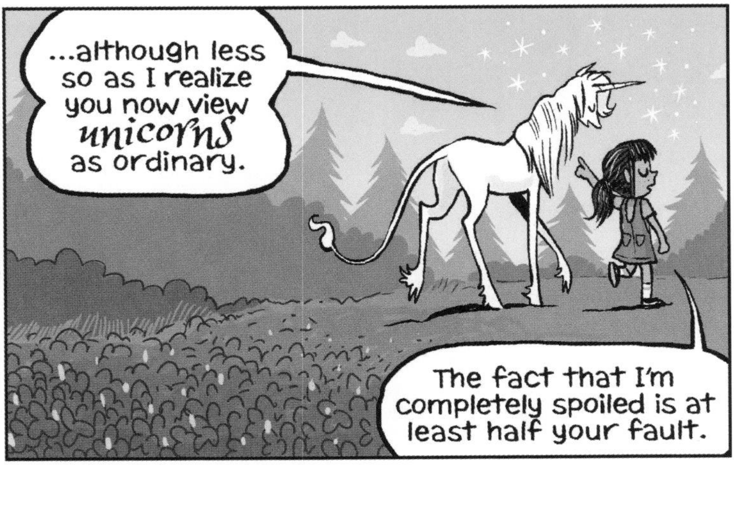
...although less so as I realize you now view unicorns as ordinary.
The fact that I'm completely spoiled is at least half your fault.

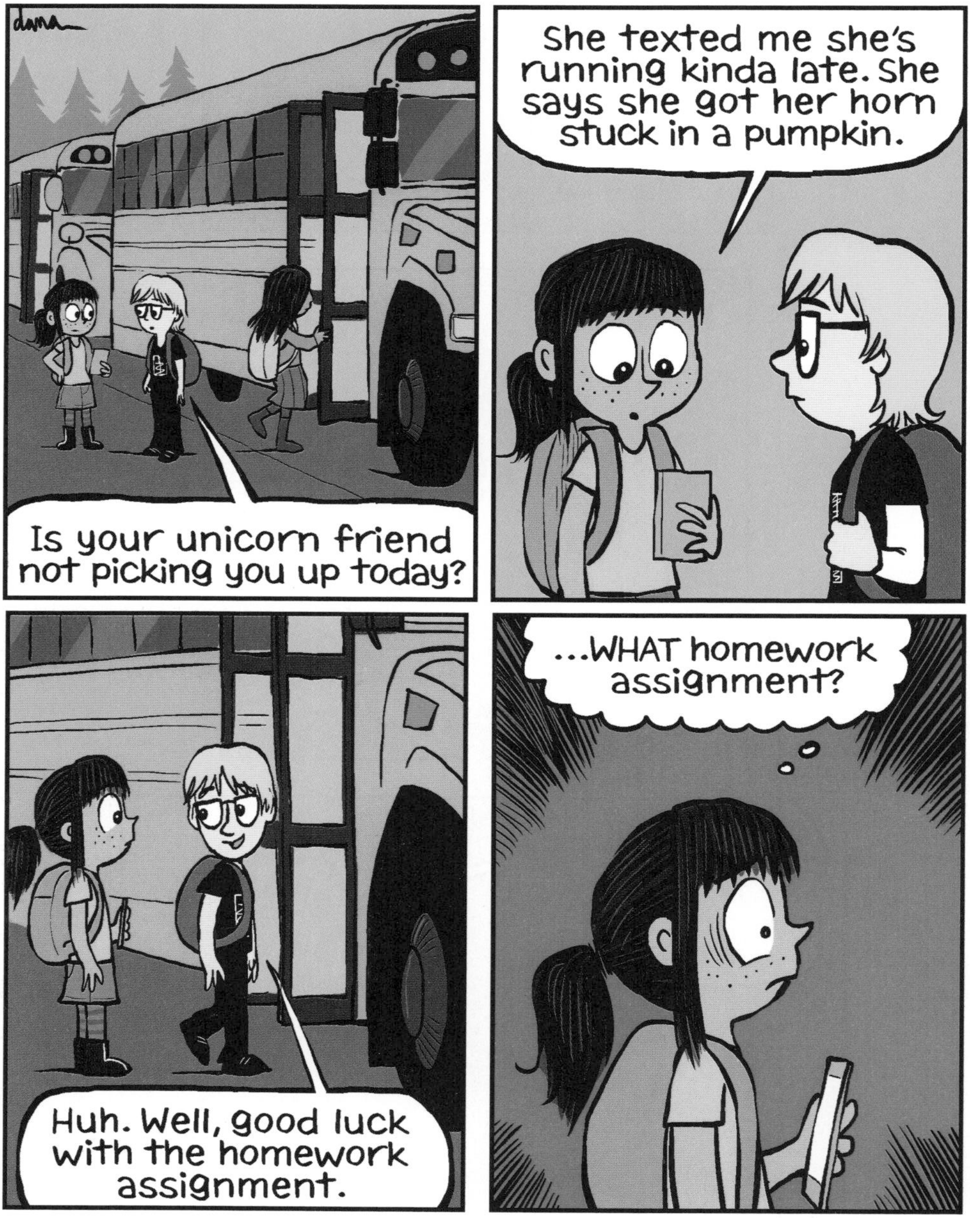
dana
Is your unicorn friend not picking you up today?
She texted me she's running kinda late. She says she got her horn stuck in a pumpkin.
Huh. Well, good luck with the homework assignment.
...WHAT homework assignment?

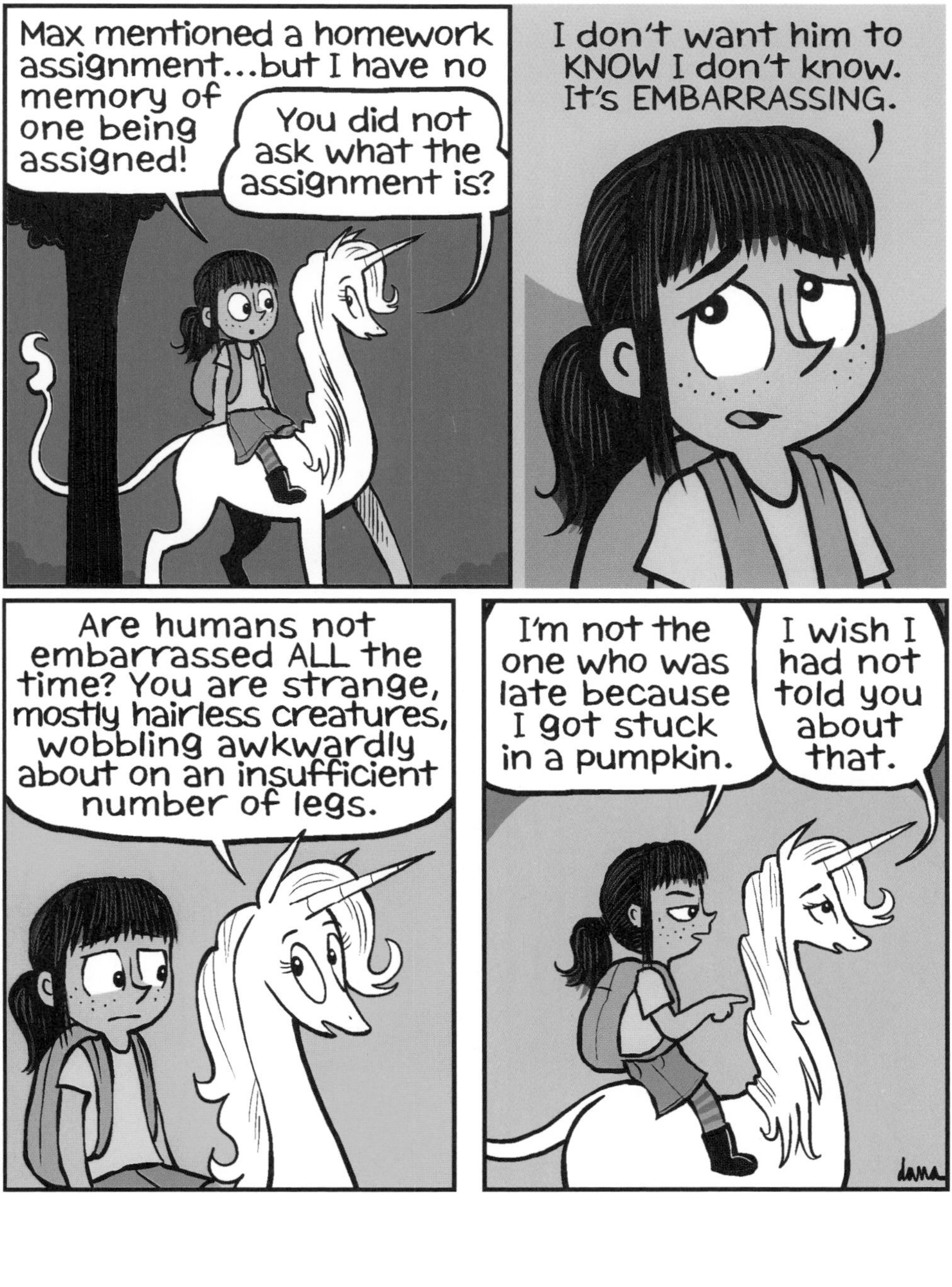
Max mentioned a homework assignment...but I have no memory of one being assigned!
You did not ask what the assignment is?
I don't want him to KNOW I don't know. It's EMBARRASSING.
Are humans not embarrassed ALL the time? You are strange, mostly hairless creatures, wobbling awkwardly about on an insufficient number of legs.
I'm not the one who was late because I got stuck in a pumpkin.
I wish I had not told you about that.
dana

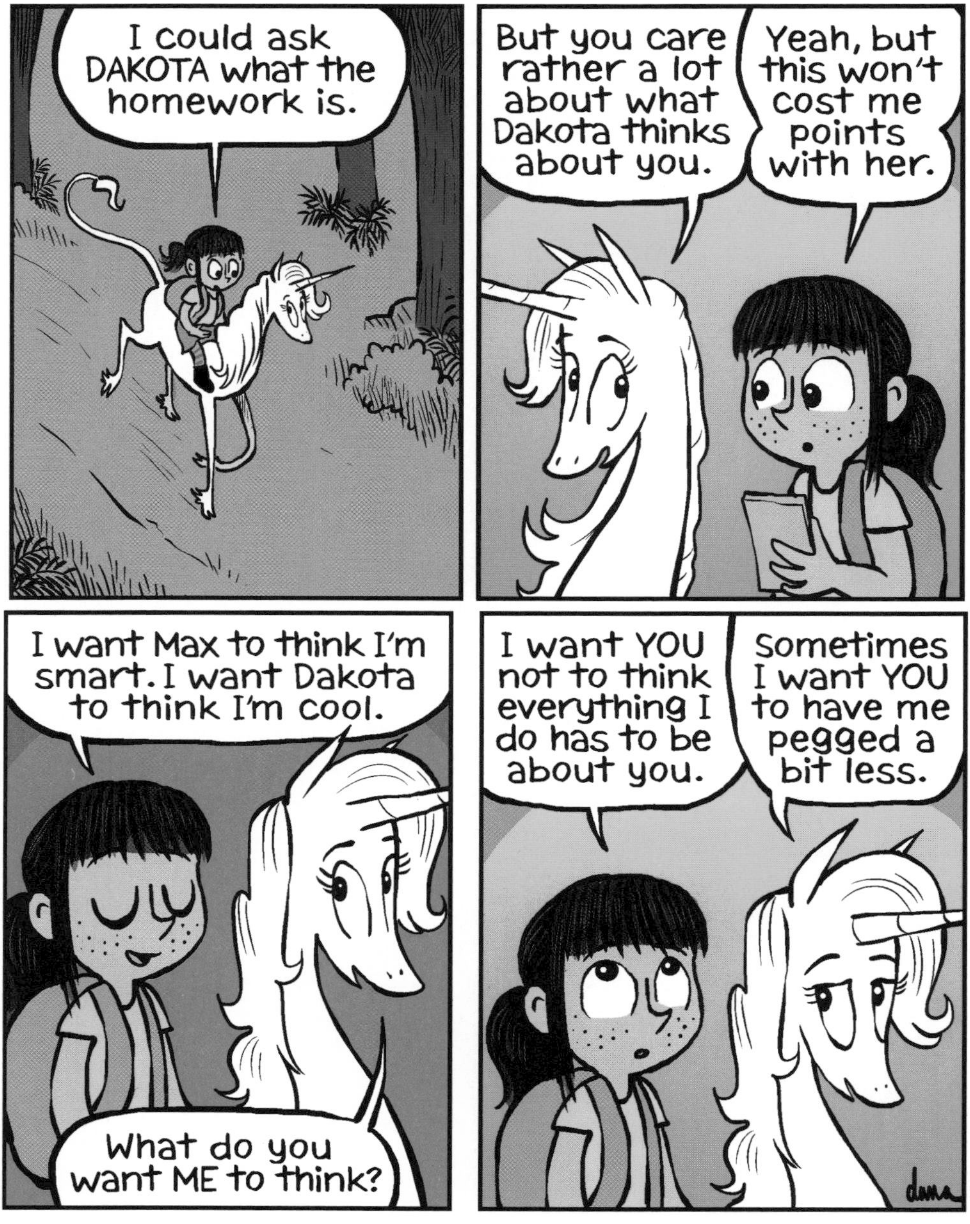
I could ask DAKOTA what the homework is.
But you care rather a lot about what Dakota thinks about you.
Yeah, but this won't cost me points with her.
I want Max to think I'm smart. I want Dakota to think I'm cool.
What do you want ME to think?
I want YOU not to think everything I do has to be about you.
Sometimes I want YOU to have me pegged a bit less.
dana

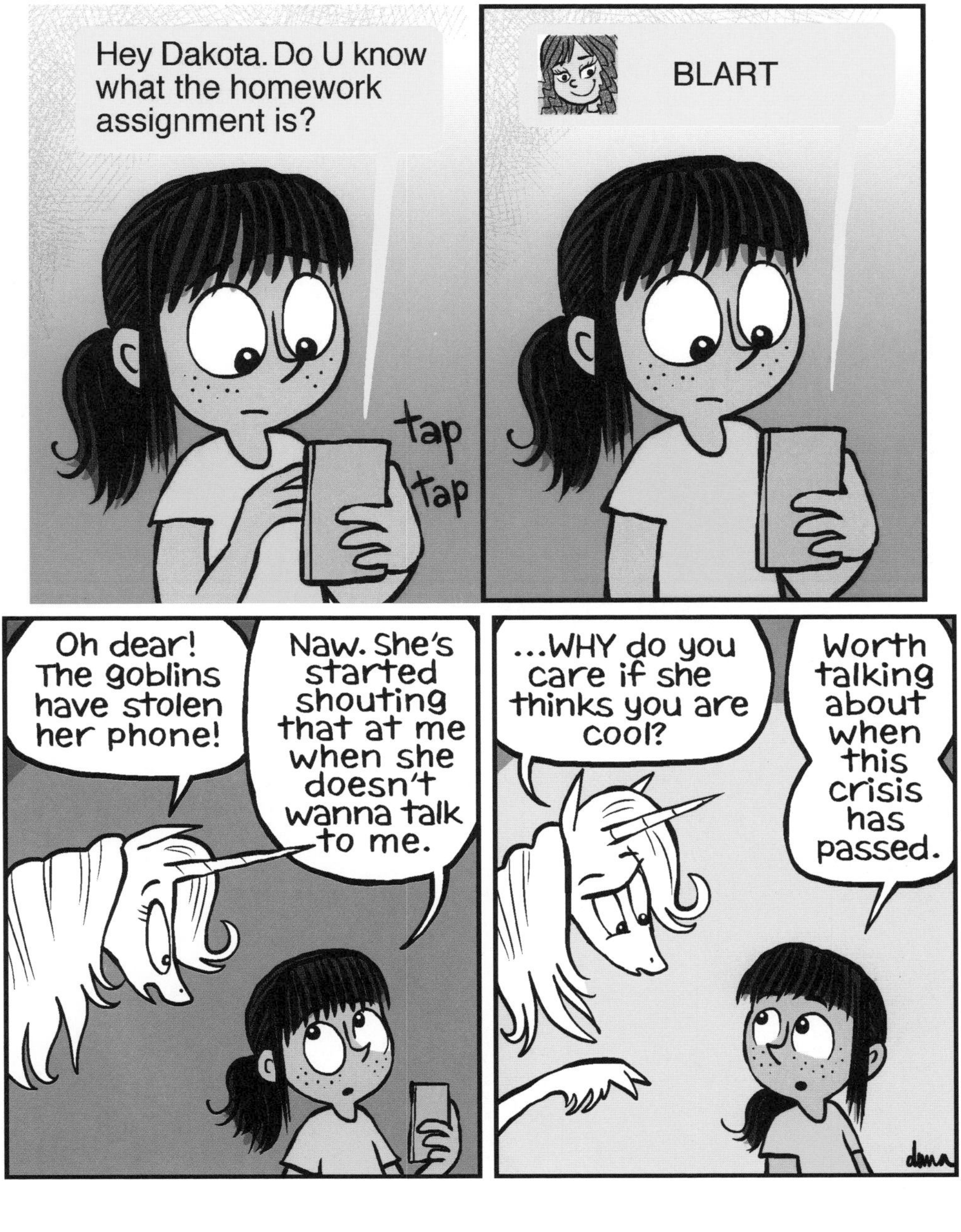
Hey Dakota. Do U know what the homework assignment is?
tap
tap
BLART
Oh dear! The goblins have stolen her phone!
Naw. She's started shouting that at me when she doesn't wanna talk to me.
...WHY do you care if she thinks you are cool?
Worth talking about when this crisis has passed.
dana

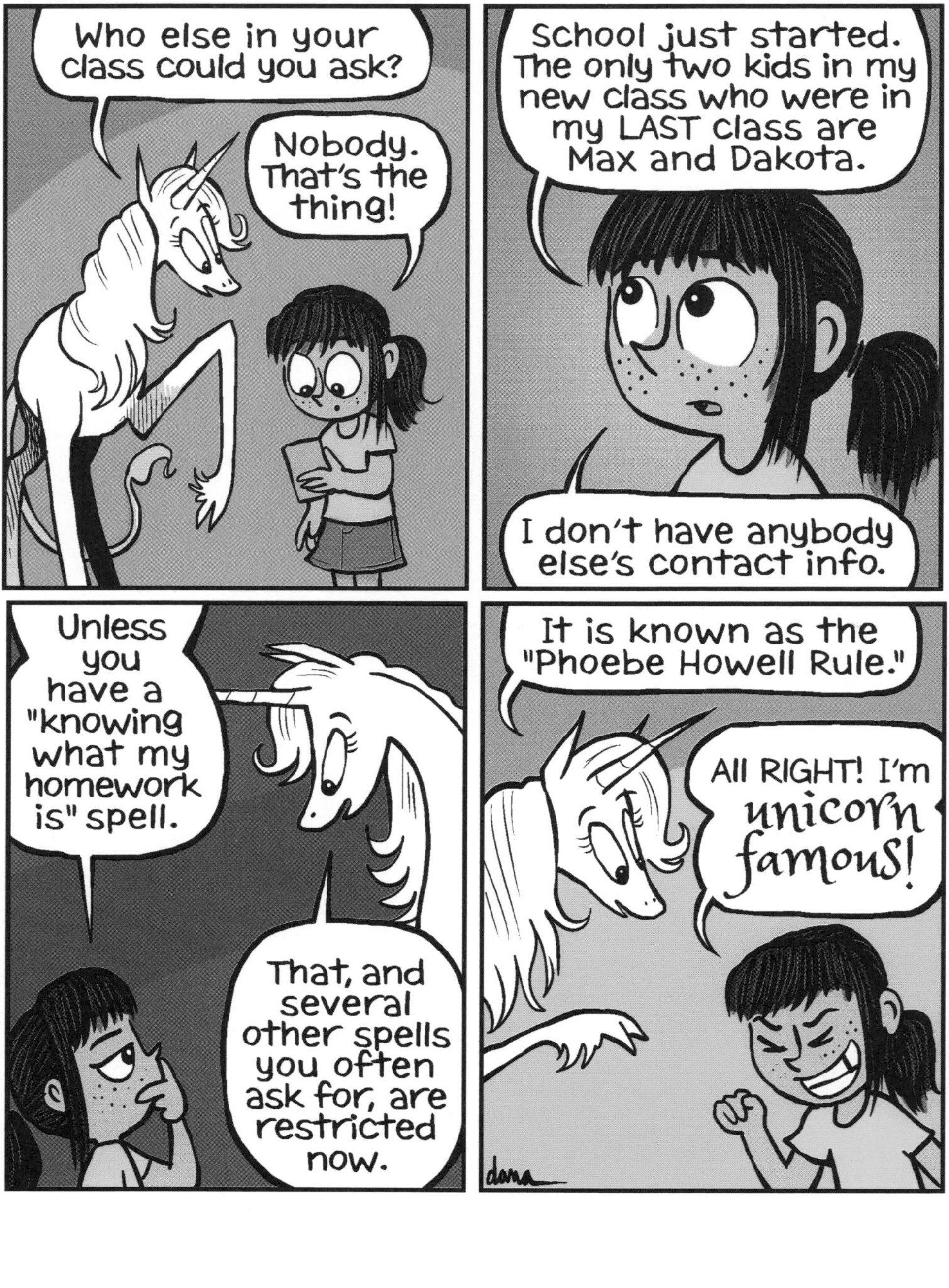
Who else in your class could you ask?
Nobody. That's the thing!
School just started. The only two kids in my new class who were in my LAST class are Max and Dakota.
I don't have anybody else's contact info.
Unless you have a "knowing what my homework is" spell.
That, and several other spells you often ask for, are restricted now.
It is known as the "Phoebe Howell Rule."
All RIGHT! I'm unicorn famous!
dana

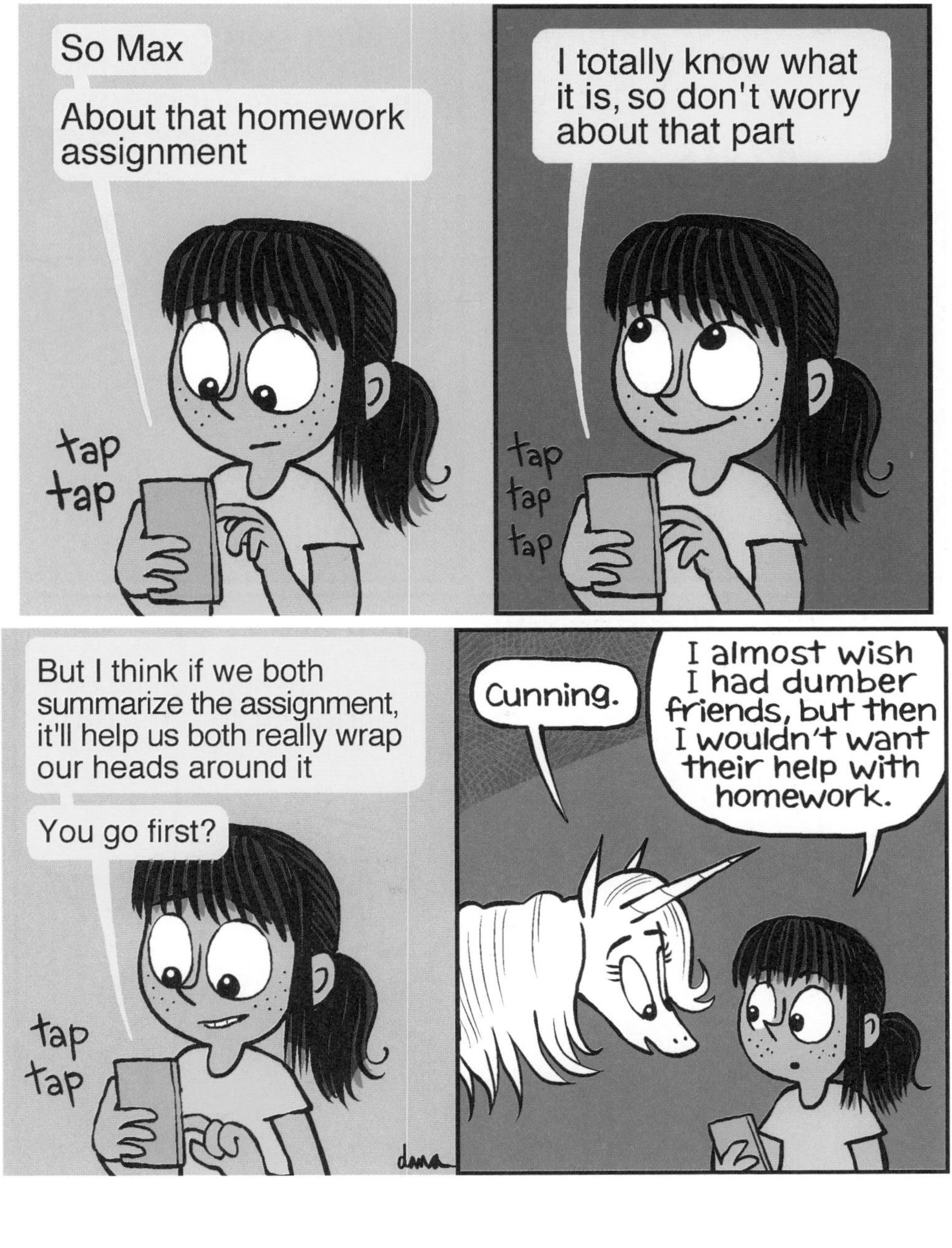
So Max
About that homework assignment
tap tap
I totally know what it is, so don't worry about that part
tap tap tap
But I think if we both summarize the assignment, it'll help us both really wrap our heads around it
You go first?
tap tap
Cunning.
I almost wish I had dumber friends, but then I wouldn't want their help with homework.
dana

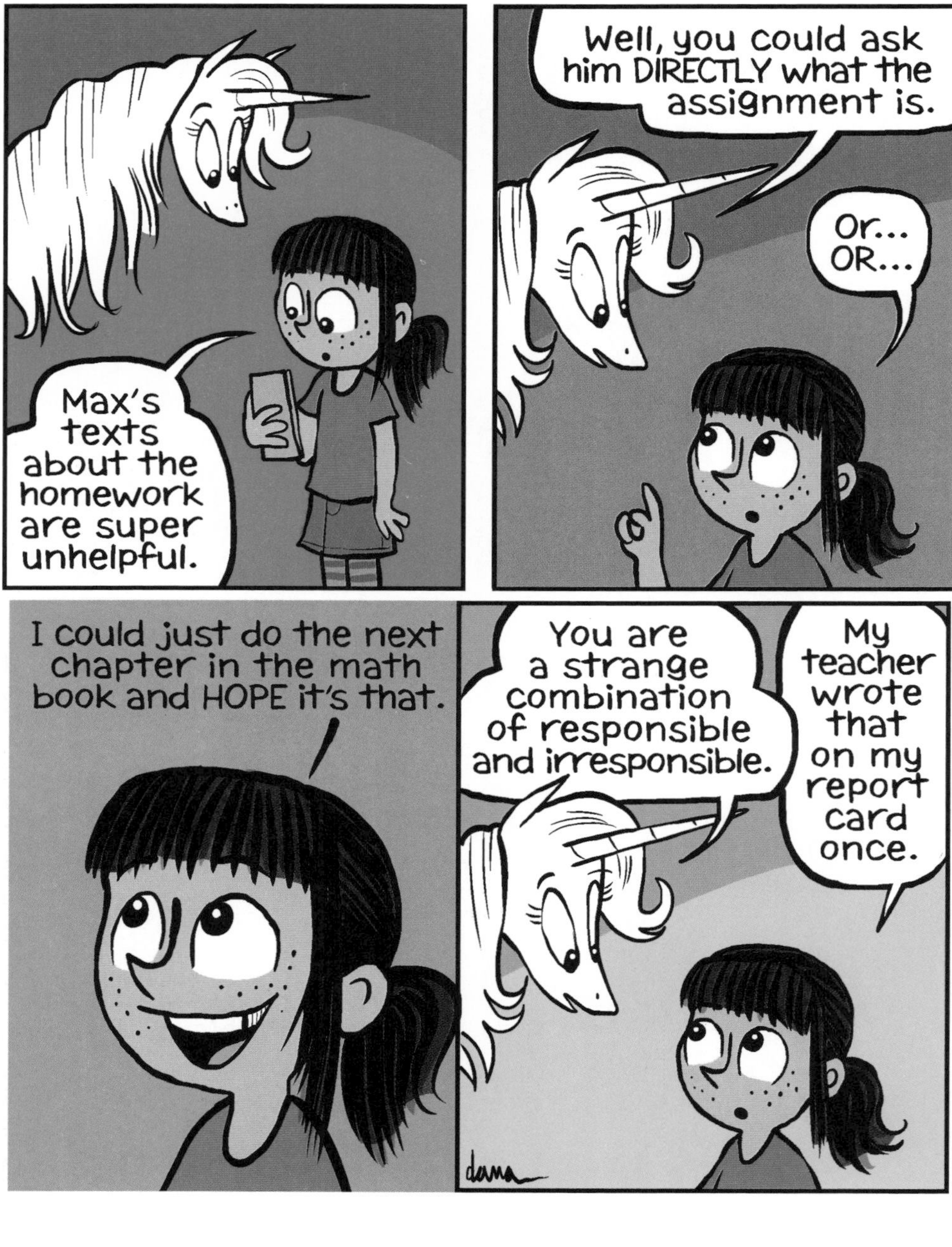
Max's texts about the homework are super unhelpful.
Well, you could ask him DIRECTLY what the assignment is.
Or... OR...
I could just do the next chapter in the math book and HOPE it's that.
You are a strange combination of responsible and irresponsible.
My teacher wrote that on my report card once.
dana

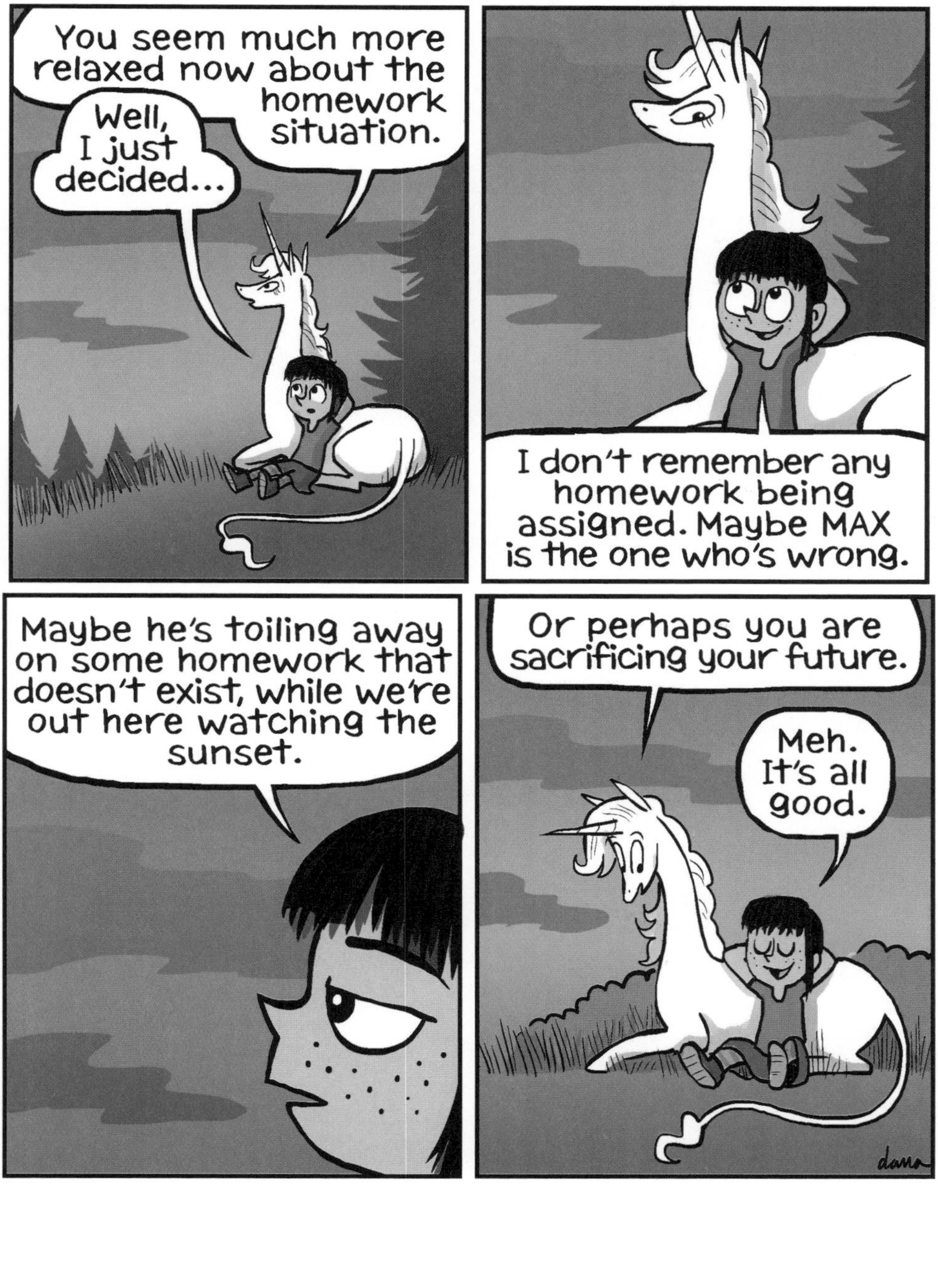
You seem much more relaxed now about the homework situation.
Well, I just decided...
I don't remember any homework being assigned. Maybe MAX is the one who's wrong.
Maybe he's toiling away on some homework that doesn't exist, while we're out here watching the sunset.
Or perhaps you are sacrificing your future.
Meh. It's all good.
dana

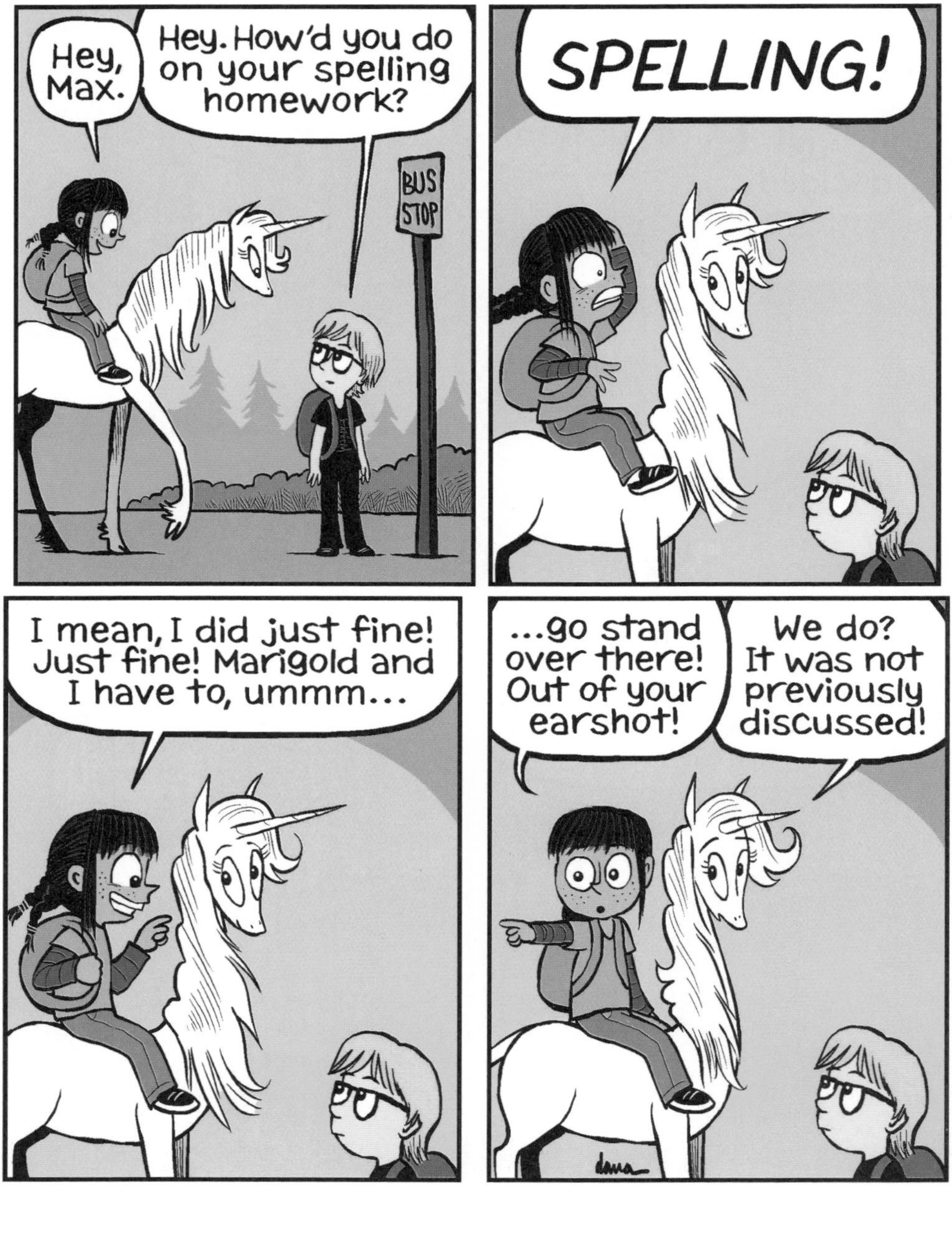
Hey, Max.
Hey. How'd you do on your spelling homework?
BUS STOP
SPELLING!
I mean, I did just fine! Just fine! Marigold and I have to, ummm...
...go stand over there! Out of your earshot!
We do? It was not previously discussed!
dana

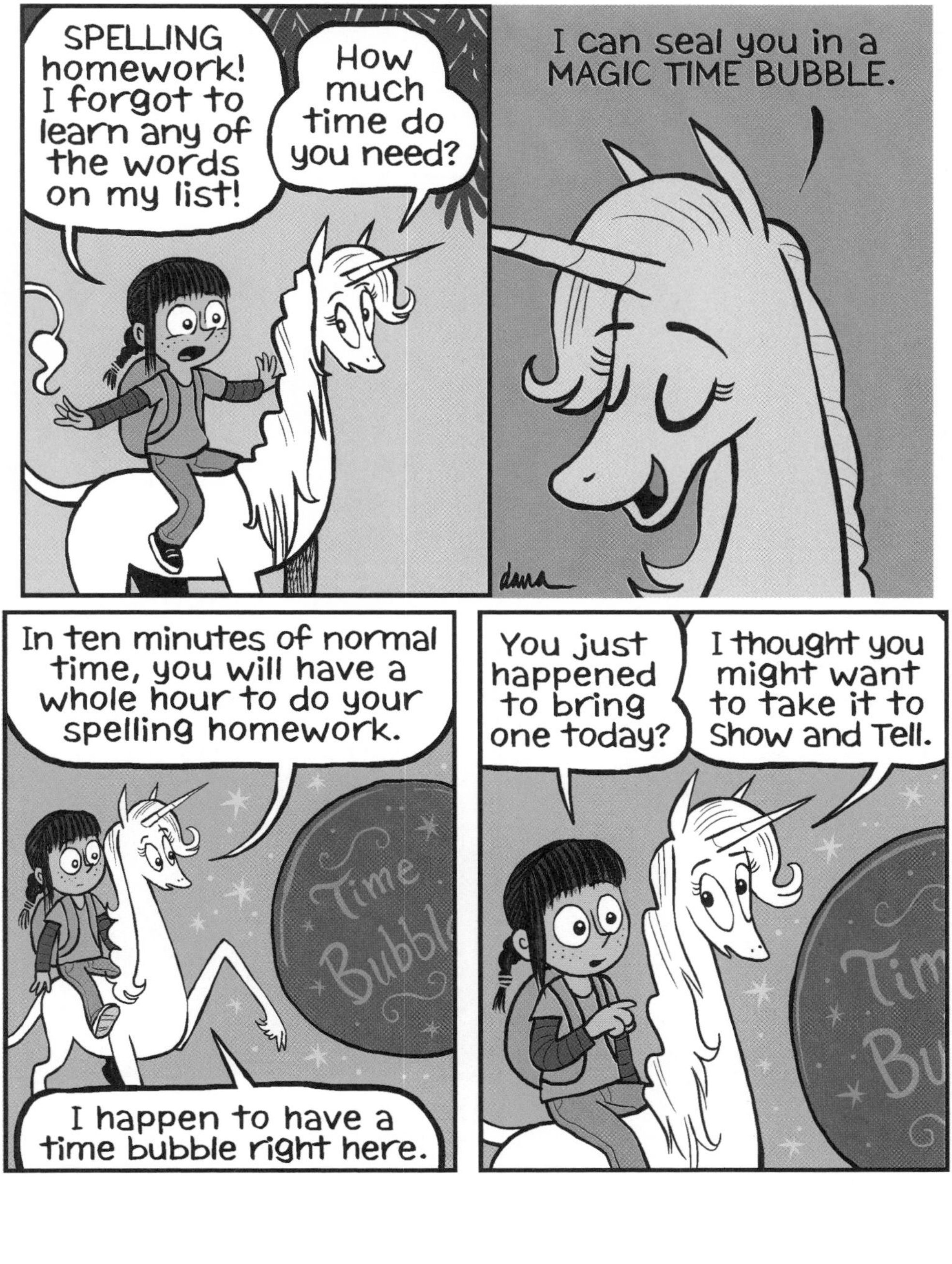
SPELLING homework! I forgot to learn any of the words on my list!
How much time do you need?
I can seal you in a MAGIC TIME BUBBLE.
In ten minutes of normal time, you will have a whole hour to do your spelling homework.
Time Bubble
I happen to have a time bubble right here.
You just happened to bring one today?
I thought you might want to take it to Show and Tell.

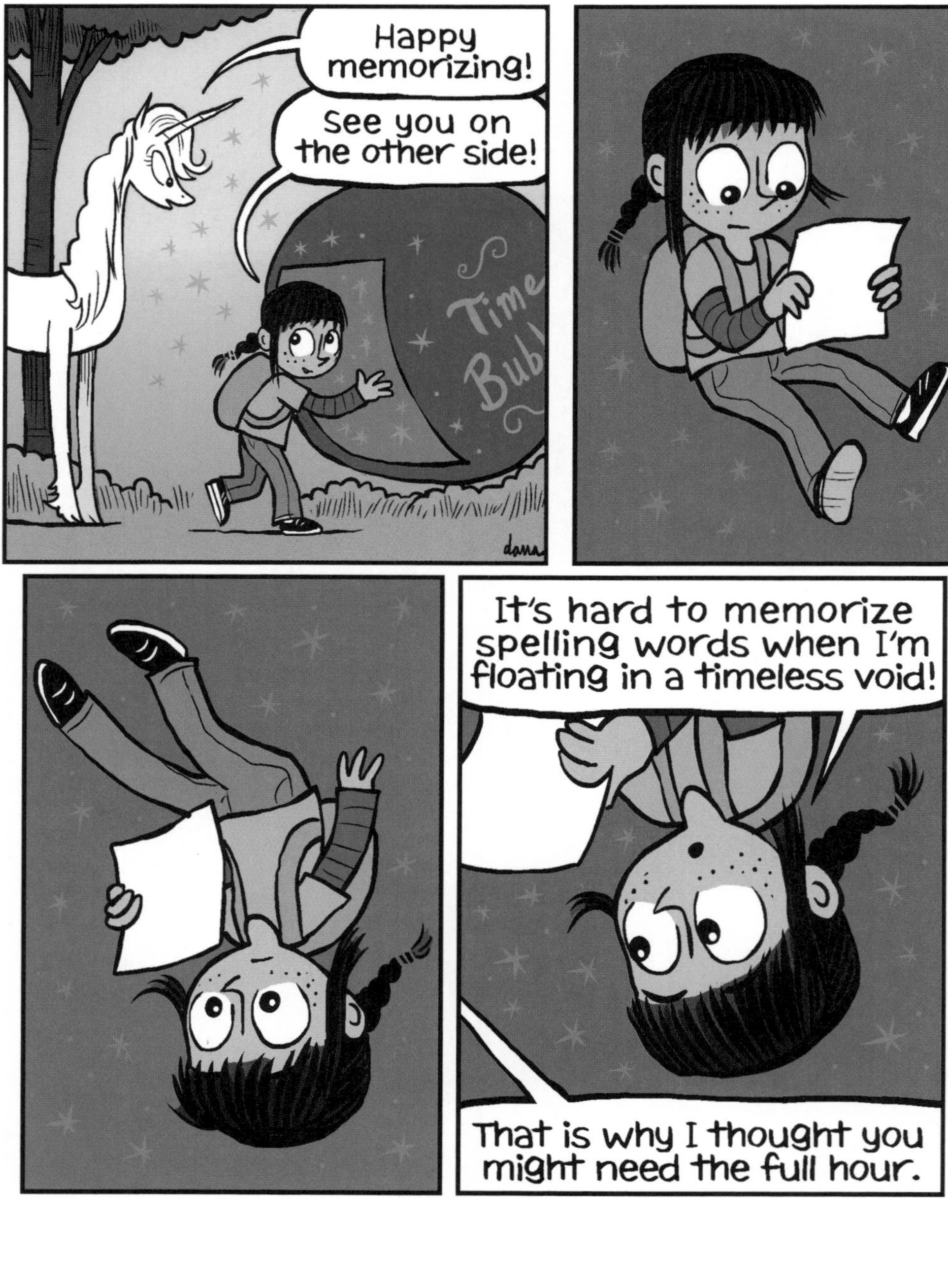
Happy memorizing!
See you on the other side!
Time Bub
It's hard to memorize spelling words when I'm floating in a timeless void!
That is why I thought you might need the full hour.

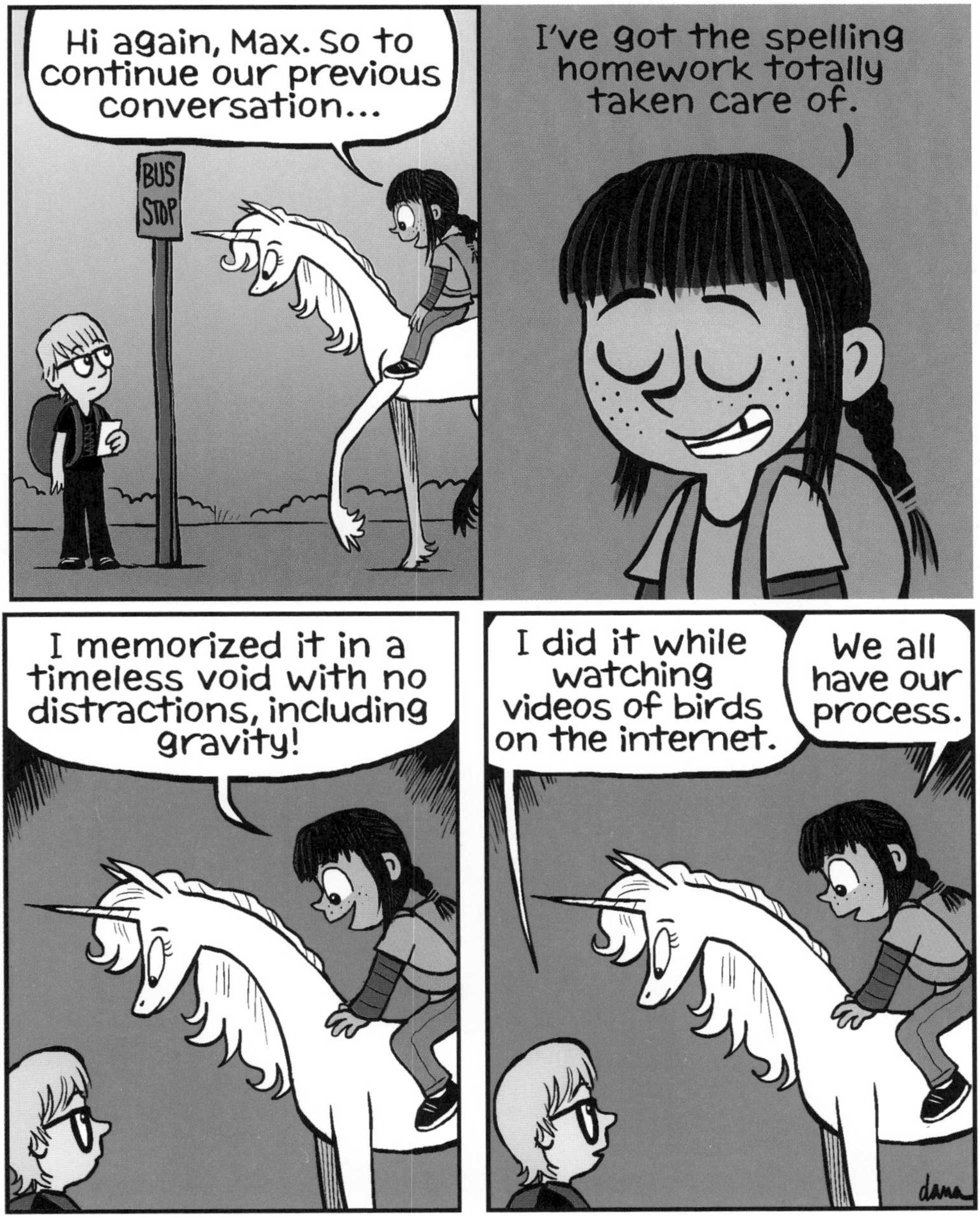
Hi again, Max. So to continue our previous conversation...
BUS STOP
I've got the spelling homework totally taken care of.
I memorized it in a timeless void with no distractions, including gravity!
I did it while watching videos of birds on the internet.
We all have our process.
dana

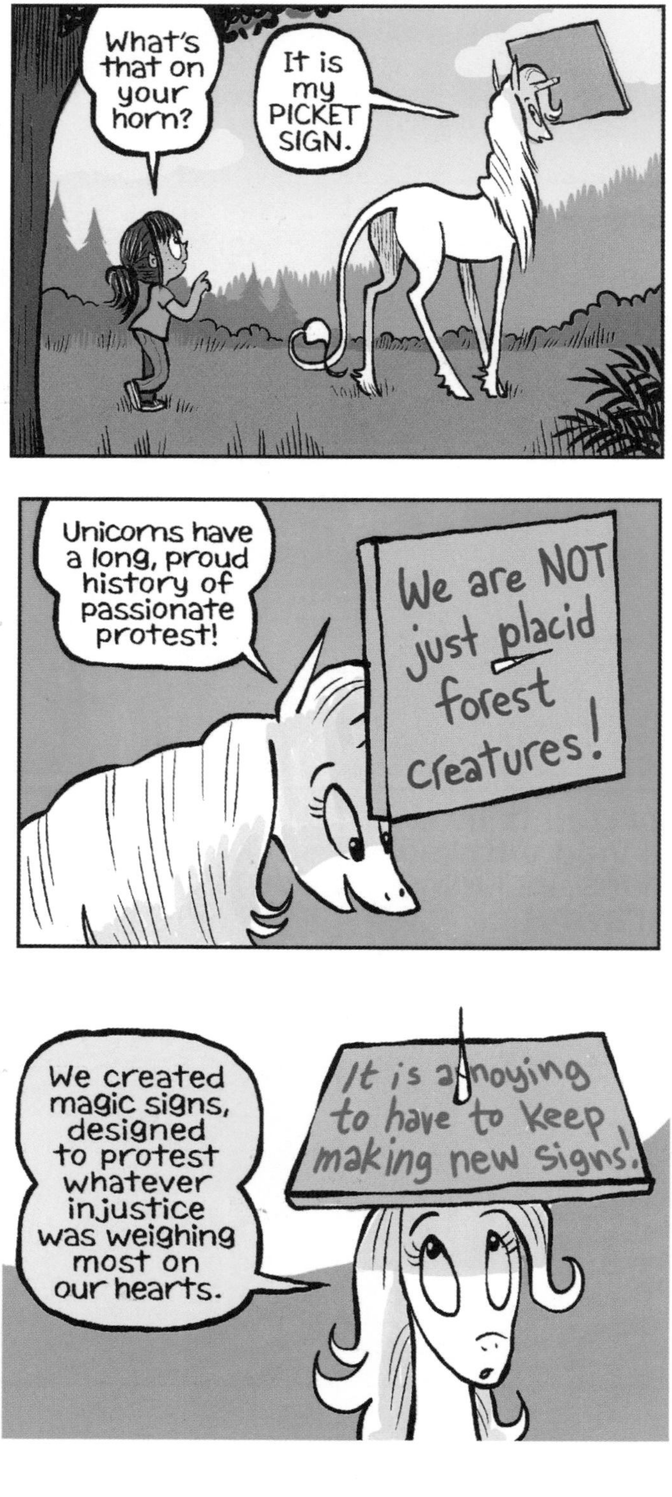
What's that on your horn?
It is my PICKET SIGN.
Unicorns have a long, proud history of passionate protest!
We are NOT just placid forest creatures!
We created magic signs, designed to protest whatever injustice was weighing most on our hearts.
It is annoying to have to keep making new signs!

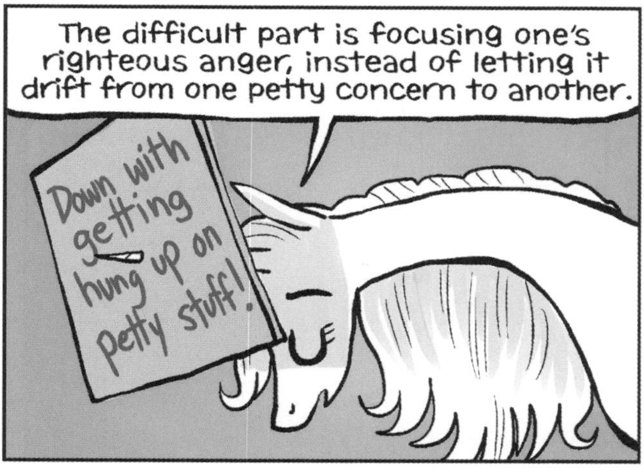
The difficult part is focusing one's righteous anger, instead of letting it drift from one petty concern to another.
Down with getting hung up on petty stuff!

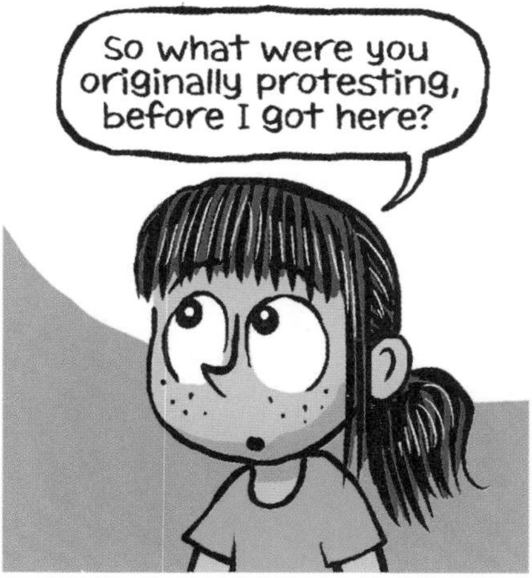
So what were you originally protesting, before I got here?

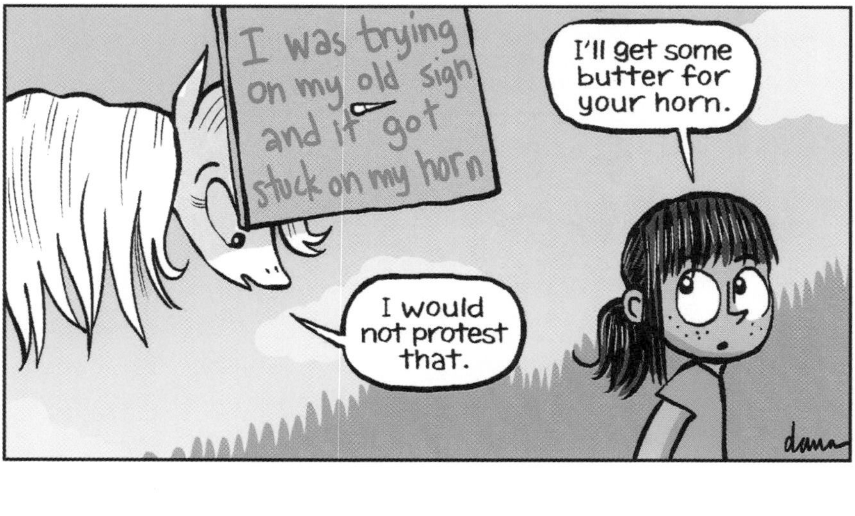
I was trying on my old sign and it got stuck on my horn
I'll get some butter for your horn.
I would not protest that.

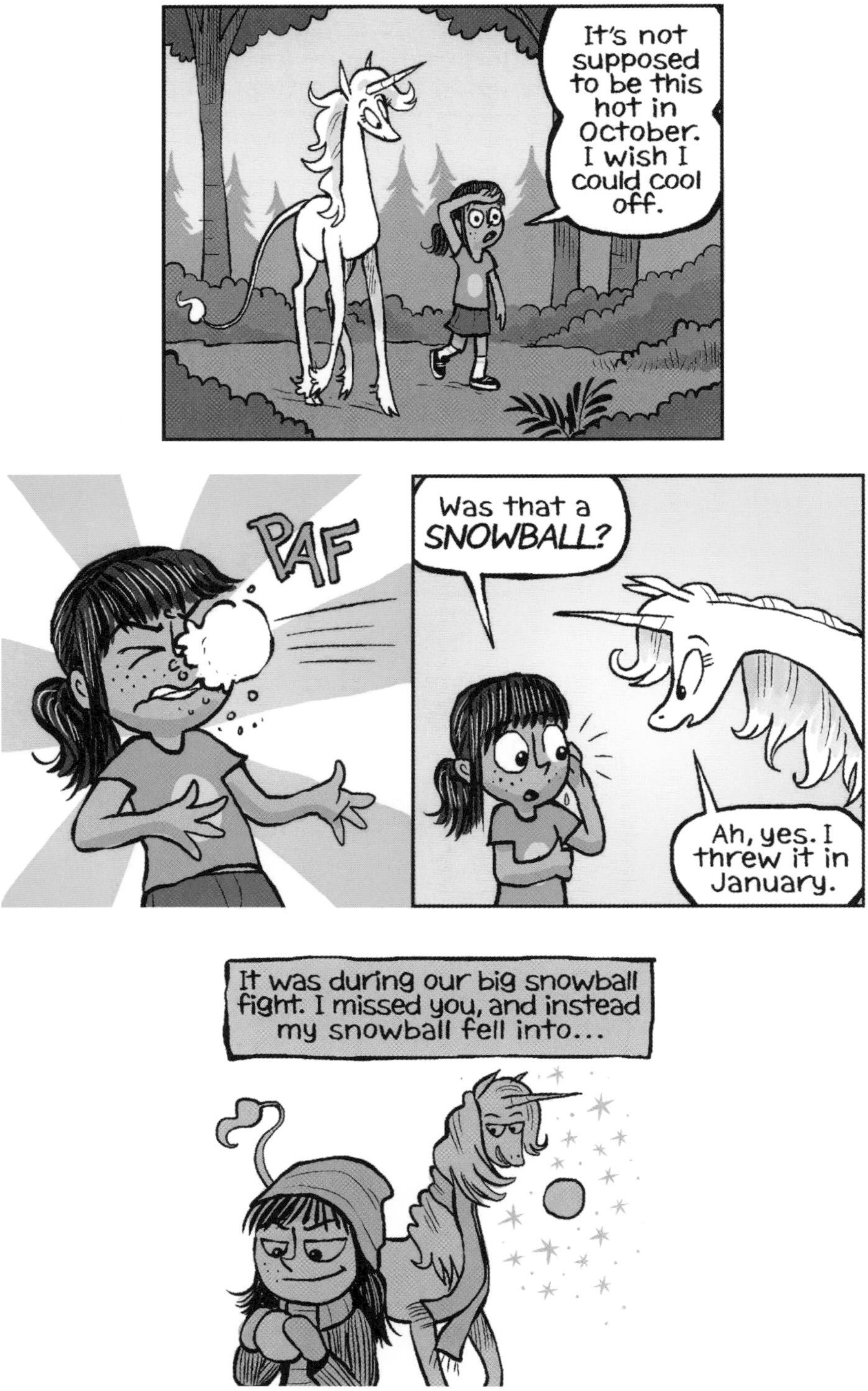
It's not supposed to be this hot in October. I wish I could cool off.
PAF
Was that a SNOWBALL?
Ah, yes. I threw it in January.
It was during our big snowball fight. I missed you, and instead my snowball fell into...

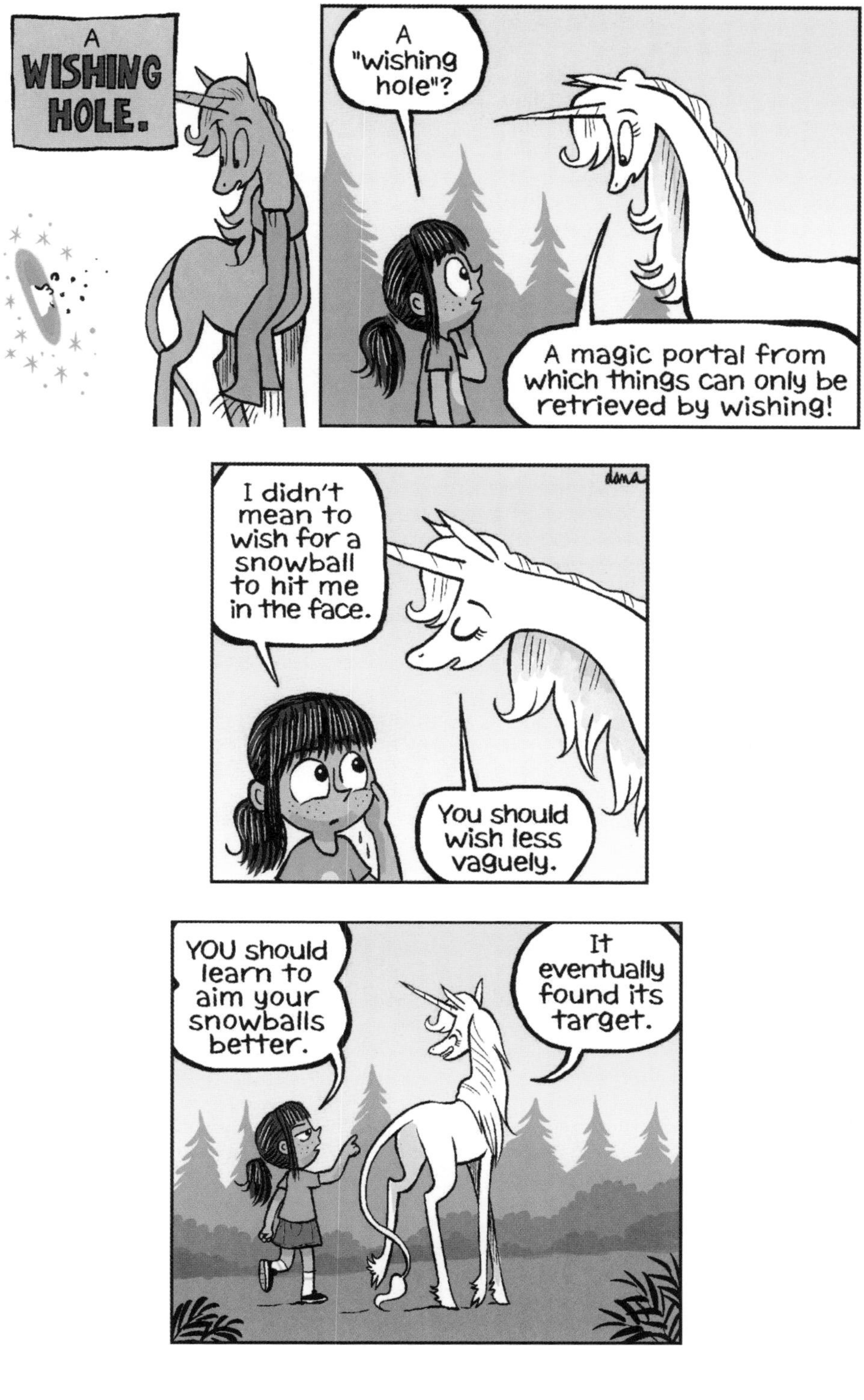
A WISHING HOLE.
A "wishing hole"?
A magic portal from which things can only be retrieved by wishing!
dana
I didn't mean to wish for a snowball to hit me in the face.
You should wish less vaguely.
YOU should learn to aim your snowballs better.
It eventually found its target.

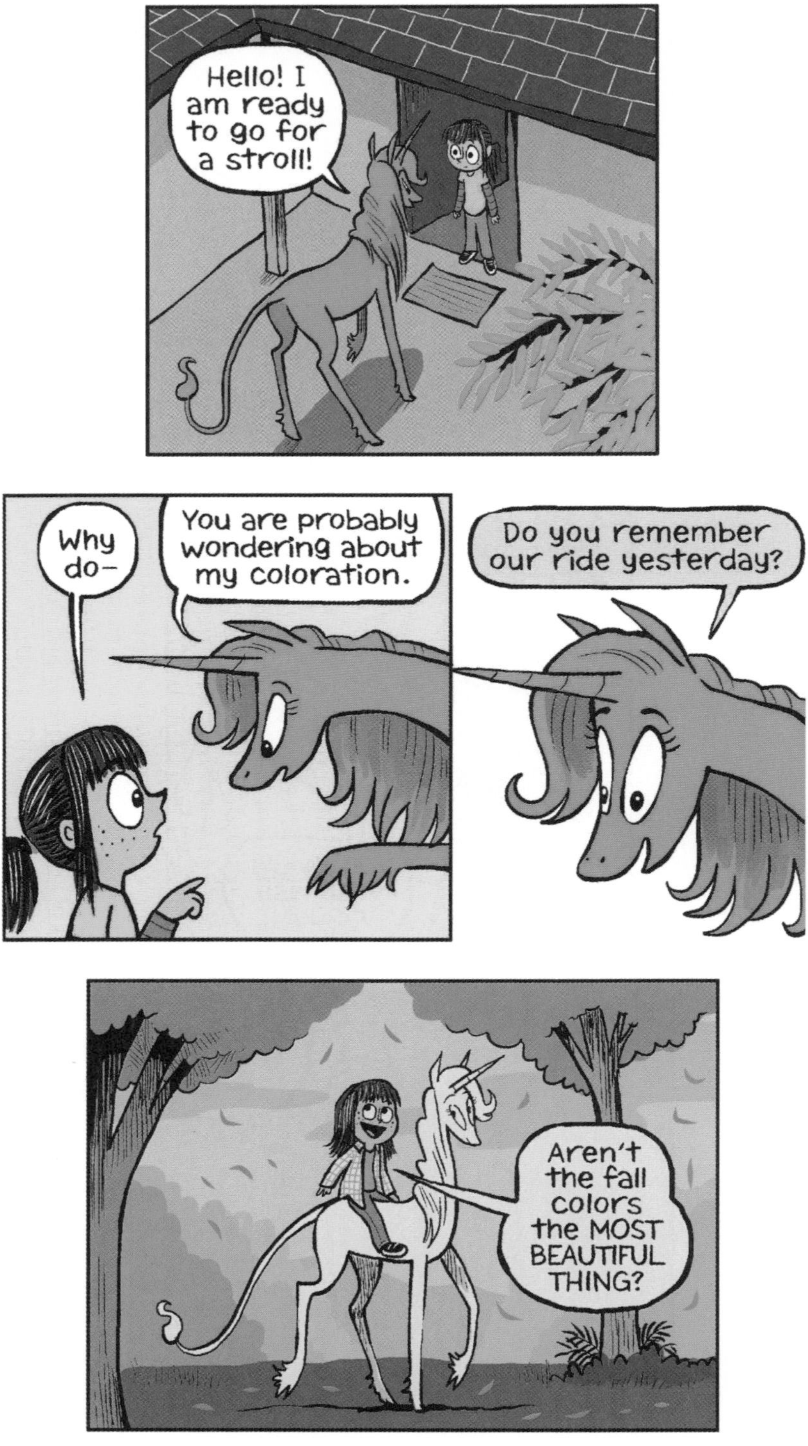
Hello! I am ready to go for a stroll!
Why do–
You are probably wondering about my coloration.
Do you remember our ride yesterday?
Aren't the fall colors the MOST BEAUTIFUL THING?

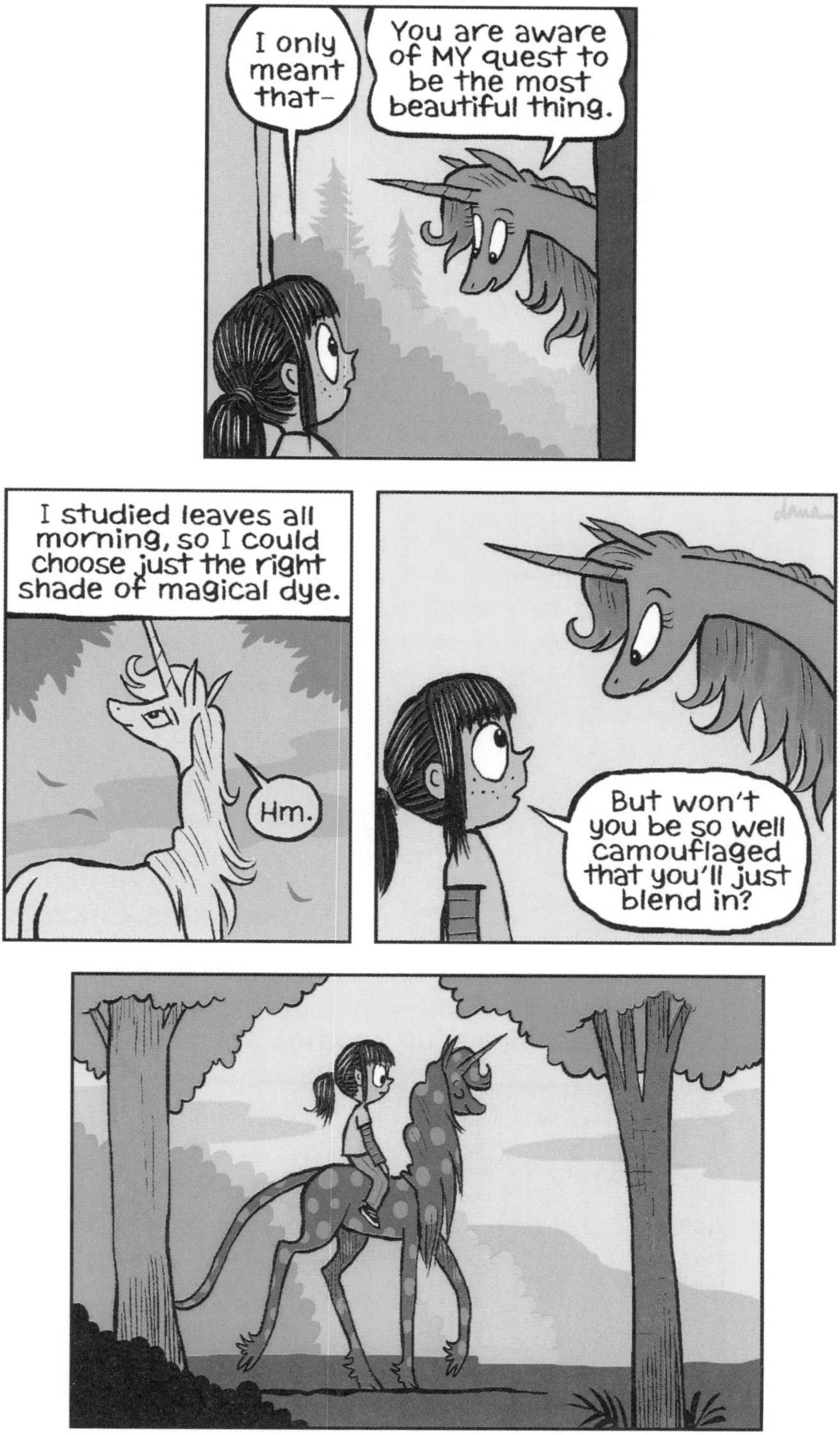
I only meant that-
You are aware of MY quest to be the most beautiful thing.
I studied leaves all morning, so I could choose just the right shade of magical dye.
Hm.
But won't you be so well camouflaged that you'll just blend in?

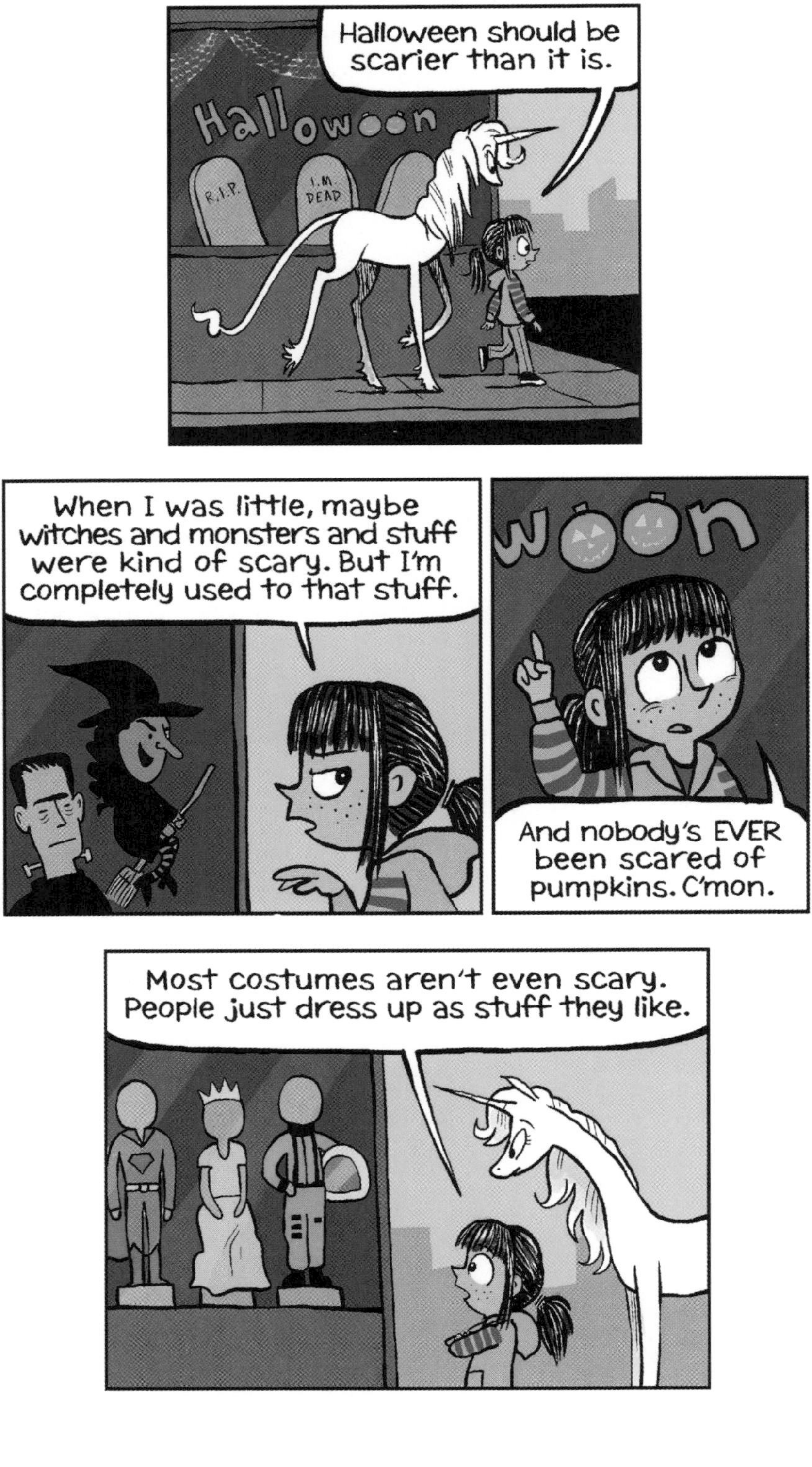
Halloween should be scarier than it is.
Halloowoon
R.I.P.
I.M. DEAD
When I was little, maybe witches and monsters and stuff were kind of scary. But I'm completely used to that stuff.
woon
And nobody's EVER been scared of pumpkins. C'mon.
Most costumes aren't even scary. People just dress up as stuff they like.

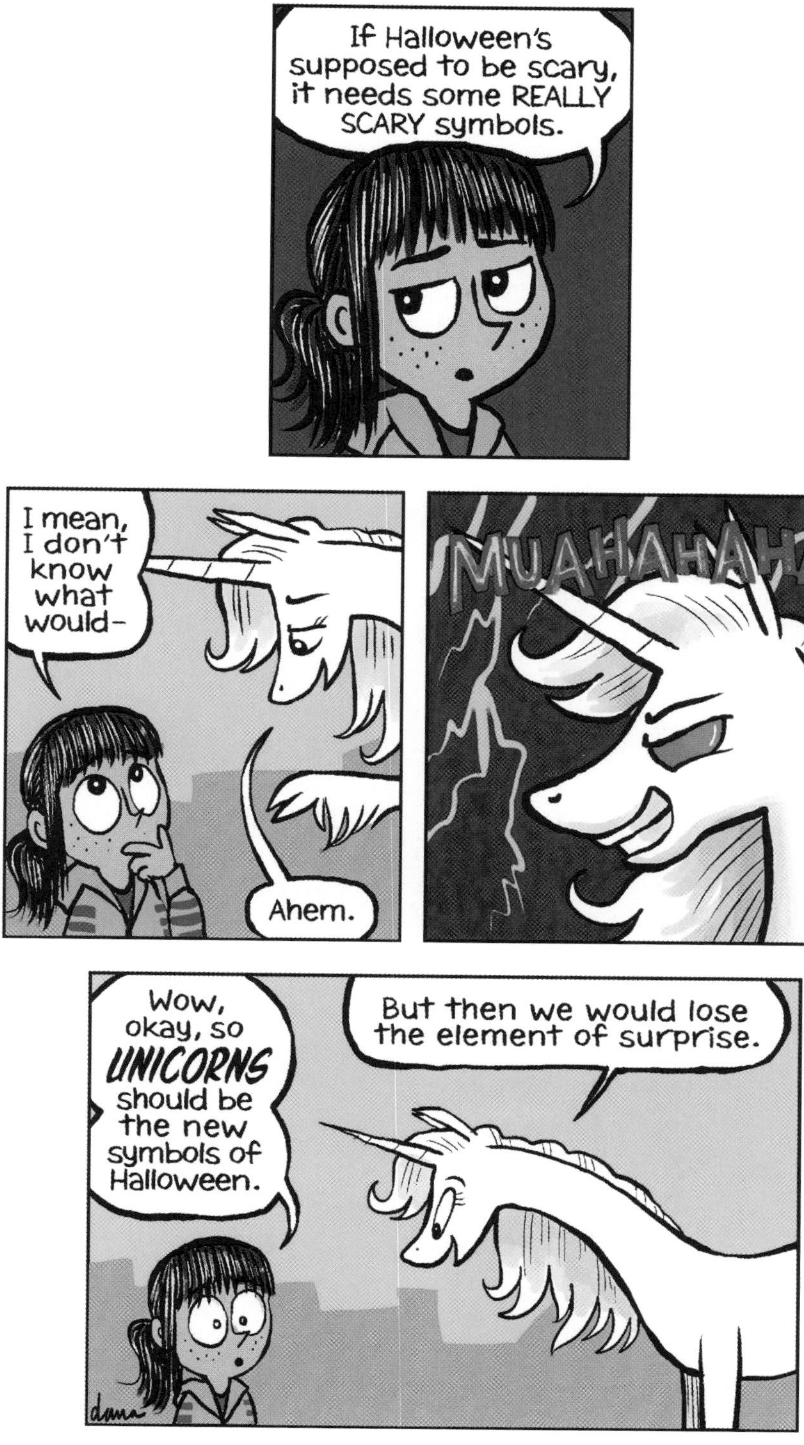
If Halloween's supposed to be scary, it needs some REALLY SCARY symbols.
I mean, I don't know what would-
Ahem.
MUAHAHAHA.
Wow, okay, so UNICORNS should be the new symbols of Halloween.
But then we would lose the element of surprise.
dana

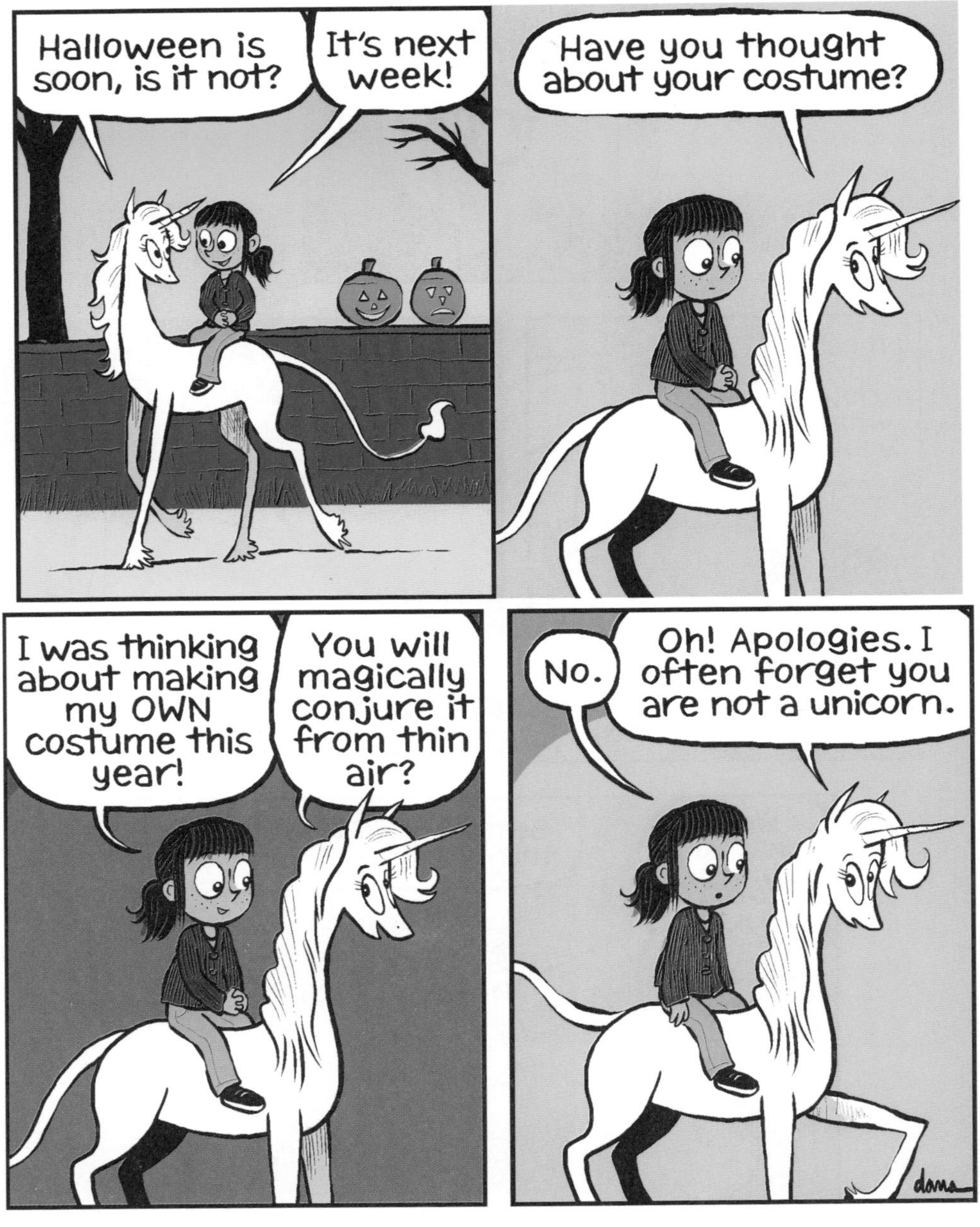

Halloween is soon, is it not?
It's next week!
Have you thought about your costume?
I was thinking about making my OWN costume this year!
You will magically conjure it from thin air?
No.
Oh! Apologies. I often forget you are not a unicorn.
dana

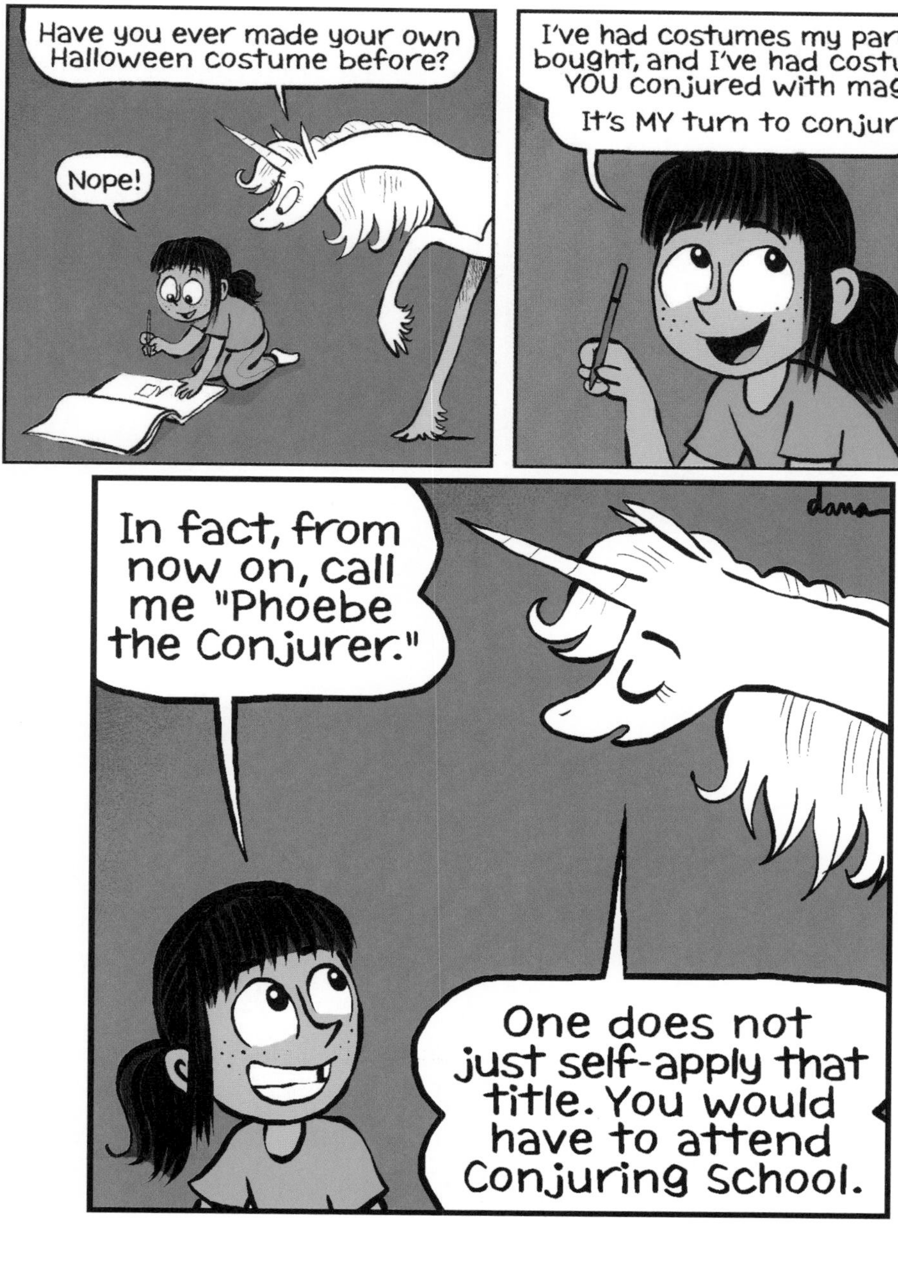
Have you ever made your own Halloween costume before?
Nope!
I've had costumes my parents bought, and I've had costumes YOU conjured with magic.
It's MY turn to conjure!
In fact, from now on, call me "Phoebe the Conjurer."
One does not just self-apply that title. You would have to attend Conjuring School.
dana

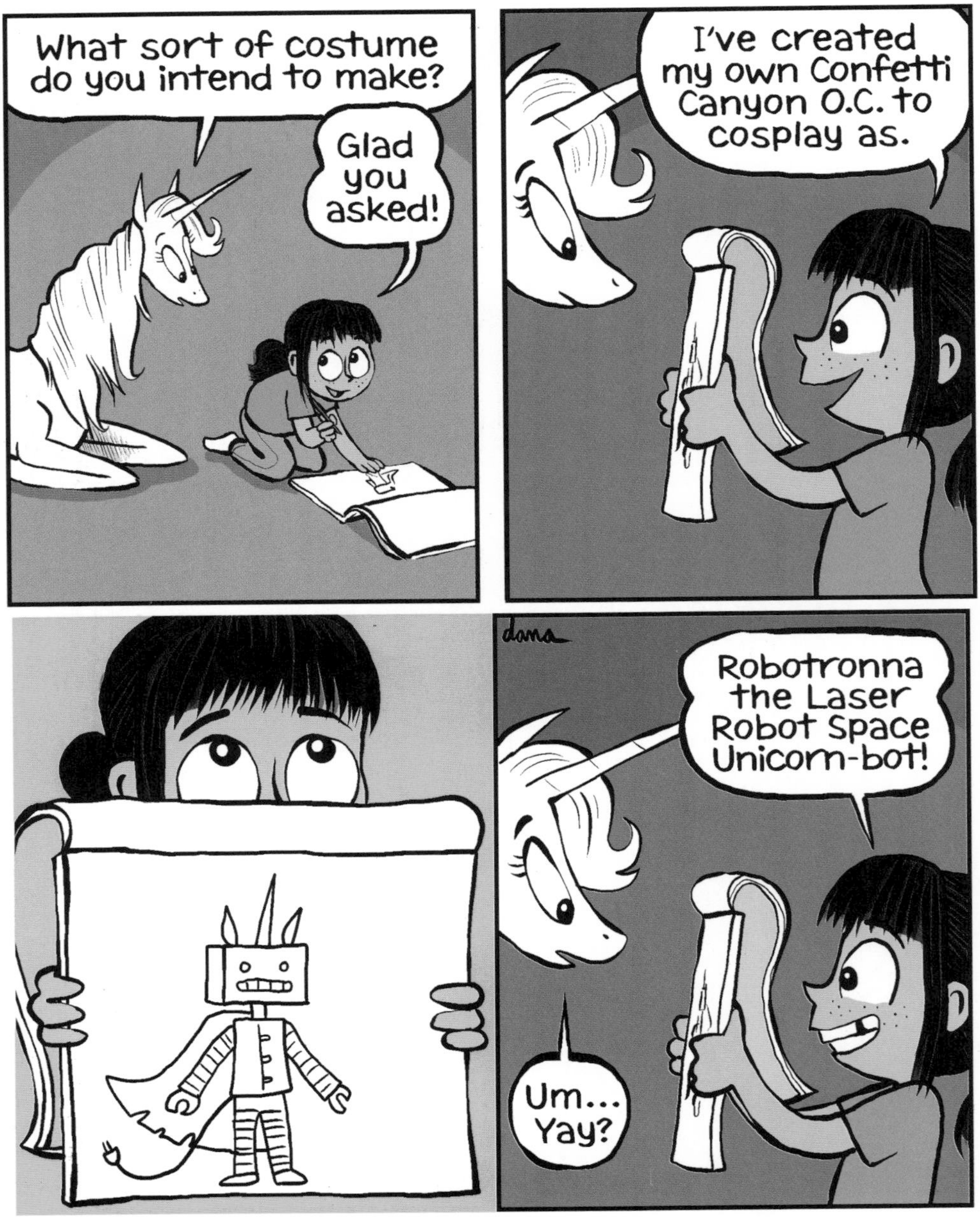
What sort of costume do you intend to make?
Glad you asked!
I've created my own Confetti Canyon O.C. to cosplay as.
dana
Robotronna the Laser Robot Space Unicorn-bot!
Um... Yay?

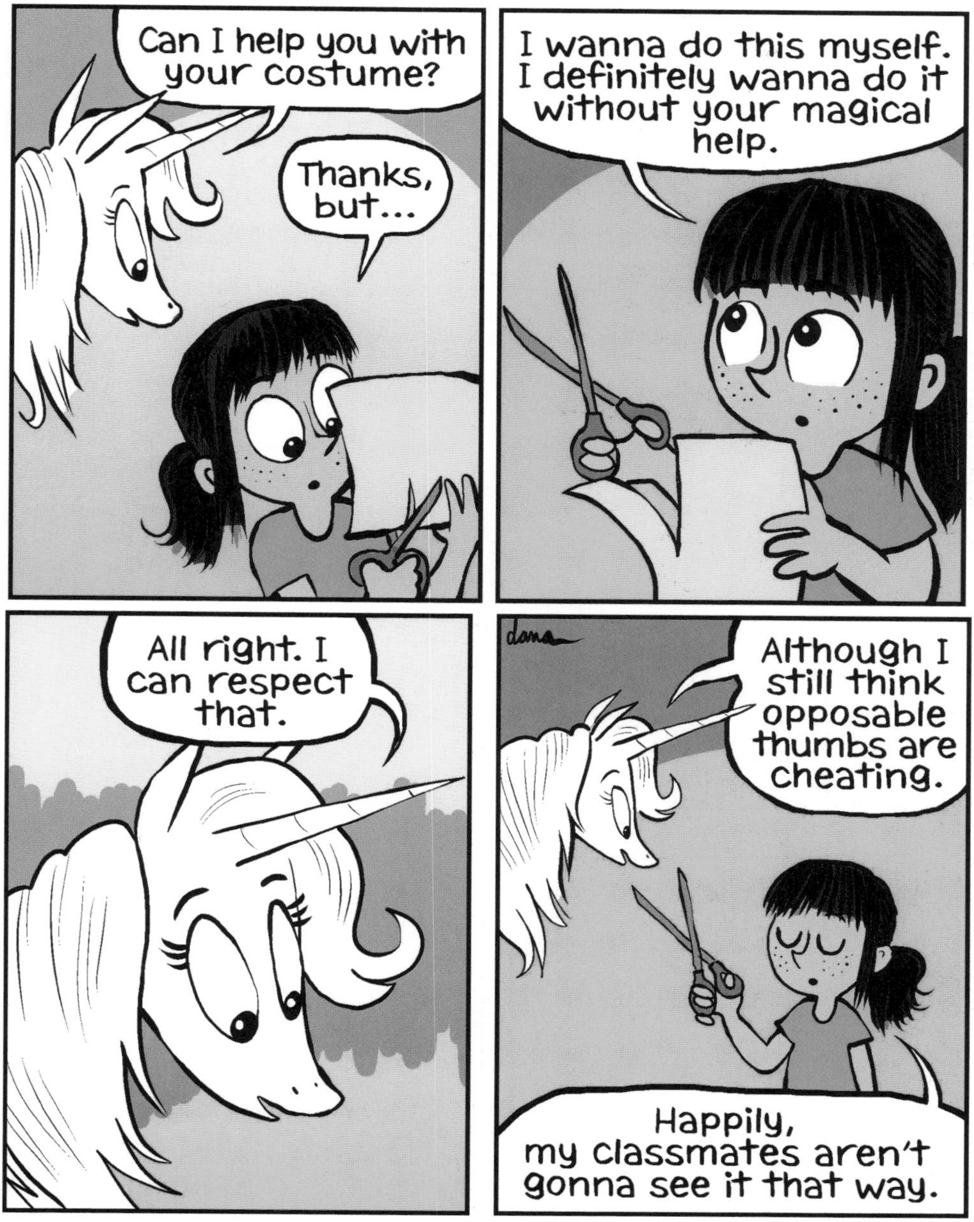
Can I help you with your costume?
Thanks, but...
I wanna do this myself. I definitely wanna do it without your magical help.
All right. I can respect that.
dana
Although I still think opposable thumbs are cheating.
Happily, my classmates aren't gonna see it that way.

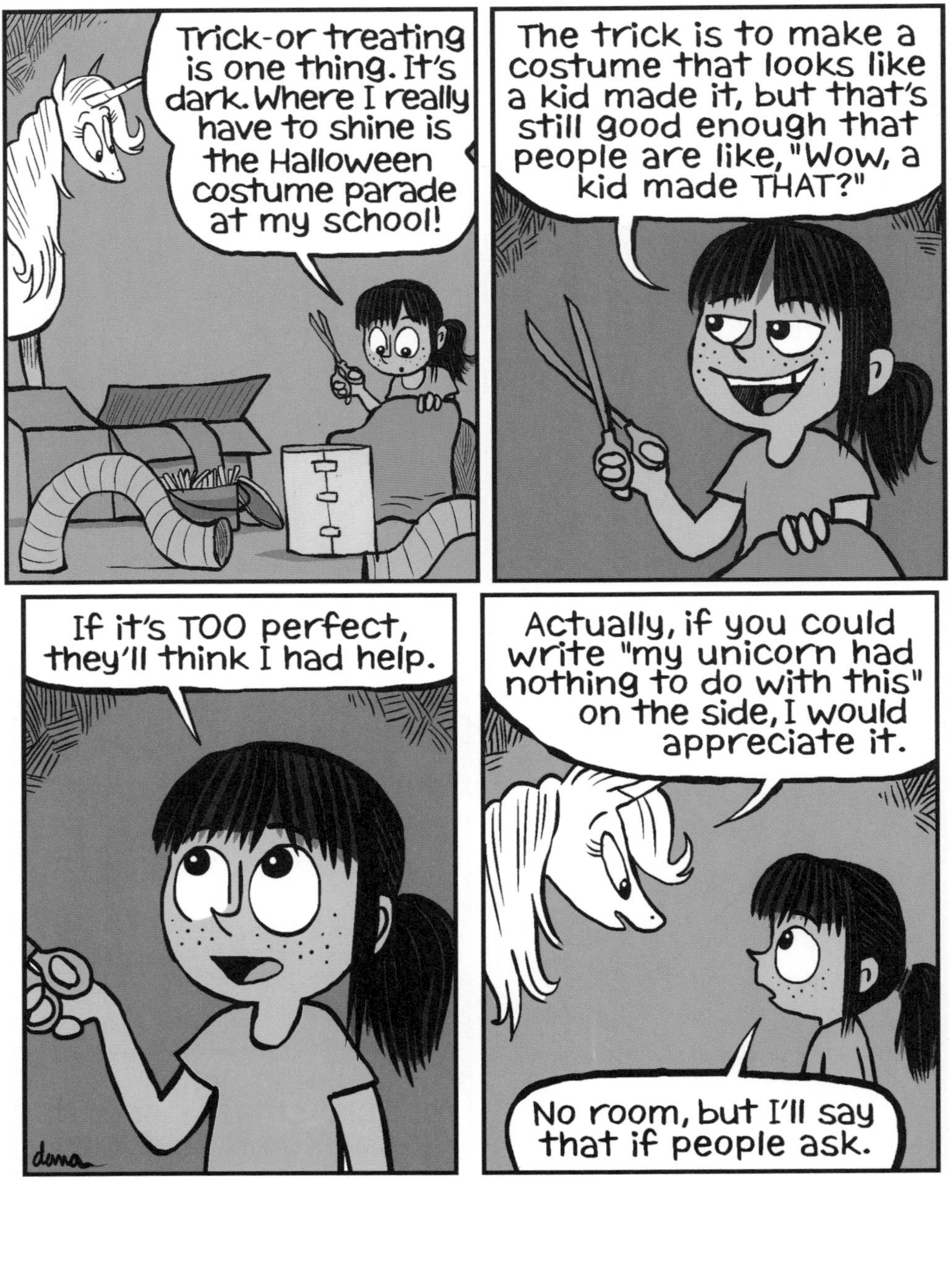
Trick-or treating is one thing. It's dark. Where I really have to shine is the Halloween costume parade at my school!
The trick is to make a costume that looks like a kid made it, but that's still good enough that people are like, "Wow, a kid made THAT?"
If it's TOO perfect, they'll think I had help.
Actually, if you could write "my unicorn had nothing to do with this" on the side, I would appreciate it.
No room, but I'll say that if people ask.
dana

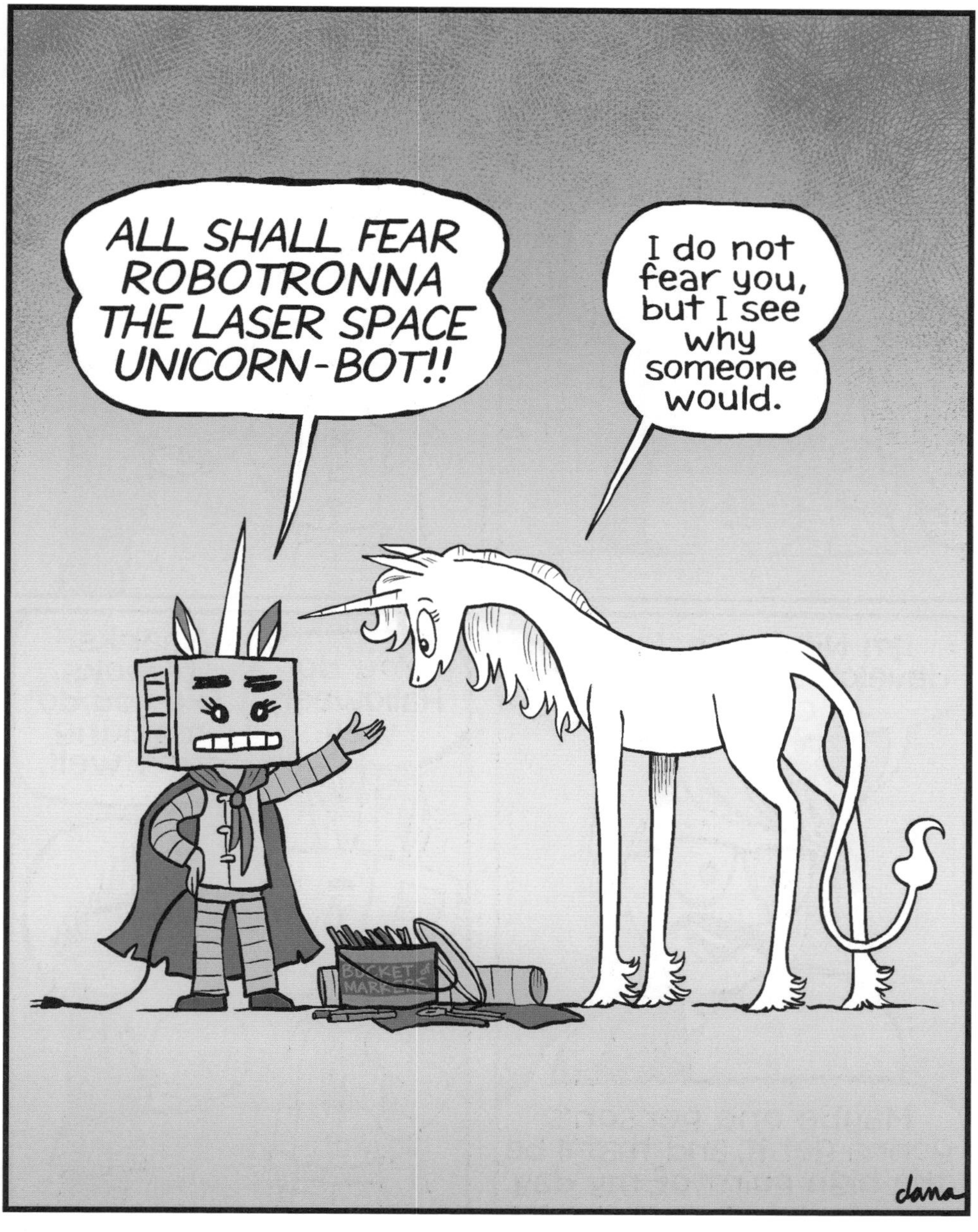
ALL SHALL FEAR ROBOTRONNA THE LASER SPACE UNICORN-BOT!!
I do not fear you, but I see why someone would.
BUCKET of MARKERS
dana

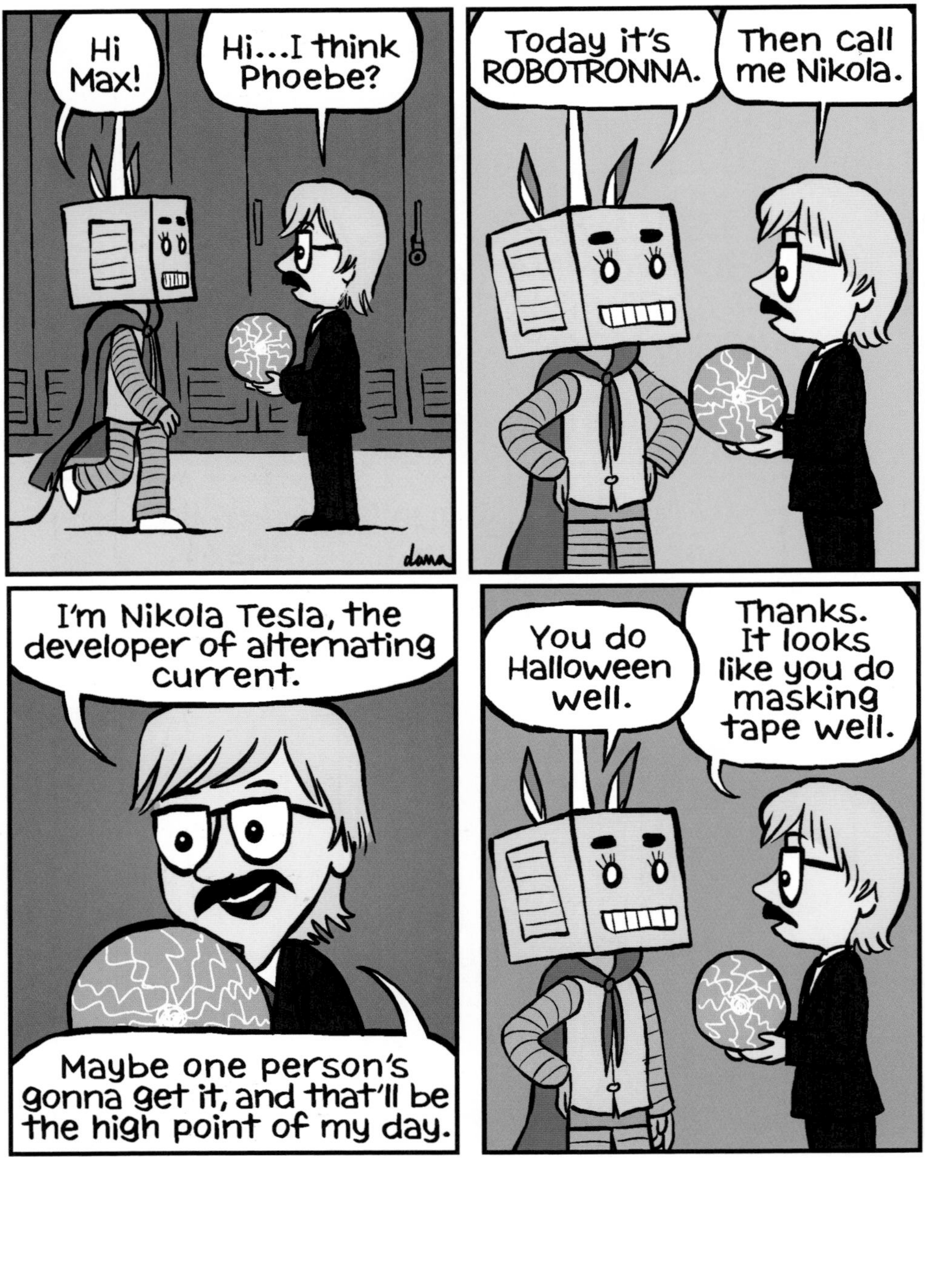
Hi Max!
Hi...I think Phoebe?
dama
Today it's ROBOTRONNA.
Then call me Nikola.
I'm Nikola Tesla, the developer of alternating current.
Maybe one person's gonna get it, and that'll be the high point of my day.
You do Halloween well.
Thanks. It looks like you do masking tape well.

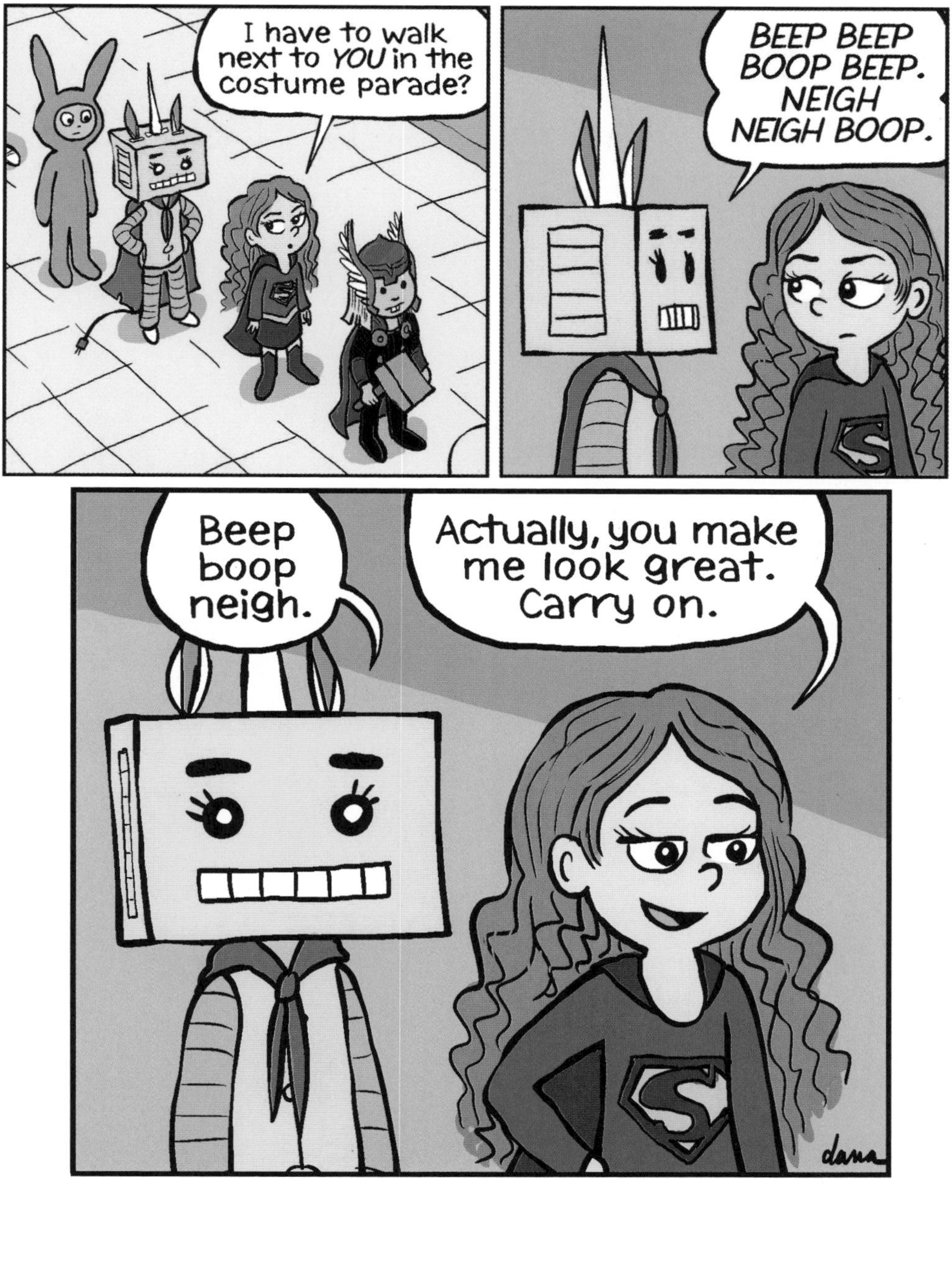
I have to walk next to *YOU* in the costume parade?
BEEP BEEP BOOP BEEP. NEIGH NEIGH BOOP.
Beep boop neigh.
Actually, you make me look great. Carry on.
dana

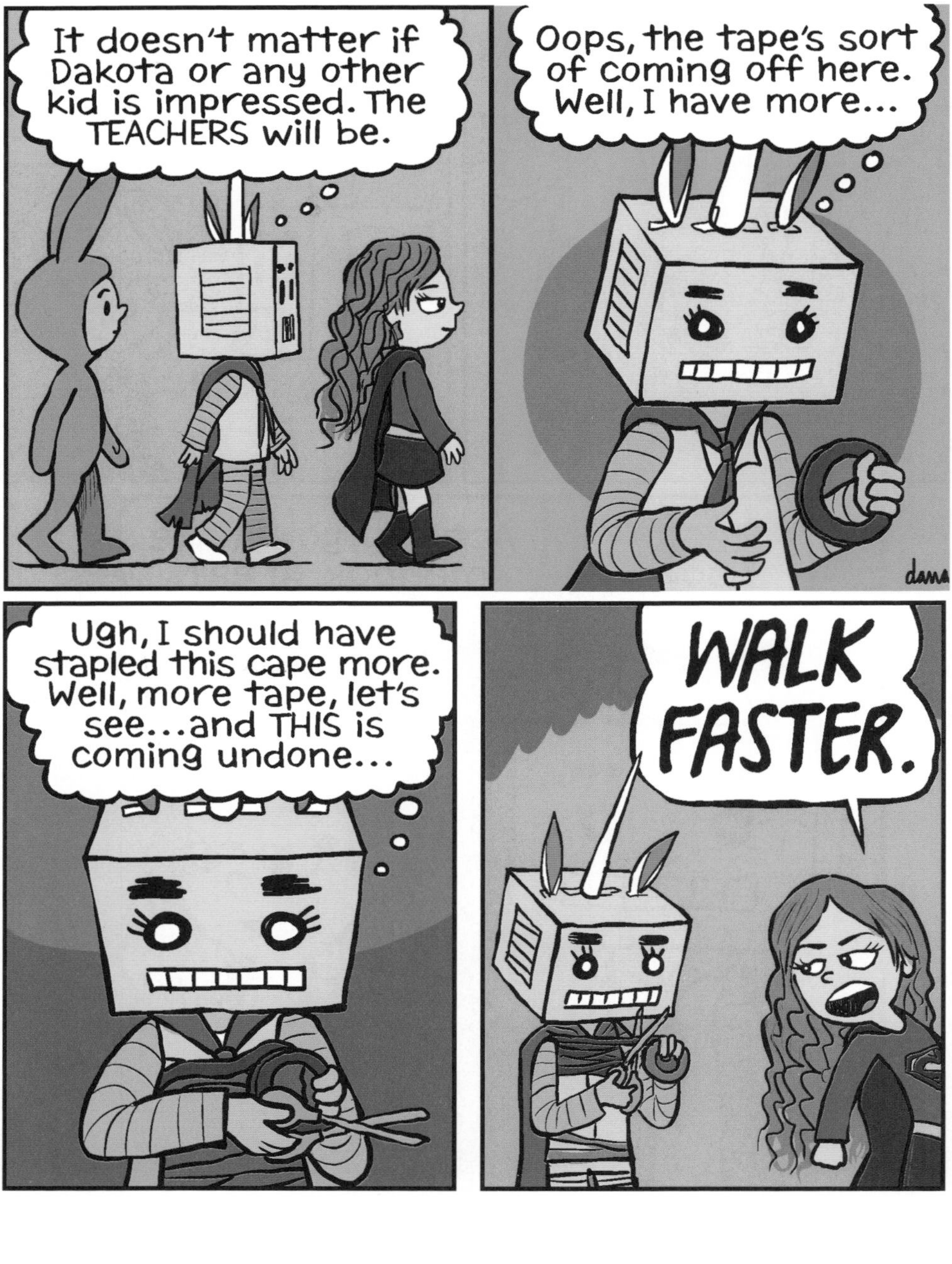
It doesn't matter if Dakota or any other kid is impressed. The TEACHERS will be.
Oops, the tape's sort of coming off here. Well, I have more...
dana
Ugh, I should have stapled this cape more. Well, more tape, let's see...and THIS is coming undone...
WALK FASTER.

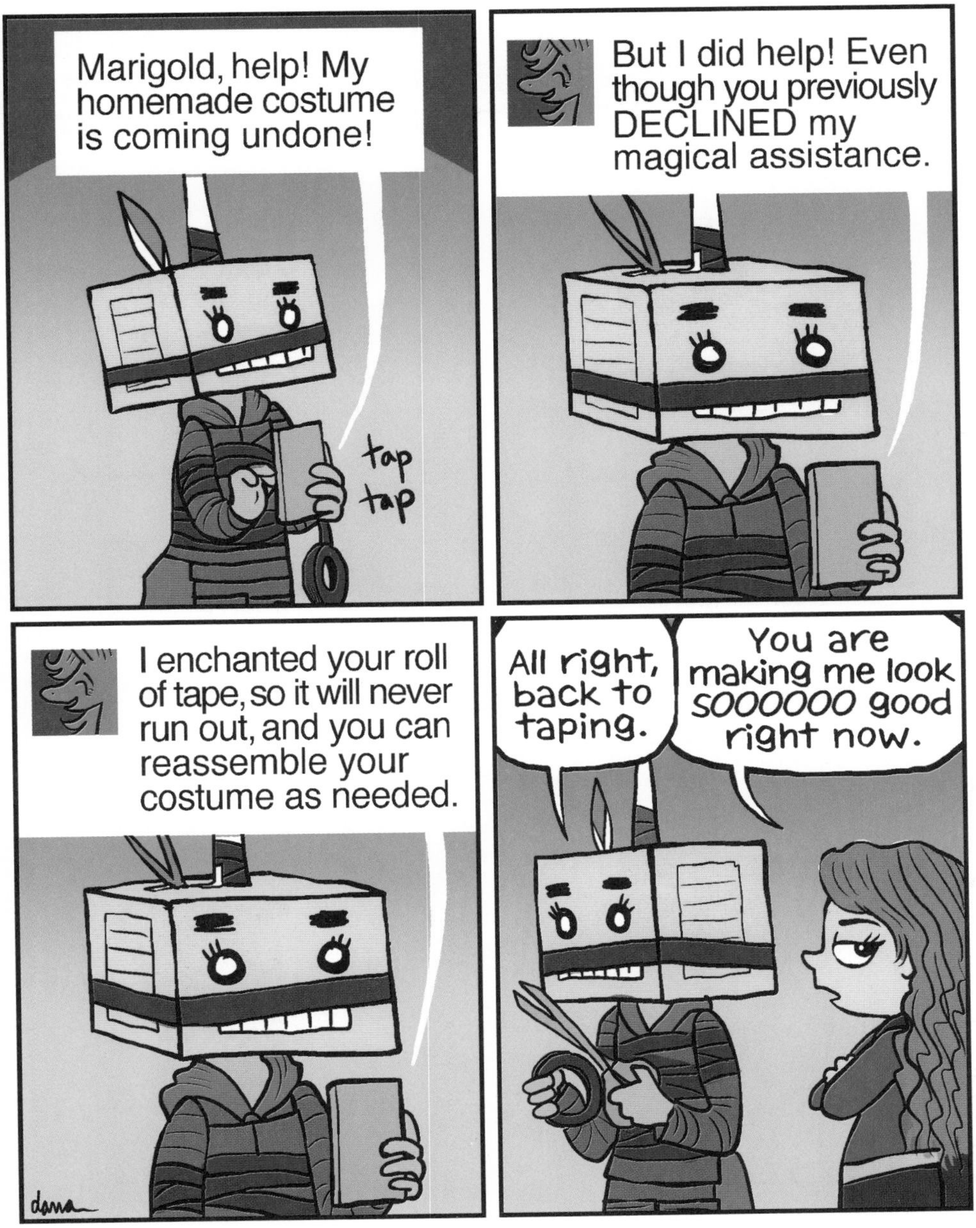
Marigold, help! My homemade costume is coming undone!
tap tap
But I did help! Even though you previously DECLINED my magical assistance.
I enchanted your roll of tape, so it will never run out, and you can reassemble your costume as needed.
All right, back to taping.
You are making me look SOOOOOO good right now.
dana

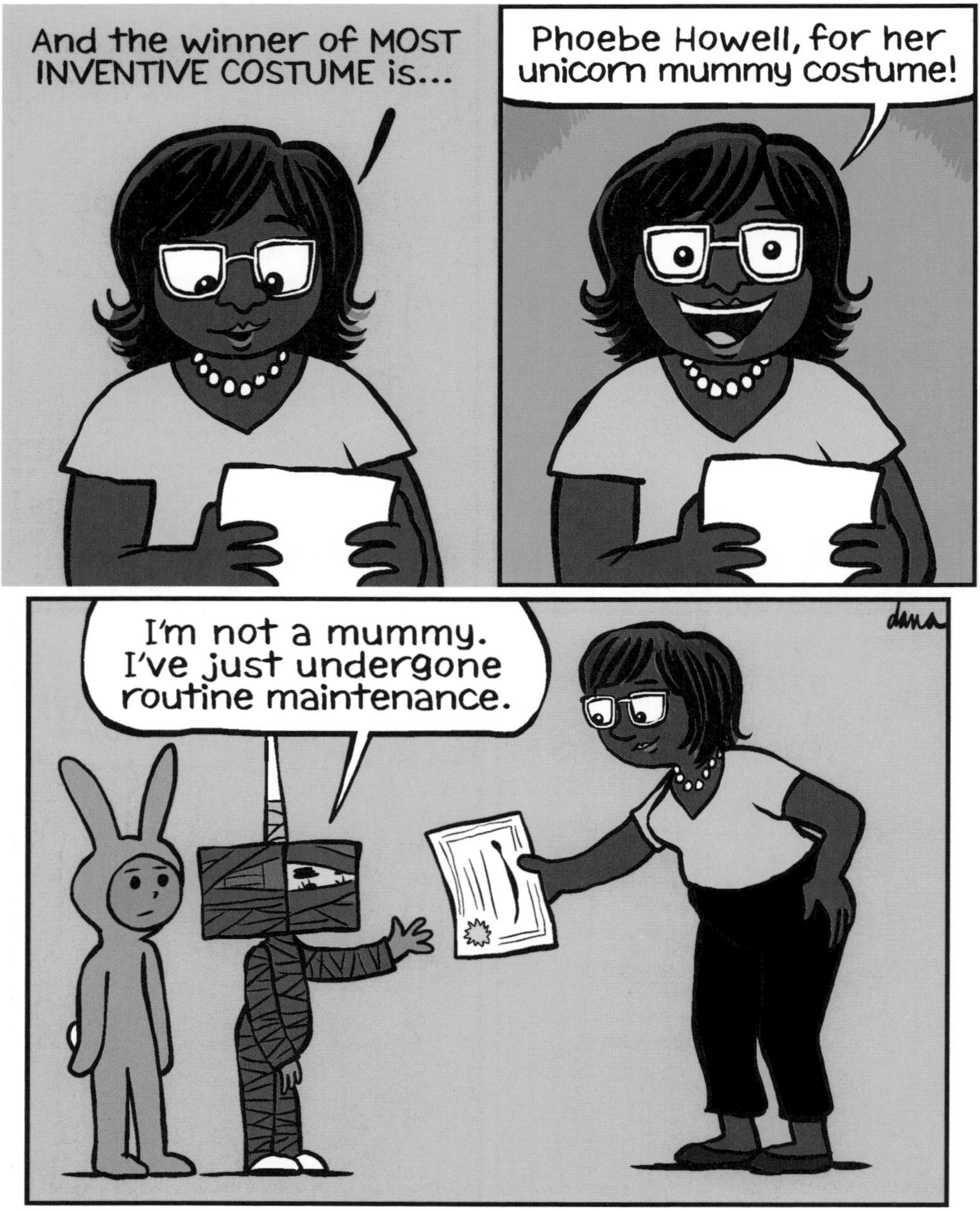
And the winner of MOST INVENTIVE COSTUME is...
Phoebe Howell, for her unicorn mummy costume!
I'm not a mummy. I've just undergone routine maintenance.
dana

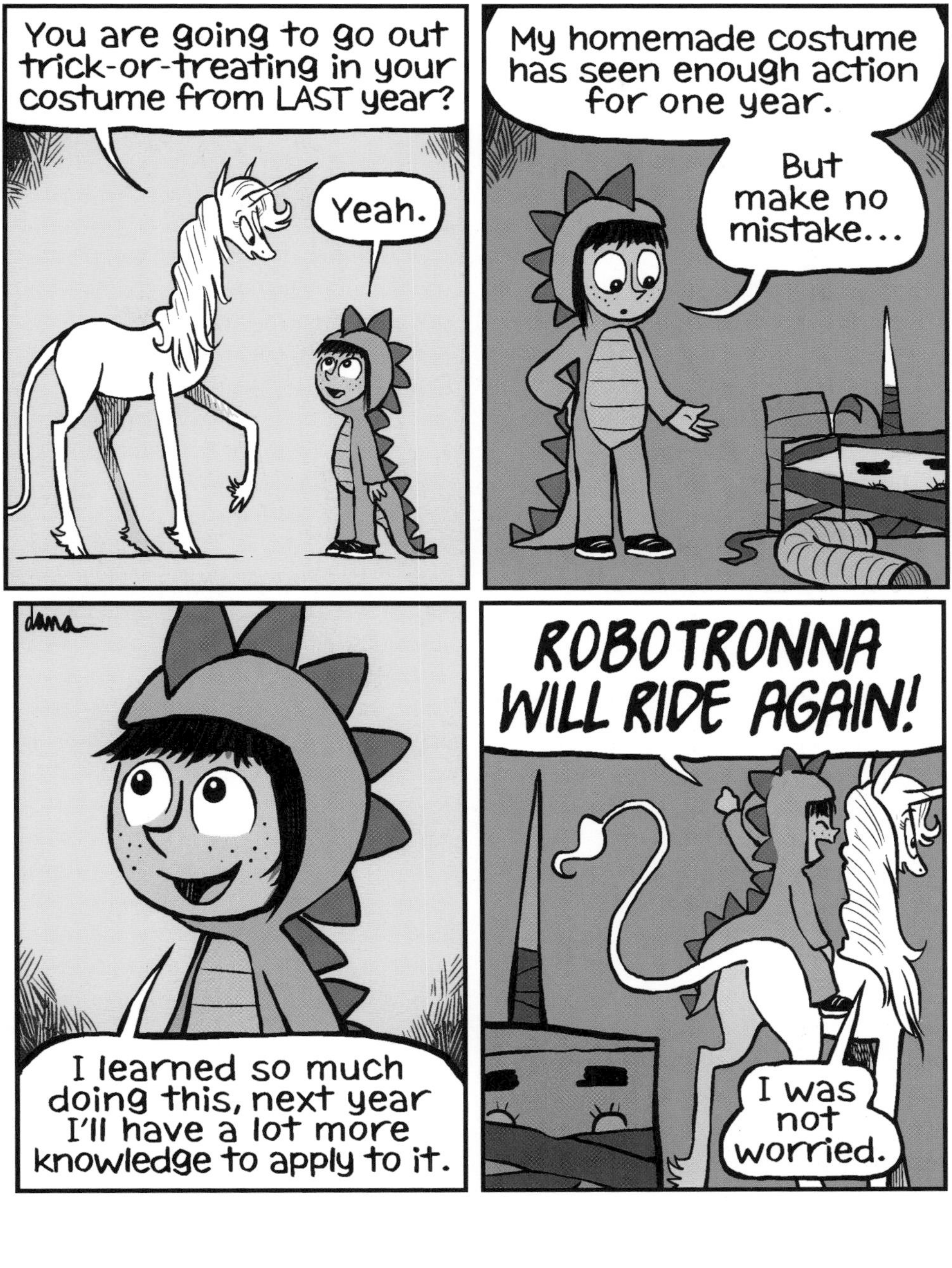
You are going to go out trick-or-treating in your costume from LAST year?
Yeah.
My homemade costume has seen enough action for one year.
But make no mistake...
dana
I learned so much doing this, next year I'll have a lot more knowledge to apply to it.
ROBOTRONNA WILL RIDE AGAIN!
I was not worried.

MORE TO EXPLORE!
A special section featuring words to learn!

GLOSSARY

awry (uh-rye): pg. 23 – adjective / out of sorts or off course ("to go awry")

basking (bask-ing): pg. 74 – verb / to lie exposed to the light or warmth, usually of the sun

biped (by-ped): pg. 79 – noun / an animal that walks on two feet, usually a human

bolster (bull-stur): pg. 90 – verb / to support or strengthen

charismatic (care-iz-ma-tick): pg. 119 – adjective / showing a charm and inspiring an attraction in other people

chide (chyd): pg. 102 – verb / to scold or voice disapproval

conjure (kon-jur): pg. 160 – verb / to call upon something or make it appear, usually a spirit or a ghost; to imagine

crystalline (kri-stuh-len): pg. 72 – adjective / clear and sparkling, resembling a crystal

exploits (ek-sploy-ts): pg. 72 – noun / daring feats, adventures, and accomplishments

extortion (ik-stor-shun): pg. 53 – noun / trying to get something, such as money, through force or threats

gloating (glow-ting): pg. 50 – verb / "to gloat" is to celebrate one's success in the face of another's misfortune

glockenspiel (glah-kin-shpeel): pg. 28 – noun / a musical percussion instrument resembling a small xylophone, with metal pieces mounted in a frame and struck with small mallets

moot (moot): pg. 127 – adjective / debatable, or not relevant

objectivity (ahb-jeck-ti-vi-tee): pg. 31 – noun / the condition of being neutral—not favoring one side or another; not biased

obsolete (ahb-suh-leet): pg. 114 – adjective / outdated and no longer in use

omen (oh-min): pg. 59 – noun / a sign of things to come in the future

osmosis (ahz-moh-sis): pg. 15 – noun / the process of molecules passing through a membrane into another one; often used to describe the transfer of ideas and knowledge into a person's brain

placid (pla-sid): pg. 152 – adjective / peaceful, calm; free of interruption

scourge (skurj): pg. 105 – noun / something that causes trouble or suffering

snarky (snar-key): pg. 122 – adjective / snide, sarcastic, and critical

synthetic (sin-theh-tick): pg. 30 – adjective / made up of materials that are combined to imitate a natural substance

vicinity (vi-si-nuh-tee): pg. 59 – noun / area; "in the vicinity" means to be relatively nearby

void (voyd): pg. 86 – noun / an emptiness or abyss

Andrews McMeel Publishing
a division of Andrews McMeel Universal
1130 Walnut Street, Kansas City, Missouri 64106

www.andrewsmcmeel.com

21 22 23 24 25 SDB 10 9 8 7 6 5 4 3 2 1

ISBN: 978-1-5248-6476-7

Library of Congress Control Number: 2020946298

Made by:
King Yip (Dongguan) Printing & Packaging Factory Ltd.
Address and location of manufacturer:
Daning Administrative District, Humen Town
Dongguan Guangdong, China 523930
1st Printing—12/28/20

ATTENTION: SCHOOLS AND BUSINESSES
Andrews McMeel books are available at quantity discounts with bulk purchase for
educational, business, or sales promotional use. For information, please e-mail the
Andrews McMeel Publishing Special Sales Department:
specialsales@amuniversal.com.

Look for these books!

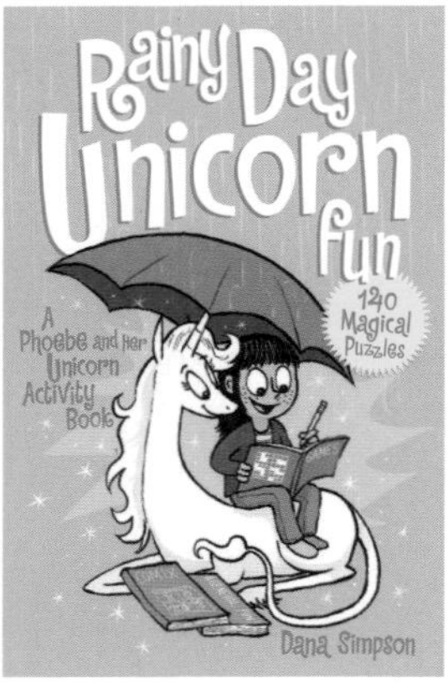
Rainy Day Unicorn fun
140 Magical Puzzles
A Phoebe and her Unicorn Activity Book
Dana Simpson

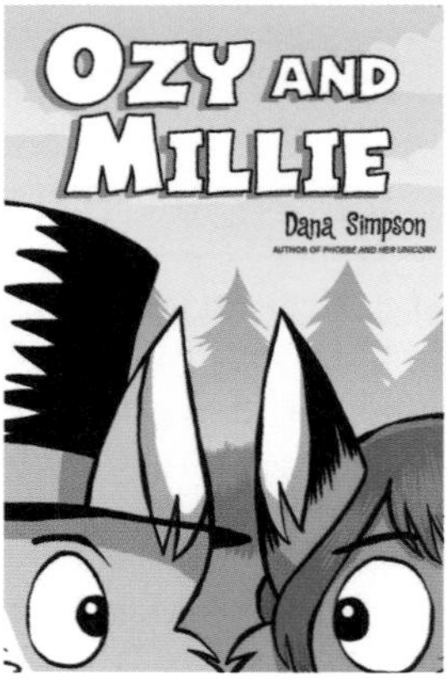
OZY AND MILLIE
Dana Simpson

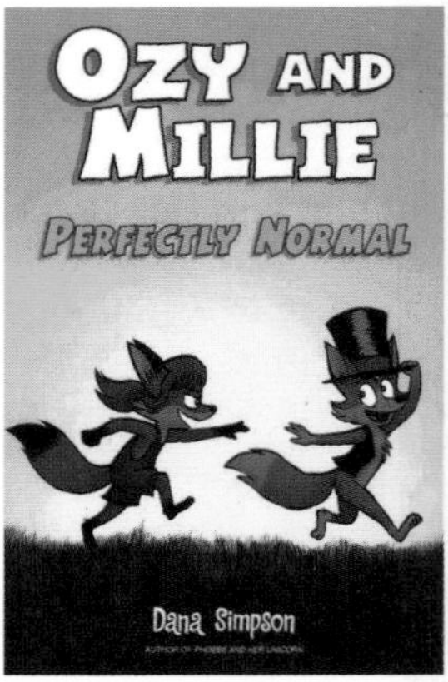
OZY AND MILLIE
PERFECTLY NORMAL
Dana Simpson

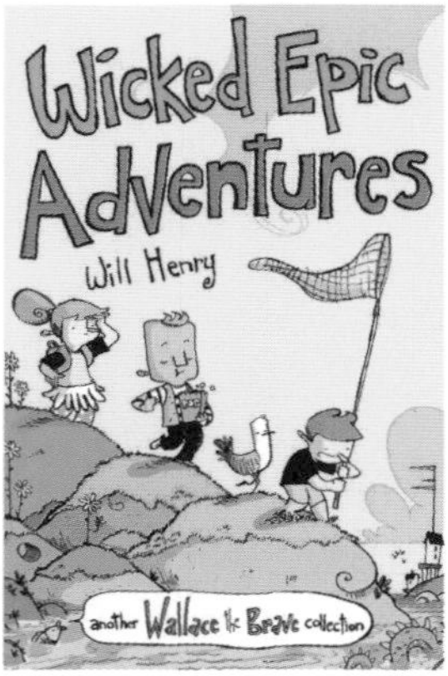
Wicked Epic Adventures
Will Henry
another Wallace the Brave collection

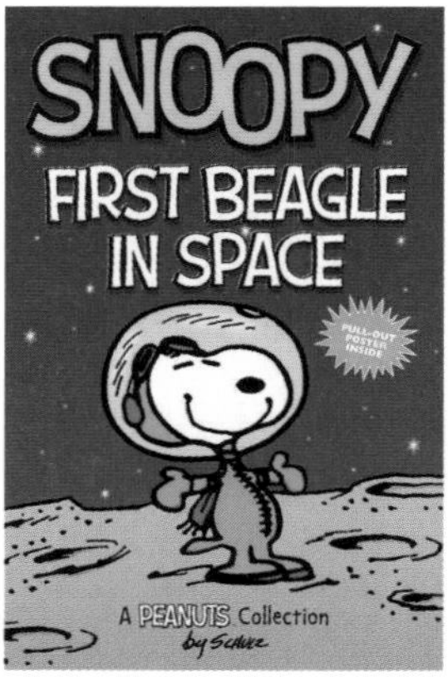
SNOOPY
FIRST BEAGLE IN SPACE
PULL-OUT POSTER INSIDE
A PEANUTS Collection
by Schulz

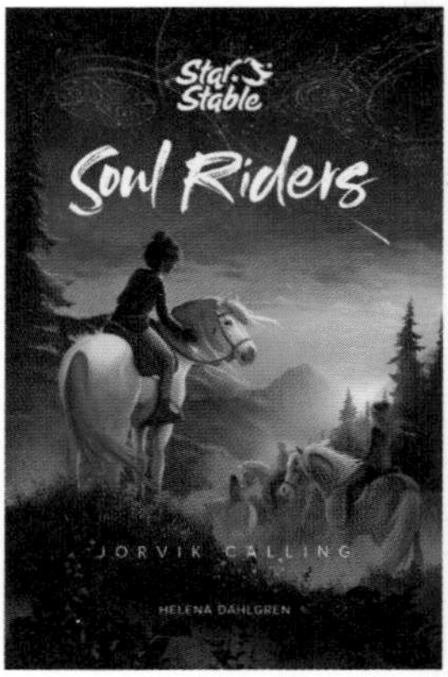
Star Stable
Soul Riders
JORVIK CALLING
HELENA DAHLGREN

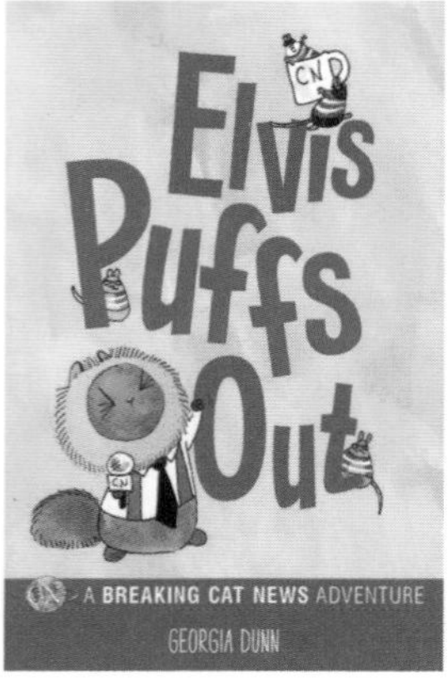
Elvis Puffs Out
A BREAKING CAT NEWS ADVENTURE
GEORGIA DUNN

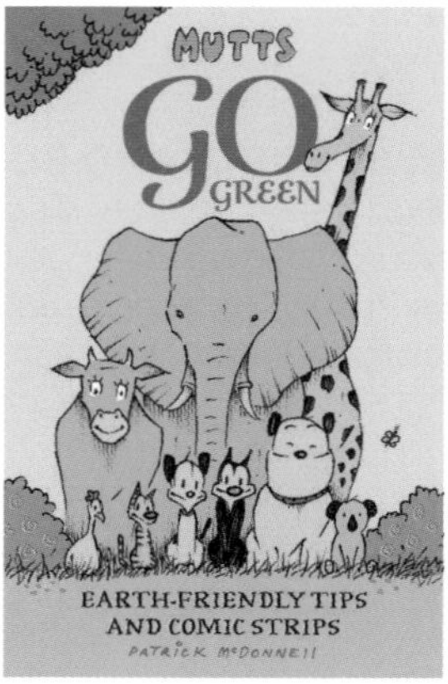
MUTTS
GO GREEN
EARTH-FRIENDLY TIPS AND COMIC STRIPS
PATRICK McDONNELL

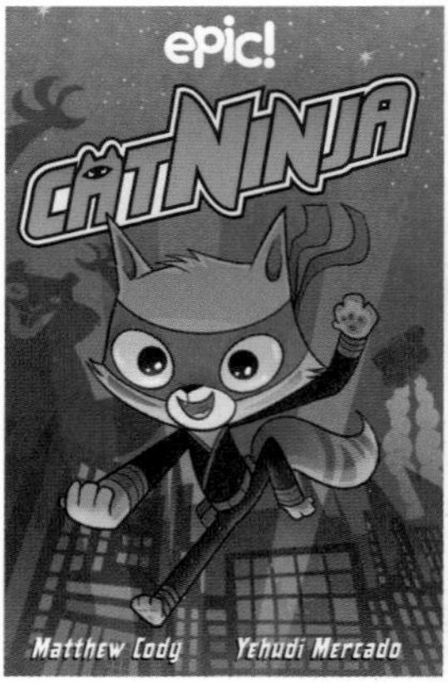
epic!
CATNINJA
Matthew Cody
Yehudi Mercado